BREAKING THE REIGN OF THE DEAD

A Pathfinder Novel

H. Rad Bethlen

Rooster & Raven

Published by Rooster and Raven Publishing, LLC

hradbethlen.com
roosterandravenpublishing.com

For the Daughters of Zeus and Mnemosyne

Author Statement Concerning Artificial Intelligence

The way I write consist of several phases.

1. Idea generation.
2. Research.
3. Story development.
4. Outlining.
5. Writing the rough draft.
6. Editing and rewriting.
7. Editing and polishing.
8. Copy editing.

I will *occasionally* use AI during the research phase if I can't locate some bit of information on my own—but I try to locate it on my own first.

I will *occasionally* use AI during the story's development if I get stuck on something—but I try to resolve my own story issues first.

I *intentionally* use AI during the copy editing phase as a stand-in for a copy editor, which I can't afford to pay for yet which I don't want to go without.

A copy editor is the last set of eyes to look at a manuscript to check for grammar, usage, spelling, and punctuation mistakes. I ask the AI copy editor to make suggestions on corrections. I evaluate those suggestions. If I agree, I make the changes.

I don't use AI for anything else.

Be comforted that this story was written by a human being for other human beings.

H. Rad Bethlen

Author's Preface

Readers will find that this work diverges from the orthodox—what has been published by Paizo. I have taken as my starting point the information contained in the *Pathfinder Campaign Setting: The Inner Sea World Guide*, yet, even as far as that goes, if the story needed to diverge, it did so. Having said that, I hope the story that follows is both acceptable and enjoyable to most people who tell their own tales in the Inner Sea.

This work was done independently of Paizo and its editorial staff. They are not to blame for anything contained herein. Indeed, they most likely have no knowledge of this book's existence. And while the intellectual property associated with the Pathfinder game is theirs, all faults are my own.

I went back and forth on whether to write this book. First, the information in the *Pathfinder Campaign Setting: The Inner Sea World Guide* is not my intellectual property. I could be sued for using it *if* I attempted to claim it as my own and profit from it. My solution is to fully acknowledge that while I created many of the characters and wrote the novel, the world the characters act in is not mine. Nor do I wish to profit financially from this work. I'm giving it away. If you paid for it, someone has cheated you.

This raises a question: it takes months, sometimes years, to write, rewrite, edit, polish, and publish a novel-length work. Is it wise to spend my time on something unprofitable when I could work on a marketable project? Here I must admit to being a slave to the story. This story wanted to be told. Besides, I saw in the story a challenge. I saw an opportunity to push myself as a writer and advance my understanding of craft. That alone is worth the effort and is its own reward. hope at least one person discovers and enjoys this story. If so, I shall be doubly rewarded.

I would rather be a slave to the poorest peasant than reign over the dead.

- Homer: *Odyssey*, XI, c. 800 B.C.

A Pressed Flower, Grain Exports, Aired Thoughts, and a Warning

The Cinerarium, Mechitar, Geb, Pharast, 4711

A cinerarium is a container in which to keep the ashes of a cremated body. It was Geb's morbid sense of humor that inspired him to name his palace so ignobly. It is an apt name, however. The immense pyramid—made not from sandstone blocks like those in Osirion, the country that birthed and exiled the immortal Geb, but from feldspar, a stone of granite, gneiss, basalt, and other crystalline rocks—was to be his eternal home, just as a true cinerarium holds one's mortal remains until time empties it.

Those massive blocks, quarried from the Shattered Range Mountains, were a plagioclase feldspar and thus were tinted red. The dawn sun made the massive pyramid —it dominated Mechitar's skyline, dwarfing the other pyramids, dwarfing even the Cathedral of Epiphenomena, Urgathoa's temple—pink. The noonday sun made it glow reddish-orange. The evening sun turned it the color of dried blood. The moon drained it of all color, turning it as pale as lifeless flesh.

Geb no longer occupied the pyramidal palace. He cared not for any of his palaces, libraries, summoning chambers, or macabre workshops; where, when he did care, he assembled rotting remains into semblances of life that more properly insulted it. Geb gave all such concerns over to his Harlot Queen, Arazni. She ruled the nation of Geb—he would, of course, name it after himself—in conjunction with Geb's hand-picked Chancellor and one-time confidant, Kemnebi, and the Blood Lords, a collection of sixty elites, many undead, but not all.

The Blood Lords met in what Geb nicknamed "the mortuary" but what was really the grand hall of the Cinerarium. Off one side of this grand hall was Arazni's personal chambers, the other, Kemnebi's offices. Kemnebi had a home of his own, a pyramid a fraction of the size of the Cinerarium—one does not upstage Geb—yet he visited it so infrequently he often forgot about it. No Blood Lords lived in or worked out of the Cinerarium, only Arazni and Kemnebi. It was a cold, silent, lifeless palace: a massive, empty tomb.

On this night the dead met. A meeting of the Blood Lords was just concluded. The business of the dead, old and new, considered. The reign of the dead continued unabated. These meetings were usually presided over by Kemnebi, with Arazni seated in a throne just behind him and a statue of Geb peering over her shoulder. Not this one, nor the two previous. Arazni was annoyed at the Chancellor's repeated absence, which forced her into bureaucratic duties she despised. The Blood Lords did not comment. They were not given to gossip. When the meeting was concluded they left—all but one.

. . .

Kemnebi had the keen senses of a predator. He was a predator. Geb bestowed upon him the blessing of vampirism. It was due to these vampiric senses that he heard the hinges of the iron door squeak, pause, then squeak again. He felt the air pressure in the room drop. He felt the warmth of life come into his space. Above all these sensations was the beating of a mortal heart, the rush-and-pause of blood in mortal veins, the iron-taste of blood on his tongue.

He knew a great deal from these clues. There were few beings, living or dead, but especially living, who had the courage or brazenness to enter his offices unannounced and uninvited. He knew, therefore, it must be one of the

Blood Lords. There were only nine mortal Blood Lords. This narrowed the possibilities. As he ran through the list of potential visitors he heard the *clack-clack* of heels. A floral fragrance came to his nostrils. Still more clues.

He thought first of Narcisse, the former Duke Between the Rivers. He sometimes wore boots with heels, sometimes wore perfume, even cosmetics, but the lightness of the *clack-clack* ruled out the grossly obese cleric of Urgathoa. There was a tiefling, that is, a human with demonic blood somewhere in her lineage, also a worshipper of Urgathoa, who—while mortal—shared a supernatural tie with a phantom, but he could not recall the tiefling's name, even though she was a Blood Lord. She would never assume enough familiarity with him to enter his offices without his personal invitation.

He thought next of She-mah-hon, an ostirius kyton, emissary from the Abbey of Nerves, sent to Geb by Aroggus to welcome those few undead who can still feel and those remaining mortals in Geb to the glory of the Abbey's lightless halls and endless tortures. She was an unsettling presence, like all kytons, a race given to disturbing body modifications, and was crazy enough to desire an impromptu meeting, but Kemnebi ruled her out. She was mortal, or so he surmised, but her blood held an otherworldly and disagreeable odor. He would have tasted it in an instant.

There was Baya-Iza, a noble from Zirnakaynin, the greatest of the drows' subterranean cities, come to Geb to study in the Ebon Mausoleum and continue the ingrained habit of merciless social climbing, of which, she proved a great success. Or perhaps Kimberly Silent Eyes, a Vishkanyas assassin clever enough to realize that if she killed her employer and took their place few would object. Both were recent additions to the ruling elite of Geb, but neither seemed likely. They were minor powers in the hierarchy of Geb, like the nameless tiefling, and could be ruled out. As the *clack-clack* neared he decided from the few remaining candidates.

"Saskia."

"Chancellor." Saskia Kalff stepped into the circle of light created by the candles on the shelf above Kemnebi's desk. "I hope I'm not disturbing you."

Kemnebi set down the pressed flower he had been contemplating and turned his head to look at his unexpected visitor. A moment of silent observation passed between the two.

Saskia was no more a friend to Kemnebi than was She-mah-hon or any of the others. This was the first time she had been in his office alone, or really, with the Chancellor alone in any setting. She knew him, of course, being a Blood Lord, but he was as unapproachable as any truly powerful leader is. By all rights she was as entitled to his time and attention as any other Blood Lord, but to act upon that right was dangerous.

She found it odd that Kemnebi was contemplating a pressed flower. It brought so many questions to her mind she nearly forgot her purpose in coming. Of all the things she expected the undead Chancellor of Geb to be doing, pressing flowers was not amongst the likely activities. She looked down at him but made a conscious effort not to possess the demeanor of one looking down on another.

He had once been human, of the Mwangi people. Specifically he was of the Mauxi people, who denied kinship with the other tribes of the great Mwangi Expanse; a dense jungle cradled by mountains. The Mauxi people still speak the Osirioni tongue and unlike the brown-skinned Mwangi their skin often showed a tint of gray. Also unlike the kink-haired Mwangi, their hair was straight. The one trait they willingly shared with the Mwangi was patience.

Kemnebi was tall and athletic without appearing overly muscular. The nobility of his features fit him well as chancellor but would be equally noticed were he a common beggar. His nobility did not come from his station but from his being. His dark eyes were made still more enchanting by the gift of vampirism. He was handsome in a way that promised delightful ruination of any seduced by him.

That he was a practitioner of the arcane arts was well known. To be a one-time confidant of Geb was to share a love of necromancy with the immortal wizard-king. To rise and stay above the Blood Lords required a true mastery of the arcane, for the Blood Lords culled the weak from their own herd. Kemnebi had learned his necromancy from Geb himself, who, in turn had learned it from Hent-er-Neheh, one of his now mummified ancestors who taught him many a millennia prior, when both were still mortal.

That Kemnebi prickled with power was obvious to any who came near. To be chancellor of Geb required a keen knowledge of protective magics. What struck Saskia the most was not Kemnebi's power but his powers of observation. His gaze was attentive which made it unnerving, unnerving because he saw what was before him, not merely the reflection of his own desire. Kemnebi, seated, looked up at Saskia.

She was one of those rare practitioners of necromancy who did not lean upon that dark school of magic in order to surpass life, but to prolong it. Nor was necromancy her obsession, as it was for so many of her peers. She knew just as much about transmutation and alteration as she did about the school of death. In mortal years she was approaching seventy. In appearance, she was approaching thirty and had remained so for a long time.

She was a native of Qadira via Taldor. Her face was squarish with high cheekbones, framed by a mass of luxurious black hair. Her eyes were large and alluring, her eyelashes long and dark, lips full and red. A beauty mark lay just below the center of her right cheek. All that was seen of her creamy white flesh was her face, neck, and upper chest, as she wore a dark blue dress, a black corset, black satin gloves, and black leather boots. About her neck was a simple gold chain and an amulet with a blue stone. Tucked somewhere in her clothing was a song bird, now quietly nesting in its mistress's pocket. This was her familiar.

"Lilith?" inquired Kemnebi. Lilith was a fellow Blood Lord, a member of the clique that had long ago formed around Arazni, a lich, like Arazni, and Saskia's mentor.

"She is well," answered Saskia. "Our dear Marquis?" The Marquis Chevonde Garron was a vampire, Kemnebi's grandchild, in a sense. His sire was one of Kemnebi's "children," that is, a mortal he had embraced and turned into a vampire. Her name was Leah Ben-Reuven. Her memory was a painful one to Kemnebi as he had destroyed her in a rare fit of rage. Ever since then he had been especially kind to the Marquis and tolerant of his eccentricities. It was only by Kemnebi's leave that Chevonde was allowed to live beyond the borders of Geb. He had both a mansion in Katapesh and a pleasure barge in its harbor. He came to Geb only to attend the meetings of the Blood Lords. At all other times he kept livelier company.

It had been the Marquis Chevonde Garron who purchased Saskia from the slave markets of Katapesh. She was only seven at the time and Chevonde had elaborate plans for her. Thus began her tutelage in courtesan-ship and espionage. When Saskia was thirteen, polished in manner and speech, and knew what to look for in Arazni's court and how to secretly communicate that to the Marquis, she was sent to Arazni, the perfect child courtesan. Lilith put an end to it.

"A cute trick, Chevonde," she said during a meeting of the Blood Lords five decades prior.

"An amusement, nothing more," he replied.

"Would Arazni agree?"

"If she knew," responded the Marquis, "the child would be destroyed. Am I mistaken in believing you've taken a motherly role?"

"Don't expect any courtly gossip from our lovely Saskia."

"I would never. I only hope she remembers her eccentric uncle Chevonde favorably."

Much had transpired since then. Lilith had groomed Saskia for far greater things. At Lilith's insistence Saskia became a Blood Lord. Arazni was not hard to convince. She almost always took Lilith's advice.

"Has Lilith sent you?" asked Kemnebi. The smile on Saskia's face gave him pause. "I do not mean to imply —"

Saskia stepped more into the candlelight. She reached down, her eyes and smile on him, and picked up the pressed flower. She contemplated it. "Perhaps a delicate necromantic spell," she said, twirling the flower in her gloved fingers, "has taken the life from this yet kept it whole." She looked from the flower to Kemnebi. "Is that what occupies our Chancellor and causes him to miss three meetings in a row?"

If Kemnebi could blush he would have. He had forgotten about the meeting. He had not, so engrossed had he been, even heard the Blood Lords just outside his door. As if reading his thoughts, Saskia added, "You failed even to send a representative to make your will known," before setting down the flower, sitting on the edge of his desk, and folding her hands in her lap. The song bird chirped at the disturbance but tucked its face beneath a wing and resumed its slumber. "I make no accusations," said Saskia. She reached out and placed a hand on Kemnebi's. "I worry."

It was a bold gambit on her part. Kemnebi looked at her gloved hand, his expression unchanged. His eyes, though, spoke what his countenance did not. Saskia removed her hand to her lap but retained her casual seat. Despite her studied nonchalance, beads of sweat began to form on her brow.

Kemnebi's gaze moved to the flower. "In one of those," he said, looking now at the books. Saskia glanced at them and saw at once they had nothing to do with the arcane. "The legal codes of every nation of the Inner Sea," said Kemnebi, "that has a legal code." He looked up at Saskia. "Some do not. Some are not written down. Some legal codes are comprised only of parables and folk-wisdom kept in the heads of the village elders."

"Cheliax?" inquired Saskia.

"A labyrinth." Both chuckled at this and for a moment the tension between them lessened. Kemnebi reached out and picked up the pressed flower. "No doubt the wife of some scholar found a better use for her husband's books." He set the flower down.

"This?" Saskia picked up a single sheet of parchment marked with columns of numbers.

Kemnebi glanced at it. "Grain exports to Nex." His gaze shifted, as if he now looked to Geb's northerly neighbor. "The population of Nex grows."

"Good," announced Saskia. "We've an excess of labor and land." Both knew that legions of zombies worked the wheat, oat, and corn fields of Geb, the bounty of the land passing through decayed hands to Nex, Geb's former enemy. The soil of Nex could barely sustain life. Geb had seen to that in the millennia-long war between himself and his closest rival, Nex. Rare was it that two such wizard-kings should stomp about the land at the same time. That they did not keep a continent between them was due to ego. That they once shared a border and warred over it was due to folly. Saskia studied the null effect her words had on the Chancellor. "If economic matters make for poor—"

Kemnebi stood and began to pace in and out of the circle of light, alternately retreating and advancing. Saskia watched as he disappeared and reappeared. "Nex grows," he said. "Nex thrives. Nex evolves." He cast his glance at Saskia. "What of Geb? There is precious little life in Geb—"

"Precious?"

Kemnebi paused. "Yes, life is precious. You must certainly believe so. Given your—"

"I do."

Kemnebi resumed his pacing but did not speak. Saskia picked up the dropped thread.

"When any mortal within the boundaries of Geb dies," she began, speaking of a law Kemnebi certainly knew of, "they are raised as undead."

"Of course," mumbled Kemnebi.

"The poor go on to work the fields or have their skeletons added to the Bonewall. Those who can afford it, or who have secured favor, are brought back as higher forms of undead." When Saskia said higher forms a smile flashed across Kemnebi's face. He knew that those of wealth and station endeavored to secure a higher place in the hierarchy of Geb by becoming various types of undead, the more powerful the better. To be a mindless undead, or a type of undead devoid of freewill, was the greatest fear of all of Geb's mortal inhabitants.

Again a moment of silence passed. Kemnebi was occupied by his thoughts. Saskia bent and looked once more over the open books. "I forgot," she said, turning a few pages. "You're redefining Geb's legal code." She looked up at Kemnebi. He met her gaze but said nothing. "It must be difficult," she added, ceasing to finger the pages. "Is it this that occupies you so?"

"All nations founded and ruled by individual personalities share the same fate," said Kemnebi. "When those individuals no longer lead, they leave behind a vacuum."

"But Geb—"

"You must remember," interrupted Kemnebi, "that for almost all of Geb's history as a nation we were at war. Now we suffer peace." He smiled, but it was a forced smile. "A warring people know not how to manage peace."

"And so?" asked Saskia, glancing at the legal books.

"And so I must establish the rules that shall govern peace, so long as it lasts." He shook his head. His pacing took on a more violent motion, an external sign of internal emotion.

"Geb hasn't fallen apart—"

"Nor will it," announced Kemnebi, stopping at the edge of the candlelight, his face defined by the flickering flames. "It will stagnate. It will decay. It will die slowly, agonizingly. Finally, it will calcify. Meanwhile," he said, resuming his pacing, "the other nations of the Inner Sea will outgrow us, evolve beyond us." He stopped again at the edge of the candlelight. "And then—" But the look on Saskia's face alarmed him. She rose and looked past him to the door but Kemnebi knew it remained closed. She looked at him.

"No other Blood Lord would tolerate such heretical talk," she said. "Let alone Arazni or—Geb," she whispered the last, as if Geb would hear. She stepped to Kemnebi who stepped forward to meet her. Her movements were those of a panicked animal and she fell into him. He caught her, his hands around her waist, her hands on his chest. She looked up into his dark eyes and saw both the multitude of flickering candles and her own miniaturized self reflected within. "I pray you speak to no other as you've spoken to me." She parted from him, passed him, and hurried to the door. He watched her pull the heavy iron door open and slip out.

A Visit Denied, a Queen in Her Chambers, Hunting, and the Stirrings of Life

The Cinerarium and the streets of Mechitar, Geb, Pharast, 4711

Saskia stumbled partway across the great hall, paused to steady herself as best her emotions allowed, then continued. She looked over her shoulder, searching the gloom. She advanced until she arrived at Arazni's door, here she stopped, her gloved fist in the air, contemplating a knock. She looked once more across the hall toward Kemnebi's offices. She listened but heard no sounds. She turned and looked at Arazni's door and was coming to a decision when it opened.

What had once been an Ulfen warrior of great prowess and courage, but what was now a type of undead commonly called a grave knight, stood in the doorway. Grave knights were powerful undead whose souls were anchored not only to their past glories and now fallen statuses but also, in a material way, to the armor they wore. They could not be sent to the hereafter unless their armor was utterly destroyed. If they were slain by battle or magic and their armor remained, they would return to seek vengeance.

The Ulfen grave knight was seven feet tall but was hunched to six. His massive shoulders were broadened by the thick bearskin cloak he wore, even in Geb, where cloaks were unneeded. Not that the dead get uncomfortably warm. Yet his wrists and hands were delicate, made slender, even effeminate, by death. His blonde hair had fallen from the pate but hung long and scraggly from the sides and back. Unlike most undead he retained the whole of his flesh, which made him unnervingly human. He had the look of a corpse pulled from a bog, indeed, he had spent many years so mummified before freeing himself and seeking his armor; which, shown dully from beneath the bear's brown fur. His eyes were sunk deep in their sockets but their green color could still be seen, even in darkness, lit from within by foul magic.

He advanced, forcing Saskia in reverse, her fist still held aloft but now trembling. The door shut behind him, although no force seemed to have been applied. The sound of its closing reverberated throughout the hall. The grave knight planted the tip of his claymore and leaned heavily on its cross guard. His green eyes studied Saskia, his mouth hung open as if he were beyond fatigue, or perhaps beyond caring, but he did not speak.

Saskia knew the grave knight to be one of five such warriors that comprised Arazni's personal bodyguard. Even a lich, perhaps the most potent undead of all, would pause before challenging a grave knight. For one such as Saskia, a mortal, even a mortal in Arazni's good graces, being in such close proximity to one of her bodyguards was terrifying. When Saskia regained her composure she gathered the hem of her skirt and hurried from the hall. The grave knight's glowing green eyes followed her. She did not look back to see.

. . .

The four remaining grave knights stood in Arazni's large, luxuriously appointed chambers. They remained at the periphery, like so many statues, but their presence could be felt. They stared at Arazni, watching her. They had not the demeanor of bodyguards but of jailers. They did not move. They did not blink. They did not take their baleful gazes from their Queen.

Arazni was a queen but she acted at times like a princess. She sat crosslegged in the center of a massive, plush bed, surrounded by pillows and blankets. A canopy of pink gossamer failed to conceal her from the grave knights' combined gaze. She gathered around her dolls that had cloth bodies, elaborate, colorful, bejeweled outfits, and delicate, painted porcelain heads. They were a gift from Lilith and had come from far away Brevoy.

"Mother is good to us," said Arazni to her dolls. She often called Lilith "Mother," as did many others in the clique that surrounded the Queen. Lilith had nurtured and protected so many of them. She was not a loving mother—she was a lich, after all—but she was a stalwart presence. She protected her brood like a tigress protects its cubs.

For a few minutes Arazni described an imaginary world of ballroom dances, costumed parties, and entertainments of all types, running her dolls through the dances and romances of her imagination. The grave knights listened and watched. A mood came over her and she slammed her dolls into the mattress, only the thick coating of pillows protected them.

"No! No! No!" she screamed. "Damn you, Aroden! How could you abandon me?" She reached out and yanked aside the pink gossamer to stare at the grave knights on that side of the chamber. "And you," she hissed. "Always watching, always lurking like so many filthy rats. That's what you are, you know? Rats in a prison. Waiting for the prisoner to fall asleep so you can chew on her. You're nothing! You're—" She tilted her head, hearing a familiar voice. She yanked the gossamer closed.

She stared at the dolls just under her hands, not seeing them. She began to tremble. She began to weep. She did not attempt to stop herself. She did not try to clear the tears from her face. They fell on her hands. They fell onto the porcelain faces of her dolls. They discolored the satin of her coverlets. She was undead, ripped from the afterlife by Geb and dumped back into her body, a body that was not whole, yet she could still cry. That was Geb's doing. He wanted her to cry.

She reached up and began to touch her face, feeling the wetness, looking at her fingers, confused. She pulled up the edge of a coverlet and wiped her eyes, laughing. She leaned to the side and slipped her fingers through a gap in the gossamer, parting it and peering through. She studied the grave knight closest. He stared back but she pretended he could not see her from behind the cloth.

"I've got a dagger," she whispered. "I've got a dagger under my pillow. Do you hear me?" She giggled. "I'm going to slit my wrists. I'm going to kill myself. Do you hear me?"

The grave knights stepped forward in unison, all moving toward the bed.

"No, no," whispered Arazni. "Don't come close or I will," now she yelled, "slit my wrists!"

The grave knights pulled back the gossamer and began to pluck the pillows from the bed. Arazni leapt from one pillow to another, pinning them in place. "Not that one!" She laughed. "Not there!" She rolled over as the pillow she was clinging to was yanked from under her. She laughed like a child. "Which one is it under?" she cried. "Find the dagger or else!"

The grave knights cleared the bed of pillows. They found no dagger. They turned to look in unison at Arazni. She climbed to her knees, clutching a blanket to her breasts. She pouted, as if she were in trouble. "I was fibbing," she whispered. "Don't be mad. Just a little game. That's all. Don't be mad."

The grave knights turned and walked once more to the room's periphery. They turned again and stood, silently watching.

"Geb?" asked Arazni. "Is that you?" She spun on her knees and looked toward the door of her room. "Are you out there?" She rose from the bed and tip-toed to the door. The grave knight closest headed her off. She looked at him. "It's Geb. He's out there. We must go to him." She stared into the grave knight's unblinking eyes. He stood before her, blocking the door. Arazni screwed up her features. "You fool!" She slammed her fist into his armored chest. "Get out of my way! I can't keep him waiting! I can't! I must—" Again she tilted her head and listened. She smiled, reached out and petted the armored chest, as if smoothing ruffled fur. She looked from the grave knight's chest to his eyes. "No, no, that won't do, little brother." She backed toward the bed, shaking her finger at him.

Arazni crawled onto her bed and curled up, clutching the coverlet. "Aroden," she whispered. "Geb." She kept repeating these two names, over and over, as if the spell they wove could fulfill her desperate need for meaning.

. . .

The servant entered Kemnebi's chambers, after knocking and being granted permission to do so. He was a blood thrall, a mortal addicted to vampiric blood, drinking it from his master's wrist. Kemnebi's blood prolonged his thrall's life, granted him durability and strength, even a touch of vampiric power, but it also hopelessly bound him. If the blood thrall went a day without his master's blood he would begin to wither and perish, like a leaf pulled from a tree.

Wamukota, the blood thrall, was also Mwangi, not of the Mauxi but of the Zenj. He was once a fisherman, casting his flint-tipped spear into the streams and ponds of the Mwangi Expanse. He once lived in a grass hut. He once had many wives and many children. He once bickered with monkeys that threw fruit at him. He once feared the jaguar and the python. He once told his children stories of the deep jungle, where apes ruled and where man hid in trees. Those experiences seemed so unreal to him now that he doubted they had ever been true. He served Kemnebi and it had always been so. He knew nothing else.

"Master?" asked Wamukota. As he spoke he pushed to the floor a naked woman. Her skin was blotched and scabrous, although Wamukota had done his best to scrub the grime from it. She was hairless, not by being clean-shaven but by being bred to have no hair. Hair got filthy, hid lice, and was unsightly. The woman, now on all fours, had the intelligence of a toddler. Her simple mind could keep no language and, should her bare intellect spur her to self-expression, she possessed only grunts and hand-motions as a means of making her needs known.

She was food, bred to be consumed by one of the many flesh-hungry undead of Geb. On this night she was lucky, she might survive a vampire. Others were not so lucky, they went to feed ghouls, who consumed dead flesh, or still worse, those undead who drained the essence of life itself, reducing their meals to husks.

"Master?" asked Wamukota. "Why do you keep candles?" He made his way to the shelf, squeezing himself between the desk and Kemnebi. "You've a spell for light." He glanced over his shoulder at his master. "Need you light at all?" He turned and began to trim the candles and check the free-flowing of their wax.

Kemnebi did not answer. Instead, he studied the woman. It was difficult for him to see her as human. She was really not so different from him but he could not acknowledge that fact. She gazed at him with child-like wonder. She did not see him as a threat. She could not comprehend that she had been taken from the pens and brought here for him to feed upon. She saw only a strange man with dark skin and dark eyes. She smiled at him, drool spilling from her open mouth.

"Take it away."

"Master?"

"I'm going out to hunt."

"But Master?" asked Wamukota, abandoning the candles and coming around the woman. "Hunt?"

"Is that so strange, Wamukota?"

"It's—" But Wamukota did not finish his thought. It was illegal to hunt. That is why the chattel were bred. No mortal would dare visit Geb if she knew she might not survive her first night there. It was illegal even for Kemnebi to hunt the living. He was not above Geb's laws, such as they were. "It's only, you haven't hunted in so long, Master."

"You fear I've forgotten how?" asked Kemnebi. "A vampire does not forget the night and how to use it."

"Of course not, Master."

"Take it away, I said. It stinks."

. . .

Mechitar is a coastal city. The Obari Ocean laps against its feet. The Cinerarium lies at the heart of the capital but it was toward the docks that Kemnebi walked. He had dug through the closet in his office, attempting to find a robe that was less than regal. He found a robe of gold-colored cloth that was so aged and moth-eaten it had turned brown and was full of holes. He took off his leather sandals, preferring to go barefoot in the muck of the streets. He removed all rings and necklaces that were for ornament alone, including that which denoted him chancellor. He tucked his magical amulets beneath the moth-eaten fabric. He turned his magical rings gem-side down. He left his enchanted staff leaned against the wall.

Nights in Geb can be cool, even in summer. This night was especially cool, as winter had just lifted its oppressive hand from the Inner Sea. The bracing air was a pleasant change from the stuffy atmosphere of the

Cinerarium. Mechitar was not a well-lit city. The dead did not often need light to see. Nor did they cherish the security light offered for it did the opposite to them, it threatened to expose. When the sun passes over the horizon fully two-thirds of Mechitar drops into absolute darkness. The remaining third is well-lit, lit enough to make up for those parts that welcome the night. It is in this well-lit third that the living huddle against the darkness and its denizens. It was this well-lit, life-filled third that Kemnebi skirted, circling like a wolf at the edge of an isolated human habitation.

He could hear them, the living, crowded in their houses. He could hear them finishing their meals, cleaning their dishes, snapping sticks for the hearth, commanding their children to bed, the children resisting. He could hear them cursing the night, begging the gods to hold the door against the darkness on the other side. Few lived alone. Solitude was an indulgence allowed to those who feared not the night. In Geb the living slept in the light.

There were some—either foolish or unlucky—who found themselves outside of the light. A merchant, who had been delayed in an important sale, hurried home, rushing through darkened streets, holding a burning torch, but one that did not burn bright enough for comfort, whispering prayers to Iomadae and Desna, clutching the handle of his dagger with his other hand. Young lovers who foolishly risked everything on an evening tryst now rushed through the streets, leaping between pools of light, frightened, exhausted, and exhilarated. Kemnebi heard them, saw them, and wondered at the flavor of their blood but let them pass.

Kemnebi kept to the darkness but watched the light. He approached the docks and turned to look out over the Obari. Waves beat their rhythm upon the shore. He heard a hound howl. It was joined by another. Kemnebi did not stay at the docks but turned and walked north, wishing to walk along the Axanir River, despite his vampiric fear of running water—a fear he never understood but could do little to counter. Once arrived at the mouth of the river he saw movement in the darkness.

He heard the hounds again, baying. He became aware that someone was watching him. Two hounds emerged and he realized they had been paralleling him. The man who was following him came closer. Kemnebi realized that the man, who was dressed as a sailor on leave from his ship, was not walking, but gliding. Nor was the man whole. There was little of legs under him. Kemnebi laughed. He was being hunted.

Kemnebi's laughter both surprised and annoyed the ghostly sailor. He was now close enough to Kemnebi to recognize that he was not living, but some other kind of undead. When Kemnebi turned to face his pursuer his attitude of amusement so unnerved the incorporeal undead that it eyed him suspiciously, whistled its hounds close, and turned back toward the docks.

"Not a sailor," it mumbled to its hounds. "A land-lover."

Kemnebi watched the fellow hunter go. 'Another who does not keep the Dead Laws.'

He continued from one neighborhood to the next, working his way toward the commercial center of the city. Merchants brought out their wares only under cover of darkness; they displayed strange things: ghastly spell components for necromancy, mementos from cultures remembered only by the dead, tomes in forgotten languages, and items unpleasant to identify yet more valuable than gold to those who sought them.

Kemnebi walked the midnight bazaar. He observed the few merchants and the scarcely more numerous undead customers. The bazaar had the atmosphere of one that took place in a war-ravaged city. The shoppers moved silently from stall to stall. When they spoke to the merchants they whispered. When the merchants replied they whispered still lower. There was no dallying, no friendly chatter between shoppers. None commented on the weather. The undead were not given to idle chit-chat.

'What do the dead need?' Kemnebi asked himself. 'The living need much and they desire still more than they need. But the dead?' He left the bazaar, lest he be recognized.

While his confessed purpose was to hunt, and while the unnatural beast within him hungered, Kemnebi made no effort to capture prey. He told Wamukota that he remembered how to use the night but something in him desired contemplation more than killing. He roamed the streets of Mechitar, both dark and lit.

He heard the deep breathing, snoring, and night-tossing of the living. From the houses of the dead he heard nothing. He came upon a group of ghouls leaping wildly over a kill. The taste of fresh blood called to his vampiric curse but he hurried away before he lost control of the beast within. He felt one of his own amongst the houses of the living and his curiosity carried him to her.

There were few shadows amongst the habitations of the living but he found them. The offensive odor of garlic struck his nose like a fist. He could see that it hung all around him in bunches. This was not the only defense the living employed. Talismans were set on every window sill. Bundles of sage hung from eaves. Scraps of paper with prayers had been nailed to every door. Holy symbols—enchantments laid upon them in layers—hung from nails by silver thread. All this irritated him and nearly drove him from the area, but he persisted.

He heard her hissing before he saw her. He stepped through a garden gate and looked down and to the side.

She was seated with her back against the low stone wall. She pulled her victim closer to her, shielding her body with his semi-conscious form, and bared her fangs at Kemnebi. Her prey was a young man, a laborer of some kind, for Kemnebi could see, even in the shadow in which the man lie, that his hands were calloused and the knees of his pants worn and dirty. His clothes were of simple make, as were his sandals.

Kemnebi stepped toward the vampire. She hissed still louder. He held his hands out, proffering peace. The man stirred, his eyes fluttering, but fell back into unconsciousness. Blood spilled in twin trails from the puncture wounds in his neck, joining just above his collar bone. The sight of it, the smell of it in the air, the imagined taste of it almost drove Kemnebi to action, but movement drew his attention. The feeding vampire, more like an animal at that moment, held out one clawed hand. She combined this with a primal growl.

Kemnebi felt the challenge she was issuing. He felt the beast within him longing to respond but he suppressed it. "You break the law," he said, his voice low and controlled. The vampire, caught mid-feed, was beyond the reach of reason. Since she failed to frighten her competition she now prepared to defend her catch. She slid the man from her lap, got her feet under her, and crouched, ready to pounce.

Now that Kemnebi could see her he was stunned. Her elaborate and costly dress was ruined by the mud and vegetation of the garden through which she had scooted, the man in her lap. Her sandaled feet were muddy to the ankles. Her jewelry was caked with a mixture of mud and blood. Her hair, once combed and perfumed, was unkempt. Her face, which, at all other times must be regal and poised, had lost all that was civilized, becoming wild.

Kemnebi took a reflexive step back, not because of the danger she posed, which, to him, was minuscule, but because she so perfectly embodied his concerns at that moment that he was unnerved. He turned and stepped through the gate, paused, looked once more at the crouched, growling, feral form, then hurried from the scene, leaving the neighborhood entirely.

He was surprised at the number of undead who willfully broke the Dead Laws. He knew many consumed the chattel provided for them. He saw the numbers bred and the numbers consumed. He had no idea so many undead eschewed such easy meals in favor of stalking and killing their prey. The unexpected insight disturbed him.

He wondered what he, in his role as chancellor, should do about it. Yet it was Geb himself who had defined the Dead Laws. It was Geb who had instituted breeding programs to feed his own kind. If a determined minority were defiant of Geb's will, Kemnebi wondered, what could he do? If they did not fear Geb why would they fear him? If Geb did nothing, should anything be done?

Every vampire possesses a supernatural sense that tracks the position of the sun. The dawn surprises no vampire. Should a mortal lie exposed to the sun they will feel its heat and in time be scorched by it. What a mortal would experience from a day of such exposure a vampire feels in an instant. Two such moments of exposure would be the end. The sun is the giver of life. It burns away sickness. It is an antiseptic. The sun abhors death, rot, decay, and darkness. Vampires are of death and darkness and so the sun is their enemy.

It was due to this sense that Kemnebi realized that dawn was fast approaching. He had walked Mechitar all night, feeding not, but observing much. He turned toward the Cinerarium and saw that its tip glowed pink. He began toward it. As he walked, the city awakened.

The sun was the protector of the living in Geb. They kept to its schedule, rising when it rose, settling when it set. There was much activity to fit into the day's allotment of protective warmth and light. The living were quick to rise and become industrious. Kemnebi—taking a terrible and foolish risk—clung to the shadows and watched as shutters opened, doors were unlocked, and faces appeared. He saw the smile on a man's face when he beheld his neighbor peeking from the doorway adjacent. The smile was returned. He continued on, clinging to the shadows.

"Where's that rooster of yours?" asked one woman of her neighbor. Kemnebi heard them as he passed on the other side of the wall by which they spoke.

"He got over the wall yesterday," answered the other woman, "most likely eaten by ghouls."

"Not ghouls," said the first woman.

"Oh? Why not?"

"They only eat *our* flesh."

The two women laughed.

Kemnebi moved on, now desperate to get behind the windowless walls of the Cinerarium.

"Are you going to make bricks today?" He heard one man ask another.

"Aye," answered his walking companion. "If the clay is not too wet."

"How can you stand to be down at the river's edge? Who knows what kind of undead lurk beneath the surface, ready to leap out."

"Only the rotten corpses of old brick makers like me, drowned themselves on purpose to end their miserable labors."

"What keeps them from grabbing you?"

"They've no sense of charity."

The two men laughed and parted.

Kemnebi arrived within the protective shadow the Cinerarium and could relax. He paused before entering and looked out over the city. 'They've a gallows humor,' he thought of those he had overheard.

He operated under the assumption that the living in Geb huddled together like so many frightened mice. That they laughed, that they walked erect, that they went about their business with unburdened hearts, that they acted like free men and women, not like cowed slaves, shocked him. Was the light of day so uplifting that the mortals of Geb forgot they served the dead, he wondered. Or was he mistaken?

. . .

Wamukota was waiting for him and could see at once that his master was upset. He would have scurried from his master's chambers, avoided his foul mood, but he hadn't fed. Kemnebi seemed surprised to see Wamukota or perhaps surprised that his thrall remained, looking plaintively at him. He realized why and raised his wrist to his mouth, let his canines drop, and punctured his wrist.

Kemnebi fell into his chair and let his arm fall to the side. Wamukota sunk to his knees, gently took up his master's arm, and raised the bleeding wrist to his lips. A look of ecstasy came over his face as soon as the blood splashed against his tongue. Kemnebi paid no heed to his thrall. He looked over the open books on his desk.

"Their laws are defensive," he said, speaking as if Wamukota could hear him. Even if the sound of his master's voice penetrated the intoxication of the blood the words were not for him, but were for the speaker. "Their laws protect life. That's why they have laws, because their lives are fragile." There was something charming about their laws, something he had come to admire. "They work so hard," he continued. "To pile up the twigs of safety and security around themselves; so many nest-building birds, hollow-boned and weak, but able to fly." He smiled to himself. "And how diligently they protect their nests." He felt a pang of discomfort and looked to Wamukota. "Greedy, are we?" His blood thrall did not open his eyes. "Wamukota!"

Wamukota opened his eyes and looked up at his master but did not remove his lips or cease his drinking. He had a strange look in his eyes, a look that mingled love, lust, shame, and hatred. Kemnebi had seen the look so many times from so many different mortals that he ceased to be swayed by it.

"Do you ever go amongst the living?" asked Kemnebi. Wamukota furrowed his brow, as if the question was absurd. "But you are living, Wamukota." The richness of Kemnebi's blood overtook Wamukota and he closed his eyes, no longer listening. "Or are you?" asked Kemnebi. "Have I made you dead, like me? Enough. Enough, Wamukota!" Kemnebi yanked his arm free and Wamukota fell back. He lifted his hand to his chin and wiped the remaining blood from it. This he licked from his fingers.

"Go out today," commanded Kemnebi. "Go out and be amongst your own kind."

"But, Master," protested Wamukota. "Whatever for?"

"Damn you, Wamukota. Go out, I say. Go out and be alive!"

Broaching a Sensitive Subject

Master Castelli's Estate, Ecanus, Nex, Sarenith, 4710

Master Castelli sat in an overstuffed chair, rotating a glass of wine by its stem as he watched the svirfneblin's blue eyes dart around the room with a bemused smile. In an adjoining room his youngest daughter, Basimah, sat on a bench beneath a window, strumming her harp and humming a song to herself. If he cared to look he could see her through the archway. Her delightful notes filtered into the room, granting it an air of peace and calm.

"How fares the Mana Waste?" asked Master Castelli.

The svirfneblin—that is, a deep gnome—was quite unlike the fey-touched illusionists, tricksters, and indefatigable explorers found on the surface. Deep gnomes dwell in underground caves far below their sun-loving kin, eschewing others' company. He rested his ever-active eyes on his host for a second, then continued cataloging the room's shapes, shadows, features, and contents.

This was the third meeting between the two men. Among humans that is enough to establish a familiarity and a certain amount of trust. Yet, the svirfneblin seemed as guarded and distrustful as he had been from the first. Castelli wondered if it was a natural trait of that people or particular to this individual. His gaze drifted to the movement of his wine. He sank into his thoughts as the red liquid rose and fell, a miniature ocean contained in glass.

In time he felt the full weight of the other man's eyes on him. He glanced from his glass to the small, dark presence sunk like a child—for he was no bigger than a child—in the twin to his own gratuitously padded chair.

The svirfneblin's eyes were motionless, boring into him like ice pressed against unprotected flesh. In that moment, Master Castelli, an accomplished practitioner of the arcane arts, a deft political operative, and a man of wealth and public esteem, felt as vulnerable as an infant.

"How do you do it?" he asked, his voice cautious, out of fear of what he might learn. "How do you survive that hellish expanse?" Basimah halted her harp-play. Into the resulting silence, Master Castelli continued. "Geb and Nex, those two god-like wizards, tore apart reality itself in their millennia-long war. The Mana Waste, their battlefield, is a living wound upon Golarion."

The knowledge that the nature of magic itself had been rent and twisted, made aberrant and uncontrollable, especially in the region known as the Spellscar, filled him with considerable disquiet. To sit across from one who regularly traversed, who seemed quite capable of surviving, even thriving, in such hostile environs, made him nervous.

Ilyx, for that was the name given by the svirfneblin, remained silent and unmoving. In the adjoining room Basimah's footsteps were heard. A door opened and closed. Master Castelli raised his glass to his lips, gulped down the remainder of his wine, and, with a visible shudder, cast the evil forebodings from his person. He focused instead on the svirfneblin's find. For Ilyx was much like a prospector, not panning for gold, but for something much more valuable.

The svirfneblin observed the outward signs of Master Castelli's inward change of mood and anticipated his desire. Before his host could voice his wish, Ilyx scooted to the edge of his chair, dropped to his feet, and crossed the room to the small chest sitting just inside the door. The jangling of his weapons and the metallic rustling of his chain shirt echoed about the room. His footfalls were silent.

He carefully picked up the chest, turned, re-crossed the room, and set the chest before Master Castelli. He spun the chest to face the other man and pulled open its lid. The reflected light from the chest's contents illuminated Castelli's face, coloring it with washes of orange, yellow, and pink.

"Astonishing," said Master Castelli. He looked from the lightning glass, he had no other term for it, to Ilyx. "There's more here than the last two trips combined," he observed with a sense of pleasant shock. He reached for a piece of delicate glass, but the chest's lid shut, barring his fingers. He looked to the svirfneblin. "Yes, of course." He rose and went to a sideboard.

He glanced at the space between the sideboard and the window sash. He knew that a magical creation—invisible and dangerous—stood unmoving in the space. He had created the creature himself and had commanded it to act as his bodyguard. He glanced over his shoulder, looking at Ilyx, who stood behind the chest, his child-sized hand on its closed lid, gazing back at him.

'Can he detect my creation?' Castelli wondered. He knew that gnomes, surface gnomes, the only kind he had any real familiarity with, had an innate understanding of magic. He was unsure if the svirfneblin, separated eons ago from their surface-dwelling kin, shared that natural aptitude.

"Care for a glass of wine? I've a wonderful vintage from Andoran." Castelli asked. The deep gnome did not stir. "Suit yourself." He opened the sideboard and found the small, bell-shaped bottle. He pulled it into the light. It appeared empty, yet was corked. He knew it to be magical. He also knew it to contain an endless supply of fresh air. All one had to do was un-cork the bottle and breathe, no matter the vacuum, noxious gas, or other hazards, the bottle would ensure that, at the least, the owner would not perish for want of air.

He made it himself, crafting was his first love. Ilyx requested just such an item at their last meeting. In an uncharacteristically long, precise explanation, Ilyx said the Mana Waste was frequently swept by magical storms that either sucked the air from the land or deposited their own noxious mix of gases—perhaps remnants of Geb's atrocious, killing fog—upon it. In such cases, opined Ilyx, fresh air was much desired.

Master Castelli turned from the sideboard. "This," he held up the magical bottle of air, "in addition to your usual asking price." Castelli looked to the case resting against the chair. He knew that Ilyx used a rare item, a gun, and that it resided in the case. "If you would allow me to examine—" A sharp look from Ilyx answered. "I was only suggesting I could make ammunition for it." But the offer did not interest the svirfneblin. Master Castelli crossed the room and extended the bottle to the ebony-skinned gnome.

Ilyx accepted the bottle, lifted his hand from the chest, uncorked the bottle and held his fingers over the opening. He could feel the air's force as it exited. He brought the bottle to his nose, looking at Master Castelli, and tested the air. Finding it to his satisfaction he re-corked the bottle and stuffed it into a pouch at his waist. He then made his way to the sideboard where he investigated, peering like a child up and over the edge, the other bottles, uncorking them, smelling, sometimes tasting, and re-corking. He decided in favor of a brandy from Molthune.

Master Castelli settled himself into his chair, pulled the chest onto his lap, and opened it. He gazed down at the erratically-shaped pieces of glass. He knew how they were made. In his years of crafting he had come across one or two pieces. He knew that deep in the Spellscar desert violent, magic-fueled storms raged. He knew that when lightning stuck the desert dunes the heat melted the sand, forming lightning-shaped glass. This was true of all such occurrences, whether in the Spellscar desert or out of it. However, in the Spellscar, whose sands were saturated with magic, and whose storms were not a result of any natural weather, but of the capricious whims of Geb and Nex's angry magics, such glass held amazing properties.

"Did you know," said Master Castelli to Ilyx, who was settling himself once again in the too-comfortable chair, the tumbler of brandy at his slate-gray lips, "that with this glass I can make any type of ioun stone? It's true." He laughed. "Normally crafting an ioun stone is a rather particular process, like baking a fine pastry. One must balance the ingredients carefully, in the case of an ioun stone, pairing the correct crystalline structure with the desired magical effect." He looked down at the colored pieces of glass. "This glass happily accepts whatever magics I put into it. You would think it too fragile, but once it takes the enchantment, it's shatter-proof." He glanced at Ilyx then back to the chest's contents. "I've made a gift of one such ioun stone to Iranez of the Orb, through intermediaries, of course. I received a hand-written thank you from Iranez herself, expressing delight." He waved his hand in mock-humility. "Of course, such things don't impress you, do they?"

Ilyx had finished his brandy. Master Castelli noticed and rose, stepping to the sideboard. He retrieved the bottle of Molthune brandy and refilled his guest's tumbler.

"All is in order, yes? All parties satisfied?" He looked down at the svirfneblin, who gazed up at him with his ice-blue eyes. Master Castelli smiled, but his smile faded. "If I may test your patience a bit further," he studied the smaller man's face, but could discern no emotion in its features. He continued, nonetheless, "I must broach a sensitive subject."

Ilyx tilted his head at this unexpected continuance.

Master Castelli returned to the sideboard and placed the bottle of brandy with its companions. With a bit of arcane speech and a weaving of his hands through the air he caused a bit of magic to shape itself into existence; the effect being, the room was cut off from divination, scrying, and other forms of eavesdropping, magical, or mundane.

He turned to face Ilyx. "Have you ever been to Geb?"

Ilyx, who had been savoring a mouthful of brandy, swallowed, then turned to look at his host. For the first time since entering Master Castelli's sprawling estate that morning he spoke, "Dangerous," was all he said.

"Exceedingly," added Master Castelli. "Would you consider going again?" He crossed the room and sat down in the chair across from Ilyx. "Your compensation would far exceed the difficulties and dangers you would face, I assure you." He glanced to the pouch in which the deep gnome had stuffed the magical bottle of air. "Far exceed what you're accustomed to."

"No."

Obsession

Geb's Rest, Geb, Pharast, 4711

What becomes of an individual life when time has lost all meaning? Aroden knew but he died. Nex knew but he vanished. Geb knew and he killed himself. Of the three only Geb returned, a ghost, cursed to pace the limits of his cage. He began to erect a palace near the edge of that cage, at the border of Geb and what, in time, would be called the Mana Waste, but he abandoned the effort.

The pyramidal palace stood half-erect. Massive blocks of stone lay scattered about, earthen ramps long returned to nature, wooden scaffolding rotting and occasionally collapsing, tools abandoned, their iron rusting —a centimeter vanishing every hundred years or so.

He named these ruins Geb's Rest and again we see his humor at work, for Geb could not rest so long as Nex's fate was unknown to him. Revenge is a powerful motivator. People have caused their own deaths in seeking it. They have harmed innocents to get at the object of their hatred. Some have sacrificed their morals seeking satisfaction for a wrong, real or imagined. Revenge blinds. Revenge binds. Revenge is the ugly offspring of pride, which is itself hideous.

Over five thousand years prior Nex and Geb went to war. Over a thousand years after that war began, Geb tried to end it. Calling upon the most powerful magics at his command he sent a fog over the land of Nex, a fog that hid within its vapors death.

By this time Nex had erected a refuge, a fortress that existed between the folds of space and time. It is doubtful that he feared Geb's fog. By all accounts Nex thought little of his rival. His attitude was one of an adult pestered by a persistent and obnoxious child, a child one longs to rid oneself of, but cannot. When the fog rolled down the sloping plains of Nex toward Quantium, its capital and largest city, Nex took one last look over the nation he built, the land he ruled, and the people who thought him a god, then stepped beyond the threshold of reality, entering the Refuge of Nex, never to be seen again.

Geb reveled in his victory for a time, though it was a hollow one. Had he really defeated Nex? The question plagued him. He felt he had been dismissed, as if Nex had grown tired of his presence and had departed without a word. This insult to Geb's pride grew like a cancer within him. Six decades after he had driven Nex from Golarion he drove a ritual dagger into his own heart. All for nought. He returned, more obsessed than ever. What was his obsession? To know the fate of Nex. To know he is defeated, finally, truly defeated.

This obsession consumed him. He scarcely noticed as thousands of years passed over him. Yes, he acted. Yes, he defended Geb against its enemies. Yes, he guided the nation he had created; but these were forced actions, not voluntary. They were annoyances, distractions from his obsession.

For perhaps a millennium, Geb had ceased to pace. He stood erect—or rather floated, having no material form —his gaze fixed northeast, passing over the Spellscar desert, the villages and towns of Nex, and finally the rooftops of Quantium. He stared at the Refuge of Nex, boring his eyes into the silent edifice. This was all he could do. It was a futile attempt to summon his rival from the unknown.

All this time he plotted. All this time he dreamed up methods, tactics, plans, visions of war, visions of suffering, visions of Nex's ultimate defeat. He pondered every permutation. He explored every eventuality. He scrapped plan after plan, finding deep within each a fatal flaw. Every plan took him to the Refuge's doorstep and upon it every plan failed. Knowing magic better than any other on Golarion, he understood the Refuge of Nex was impenetrable. It was a door without a key. It was a door sealed shut for eternity. He could invent no way to breach it.

This is how Geb reckoned time.

This is how Geb nurtured his cancer.

This is how Geb obsessed.

A Contemplation, a Quest

The Home of Ahrhune ag-Hashid, Aspenthar, Thuvia, Pharast, 4711

Ahrhune ag-Hashid was an aging man. His years on the Inner Sea began as an untested cabin boy on the pirate ship *The Sands* and ended—after battles, unwelcome boardings, and assaults too numerous to count—as captain of *The Destiny*, a pirate ship funded by Prince Zinlo, leader of Thuvia's second-largest city. That same prince had gifted Ahrhune the handsome home he now uneasily occupied, a burden that weighed his heart with regret.

The many seasons at sea tested Ahrhune's constitution and found that edifice impenetrable. The life of a pirate, even one operating under the secret protection of a prince as cunning as Zinlo, was so peppered with dangers that it had refined his wits into a piercing point, still sharp after two years of comfortable land-living.

Ahrhune ag-Hashid had been decorated with such honors as a pirate may get: the glory of battles won, the reputation that comes from surviving long years under sword and sky, and the wealth and trappings of a thief. Two years ago *The Destiny* was pulled to pieces by a magical storm. He had seen an angry div, an evil spirit, a genie-kin, skating the violently-pitched waves and had known it to be the cause.

Somehow he was not taken into the bosom of Gozreh, Master of the Waters, a fate he deserved, for he had lived by the largesse of that fickle god for three decades. No, he did not drown. Instead, when the div's anger was satisfied and the black-bottomed clouds departed, Ahrhune found himself on the shore east of Aspenthar, cradled by sparkling sands the color of hammered copper. The sun shown down upon him with such grandeur that he felt he had died and washed ashore in the land beyond. It was then and there that he decided upon retirement.

Now he sat, his legs crossed beneath him, on a satin-covered pillow: green, trimmed with gold threads and tassels. He balanced a sheathed scimitar on his knees, stroking his beard—more gray than black these days—nursing his doubts.

'Can an old pirate, a taker of men's lives, indulge in such a luxurious fantasy?' he wondered. 'Here I sit, in comfort, warm, over-fed, in the home of a prince,' his gaze fell from the gem-encrusted scabbard to the fine, patterned cloth of his wide-legged pants, to the tooled-leather tops of his house slippers, to the hand-woven rug, red, blue, and gold, displaying a marvelous artistry, gleaming up at him from beneath the cushion.

He was struck by the memory of his first "bed" on the ship *The Sands*. It was a fish-gut-caked patch of wood on the floor of the hold, blanketed by rats, that he fought off with a broken mop handle, and yet whose warmth he sought when the cold of the sea came seeping through the hull, pulling his life's warmth from him on those dark, moonless nights.

'They say religion comes to old men,' he thought. 'How will you take me, Sarenrae, the Dawnflower, the Redeemer? Is it you that fills me with this sense of dishonesty? Now that I am wealthy and content, or should be content, I come begging pardon. I have thrown men into the sea, hearing not their pleas for mercy, yet I beseech you for mercy.

'I ask you to forgive my dishonest life, to heal me of my guilt, to hear my cries for redemption, now that the specter of death hovers near. Am I a hypocrite? What would you, the goddess of honesty, do with a hypocrite who begs your favor? Yet, under that brilliant sun, on those welcoming sands, did I not feel your presence? Was it not you who began our dialogue? Who informed me that my wayward soul needed to be redeemed?'

Ahrhune felt self-conscious. His own troubling thoughts and doubts filled him with self-loathing. With a frown he set the scimitar on the altar and rose. A perfume of aloes wood and pastilles came from the harem. Also from there he heard many instruments, played by joyous hands. These notes mixed with the melodious warble of nightingales that floated in through the open window. The appetizing smell of many rich, fattening dishes greeted his nose.

He stood, placing his doubts aside for the moment. He straightened his shirt and sash, felt the turban on his head with his fingers, reassuring himself of the tightness of its wrapping. He touched the outside of his hip pocket, feeling the hard certainty of the wax-stopped, metal vial it held.

In that vial was a dose of sun orchid elixir, kept—he was a thief, after all—from among the booty of his trade. All such vials were to be given to Prince Zinlo. Failing to do so brought death. Ahrhune had defied the order. He knew that the elixir would pull back the heavy blanket of time. He knew that even the small amount of elixir in his possession would cause him to outlive the youngest in his harem. Such was the promise of that priceless alchemical mixture, derived from the sun orchid, that rare, delicate, desert bloom. Why he had not cut the wax and imbibed the potion he did not know. It was a mystery his wisdom wrestled with.

The pleasant odors spoke to his stomach. His mouth was eager for wine and candied dates, seasoned fowl, the crisp snap of cucumber, pleasantly warm breads, and rich chocolates, all finished with coffee. Thus was his bind, thus were the two choices before him. One, to redeem his soul and pass beyond the flesh, the other, to squeeze from life every drop of pleasure and joy. He weighed the scales, oscillating back and forth.

Now, he went to the flesh. He smiled to himself. 'One should enjoy life's bounty,' he decided. He thought to look to the altar, to, as was his custom, open Sarenrae's holy book, *The Birth of Light and Truth*, in order to take a bit of scripture to the dining hall, to his guests—for he always had guest these days—as a point of conversation, yet he did not.

. . .

That night Ahrhune slept poorly. Perhaps the rich food, which he still wasn't accustomed to after two years, caused him to toss and turn. Perhaps it was that he had retired to bed after sharing in the company of Dinarzade, that slender-waisted, giggling, long-lashed beauty from Pashow, without saying his evening prayers, the guilt of which, caused his fitful slumber.

Or perhaps it was that his questions to his goddess were being answered—as they so often are—in his dreams. For Ahrhune had, on that cool evening, his window open, admitting the salted breeze from the Inner Sea, a vision so horrifying, so menacing, so beyond even the most hauntingly memorable nightmare from his childhood, that he awoke with a scream that frightened all others in his home and brought them to his side.

"I must go," was all he said to mollify their fears. When his destination was sought by his staff, slaves, and lovers, he repeated, "I must go."

That morning Ahrhune, once a pirate, in command of a formidable ship and crew, returned all of his wealth to his prince, kept with him only what he needed for travel and battle, and set foot once again on the deck of a ship, this time as a passenger. He had as his only guides the nightmarish vision and *The Birth of Light and Truth*. In his pocket remained the vial. He had not relinquished that.

A Meeting, an Epiphany Expressed, Discord

The Cinerarium, Mechitar, Geb, Pharast, 4711

Geb designed the Cinerarium's grand hall with sensitivity to acoustics and lines of sight.There are no pillars in the room or any other features but chairs, open space, and a statue of Geb. The room is a polygon with eight faces, floor and ceiling uncounted. At one end is a dais with a throne.

The throne, like all such specimens, was too large for its occupant, too ostentatious for its setting, and too uncomfortable to be long endured. It was meant for Geb but its cushion ceased to be compressed by him. In his throne sat Arazni, the Harlot Queen, much slighter in build than Geb and so nearly disappearing into the regal chair. She tucked her legs under her like a child, twirled an enchanted wand between her delicate fingers, and looked at the assembled Blood Lords with curiosity, malice, and boredom.

The wall opposite the throne was the entrance through which the Blood Lords passed, adhering to their long-ago established order of coming and going. These elites now sat in semi-circular rows, with the most important at the front, the least important at the rear. By turning her head to her left Arazni could see Eratosthenes.

Their relationship was a complex one. Long ago, the disillusioned elf came to her. He promised everything he possessed—and everything he would come to possess—for the secret to lichdom. Before this, Eratosthenes fought to regain the elven lands from the demon Treerazer. He had been wounded and he could not be recovered by the elves, who were forced to leave him for dead. His blood seeped into the Tanglebriar and something of that cursed land flowed in reverse. He did not die but crawled free of the Tanglebriar, holding in his guts with one hand. This is how he left Kyonin. He never returned.

Arazni accepted his offer, sharing with that regal elf both her knowledge and her bed. It pained her to recall the kinds of emotions she had long ago abandoned for lesser substitutes. Eratosthenes became a lich but not through Arazni—he learned of the Whispering Way not long after arriving in Geb. In time their relationship grew cool, became official, became political.

Eratosthenes gave wise counsel. He could be trusted. But Eratosthenes desired to become a power unto himself and had. He gave wise counsel, but took none. Behind him sat those who looked to him for leadership, his fellow liches, adherents of the Whispering Way, and those violent undead that only he could control.

If Arazni turned her head slightly to the right she could see Aleksandr Kovalenko. Of elven blood Aleksandr possessed half. He was Chelaxian, born of nobility. He was Kemnebi's eldest child still "alive" and active. Having been raised in the stewing cauldron of Chelaxian power politics served Aleksandr well. His self-control was total, his erudition complete, his far seeing perception an asset to him and those he took into his confidence.

He was handsome, sender in body and face, with long chestnut-colored hair, enchanting brown eyes, full lips, and a straight nose. The elven half of his blood turned his otherwise masculine features somewhat androgynous. In soft lighting he looked a youth. In harsher lighting he could summon a sinister mien. A scar plunged from his hairline, traveling down the left side of his face to the corner of his jaw. It contrasted sharply with his delicate features, providing him an air of danger or perhaps tragedy, depending on how he used it.

Still further right and Arazni could see Hent-er-Neheh. There were few like her. She was so old that the word anachronism seemed not enough, for she was of a culture so buried by the sands of time that she was foreign in aspect, manner, language, and thought.

It was difficult to place the mummy lord. She was Geb's ancestor. (Four such relatives of Geb sat in the grand hall, all Blood Lords, all mummies.) It was Hent that formerly began to teach Geb the arcane arts. It was difficult to imagine that Geb had ever been anything less than a wizard-god. That there was one who not only held memories of such a time but who was the source of Geb's arcane understanding was bizarre. That one existed who had scolded Geb, called him out for his errors, turned his nose to his books, was unfathomable, yet there she sat.

The relatives of Geb occupied a strange place amongst the Blood Lords. They could scarcely be argued against. They could claim unrivaled knowledge of Geb's desires, for they knew him, were related to him, and had aided his rise to power. They maintained the party line, the status quo, of Geb's culture, yet they were alien in their outlook, in their concerns, in their expectations, in their dealings.

When Geb was present in Mechitar his relatives were the most powerful of the Blood Lords. With Geb's absence they have fallen somewhat. Not to say that any Blood Lord would cross Hent-er-Neheh or her father, Nakht-Neb-Tep-Nefer, himself a mummy, one generation removed from those who founded the death cult in Osirion when much of the Inner Sea was untamed wilderness.

Seated next to Hent was Latitia, the Diseased. It was no mistake that Hent sat between Latitia and Aleksandr, for they had been lovers and, when Aleksandr's feelings cooled, Latitia swore to destroy him, a promise she had yet to fulfill. Latitia was not the High Priest of the Church of Urgathoa in Geb, that role went to Sthaga. But Sthaga was a dread wraith who, although powerful, had lost all concern for politics, even, some would say religion, desiring only to slay the living. It was Latitia, and others such as Narcisse, who sat immediately behind her, and Nah-le-tah, who did not sit at all (he was a tomb giant and far too large for any available seat), who had risen to prominence in the church.

This was to be expected. She was a Daughter of Urgathoa. Amongst all the Blood Lords and all the undead in Geb only Latitia was so blessed by the Goddess of Undeath. Transformed from human into a hulking, yet somehow graceful, scythe-clawed undead who, with every wave of her arms, cast seeds of disease, rot, and death about her.

It was this quintet that formed the first row before Arazni. Behind them their followers fanned out, jostling against one another in their complicated pecking order. A ten-foot-diameter space between the throne and the first row of Blood Lords served as an arena for the careful art of rhetoric. The hall echoed with the sounds of a door opening and closing. Footfalls were heard. All turned as their Chancellor entered.

. . .

Kemnebi advanced into the open space before Arazni, turned to her, and bowed. He turned to the Blood Lords, took a deep breath, and began.

"I've called this meeting of the Blood Lords to share with you an insight I've had due to my study of the legal codes of every nation of the Inner Sea." From the middle of the room he heard a gasp. It was barely audible and few other Blood Lords heard it. Kemnebi noted it but continued. "As you know I've been tasked with redefining the legal code of Geb. Much was different when the Dead Laws were made. We were at war and, honestly, things were simpler then."

Kemnebi had practiced this speech for several nights, going up and down ladders of logic, making and adjusting word choices, and anticipating his audience's reaction. He had so internalized his argument that he spoke freely. He began to move about the confined space, certain to turn to Arazni from time to time, to show respect and to retain her attention.

"What is the nature of the Dead Laws?" he asked his audience. It was a rhetorical device, a question he himself was to answer. "To protect the living." He paused and looked into several individual faces. "We think they protect us, and in a way they do, but mostly Geb was thinking of the living, for," he held up a finger, "without the living there would be no dead." He clasped his hands behind his back, looking down as he paced. "This is tautological. Of course, without the living there would be no dead. This is not what I mean." He paused his speech, stopped pacing, and looked at the Blood Lords. "Geb knew that a nation comprised only of undead was doomed."

Several gasps now joined the first. There was a great deal of uncomfortable twisting in one's seat, and a fair number of foul oaths. Mostly this came from the rear of the room. Those in the front had better self-control.

"Let us think practically," said Kemnebi, speaking over the noise, which was not yet great. "Many of us, myself included, could not continue to exist without the life force of the living. Geb foresaw this and instituted a breeding program so that those like me, and many others as well, would be fed. This was not the extent of Geb's foresight. He knew as well that a society of the undead would become a pariah, would be set upon by all other nations, would fail to have an economy, would fail to remain cohesive in any meaningful way without the living."

Noreen Paisely, a llorona—undead known for drowning victims as they once drowned their own children, hers in the Axanir—and a member of Arazni's court, rose. "The living?" she laughed. "Despicable. Blind cattle. Why should we—" A scowl from Arazni silenced her. She sat.

Kemnebi, who was emotionally prepared for such an outburst, remained unperturbed. He allowed silence to efface Noreen's words before continuing.

"The Dead Laws fill two pages of vellum." He held up two fingers. "Can a nation be sustained by two pages of law?" He shook his head. "I've read so many legal tomes I have come to abhor them. What do they all have in common? What do those seemingly endless layers of clause upon clause have in common with our Dead Laws? They all protect life. They all protect those trappings that promote life and make life worth living." He did not speak for several moments.

"What are we?" he asked, returning to his opening device. He motioned to Eratosthenes, "lich." He motioned to Hent-er-Neheh, "mummy." He motioned to Aleksandr, "vampire." He motioned to Latitia, "a Daughter of Urgathoa." He looked over the Blood Lords. "We are the elites. We are the natural aristocrats, the unnatural aristocrats, if you will." An idea struck him and he went with it. "And so Noreen's outburst is justified. What concern is it of ours what the living do, how the living live, or if there are any living at all, so long as we can feed?"

He sensed the turn had captured his audience's attention. He spoke with increased passion. "Yet, if there were only elites, we would destroy each other in futile strife. No, we can't deny it. It's true. Or," he again raised a finger, as if an idea had just come to him, "we would find some horrible equilibrium. We would watch each other, plot and scheme, yet hardly ever act for fear of final and irreversible death.

"These are individual concerns. How do we hold on to power? How do we oppress others while ourselves remaining free? I think this way myself but," he paused for effect, "in studying the law I have gained a broader perspective. What happens when there are more dead than living in a society? What happens when there are more elites than commoners? I asked earlier what are we. I ask now, what are the living? Are they, as we've heard, cattle? Or are they more?

"I ask you, how do societies of the living grow, evolve, change over time? How do societies of the dead do this? Can they? What happens when one nation ceases to change, ceases to evolve, while all others continue to? Will not this society fall behind? Won't it perish for want of—for lack of a better term—new blood, new ideas, new modes of living? Society builds upon itself as it grows, this is a rule of nature, growth through evolution, building upon what came before." He stopped and brought a hand to his chest, as if alarmed. "How can we grow? How can we benefit from this wise and powerful system? We cannot." He paused again, to let his ideas sink into his listeners' minds. In that pause Eratosthenes rose.

"What you speak of is known to all." Eratosthenes waved his hand over the assembly. "Have we not witnessed the rise and fall of empires? Have we not watched as family lines rose to prominence, like a weed gains ascendency in a garden, until it is yanked by the root? You speak of growth, of evolution, of change." Now Eratosthenes paused for effect. "Those of us who have escaped mortality know that these are cycles. The cycles of man, nothing more." He looked at Kemnebi. "You have become enchanted with mankind. You are, by your nature, the nature of a predator, tied to them. I cannot fault you for your concern with the living. Forget the works of the living, for they are shallow. They turn to dust, fall to the ground, and regrow, only to turn to dust again. They are cycles, repeated endlessly, nothing more." He was giving Kemnebi an out, a way to save face. Having done this, he sat. But Kemnebi did not take it.

"Cycles, yes, in this you are correct, Eratosthenes. But, like the corkscrew, with each turn they rise higher." Here there were mumbled disagreements and loud scoffs. Kemnebi continued. "I have seen the future of Geb. With each passing season there are fewer living amongst us. Soon there will be none except those we keep in pens. So what? you ask. I tell you, we need them. Not as food, not as slaves, but as providers of life. For Geb to continue we need to change, evolve, and grow as every other society does. Geb knew this. It's why he protected them, only he didn't go far enough. We must go still further." With every syllable of this sentence he pounded his fist into his open palm.

There followed a murmur of questioning and incredulous voices. Many of the more excitable Blood Lords spoke out, early to denounce Kemnebi for presenting the preposterous. A few rose up, as if to leave, but it was a symbolic act and after making it they sat, more curious than enraged.

"What do you propose, Chancellor?" asked Hent-er-Neheh.

Kemnebi, caught up in his own argument, was pleased to hear the question. He believed he was changing minds. That Hent was inviting him to ruin did not occur to him.

"When there are too many elites they fight over limited resources, limited wealth and positions of power. What's the result? They whittle down their number to an acceptable level, a level the society can support. This is what happens amongst the living, at any rate. But amongst us, who have no natural deaths to prod us to act, who can wait, who can lay plans that span decades, even centuries, this natural whittling down does not occur, or it occurs too slowly. The ranks of the elites swell. The common people cannot support them. The society collapses under its own weight."

"What do you propose, Chancellor?" repeated Hent-er-Neheh.

"If the forces that keep a society in balance are no longer in play in Geb, due to the nature of undeath," he looked at Hent-er-Neheh, "we must lessen our own number—intentionally."

"Fewer Blood Lords?" asked Aleksandr. He was Kemnebi's ally, and even in this he would support him, but he was hearing this for the first time, Kemnebi not having shared his thoughts or asked for counsel. If he had, Aleksandr would have cautioned him to keep his epiphany to himself.

"Not only that—" began Kemnebi, but Latitia rose.

She was a hulking presence in the open space between Arazni and the Blood Lords. Even though all she'd done was stand, Kemnebi had to leave the space to make room for her, especially for her scythe-like claw. She did not turn to the Blood Lords or address Arazni but stared at Kemnebi, her eyes aflame.

"Fewer undead? More living?" She looked from Kemnebi to the statue of Geb. "Do you hear that?" Now she looked to the floor, as if peering through stone and soil, seeing into the underworld. "Mistress—Goddess—do you hear that?" She returned her gaze to Kemnebi. "The living are vessels, to be filled with disease. The living are to die agonizing deaths. This is Urgathoa's command. Provide life? Provide life to us? Ha!" She took her seat. Kemnebi returned to the clearing, pretending that Latitia had never spoken.

"Fewer undead in total," he announced. The Blood Lords, mostly from the third row back, erupted in protest "We must return to what we naturally are," Kemnebi spoke over the dissenters. "We must be an aristocracy, an elite, not the common people in the streets. For that we need the living. There are too many undead."

The room fell silent. Kemnebi realized that Eratosthenes had stood and, arms outstretched, brought order to the room.

"I have an army," he stated, lowering his arms to his sides. "Thousands of undead, of many different types." He looked over his fellow Blood Lords. "Many of us have such armies. Those that don't, have private guards, household servants, and so forth, all comprised of undead." He turned to Kemnebi. "Would you deprive us?"

"No, not of the kind that survive solely on necromantic energy. It is the types of undead that prey upon the living—"

"Like you?" asked Eratosthenes.

Kemnebi thought of the vampire he had surprised in garden as she fed. "Yes, like me." When no one spoke he continued. "We need more living people in Geb. The scales are out of balance. Geb must, like all other nations, be a society of the living." A rising tide of angry voices washed over him. Again, he had to speak with the fullness of his voice. "It is the only way Geb will evolve. It is the only way Geb will survive. We, us," he waved his hands, indicating the Blood Lords, "we will rule, as we should. But we must acknowledge that we need the living. We cannot rule the dead."

There was discord in the grand hall. For several minutes each Blood Lord spoke, shouting over one another. The Blood Lords, unaccustomed to such outbursts, were driven to them by Kemnebi's heresy. After several minutes the voices began to silence. It took Kemnebi a moment to figure out why. When he did he turned and saw that Arazni was standing, one hand gripping the arm of Geb's throne, her wand fallen to the floor. Her grave knight protectors came forward from the shadows and stood around her.

"Arazni, Queen," said Kemnebi. "Tell me your thoughts."

Arazni stepped down from the dais, coming close to Kemnebi. She looked up into his face, the emotions of disbelief and anger clear in hers, but also something else—fear. She turned without a word and walked to her quarters. Her grave knights followed. After a moment's pause those in Arazni's court broke ranks and rushed after her.

Kemnebi watched as the women filed through Arazni's door, slamming it shut behind them. He turned and saw that Eratosthenes and his fellow liches were filing out the rear door, as were all of Geb's mummified relatives. Many of the worshippers of Urgathoa were leaving as well, although some stayed behind—those Urgathoans who still lived—curious to know more. All of Kemnebi's vampiric allies remained, but they shared a look of dismay.

. . .

In the outer hall a young woman studied the faces of the Blood Lords as they passed. Many faces, locked in the grimace of death, provided scant information about what had transpired during the meeting. She assessed the body language of the departing Blood Lords, listened carefully to every word spoken, and from these abridged sources she took what she could, to make use of in time. She had an excellent memory. She was there, in part, because she had an excellent memory.

Her name was Elana de Oliveira and she was from Nex. She kept that vital piece of information to herself when she arrived in Geb. She was pixie-like in appearance; her dark hair cut just at her jaw-line, bangs to just above her large, brilliant blue eyes, a button of a nose, and inviting, naturally red lips. She had a beauty mark along the ridge of her cheek bone, just off the center of her right eye.

It was this beauty mark that prompted Saskia to speak to the young woman in the otherwise hushed halls of the Ebon Mausoleum (both being in possession such a mark). Elana was a first-year student, a rare beauty in Geb, and also the most brilliant caster in her class. Once the two women drew close, they did not separate. It was Saskia who now rushed from the grand hall, grabbed Elana by the elbow, and spoke into her ear.

"Come inside," she commanded, pulling Elana into motion. "You must stay close to Kemnebi." Elana turned to look, not believing she had heard correctly. How was she, a student of the Ebon Mausoleum, and a mere assistant, albeit to a Blood Lord, supposed to stay close to the Chancellor? "Yes," said Saskia, answering the question she read in her protege's eyes. "He has few friends now. He will need new ones." The pair entered the grand hall, passing along its perimeter. In the center, Kemnebi spoke to a group of curious Urgathoans and his own vampiric allies. He had the unmistakable look of a man who has been misunderstood and who labors to make himself clear. Saskia came to a halt and spoke again to Elana.

"He has called for fewer undead in Geb. No, I can't explain it all now, later. Stay close to him, listen, observe, and report to me at once. And if you should catch his eye —" She led Elana to Kemnebi, deposited her, then bent to retrieve Arazni's dropped wand. She walked to the

Queen's door, paused, looked at both her protege and Kemnebi, then entered, shutting the door behind her.

Those Who Remained

The Cinerarium, Mechitar, Geb, Pharast, 4711

Realizing their company consisted of emotionally distraught, blood-drinking undead, the few mortal Urgathoans remaining filtered out of the grand hall. This left only Kemnebi, his vampiric followers, and Elana, who remained at the periphery.

"What have you done!" demanded Rhianna Ceinwen. "Are you trying to get us all killed?"

Rhianna was, like the Marquis Chevonde Garron, Kemnebi's "grandchild." She was Aleksandr's child, though strictly speaking, vampirism has no true lineage—one is simply a vampire or not. Still, the notion of a familial bond, however sentimental, proved advantageous, offering ready-made allies, servants, masters, lovers, and enemies. She was the type Kemnebi would never embrace and give the gift—or curse—of vampirism. It would seem that this would be true for Aleksandr as well, as they had little in common. As happens so often, opposites attract.

Rhianna was once human, a Shoanti, from the Lands of the Linnorm Kings. She was of the Skoan-Quah, the Skull Clan, so called due to their too-keen interest in death. She traveled to Ustalav with the idea of learning more about necromancy. This was a convenient, and not altogether believable, fabrication made in order to convince the tribal elders to let her travel from the tribal lands rather than find a mate and contribute to the next generation of warriors. Despite her claimed motivation, book learning wasn't for her. She favored the blade. Yet, she was on an adventure, and that suited her fine.

It was in Ustalav that she met Aleksandr, who himself went to there to actually learn necromancy. The arcane school of necromancy is not popular in Cheliax. It is not banned, as it is in other places, but to those desiring power and prestige within Cheliax, the Church of Asmodeus is the only true path. As much as Aleksandr had been raised within the church, he was leery of signing his soul over to the god of contracts, slavery, pride, and tyranny. He was too cynical to believe he would win out in such a bargain. The fateful meeting between Rhianna and Aleksandr was before Aleksandr met Kemnebi and embraced undeath. He was at that time, like Rhianna, young, and looking to make his way in the world.

The pair made an odd couple. While Aleksandr was then, and remains, a gentleman of noble blood, well-spoken and restrained, Rhianna was loud, aggressive, blunt-spoken, and unrestrained. Whereas Aleksandr prefers an intellectual conversation, Rhianna prefers a drinking song. Aleksandr found Rhianna's inhibition freeing. Rhianna found Aleksandr's self-control alluring. The two shared a bed, or floor, or patch of matted grass—whatever was available when their passions overcame them. However, due to the intensity of their romance they were bound to fight. After one such fight Aleksandr vowed never to speak to Rhianna again. He left both Ustalav and Rhianna, traveling all the way to Geb to get away from her.

Four years passed before they would meet again. By this time Aleksandr had met Kemnebi, gained his trust, and had been embraced. Rhianna still loved Aleksandr and it was she who sought him out. Only her pride had kept her from doing so earlier. It was during their passionate reconciliation that Aleksandr embraced Rhianna. He often regretted doing so; however, he found her—really her brashness and impulsiveness—to be a useful tool. At this moment, it was unwelcome.

"Rhianna—" said Aleksandr.

"Although her phrasing leaves much to be desired," interrupted Trevedic Faull, "her point is valid."

Trevedic spoke as if Rhianna were a barely tolerated equal but in reality she was his sire. She had embraced him, passing to the brilliant young caster the gift —or curse—of vampirism. How this unlikely relationship came to be was due to Aleksandr.

Before undeath, Trevedic was a kayal, a "fetchling," born on the Shadow Plane. This is, as its name implies, a dark mirror of reality. The Shadow Plane is much like reality, albeit drained of something essential to life. Gray is its brightest color. It has more shades of black than a normal eye can distinguish. It is a place of whispers. Those who live in the Shadow Plane consider the brokering of secrets a noble art.

Trevedic made his way, along with many others of his clan group, to the Inner Sea. The clan settled in Oppara in Taldor. It was here that Trevedic began to study necromancy. In time he learned all he could in Taldor and sought out other centers of learning. He saw Ustalav as a dangerous backwater. He had heard of Geb the man and Geb the nation. He made the long journey to Geb and once there, sought out a teacher.

Trevedic proved to be an astute political operator. He learned who was who in Geb's convoluted hierarchy. He made himself useful to powerful people. He worked the social scene, as limited as it was, and soon met Aleksandr. The two shared many interests. They enjoyed one another's company. And even though both were aware of the backdrop of politics, they formed a genuine friendship.

Aleksandr believed that it might be useful to himself and to Trevedic if the later were embraced. However, Aleksandr didn't want to embrace Trevedic himself. He wanted his child, Rhianna, to give him the gift.

Trevedic met Rhianna and found her unfeminine. He did not relish the idea of associating with her. Trevedic asked why Aleksandr wouldn't embrace him himself. Aleksandr said that his sire, Kemnebi, had forbidden him from embracing any more mortals without permission (he was, at that time, still irked by Rhianna's unrefined presence). Aleksandr did not appreciate this. He thought it was embarrassing to have to beg permission. Yet, he was not willing to disobey his sire. Kemnebi had given Rhianna the same prohibition (fearing she would collect around her a tavern-full of uncouth immortals) but Aleksandr knew she would ignore the prohibition if the mood struck her.

What Aleksandr didn't tell Trevedic was that he wanted Rhianna's child to be his friend so that he, Aleksandr, would have a useful means of manipulating her indirectly. Also, Trevedic could be indirectly manipulated through Rhianna. Aleksandr could use each to influence the other. It was perhaps a bit too obvious, but Rhianna wasn't clever enough to catch it and Trevedic, although he saw it immediately, was too power-hungry to consider the long-term ramifications.

"Both the problem as stated and its solution, Chancellor," continued Trevedic, "seems opposed to Geb's vision."

"And what is Geb's vision?" asked Kemnebi, mental and emotional exhaustion apparent in his voice.

"To convert all of the living into undead, which he may then command," said Trevedic.

"Who cares about Geb?" growled Rhianna. "I care about myself." She turned from Trevedic to Kemnebi. "How did you put it? Decrease our own numbers intentionally? And you said that to Hent!"

There stood behind Rhianna another vampire, who had yet to speak and who was unlikely to. She had been a vampire less than a decade, a Blood Lord less than a year. Rhianna made such an intolerable fuss over her newest lover, an elven woman named Aedha "Weeping Tree"

Nijis, that Kemnebi made the poor girl a Blood Lord just to keep Rhianna from continually accosting him. He adopted a fatherly role, knowing he'd thrust the naïve elf in over her head.

Rhianna, feeling at that moment both vulnerable and angry, grabbed her lover, pulled her close, and rest her head on her shoulder, muttering to herself. All the while Chevonde was barely able to contain his laughter.

"Let us speak honestly," said Kemnebi. "Rhianna has expressed shock and dismay." He looked to Aleksandr then to Chevonde. He realized there was yet another presence and turned, seeing for the first time the vibrant, young mortal standing near. He studied her, looking at her even as Aleksandr answered.

"What you propose is sensible," said Aleksandr. He turned to Trevedic. "And while Geb may have once thought that way, and acted to make such a vision a reality," he turned back to Kemnebi and noted that his sire was smitten. This information he could do little with at the moment, but he would think much about it later. "He long ago abandoned any such goal. The reality is, Chancellor," this calling of his sire by his official title gained Kemnebi's attention. He turned to face Aleksandr. "You're right. But, how can we make your vision a reality?"

"Eratosthenes will never allow it," said Trevedic. Of all of Kemnebi's allies, it was Trevedic who was closest to the liches. He taught at the Ebon Mausoleum, worshipped Nethys, the god of magic, as did many of the liches, and was an adherent of the Whispering Way, even though he could never become a lich.

"Nor will Hent," muttered Rhianna, her face still buried in her lover's shoulder.

"Say nothing of Latitia," said Aleksandr.

"Aedha?" asked Kemnebi.

The bewildered look on the elf's face answered for her.

"You're thinking about this all wrong," announced the Marquis. The group turned to face him. He stepped closer, looking first to Elana, whom he was suspicious of, then to Arazni's closed door. "What you've done, our wise patriarch, is disguise a power play as a collective boon. Are there too many undead? Or too few? Ha! It matters not. Are there too many whom we can't control? Yes, and that is a terrible state of affairs. We must convince our fellow Blood Lords of the self-benefitting possibilities of our Chancellor's vision."

"Chevonde, that is not—" said Kemnebi but the Marquis was too excited to stop.

"We must convince Eratosthenes that he can rid himself of his rivals by agreeing to your plan," he said, looking at Kemnebi. "We must convince Latitia of the same, and Hent-er-Neheh, and everyone else. Once they realize they can use the cover you've provided them to murder those they dislike, they will gleefully do so. We must ensure we come out on top, of course, but you will have your culling, of that you can be certain."

"I am not advocating civil war," said Kemnebi. "I do not want mindless destruction or chaos. I do not want Geb to fall into strife. The destruction of Geb is exactly what I'm trying to avoid."

"Then you must be careful and deliberate," said Elana. The vampires turned to her, studying and evaluating her, as she stepped into their circle of confidence. "The Marquis is right, or at the very least, it's what the others will come to think, once the shock of your words has faded." She looked directly into Kemnebi's eyes. "You must establish your vision, clarify it, define it, and convince them that it is indeed a collective boon, not a cover for murder and strife."

"Sell it to them?" asked Aleksandr.

Elana turned to him. "Yes, convince them." She looked again to Kemnebi. "You must act now. Before they turn against you."

. . .

"Kill him!" screamed Arazni. "I'll kill him myself!" She spun and marched toward the door.

"We must be careful," said Lilith. Arazni spun to face her.

"You heard what he said. A direct challenge to my rule." She paused, looked chagrinned, and spoke again in a humbled voice, "to Geb's rule."

"To your rule, my Queen," said Lilith, coming close to Arazni and placing both hands on her shoulders. This symbolic act of support and comfort accomplished she dropped her hands and stepped aside.

"A ruse," announced Baya-Iza. "Although he seemed genuine enough, it was an act." She waved a dismissive hand. "I've seen maneuvers like it before, usually under the guise of a religious inquisition."

"He most certainly lacks support for his fantastic idea," said Moira the Disowned, a human wizard from Galt.

"You know Aleksandr well," said Jasmine, the Dead Bride, a zombie lord. She failed to notice the icy look flashed to her by Arazni.

Moira and Aleksandr had once been a romantic couple. This was known publicly, an unusual misstep by Aleksandr, who rarely allowed a weakness to be known by those who might exploit it. The romance angered Arazni, who hated to see others enjoying what was lost to her. She began to undermine it. Aleksandr knew he could not oppose Arazni and gave up the relationship, acknowledging defeat. This was not enough for Arazni. Even though Moira was still mortal, and not particularly powerful, Arazni elevated her to the rank of a Blood Lord. Arazni drew the mortal into her clique, dangling her before Aleksandr, a prize he'd lost and she'd won.

"Talk to him," continued Jasmine. "He is Kemnebi's closest ally. Perhaps he—"

"The seed falls not far from the tree," interrupted Sulah, Bones of Wood. "What could be expected from such a dialogue?"

"Who knows?" asked Jasmine. "If he retains feelings for her," she motioned to Moira, "he can be manipulated."

"No!" screamed Arazni. "No games. No intrigues." She turned to Lilith and spoke as if asking permission. "He dies. Him and all his allies."

"If he wants fewer undead," said Araminta, a Carnival of Death, who, like Jasmine, was a zombie lord. "He should offer himself up first."

Arazni went to her bed and sat. Her followers gathered around her, many climbing onto the bed and throwing their arms supportively around their queen. The grave knights watched, stepping closer.

"He's always sought to undermine me," said Arazni. "He wants the throne for himself. Does he think he can rule Geb?" She looked into the faces of those around her. "He's a glorified clerk."

"He's proven himself foolish in this," said Lilith.

"He will soon fall," added Baya-Iza.

Arazni looked between them. "What if he doesn't? What if—"

"My Queen," interrupted Lilith. "There is no profit to be had thinking thus."

The group fell into silence. Lilith made her way to Arazni's side, taking a seat on the bed in a space made for her. She took Arazni's hand into her own. "Eratosthenes spoke wisely. Kemnebi has become enamored by the living. He has forgotten himself." Arazni looked into Lilith's face. "He has given us an opportunity to act against him. My Queen, pull to you your allies. Hent-er-Neheh and her father, Latitia, Narcisse, and Sthaga." She glanced at Moira and Jasmine. "Even Kemnebi's allies can be pried from him." She rose and stood, facing the assembled group. "Outright war would be costly and foolish." She looked at Sulah. "Starve the tree of sunlight and it will die."

"Drive not your axe into the wood," said Sulah, "but blot out the sun."

Lilith looked once more to Arazni and saw that she was not quite convinced. She was prepared to continue but Arazni rose, shaking loose the arms draped over her. She walked to the cold hearth at the opposite end of her chambers and stared into its gray ashes.

"Leave me."

Lilith nodded the others to hurry from the room.

"My Queen—"

"Mother, please."

Lilith left, shutting the door behind her. Arazni was alone with her grave knights.

"Aroden," said Arazni. "I died once and took my place in the heavens. My hand ready for yours when you chose to rise to your celestial throne, rather than walk amongst men." She took up an iron rod, knelt, and began to poke the ashes. It was a futile act. There was no fire to nurture. "Geb yanked me from my celestial seat." She glanced over her shoulder as a grave knight stepped near. She looked up at him. "I remember that much." She crossed her legs beneath her, sitting like a child might. She let the iron drop from her fingers. It rapped sharply against the stone before the hearth. "But can I truly blame Geb for all that has transpired since?" She thought for a long time before speaking aloud again.

"Iomedae, it is not you I fear, although you have risen higher than I and certainly despise me now." She looked over her shoulder, toward the closed door to her room, looking out mentally toward the grand hall and what had transpired within. "I do not fear him or these reforms he proposes." She glanced again at the grave knight looming over her. "I've never feared you." She looked again at the ashes. "Nor do I fear your creator—and mine." She took up the iron rod again and contemplated its hardness, its rigidity. It seemed an apt symbol. "I fear your judgement, Pharasma. I can never again come before you."

Conquest Day

The Temple of Pharasma, Quantium, Nex, Pharast, 4711

Elder Architect Oblosk stood at the crypt's periphery, pressing a long-fingered hand against the rough-hewn stone of a pillar. It supported the arches spanning the presbytery and altar. The pillar looked as if it had been abandoned in the quarry, as if the stone was bad and couldn't be used. All four of the pillars looked that way. They were marred by chisel and hammer marks. They were crude. They weren't even straight—they bent inward as if the arches they supported taxed them near failure. But Oblosk knew that these bends obscured the solid, straight core. Their weakness was a deception.

The crypt was a part of the church to Pharasma, near the heart of Nex's capital, Quantium. The church was, due to its subtlety, his most beloved design. It was to be his last. He had expressed all he wished with stone.

Pharasma was the Lady of Graves, the goddess of birth, death, fate, and prophecy. She placed every immortal soul into the womb and sat in judgment when it returned to her. He designed the church to appear as if it was in the process of being born, of becoming; or of decaying, succumbing to the ravages of time. Which state it appeared to occupy depended on the spiritual perspective of the viewer.

"Not long now," said Elder Architect Oblosk. He was speaking to the stone, but thinking of his own remaining time. He heard a door open and shut, then heeled boots clicking on granite. He let his hand drop.

"Elder Architect, there you are."

"Here I shall remain." He smiled at his words' meaning, his back to the newcomer.

"But Elder Architect, celebrations begin."

He turned. "I know." He beckoned with a motion. His assistant came forward. "There, look." Oblosk pointed. "Do you see that corner?" His assistant looked. There was nothing special about the corner behind the rearmost pillar. He looked down at his master.

Elder Architect Oblosk was only three feet tall, not even up to the belt-line of his human assistant. He was a pech, a type of fey that few on the surface ever see. Not even the other subterranean races know much about the pech. They live deep, where Golarion resembles an alien world, so hot, wet, and suffocating as to be unrecognizable, even to those who dwell in the Darklands.

"I'll be buried there. Maybe a bronze plaque to mark off my space within the stone."

"Elder Architect! Do you feel unwell? I'm sure High Priest—"

"I feel fine," said Oblosk. He reached out and patted the pillar. He turned and began from the crypt. His assistant followed.

"I do not mean to speak out of—"

"Say what you have to say," advised Oblosk. "I'm old. I don't have time for unnecessary verbiage."

"What I mean, Elder Architect, is," the assistant glanced back to the nondescript corner, "don't you deserve a mausoleum? A grand building to mark—"

Oblosk laughed. He waved his hand. "What? Isn't this good enough?"

"Elder, I only meant—"

"You don't like the idea of me tucked away in a corner?" Oblosk reached out and patted the knee of his assistant. "I've endured a lifetime of people fussing over me." He smiled. "I think I've earned the right to be left alone for a while. Maybe even forgotten."

"Elder Architect, you will never be forgotten."

"Yes, we've a wonderful memory, us Nexians. Don't we?" The pair had passed through the church and were now under the portico. Oblosk stopped and peered up at the ribbing and the decorative underside of the roof. Sounds buffeted the two men. A crowd was gathering in the street. Oblosk waved his hand, indicating the people. "What's this?" he asked, although he knew plenty well.

"It's Conquest Day, Elder. Don't you remember?"

"Conquest Day?" Oblosk feigned ignorance.

"Elder, you worry me."

"Play along. Why do we gather?"

"To renew our resolve."

"Resolve?" Oblosk asked, tilting his head.

"Yes, Elder. Our resolve to defeat Geb."

"Why?"

"Elder?"

"Why would we want to defeat Geb?"

"Elder, must you jest?"

"Jest?"

"Elder, we renew our resolve to defeat Geb every 26th of Pharast because of what he did to us."

"What did he do?"

"Elder!"

"Tell me, dear child, what has Geb done to you?"

"Well, Elder, nothing to me personally."

"And yet you pledge every Conquest Day to destroy him and his people?" Oblosk patted his assistant on the knee. "I take matters too far, yes, I know. I remember well the atrocities Geb has committed. I remember the taste of his yellow fog. If I had breathed in a lungful I wouldn't be here. Neither would this church. Yet, I also remember when Nex caused meteors, some larger than you, to rain down on Geb for one hundred days and nights."

"But he was defending—"

"Defending? Who started it?"

"Elder?"

"Who struck the first blow? Who cast the first spell in anger? Nex or Geb?"

"Geb."

"Are you certain?" asked Oblosk.

"I—I don't really know, Elder."

"Neither do I. Only Nex and Geb know the whole truth. And yet we renew our commitment to get revenge. Why, I wonder. Nex left us long ago. Permit me to speak honestly, I knew him."

"Yes, Elder."

"He was a kind of man I can't even describe. There have been perhaps two other men like him: Aroden and Geb. To see the world and its people through such a prism of intellect. You and I, we can't even imagine it. I used to ponder over his every utterance, struggling to comprehend —" Oblosk chuckled. "Forgive me, I speak of things long passed. Come, we must renew our resolve. I'm aware a most impressive magical display is planned for tonight. The might of Nex has never been greater. I have the utmost confidence that we shall soon fulfill the vow we make this day."

"Elder," said his assistant, his tone scolding. "You jest too much."

The Former Duke Between the Rivers Receives an Unexpected Guest

The Cathedral of Epiphenomena, Mechitar, Geb, Gozran, 4711

The rivers in question were the Sellen, on Galt's western border, and the Stormflood, a hundred and fifty miles to the southeast. Narcisse claimed his family once ruled the territory until the revolution and ensuing terror. Narcisse, then a young man, foresaw the inevitable outcome. He saw his neck under the Final Blade.

He tried to convince his family to take up arms. They wrongly believed the revolution would never last. It was rabble, they said, clanging their iron pots in protest of life's unavoidable miseries. Narcisse knew better. When the courage of his parents and siblings failed to materialize, he assembled his own mercenary band. However, when the fever of revolution threatened to turn them, he issued one last order: slay his own family. Narcisse sided with the revolutionaries.

It was a choice made of bloody necessity. With his family executed, Narcisse absconded with their wealth. He burned down their estate, wished the land between the rivers farewell, and went to Geb. He was already secretly a worshipper of Urgathoa. Why not seek refuge under her black banner?

Now he rarely left the Cathedral of Epiphenomena, except to attend meetings of the Blood Lords. He had no need to go elsewhere. The church provided him with every necessity. Also, travel was tough on his knees. Not only was he no longer young, he was grossly obese. Of the three chief concerns of the Pallid Princess; disease, gluttony, and undeath, Narcisse adhered to gluttony. He was a gourmand of legendary appetite.

The Cathedral of Epiphenomena was of an architectural style alien to Geb. It had no roots in ancient Osirion. The style itself began in Cheliax and was modeled loosely on the architecture of Hell. Few study Hell's architecture firsthand—too risky—and summoning a devil to quiz it on styles feels wasteful, leaving much to the architect's imagination. This "Hell-ish" style is fully realized in what is called High Isgerian.

The exterior of the Cathedral of Epiphenomena is dominated by twin towers crowning the facade. The facade is pierced by entrance portals that are lavishly decorated with sculpture. In Cheliax and Isger this sculpture chronicles Asmodeus' rise. In the case of the Cathedral of Epiphenomena the sculpture depicts the multitude of undead propagated by the Pallid Princess. High above these sculpture-encrusted portals is a rose window, a massive circle of stained glass that has at its center the depiction of a fly. The fly's eyes are quite impressive in stained glass.

The cathedral is built around a central nave flanked by aisles with a transept, terminated by a choir, surrounded by an ambulatory with chapels. The architectural style presents contradictions. The cathedral is made of marble called Marquina Black (a calcite stone, its color resembles the night sky) but its massive, stained glass windows let in ample light. The flying buttresses allow for lofty interior spaces but the goddess to whom the cathedral is dedicated is not concerned with the soul's ascent, but with the grave.

These contradictions are ignored. The focus is on the chapels. There is one devoted to disease, one to gluttony, the final to undeath. Narcisse is the undisputed ruler of the chapel of gluttony; a feast hall. Latitia rules the chapel of disease; a refuge for lepers. Sthaga rules the chapel of undeath—where ghouls multiplied with prodigious rapidity—and, as High Priest, can command the entire cathedral.

Narcisse was in his personal quarters when the messenger came. He sat at his vanity, peering into the mirror. He was applying rouge to his cheeks when he saw the acolyte in the glass.

"Yes?" Narcisse asked.

"A visitor."

"But the feast has already begun. Ah, the sin of late arrival, oh well, find our visitor a seat. I shall greet them presently. My skin looks atrocious today." He contemplated his reflection. "My lips are the color of ash." He looked to the vanity's top, searching for lipstick.

"He does not eat."

"Huh?" Narcisse looked at the acolyte in the mirror. "He comes to our table and does not eat?" He turned on his stool, which groaned under his weight. "The Soufflé? He cannot refuse the—"

The acolyte, whose eyes were downcast, looked up at Narcisse. "Chancellor Kemnebi."

"What?!" Narcisse reached out and grabbed the wine-stained sleeve of the acolyte's light gray robe, pulling him so close the two men's knees met. "The Chancellor? Are you certain?"

"Yes."

"But—" Narcisse turned once more to gaze into the mirror. "My lips, ugh! Damn the gods." He hastily smeared some color onto his lips, rose, and began to push the acolyte ahead of him out of the room. "Hurry, to the cellar, see if we've a bottle of bloodwine. Ugh! I can't believe this. If I'd had time to prepare— Hurry, you fool!"

. . .

"Chancellor," said Narcisse, descending the stairs. He waddled across the feast hall and grasped both of Kemnebi's hands. "A great honor." He glanced over his shoulder, releasing one hand but keeping the other captive. The feast was dying down. The feasters, most of them worshippers of Urgathoa or Geb's still mortal nobility, were slumped and silent. He turned back to Kemnebi. "If I had been apprised of your coming, Chancellor, I would have—"

"Pay me no honors, Narcisse. I come not as your chancellor but as a supplicant."

Narcisse leaned back, studying Kemnebi's face. "Supplicant?" The idea made him nervous. He kept ahold of Kemnebi's hand, gently pulling him into the room. "If you'll allow me?" He did not wait for an answer. He motioned with his free hand to a decanter. "Sazerac, to be enjoyed before eating; a mixture of sugar syrup, Peychaud bitters, anisette, and bourbon. Care for a sip?" Kemnebi shook his head. Narcisse pulled him further along the table, motioning to silver platter. "Tomatoes stuffed with crab meat. With this we drink a white wine from the Carpenden Plains of east Andoran, a dry white." He raised an eyebrow, posing the question. Again Kemnebi shook his head.

Narcisse pulled him a bit further. "After the Sazerac and the tomatoes we have quail with quince preserves and curried rice. I can have the chef— No? Perhaps the next dish will entice you. Calf liver with bacon and onion, garnished with parsley and lemon." He saw the look on Kemnebi's face. He shrugged his shoulders. "Liver isn't for everyone. Ah, here," he motioned again. "Opossum." He placed his free hand affectionately over his heart. "I personally hand-fed them milk and wild cereals. This I did for ten days. Then they were roasted. As you can see they are accompanied by turnip greens. I'll send for the chef." He waved forward an acolyte.

"Narcisse—"

"No?" He waved away the acolyte. "You've eaten. I should have guessed. Well, on to dessert? I've two." He laughed. "One dessert would hardly be fitting for a feast. I've a rum chocolate mousse and," here he leaned into Kemnebi with brotherly tenderness. "A lemon soufflé. Eh?" He smiled and winked. "How dare I forget." He feigned embarrassment. "The white is only to be enjoyed with the tomatoes and crab, everything else gets a red from —"

The acolyte with a bottle of bloodwine appeared. "Finally, these scum." Narcisse turned and looked at Kemnebi. "I swear, they eat half my table before I sit. Then they drag their feet!" He laughed. "Here, here," he reached out and pulled the acolyte close. "Bloodwine." He took the bottle and blew the dust from it. "Let's see, a vintage from Taldor, fortified with the blood of Lady Josephine of House —"

"Narcisse. May we speak in private?"

"In private?" He returned the bottle to the acolyte. "Yes, of course." He shoved the acolyte away. "Allow me the honor of hosting you in my personal chambers. I've had the walls re-frescoed. The damned family crest of my predecessor assaulted me from every flat surface. I had them chiseled off. I thought it more fitting to—"

. . .

Narcisse lowered his bulk into a plush throne-like chair. It was specially made for a man of his girth. He had offered it to Kemnebi, as it was the most prominent chair in the room and Kemnebi the most prominent personage, but it was refused. Kemnebi sat in a slightly less grand chair. The attending acolytes had been commanded from the room. The two men were alone, a Blood Lord and his Chancellor. A cleric of the goddess of undeath and his vampiric supplicant.

"You were at the meeting?" asked Kemnebi.

"Of course."

"You recall what I said?"

"I cannot attest to every word," Narcisse smiled, "but I believe I caught the gist of it."

"I spoke inelegantly."

"You spoke honestly. It wasn't your words but their meaning that gave offense."

"Were you offended, Narcisse?"

"No, forgive me, now it is I who speaks inelegantly. There was some disagreement with your thesis. That is all."

Kemnebi thought for a moment before continuing.

"Have I offended the church?"

"The church?" Narcisse smiled. "You have not offended me. I cannot speak for the church, not yet. Perhaps Latitia or Sthaga—"

"Latitia's opinion is well known," said Kemnebi. "As for Sthaga, let us not kid ourselves, he cares not."

"He is a most single-minded High Priest."

Kemnebi rose and began to pace. "I want Geb to thrive. I'm thinking of all of us, not merely of myself. Nor have I become enchanted with the living, as some are wont to believe." He turned to Narcisse. "Many of Urgathoa's worshippers yet live. Certainly you see the wisdom of my words?"

"I see wisdom in much that you say, Chancellor."

"A diplomatic answer." Kemnebi resumed pacing. "How do you manage it, Narcisse? How do you keep yourself, and those who adhere to the same scripture you do, alive when Latitia wants to fill you with disease and Sthaga wants to drain the life from you? How do you walk the middle path?"

"Charm and luck."

Kemnebi eyed him.

"Okay, luck." Narcisse laughed. "Yours is a serious question, Chancellor. I wish I could give you a serious answer. In truth, my position is precarious. Not only do I have Latitia and Sthaga for allies, my own goddess would rather I be a ghoul than a man." He held out his hands. "I suppose it is only a matter of time until I join Sthaga's increasing brood. Until then, I shall eat, drink, and be merry."

"Well put, Narcisse. But, when you join your High Priest, what shall you feast upon when there are no more corpses in Geb and no more living to produce them?"

"There are living elsewhere."

"Is that our fate?" asked Kemnebi. "To devour our resources with no thought to their replenishment? To do so would force us to war. Can we take on every nation in the Inner Sea?"

"Need we?"

"We could not even defeat Nex. Now we feed them."

"Chancellor, I—"

"Yes, yes, this is circular and frustrating."

"I merely meant to say that I am not wise enough to know the answer."

Kemnebi stopped pacing and faced Narcisse. "Yes, you are. You know I'm right."

"Would you have me say it?" Narcisse studied Kemnebi's face. "Very well, yes, you're right. Gebbian society is unsustainable. The road we walk leads to total collapse."

"Then you agree? We must decrease our numbers." Kemnebi sat on the edge of his chair, leaning toward Narcisse. "We have to begin with—"

"Forgive me for saying so, Chancellor. There is no where to begin, for there shall be no beginning to such a plan, only an end."

Kemnebi looked at Narcisse. He rose and resumed pacing. "You agree with me, but you will not support me."

"Oh, don't get me wrong, Chancellor. You have my complete support." Kemnebi looked at Narcisse, who continued. "And were I to claim so publicly, I would not live out the day."

"You won't be alone. Aleksandr, Trevedic—"

"All know you have their support. What of Arazni, Hent-er-Neheh, Eratosthenes? What of Geb?"

"An obsession on short term profit," said Kemnebi. "Leads to long-term ruin."

"I agree," said Narcisse, patting his stomach. He knew well the harm caused by too intent a focus on the gains to be had here and now.

"Yet you do nothing to stop it?"

"What can I do, Chancellor?"

"You're a Blood Lord. You're one of the most influential clerics in Geb. You have many friends and allies. Go to them, speak to them, convince them."

"Convince them to do away with their servants, their armies, the source of their power and influence?" asked Narcisse. "What should I tell them is the reason? To avert an uncertain fate? Think of it, Chancellor, who would be the first to divest themselves of their power? What would happen to, say, Khamati, Geb's very own cousin, who, I might add, has made many enemies, should his house fail to be guarded my those mummified monsters he calls pets? What if he were the first? How long before he's destroyed? I happen to know Latitia hates him. She hates so many. She wouldn't hesitate to destroy him, if she could do so without taking unreasonable personal risk."

"It has to come from above, Narcisse. We must lead the way—us. The lesser undead look to us. We set the precedent." Kemnebi read the cynicism on Narcisse's face.

"Yours is the attitude I expected to encounter. Agreement in private, unwillingness to act publicly."

"There is still time, Chancellor—recant, reverse yourself. It will not be a graceful exit, not now, but you can exit." Kemnebi looked at Narcisse. The latter continued. "Would you have me say this, too?" Narcisse frowned. "How long have you been chancellor?"

"Step down? Is that what you're— No! How can I? When I see Geb's ruin so clearly? I have to save Geb from itself, not abandon it!" Narcisse remained silent. "If one of the others, Hent or Eratosthenes, if they come to see what I see, if they act, will you—"

"If you can convince them, Chancellor, you will not need me."

The Boon of Observance

Central Oenopion, Nex, Rova, 4703

Castelli—not yet titled "Master"—was handed a scroll by a messenger. He examined the wax seal. It showed a stylized black bird, head tilted back, beak open, its taloned feet tearing a scroll in two. The symbol had multiple secret meanings, all of which he knew. The symbol's acknowledged meaning was that the dispatch had come from, and was the property of, Nex's intelligence service.

The seal was unbroken. He nodded the boy's dismissal. Feeling an ache in his lower back (he had been bent over paperwork all morning), he rose from his desk. He thought of the few errands he personally felt like handling, mentally composed a route, and left the cramped, but nondescript, house, tucked in an unremarkable neighborhood on the outskirts of Oenopion, in central Nex.

He began toward the center of town. On the way he broke the seal and read the brief note scribbled on the parchment: a thirteenth kraken, eyes gouged out, like the twelve preceding, had washed up on the western shore of the Isle of Kortos.

Castelli kept the scroll in hand. 'Another kraken,' he thought. 'All coming in the same month, Rova.' He frowned; the omen's meaning—if it was one—remained a mystery. It was one of a number of mysteries that it was his duty to gain information about, if any was to be found, ponder over, and later, to advise the Council of Three and Nine on, if he had any wisdom to impart, and he had better.

He made an alteration to his route, turning down a wide avenue toward the miasmic lake at the center of town. The overpowering chemical smell, the result of the toil of hundreds of alchemists, that hung over Oenopion, unmoved by wind, could scarcely mask the odor of the ooze colony that inhabited the lake.

The avenue narrowed as it angled down, terminating at a low stone wall. Castelli cast his gaze over those odd waters. An island, not of stone or earth, but of undulating, gelatinous bodies, mingling together, thrashing about in slow-motion, rose at the center of the lake. Few stood gazing, like him, over the waters, for they were not waters one looked at for leisure or to soothe one's troubles. It was not that kind of lake.

He peered over the edge of the wall. A thin film hid all that was beneath. The film, seemingly aware it was being looked at, began to bunch against the stone, as if it were endeavoring to climb out and greet its rare visitor. Castelli felt a presence. The "other" was not physical, but mental. He felt it not near his person, as one feels the approach of a friend or lover, but in his person, in his mind, an unwelcome sensation.

He had felt it before, when he first arrived in Oenopion from Quantium. As he entered town, long before he neared the lake and its colony of oozes, he felt a probing. His companion and working-fellow laughed when he saw the expression of violation and horror on Castelli's face.

"The oozes," said the man between bouts of laughter, "welcoming you, in their own special way." The man had been compelled to grab Castelli by the arm and drag him into town, so deep was his shock at the "greeting."

"An individual ooze," explained his guide, "is a mindless, detritus-eating paste," the man laughed at his own descriptive powers. Castelli did not. "Get a few hundred together and you find yourself with a hive mind of considerable intellect, and no little amount of meanness."

That meanness Castelli now felt. He tossed the dispatch onto the film covering the water. Both the paper and its contents were digested by the film. Strangely enough, the ooze colony, as alien as it was, formed the backbone of Nex's intelligence service. It was fed—literally —all available information, and added to it the results of its own "natural" powers of divination. The colony then rudely inserted the answers into the minds of those unfortunate enough to interface with it.

Castelli turned away from the lake, nearly forgetting his list of chores, and nearly rushing back to his desk, where, after his brief encounter with the colony's hive mind, he would feel a bit more protected. He caught himself, calmed, then directed himself instead to Stilgar's Scrollworks.

He found the dwarf on a stepladder, facing a towering, doorless cabinet of packed shelves, sliding long, narrow pieces of paper into place.

"I've never once heard of a dwarven magician of any renown," he announced to Stilgar's square-shaped back.

"There aren't any," grumbled the surly dwarf, who was, as rare as the breed is, a talented wizard. "But," he glanced over his shoulder, looking eye-to-eye with the taller human, "if it's a craftsman ye be after, best stay away from yer own kind."

"That's why I get all of my scrolls made here," Castelli smiled, "by the humans, elves, gnomes, and halflings that you employ." He touched his chin, "hmmm, no dwarves."

Stilgar stomped down the ladder's rungs and pushed his way past Castelli. "Still dwarven craftsmanship".

"Yes, of course," chimed Castelli, following.

"Ye've five scrolls," said Stilgar, as if condemning his regular customer for the spendthriftness of his order. He went to a scroll-crowded shelf and began turning the paper tags attached to them by string. While Stilgar familiarized himself with his ever changing inventory, Castelli peered through an open archway.

On the other side was a long room with a low ceiling. Within, tables were crowded together with barely enough space between them for the multitude of chairs or their occupants. Castelli saw members of many races bent over the finest paper available, dipping quill pens into reservoirs of ink more like horse troughs in length and width, lacking only depth.

It was a room full of apprentices who learned the basics of the wizard's art in the most commercial of ways. Stilgar, although both a dwarf and a wizard, was far from stingy. He may charge more than was reasonable, and demand more than could be met even by the most over-achieving student, but those wizards who he "graduated" were not only expert scroll-crafters, the finest in all of the Inner Sea, one might believe, but were lightning-fast casters, for they had many spells so well known, due to the long hours of copying and recopying them, so completely committed to memory, that they were in danger of casting them in their sleep.

Not only were they well-trained, Stilgar was sure to give them their proper cut from the copying, sending his students into the world well-outfitted. His fairness in that matter ensured he had his pick from among the limitless pool of would-be casters.

In that body-packed room of young wizards, Castelli's eyes alighted on one, causing the others to fall away. She was little more than a girl, just handed off by her nervous father to the none-too-friendly dwarf. There was something about the way she sat, on her knees, bent forward, her whole body engaged in joyous concentration —she wrote with a careful hand, her tongue stuck in the corner of her mouth—told Castelli she was the sort of raw material he could make much of. He knew at once, in that prophetic way one comes upon such certainty, that he was going to steal a student from Stilgar, shape and mold her into a formidable caster and operative, and make her his protege. He only hoped the dwarf would forgive him.

"On credit or paying now?" asked Stilgar, speaking too loudly to catch the attention of his customer.

Castelli forced a smile, "Stilgar, old friend," he began. The wily dwarf narrowed his eyes then turned them to the apprentice Castelli had taken notice of. He returned his iron-flecked eyes to Castelli and growled.

Four Meetings Under a Full Moon

Various locations, Mechitar, Geb, Gozran, 4711

The Marquis Chevonde Garron looked to his left and saw an eye bigger than his fist staring back. It belonged to one of Khamati's mummified "pets." Chevonde saw, in his reflection, that his hair was a bit flat, ran his fingers through it, then tossed his head to give his black mane a bounce. He could not see himself well enough to discern his features to any degree, so he could not admire himself, as was his pleasure. Instead he glanced up, looking at the full moon through the compound leaves of the date palms.

"A bulette," came the gravel-voice of Khamati. "A burrowing monster."

Chevonde looked at the mummified beast. "That burrows?"

The quadrupedal monster resembled a massive, armor-plated lizard with a shovel-shaped head and a maw overflowing with teeth. Chevonde leaned to the side to examine its claws. They were long and thick, useful for digging and killing. The beast was somewhat emaciated, having had its internal organs removed. It was still formidable. The linen wrappings were less prevalent than they were on most mummies, due to the natural armor-like plating. Chevonde sat upright and regarded his host.

Khamati was wrapped in age-browned strips of linen. He too was mummified, although his head was bare. The flesh of his bald head was mottled brown and gray. His eyes had been removed, or had disintegrated, but he still "looked" from the sunken hollows, somehow seeing. His teeth had been "fanged," sharpened, the teeth of a predator. Chevonde heard a rumor that She-mah-hon, the ostirius kyton, had performed the dental surgery and had taken an inappropriate pleasure in doing so.

Khamati wore a necklace of gold and lapis lazuli. A holy symbol, made of gold, shaped like a medallion, and honoring some long forgotten god, hung from the necklace. Khamati wore a dark blue skirt in the ancient Osirian style and a crimson-colored waist-sash. Tucked into the sash was a dagger in a gilded, bejeweled sheath and a wand of ebony wood, topped with a gleaming silver ball. He was standing with one linen-wrapped hand on the back of the chair opposite the Marquis. Chevonde had been led, by an armed and armored skeleton, who regarded him with a sinister intelligence, to the oasis behind Khamati's pyramidal home.

Geb's mummified relatives occupied between them three such pyramids, all close to the Cinerarium. Nakht-Neb-Tep-Nefer, the eldest of Geb's relatives (which, made him perhaps one of the oldest beings in the Inner Sea) occupied the largest of these family pyramids. He shared it with his daughter, Hent-er-Neheh and her student and personal attendant, Uoser.

Nakht had long ago removed himself from Gebbian society. He rarely attended the meetings of the Blood Lords. After living thousands of years, after witnessing so much human folly, Nakht longed for the end to the entire farce. He was drawn to Groetus, the god of end times, an event which Nakht contemplated with much satisfaction.

Khamati occupied the neighboring pyramid, which was smaller than Nakht's. He needed the smaller footprint to allow room for his garden. Despite the fact that Khamati was both undead and hated sentient life, he lavished attention on his personal oasis. It was home to many of his mummified pets. Another of Geb's relatives was Khufnu.

Khufnu was many generations removed from Geb. He did not know Geb personally, despite their familial tie.

By the time Nakht mummified Khufnu, Geb had committed suicide. Khufnu was the most secretive of all of Geb's relatives. He had some private obsession that few knew or understood. He wasn't power-hungry or political. He had no known friends, allies, or enemies. There were rumors that Khufnu worshipped Shax, the swan-headed demon lord of sadistic murder, but anyone who spread such rumors was soon found cut into gory pieces. It was also rumored that Khufnu acted as an assassin for Geb and his relatives, but even fewer spread this rumor.

If Nakht was removed from society, Hent politically astute and cautious, and both Khufnu and Uoser politically irrelevant (although still both Blood Lords), Khamati was the dangerous instigator of the family (not counting Geb himself). He rounded the chair and sat. As he did so the mummified bulette turned and disappeared amongst the date palms.

With the bulette's bulk now absent, Chevonde could see that there stood nearby two other mummified monsters. One was a type he knew, a lamia. The lower half of a lamia is that of a lion. Her upper half is of a shapely woman. She retained her feline eyes. Not far from the mummified lamia stood another half-beast, half-woman that Chevonde could not identify. Here again was a leonine lower portion but as opposed to all four legs this had only two. The human upper half was further adorned with a pair of large hawk's wings.

"You've quite a collection," said Chevonde. The compliment drew no reply. Chevonde studied the garden about him. A gurgling pool was to his right, surrounded by lush vegetation. The date palms were so numerous they hid the pyramid. "Despite my admiration, I did not come to critique your husbandry."

Chevonde was interrupted by a fear-filled screaming. The same skeleton that led the Marquis to his seat now drug a terrified woman into the clearing. She was the first living being Chevonde had seen anywhere near Khamati. The skeleton shoved the woman to her knees.

"I do not often host," said Khamati. "I have no food or drink. I have no blood to offer you, except—" He motioned to the woman, a slave, wearing only rags and an iron collar around her emaciated neck.

"Your consideration of my needs is noted," said Chevonde. "And lest I show poor etiquette by turning you down, I have already, ah, dined this evening."

Khamati turned to "look" at the skeleton. The skeleton grabbed her arm, yanked her up, and led her off. Chevonde watched them, then turned to Khamati.

"I speak on the Chancellor's behalf." Chevonde studied Khamati in the hopes of getting a read on him, but the other man's face offered no emotion. It perhaps could not. "You were at the meeting, yes? As you know, the Chancellor shared some, ah, unexpected revelations." Again Khamati did not speak or otherwise reveal his thoughts. Chevonde continued. "It was a shame that the meeting adjourned before the Chancellor could add nuance to his vision. With your permission I shall do so." Chevonde smiled but received nothing in reply. His audience was immune to his charms.

"You see," he began, "the idea of increasing the amount of life in Geb, and doing so by decreasing the number of undead who prey upon the living, is a helpful screen. What lies behind this screen? Opportunity. Who decides which undead are to be, ah, gotten rid of, to use a vulgar term? Who must give up what they have for the greater good? Who is to be weakened and by how much? These questions must be answered." Chevonde detected a show of comprehension and interest from his host.

"You see, what the Chancellor meant to say, but for obvious reasons could not, is that there are too many young hot-heads breathing down our necks. Also, the powers that be are too entrenched to dislodge. We can't advance, yet the rearguard rushes forward. This political situation does not bode well for Geb. Now—" But Chevonde's keen ears picked up a scuttling sound.

From the shadows cast by the palm fronds came another of Khamati's mummified pets. It was as large as the bulette but otherwise quite different. It resembled a scorpion but without the stinger or claws. In place of these weapons it had a pair of massive pincers, large enough to go around a man's waist, sharp enough to bisect him.

The mummified ankheg moved behind Khamati and stood between him and the path that led from the oasis. The lamia moved forward, producing a kukri from a previously unseen sheath. Chevonde paused and studied the foliage to his right. Khamati made no response.

Master?" a voice whispered from the shadows. Khamati tilted his head. A man stepped from the shadows. He wore dark clothing and soft-soled boots. A bandolier, heavy with daggers, was stretched across his chest. He pulled his scarf to his eyes, hiding his face.

Chevonde picked up the distinct taste of fresh blood about the man but didn't see any obvious source, nor did the man act wounded. The messenger approached Khamati, carefully stepping around the ankheg, bent, and whispered into his master's ear. Despite listening, Chevonde could make nothing of the messenger's words. Having delivered his message, the man departed the way he had come, taking the delightful smell of fresh blood with him.

Chevonde was well aware that Khamati had an elaborate network of spies spread throughout Geb. No doubt, some bit of information had been deemed important enough to deliver, despite the presence of an outsider.

Khamati made no acknowledgement of the interruption nor did he beckon Chevonde to continue. He sat, gazing at his visitor with empty sockets. The lamia re-sheathed her dagger. The ankheg turned and re-joined the bulette in the darkness. Chevonde took this as a prompt to continue.

"Those who endorse the Chancellor's vision will have a greater say. Perhaps you, Khamati, can think of," he glanced at the foliage about him, "areas to be pruned."

"To rid myself of my enemies with the Chancellor's blessing?" asked Khamati.

Chevonde held out his hands and smiled. "There are many ways to accomplish the Chancellor's goal."

"Is that his goal?"

"It's my, ah, interpretation."

"I took him at his word," said Khamati.

He rose and went to the gurgling pool. He knelt and reached into the water. The ends of the linen wraps spread out on the surface. Chevonde saw movement. Several blue-shelled crabs came from the pool's depth, coming to Khamati's fingers. "These crabs chew the flesh from my bones." For a moment Khamati's voice betrayed his affection for the crabs. "They don't fear me." He turned and glanced at Chevonde. "They don't comprehend what it is they consume. They're driven only by hunger, nothing more." After allowing the crabs to gnaw on his flesh for a moment Khamati stood, the linen dripping. The crabs scuttled back into the security of the pool. Khamati looked over his shoulder. "You know what that's like, don't you?"

"Certainly."

Khamati turned to face his guest. "I'm driven by hunger, too. The hunger for power." He returned to stand by his seat. "There is above me a ceiling I cannot pierce. Nakht-Neb-Tep-Nefer, Hent-er-Neheh. They are allies, yes, but also steps which I must tread on my way higher. I do not fear telling you this, for you no doubt feel the same about Aleksandr and even Kemnebi."

"In this regard we differ."

"Do we?" Khamati sat. "What is it you hunger for?"

"Entertainment."

"Will slaying your enemies entertain you, Marquis?"

"I have no enemies."

"I am your enemy."

"Oh? I wasn't aware we had quarreled."

"You are not a member of the ancient order, so you must be destroyed."

"Now?" asked Chevonde, half in jest.

"I gift you more time." Khamati waved a hand benevolently.

"I appreciate—"

"But soon." Chevonde felt the approach of Khamati's mummified pets. The mood turned menacing. "However," said Khamati. "I find your interpretation more to my liking than my own." He rose and began toward the path out of the garden. The lamia and maftet joined their master. The ankheg and bulette were too large to follow down the winding path, but they came forward anyway.

"Does the Chancellor have your support?"

Khamati turned. "Tell the Chancellor we shall be working toward the same ends, albeit through different means." With this Khamati walked the winding path, disappearing into darkness. He was followed by the two mummified half-lion women.

"I shall," said Chevonde. He felt a presence and turned, seeing again one of the bulette's massive eyes regarding him.

. . .

Not all of the members of the Whispering Way in Mechitar taught at the Ebon Mausoleum. Not many had the patience for it. However, in a circular chamber beneath the school for necromancy the Whispering Way held council. Off of this chamber were six doors and two sets of stairs, one leading up into the Ebon Mausoleum and one down to a locked door. Behind this locked door was a secret only Eratosthenes knew.

Trevedic Faull stood in the center of this circular chamber, fretting. His was a disagreeable task. He was a member of the Whispering Way, an adherent of its code, a believer in its mission, yet he was preparing to preach the exact opposite of its beliefs and he knew it.

One of the six doors opened. The unnerving smell of chemicals poured forth. The hissing, bubbling, gurgling, and sizzling sounds of ongoing alchemical experiments joined the odors. A ratfolk stood in the doorway, one hand on the door, his back to Trevedic. He was watching his experiments, loath to leave them unattended. He paused, looked over everything, then cautiously shut the door.

He turned, saw Trevedic, and held a finger up to his muzzle. He gingerly stepped to Trevedic and spoke in a low tone. "I hope no one yells or slams a door." He glanced back toward his lab. "If you hear an explosion I'll need to request more funds from the general pool to build a new laboratory."

Cassius Allius was the most unique lich in the Whispering Way's long history. The art of necromancy played only a supporting role in his successful attempt to become a lich. The main player was alchemy. Beneath Cassius's black robe was a network of tubes, vials, magic-powered pumps, and similar inventions that filled the ratfolk's body with the chemicals that kept him between life and death.

Another unique feature, and one that intimidated many, was that Cassius had begun his alchemical research under the guidance of Tar-Baphon, the Whispering Tyrant. It was Tar-Baphon who provided the needed necromantic additions to Cassius's alchemical inventions. However, a falling out between the two meant that Cassius was long removed from the Whispering Tyrant's company when the Whispering Tyrant's neighbors finally united to defeat and imprison him.

Another door opened. One of Trevedic's fellow professors emerged, a human wizard named Dagillus. He was not yet a lich but was being led down the path by Eratosthenes. He was from Isger and was once the consort of Lady Kaltessa, of Iron Rose. However, a diplomatic visit by Eratosthenes provided an opportunity to leave Isger for Geb and leave Lady Kaltessa's bed for a stone slab beneath the Ebon Mausoleum.

"Trevedic, Cassius—"

"Keep your voice down," said Cassius, albeit in a polite tone.

"Ah, got something brewing, do we?"

"Brewing? Not quite. I've got—"

"Are you going to blow up your lab again?" asked Dagillus, joining the pair in the center of the room.

"No—well, I hope not."

Several other doors opened and the remainder of the Whispering Way adherents entered. This consisted of four liches who spent the majority of their time either in their chambers, taking the study of necromancy to rarified heights, or in the outer planes, perusing the libraries of Abraxas, the demon lord of forbidden lore, magic, and snakes, or bargaining with Orcus's demons for an introduction to the lord of death, necromancy, and wrath. They nodded respectfully to the trio, advanced to stand near, but did not speak. Only Eratosthenes was absent.

"What's this all about?" asked Dagillus.

"Perhaps we should wait for Eratosthenes," said Trevedic.

"He said he'd be a moment and that we should begin without him," said Dagillus.

"I would rather—"

"Does this concern the Whispering Way?" asked Masgava, one of the quintet of liches, not counting Cassius.

"Not directly," said Trevedic, "but indirectly, yes, it does."

"Then begin," said Masgava.

Trevedic knew his audience was impatient, having been forced from their studies. He also worried they might react poorly to his message. He didn't want to irritate them by requesting they wait.

"Many of you were at the most recent meeting of the Blood Lords. Those of you who weren't," he looked to Dagillus, "have by now heard that Chancellor Kemnebi has—"

"Blasphemed," interrupted Neacal Aodhan, another of the liches.

"He has challenged the status quo," said Trevedic.

"Fewer undead?" asked Dagillus. "That's what I heard."

"Not fewer liches, not a weakening of the Whispering Way. What the Chancellor—"

"What he said was irrational," said Ashoka, another lich.

"What he meant," countered Trevedic, "was that there are too many violent undead like ghouls, wraiths, and so on that prey on the living."

"So?" asked Masgava.

"For a nation to survive," said Trevedic, "it needs the living. The Chancellor is thinking in terms of an economy, of production and consumption, of law and order, of—"

"His thinking is misguided." It was Eratosthenes. He stood on the bottom step of the stairs that led up to the Ebon Mausoleum. He stepped down and walked into the circular chamber. "Everything that needed to be said, Trevedic, has been said."

"With all due respect, I don't believe it has."

Eratosthenes nodded to the other liches. He turned to Trevedic. "We have in this room now six who have realized the promise of the Whispering Way and one," he motioned to Dagillus, "who walks the path." He looked at Trevedic. "We allow you to stand among as even though you cannot walk the path to its final destination."

"If my loyalty is in question—"

"Need we question your loyalty, Trevedic?" asked Ólchobar Yevan, the final lich to speak. All looked to him, then to Trevedic.

"My devotion to the Whispering Way has never before been in doubt."

"Yet your Chancellor," said Eratosthenes. He paused, "our Chancellor has expressed a vision for Geb's future that is diametrically opposed to the goals of the Whispering Way. Need I remind you that we believe life does not truly begin until death?"

"You needn't," said Trevedic.

"Kemnebi feels that Geb was and is concerned for the living," said Eratosthenes. "I can assure he is not. Kemnebi believes that without the living the nation of Geb will crumble. I can assure you it will not. Kemnebi believes that we are on an unsustainable path, that a nation of the dead will be a travesty, or at the least, a failed experiment. I can tell you—with great confidence—that the nations of the living have been and always will be failures. A nation of the dead will prove a success. Only," he held up a bony finger, "if we avoid the kind of self-sabotage we now face."

Trevedic was flustered but gathered his thoughts and tried again. "What Chancellor Kemnebi feels is that our true role is to rule, to be the aristocracy. We belong at the pinnacle of social and political power. We, I mean undead in general, cannot be the common man. We will not—or cannot—do the work the common people must. We, the dead, cannot sustain a society. There are things even we need. Since we will not provide them for ourselves we must rely on the living. If we have no living —"

"I need nothing from the living," stated Eratosthenes, "except corpses."

. . .

Aleksandr waited between twin Taotiehs. The tiger-shaped constructs, made of marble and magic, were covered with hieroglyphs. Each, although seated on their haunches, was taller than he. A naïve visitor might assume they were statues. Aleksandr knew better. He tried not to look at them. Instead he peered up the sandstone stairs toward the ever-changing glow of firelight. He was conscious of the fact he had never before been made to wait.

Aleksandr saw a shadow race down the stairs toward him. Someone was passing before the braziers at the top. A moment after, he heard footfalls. A robed figure came into view. It was Uoser, Hent's long-time student and personal attendant. The two shared a mother-son dynamic, even though thousands of years separated them. Hent performed the mummification ritual that carried Uoser beyond life into undeath, that joined him to the ancient order. He had spent a millennia thanking her.

Uoser was a young man when he was killed and brought back. In many ways he resembled a teenager, not yet fully grown into his own body. The mummification process had slimmed him down even more so. He was a slight figure who relied on copious amounts of fabric to give him presence. He also retained the immature man's fetish for skulls and other markers of evil and death. He wore a necklace of cat skulls, their eye sockets filled with rubies, their teeth gilded. A collection of human and animal skulls hung from his belt, clanking as he descended the stairs. His staff was topped with a gilded ram's skull, its eyes replaced with emeralds. Aleksandr was aware of another troubling truth: Hent had always greeted him herself. This time she sent a lackey.

"Hent-er-Neheh will see you now," said Uoser. He turned and began back up the stairs. Aleksandr followed. One of the human skulls from Uoser's belt stared back at him. He thought it an ill-omen.

The pair arrived in the massive central chamber of the pyramid. It took some time to cross it. As they did so, Aleksandr glanced to either side. The painted walls always impressed him. They were lit by braziers. The color of the paints remained vivid, despite their age. He felt a desire to abort the entire mission and pretend he had come to admire them. He frowned at his lack of resolve and looked toward the group at the end of the chamber. He hadn't expected Hent to be entertaining visitors.

"Aleksandr Kovalenko, Blood Lord," announced Uoser. He pointed to a spot in which Aleksandr was to stand. His duties discharged, he stood next to Hent.

Aleksandr looked over the group. He was pleased that Nakht-Neb-Tep-Nefer was not among them. The ancient mummy was impossible to deal with. He dismissed everything he heard as the ignorance of youth. Nothing interested him, except the dissolution of material reality. He had no motivations or desires that could be leveraged or manipulated. Despite being immortal, he was impatient. In fact, other than Hent and Uoser, none of Geb's relatives were present. However, Aleksandr was not pleased to see Viratus, Vocorix, and Vennonius, the trio of diplomats from Nemret Noktoria.

Nemret Noktoria is an ancient necropolis buried deep beneath the sands of Osirion. There is, so far as Aleksandr knew, no life in Nemret Noktoria. There are only tombs, graves, and ghouls. How the necropolis came to occupy the cavern, how it had survived for so long under sand and stone, and why the ghouls of that dead city cared about events on the surface, Aleksandr couldn't fathom.

Aleksandr did not know that thousands of years prior, when a cult arose amongst the Pharaoh's royal embalmers—a cult that sought to corrupt the mummification process so that undeath became the final realization of technique—those cultist searched for lost knowledge in the tombs and crypts of Nemret Noktoria. The members of this cult were exiled from Osirion by the Pharaoh. Those who weren't quick enough out of Osirion were executed. The cult was comprised of Geb and his relatives. The relationship with the necropolis was long and lasting.

"Aleksandr," said Viratus, "it has been too long since we last spoke."

Aleksandr half-bowed. "A pleasure Viratus, Vocorix, Vennonius. I did not expect to see you here."

"We are here at Hent-er-Neheh's pleasure," said Viratus.

"I thought they would like to hear what you have to say," said Hent. "I have apprised them of Chancellor Kemnebi's recent," she paused, "revelations."

"He no doubt discussed them with you," said Vocorix. "Before making his case to the assembled Blood Lords."

"In this matter the Chancellor kept his own counsel."

This bit of news interested Hent. She sat forward. "Is that true?"

"Yes."

"We understood that you were his closest adviser," said Vennonius.

"I have that honor," said Aleksandr.

The three diplomats looked to Hent. It was obvious that they had already discussed this particular topic.

"Were you surprised by his," Viratus returned his gaze to Aleksandr, "revelations?"

"I admit that I was."

"So you were in much the same position as I," said Hent. "Tell me, what did you think of the Chancellor's speech?"

"Shocked, then worried," said Aleksandr. "I have spoken with Chancellor Kemnebi, gained insight into his, as you say, revelations, and I now see the wisdom in his words."

"You agree with him?" asked Hent.

"Yes."

"Don't you feel," asked Vennonius, "that due to your relationship with Chancellor Kemnebi you are biased?"

"It is not unreasonable to be so," said Vocorix, looking to his fellow diplomat.

"Of course not," said Vennonius. "I merely meant that," he turned to face Aleksandr, "one in your position must weigh loyalty to an individual against loyalty to a state."

"Yes, I understand," said Aleksandr. "I believe that Geb will benefit, in the long run."

"If there are fewer undead?" asked Viratus.

"Yes."

"What I believe the Chancellor said," began Hent, "was that there needs to be more living in Geb. The only way to ensure this is for there to be fewer undead."

"I see the nuance," said Viratus, turning to Hent and bowing his head.

"The Chancellor," continued Hent, "is wrong." She turned to Aleksandr. "I've always appreciated your intelligence. I've been watching you for a long time and you've made few mistakes."

"Thank you," said Aleksandr.

"You've admitted that you were worried." Continued Hent. "Why?"

"Geb is a nation built on necromancy," said Aleksandr. "The goal of necromancy is the manipulation of death. Necromancers create, collect, and command the undead. To say that there needs to be fewer undead—" He held out his hands.

"I do not understand," said Vocorix. "Why must there be more living in Geb?"

"Chancellor Kemnebi," said Aleksandr, "is worried that without the living to fulfill necessary roles in the economy, in society, in everyday life, Geb will cease to grow and evolve as the other nations do. We will fall behind. In time we will no longer be able to compete. We —"

"Change?" asked Vocorix. "Evolve? I do not understand."

Viratus spoke. "Nemret Noktoria has not changed or evolved. We have no need."

"You do not interact with other societies," said Aleksandr. "You are not surrounded by the living, by enemies, current or potential."

"What does that have to do with anything?" asked Vennonius.

Aleksandr thought for a moment. He did not have his sire's deep understanding of these issues, nor, truthfully, did he agree wholeheartedly with Kemnebi. As a vampire he knew he needed the living. But his audience, comprised of ghouls and mummies, did not. He had no idea how to persuade them, how to play to their needs. He was struck by a thought.

"I do not mean to be rude, but, you consume corpses, do you not?" He directed the question at Viratus, the chief diplomat.

"I take no offense. We do."

"So you could say that, as a society, corpses are your greatest resource and need?"

Viratus looked at his companions. "You could phrase it that way, yes."

"What if there were too many ghouls? What if they consumed so many corpses that the supply ran out? If you had no way to replenish your supply of corpses, what would happen?"

"We ran out of corpses long ago," said Vocorix. "We get fresh corpses from the surface."

"What if you couldn't? What if the tunnels that led to the surface caved-in? Or some other danger or obstacle prevented you from reaching the surface? What then?"

"Aleksandr," interjected Hent. "Are you here to discuss Nemret Noktoria or Geb?"

"I am here to discuss Geb."

"Then it is time we do so," said Hent. "What the Chancellor asks is impossible. Furthermore, it is not certain that more living in Geb would be beneficial. Indeed, if we are hard-pressed by enemies, now and in the future, I would argue that more undead, not fewer, is the solution." Hent looked to the trio of ghouls, who nodded in agreement.

"Whether the Chancellor is correct or incorrect," continued Hent, "is an academic matter. One could waste endless nights with such philosophical talk, but to guide a nation like Geb by it is—suicide." She leaned toward Aleksandr. "My nephew did not found a nation so that the living could multiply and prosper. He founded a nation so that the dead could do so. It was Geb's wish that undeath no longer be hidden, as if it were a condition of which one is to be ashamed." She looked to the ghouls, who nodded. "Add to this that Kemnebi's argument is defeated by the fact that Nemret Noktoria has existed for thousands of years, as has Geb itself."

"I understand," said Aleksandr. "But there have been living in Geb that entire time, more living than dead. In order for Geb—"

"You must no longer think of Geb," interrupted Hent-er-Neheh. "The point has come in which you, Aleksandr, must think of yourself." She sat back and turned to Viratus. "Soon there will be a new chancellor." She looked at Aleksandr. "We must acknowledge that Kemnebi has disqualified himself for the role. Arazni is queen, this is not in dispute. But this nation is Geb's. It is high time that one of his relatives, all of whom share his vision, takes a leading role in furthering it."

"I can think of none better than you," said Vennonius.

Hent let escape a haughty laugh, but checked herself. "That has yet to be determined." She again looked at Aleksandr. "Your loyalty is commendable. Indeed, loyalty is in scarce supply in every nation, living or dead. A chancellor cannot rule without the loyalty of those he—or she—rules. I reward loyalty, Aleksandr. You must ask yourself to whom and to what you are loyal. Are you loyal to Kemnebi? Or are you loyal to Geb?"

. . .

"Why send us to Nah-le-tah?" growled Rhianna. She walked with long strides, tugging Aedha by the hand, who half-jogged to keep up. "Why send us to talk to anyone? I hate talk."

"The giant seems polite," said Aedha.

Rhianna looked at her. "Polite?"

"He's always been respectful to me."

"He worships Urgathoa," said Rhianna, looking ahead. "Whatever else you think about him, remember that."

"But, we're vampires, so we should be safe, right?"

"Safe?" Rhianna stared at her lover, then looked away. She patted the hilt of her enchanted bastard sword with her other hand. "I'm always safe. What I'm saying is he's too—" She searched for the right words to describe the tomb giant but couldn't find them. "He's too much like Aleksandr."

"Your ex?"

"Don't remind me."

"How is he like Aleksandr?"

"They're both too damn civilized."

The pair turned onto the avenue that led to the Church of Epiphenomena. The twin black towers loomed over the intervening buildings. The moon was full, bathing the wide avenue in light. Rhianna did not turn her gaze from the middle distance. She had a warrior's well-honed instincts. She saw without having to look. She heard without actively listening. She felt danger approaching before any single sense gave evidence. When she stopped, Aedha jogged past her and was yanked to a halt.

"Your bow," said Rhianna, her voice low. She released Aedha's hand and reached for her sword.

"I—I left it at home."

"You what?"

"I—"

Both vampires heard the cluster of footfalls and saw the swaying lights of torches before the group walked out onto the avenue. There were a dozen of them. They turned, saw Rhianna and Aedha, and slowed to a stop. In the near silence—only the crackling of torches supplied sound—more footfalls were heard. Aedha turned and saw another dozen appear behind them. She reached out and grabbed her lover's arm.

"Rhianna—"

Rhianna drew her sword. "Do you fools know who I am?"

"Rhianna Ceinwen!"

Rhianna spun to face the speaker. He held no torch. Instead his hand glowed with divine light. He raised his other hand and held aloft a holy symbol made of gold, carved in the shape of a fly. He said no more but raised his divine-fire-wreathed hand. Before Rhianna could react a beam of light shot from his palm, striking her in the chest. She felt the angry heat of it.

Rhianna growled, pushed away the pain, and charged the cleric. He thrust his holy symbol forward. Rhianna ignored it and lifted her sword. Just as she was about to strike, two men lunged in front of her. One of the two men thrust out his torch, intent on blocking her downward chop. Her sword cut through it, lopping off the burning head, and struck the second man in the shoulder, but it was a glancing blow.

Aedha turned toward the other group, the first that they'd seen. She did not have her bow but she had her sword. She drew it as three men advanced. They held torches and swords and seemed practiced in the use of both as weapons. It may have been that the moon was full, reflecting off the blades, but Aedha felt that there was something odd about their swords. The metal was too white in color, not like steel. However, she didn't have time to contemplate the metallurgy of her attacker's swords.

The trio fanned out. One lunged but Aedha knocked his sword away. Another threw his torch at her face, causing her to wrench awkwardly to the side to avoid being struck. The third, seeing she was off-balance, stabbed forward. His sword pierced her side, the tip poking through her back. It was not the first time since being turned into a vampire that Aedha had been stabbed, but the wound seemed more significant than it should have been, given her vampiric durability.

She stepped back, both regaining her balance and un-skewering herself. The wound bled and didn't want to close, despite the self-healing power of her vampiric gift. It was then that she realized the sword was made of silver, to which vampires were weak.

"Rhianna—"

"Aedha!" yelled Rhianna, interrupting the other vampire's warning. Rhianna was also backing up, as the dozen attackers advanced. "Get out of here."

"I'm not leaving you."

The two women were back-to-back, each facing a dozen attackers, including clerics of Urgathoa, something that surprised them both.

"Leave these chumps to me," said Rhianna over her shoulder. "Twenty-four to one is nothing, mere exercise." As she bragged she parried swords and torches. Still, the wound in her chest worried her.

The attackers spread out, forming a circle around the women. Aedha waved her sword in wide arc, keeping those close to her at bay. Something began to unsettle her, however, more so even than the silver blades. She heard a woman's seductive voice over the growing din of battle. She couldn't concentrate hard enough to pick up the words but they pressed on her mind, smothering her thoughts. The movements of the men before her took on an exaggerated slowness, as if they were pantomiming battle.

Over the shoulders of the men she saw a figure in a gray, tattered robe. A gleaming gold fly hung from a gold chain around her neck. The holy symbol was the size of a fist and just as menacing. The sleeves of her robe ended at her elbows; her arms were wrapped in blood-spotted bandages. Her fingernails were long and black. The cleric's raised hood hid her face in shadow. From that darkness came the words that enchanted Aedha. She heard a command, spoken in a whisper, but which rode over the shouts of combat.

Embrace your lover.

Rhianna feinted to her right, shifted left, grabbed the sword arm of the man closest, pulled him off-balance, and ran the point of her sword into his ribs. She was surprised to see, and feel, that under his loose cotton shirt the man wore one of chain. Her thrust was strong enough to shatter the links, shatter his ribs, and pierce his heart, but that he was armored, and trying to hide it, was yet another surprise. She yanked her sword back and was preparing to shift to her right when she saw, in her peripheral vision, Aedha's sword clatter to the ground. She halted her movement and was about to turn when she felt a pair of arms wrap around her. She saw and felt that Aedha was clinging to her.

"What are you doing?"

Just then another beam of searing light struck her, this time in the hip. At the same moment she felt several swords tips thrust into her. Rhianna was not only a practiced fighter, she was a vampire. Her body was fortified by powerful necromantic magic. She should have been able to shrug off the blows, but these were different.

Her vampiric toughness did nothing to stop them. She too realized that her attackers were equipped to kill vampires.

Rhianna looked into her lover's eyes and saw that they were rolled up, the pupils nearly disappearing. Aedha wasn't present in the normal sense of the word. She clung to Rhianna but other than that she was unresponsive.

The beast at the heart of every vampire is a survivor. Rhianna, feeling her wounds, and knowing that she was outmatched, welcomed the beast. She shook-off Aedha, spun—the silver blades dislodged by her movement—and with a primal growl, lashed out with her sword. She knew she hit something, she felt the drag of it on her blade, she tasted the blood that splashed onto her face, but the beast prevented her from knowing fully what was transpiring. The beast did not operate by conscious thought, it did not plan or calculate, it killed and didn't stop until the killing was done.

Rhianna moved and struck. Rhianna killed. But she was only partially present for the slaughter. It was the familiar touch of Aedha's hands that drew Rhianna away from the beast. She became aware of her surroundings and saw that, as before, Aedha was clinging to her, attempting to still her sword arm. However, her grip was tentative. Rhianna was too strong and too wild to control. The beast surged forward. Rhianna cut down two men with one horizontal slash. One of her attackers lunged toward her. She felt his blade enter her right thigh, but the pain was distant. The wound only made the beast angrier.

Still, the beast didn't have total control. Rhianna realized that Aedha was being pulled away by two men, each of whom held one of her arms. Her eyes were still rolled up into her skull. She made no effort to fight off her attackers. Rhianna pulled her sword from a corpse at her feet and advanced toward the pair that held Aedha. Another man stepped between her and the trio, his back to

Rhianna. He lifted something and held it to Aedha's chest, then stepped to the side. Rhianna lashed out, slashing the man's back. He screamed and reached behind him to feel the severity of the wound. Miraculously, he kept his grip on the stake poised just above Aedha's heart.

A second man was in the process of swinging a heavy wooden mallet. Rhianna reached forward in an attempt to grab it but she was too late. The mallet slammed against the flattened end of the stake, driving it into Aedha's heart. Aedha collapsed, paralyzed by the wood.

Rhianna grabbed the mallet, yanked it from the man's hands, tossed it aside while at the same time stabbing him in the gut. She yanked out her blade, spilling his intestines at her feet. She knelt and reached for the wooden stake, intent on pulling it free. The man's body dropped at her side. He lay next to her, moaning. A moment later she heard his death rattle. Although the sound should have encouraged her, it didn't. Rhianna was able to grab the stake but her strength was failing. She was not even aware that a sword had run her through until she glanced down and saw the tip.

Rhianna heard a woman's voice. "Give up, you cannot win."

She looked and saw the speaker. A female cleric of Urgathoa pulled back her hood. Her skin resembled ancient parchment; unevenly discolored with pieces flaking off. Hers was the skin of a leper. Her hair was limp and black. Her eyes were bulging, bloodshot, and fanatical. Yet, she was young, it wasn't age that disfigured her; it was disease. The cleric raised her hand and the remaining attackers stayed their blades. The sword's tip withdrew from Rhianna's stomach. Blood spurted from the wound, spilling over her thighs. The beast cried out for her to flee, to seek the safety of her coffin, but she refused.

Rhianna was too weak to do anything but kneel. It took all her strength to keep from toppling over. Really, it wasn't her strength, but her pride that kept her upright. The cleric studied Rhianna's wounds, cataloging them, a bemused expression on her face. She looked from the wounds into Rhianna's eyes.

"Come over to our side. Renounce Kemnebi. Embrace Urgathoa."

"Fuck—you," growled Rhianna. Blood spat out with each word, coating her chin.

"I was told to make the offer," said the cleric. "I'm glad you refused." With this she drew a silver dagger from the folds of her robe. She grabbed the top of Aedha's head with one hand and placed the blade against the helpless vampire's throat. Rhianna reached out and grabbed the cleric's wrist, but she was too weak to stop what came next. The cleric cut off Aedha's head.

"No!" screamed Rhianna.

"Kill her," commanded the cleric, who shook off Rhianna's hand and rose.

. . .

From the mouth of a nearby alley a man crouched amongst the refuse. He wore dark clothing and soft-soled boots. A bandolier, heavy with daggers, was stretched across his chest. He hadn't seen the beginning of the ambush, but he had heard it. Now, from the safety of the shadows, he watched. He knew his master would be interested. Maybe, thought the spy, his master would reward him. Being turned into a mummy upon death was better than ending up in the Bonewall.

The spy could barely see what happened next, there were too many corpses piled up, but he could guess. One of the two vampires was beheaded. A cleric doused her severed head in holy water and the vampire, head and body, turned into ash.

Once this was accomplished those who still lived prepared to cut down the remaining vampire. The spy had overheard the name Rhianna Ceinwen. It was a name he knew, even though he had a hard time believing it was a Blood Lord being murdered in the streets of Mechitar.

The men lifted their swords and struck. But Rhianna did not fall into the pile of ash that had been her lover. Instead her form melted away, becoming a cloud of gas. Although she was hard to see in her new form, the spy could follow her by the displacement of objects she passed before. She rose over the heads of her attackers and floated away. He lost sight of her and returned his attention to the group in the avenue.

Two gray robed figures approached one another, one hunching forward, his hands clutching his stomach.

"Jenya is dead," said the hunched-over cleric. There was pain in his voice.

The leprous cleric looked over the corpses until she spotted Jenya's. She shrugged her shoulders and looked back at her fellow cleric.

"She cut me."

"Let me see." The female cleric knelt and examined the wound, poking her black nails into the bloody slit. The male cleric grimaced at the unwanted probing. He returned his hands to his stomach as soon as she was done tormenting him. "I'll sew you up when we get back to the church." She stood. "Try not to bleed to death before then." She turned to the surviving men. "Gather up the corpses. Hurry. We take everyone with us. Leave nothing behind. Nothing."

"She got away," said the male cleric.

"So?"

"Latitia said—"

"Shut up. Don't say her name."

"But now they'll know, the Chancellor and the other vampires."

"Good. It's more," the female cleric laughed, "interesting that way."

"There's too many to carry," protested one of the men, interrupting the dialogue. "We're wounded. Heal us."

"Heal you? Would you prefer I command your corpses to carry theirs." She pointed to the scattered bodies in the street. The men did not require any more motivation and, despite their wounds, began to gather up the dead. The spy backed deeper into the alley, turned, and ran out the other end, eager to report what he had seen.

A Growing Intimacy, a Departure, and an Unwelcome Interruption

Various locations, Mechitar, Geb, Gozran, 4711

"How did you—"

Kemnebi laughed. Elana was attempting to ask a question so complex she couldn't put it into words. The pair had settled into Kemnebi's living room. He tried to remember the last time he had set foot in his pyramidal home. The trophy collection reminded him how much he'd forgotten. He turned at movement. Wamukota handed him a goblet of bloodwine.

He looked down at his master, offering his opinion through his eyes. He was suspicious of the girl, but, being a loyal retainer, he didn't question his master's judgment. He went to Elana and handed her a goblet of wine. He left to fetch a tray of food and returned, setting it before Elana. She leaned forward and sorted through the fruit and cheese. Kemnebi wiped a line of clean in the dust on the table and looked at his fingertip. He blew the dust from it.

"How did I begin my necromantic studies?" he asked. "How did I become a vampire? How did I become chancellor?"

Elana smiled. "Yes." She sipped the wine. "But, what I'm most curious about is," she studied him with her large, blue eyes, "how did you befriend Geb?"

"I didn't."

"But—"

Kemnebi rose. He went to a small teakwood cabinet and opened it. "If I remember—ah, yes, here." He pulled out a gold medallion that depicted a god long forgotten to mankind. He walked to Elana and handed it to her.

"My great great grandfather's."

Elana studied it. "I don't recognize the depiction."

"Few would," said Kemnebi, resuming his seat. "I must take you back a long way." The statement was also a question. He was requesting patience from the young woman who sat across from him. She nodded that she understood.

"My great great grandfather advised Geb, back when he was a mere mortal. Well, really, he was an advisor to the Pharaoh. When Geb's relatives began a cult amongst the royal embalmers my ancestor joined them. In time Geb proved the most influential in the cult. He was the rising star, and the most aggressive. He relied on my ancestor to inform him of the Pharaoh's desires and weaknesses.

"Geb had the idea of convincing the Pharaoh of the cult's aims. You see, the belief back then was that life was a preparation for the afterlife. Life was short, the afterlife was eternal. But the cult didn't trust the gods. They doubted the accuracy of the afterlife as depicted on ancient tomb walls. They were the royal embalmers and they alone knew that the mummified remains they created were nothing more than elaborately dressed corpses. What the ancient order wanted was to live forever—here. They embraced undeath.

"My ancestor advised Geb against approaching the Pharaoh. Geb ignored him. When the Pharaoh learned of the cult he flew into a rage. He told the cultists, most of whom were Geb's relatives, to leave Osirion or face his wrath. Many fled, including my ancestor. But Geb and his family were stubborn. They thought they could kill the Pharaoh and take his place. They were wrong." Kemnebi smiled and sipped his bloodwine.

Elana sipped her wine and ate a grape.

"The Pharaoh's men hounded Geb and his relatives out of Osirion," continued Kemnebi. "They fled south, into what was then wild country. But the Pharaoh pursued them still further. They had no recourse but to mount the Shattered Range and cross over into the Mwangi Expanse. There they joined those who had already fled. I can only imagine how furious Geb must have been at such a humiliating retreat. He and his relatives were not going to stay in the jungle for long. They crossed back over the mountains, but not everyone went with them. Many stayed in the Expanse, including my great great grandfather.

"Those that stayed behind abandoned not only Geb but their beliefs in the ancient order. They took up their old religion. They mingled these beliefs with the strange spiritualism of the people of the Mwangi. The exiles intermarried and within generations the Osirion blood had thinned.

"I was born in the Mwangi Expanse. Geb, the ancient order, the Pharaoh's wrath, exile from Osirion," Kemnebi laughed, "to me they were myths. I didn't believe them." He nodded to the medallion. "Until my father showed me that." Elana studied the medallion a moment longer then handed it back. Kemnebi held it up and Wamukota emerged from the shadows, took the medallion, and stowed it in the cabinet.

"But Geb did not forget that some of his followers had abandoned him. Geb does not forget a slight. He returned to the Mwangi Expanse. My ancestor was long dead. I was a boy. I had an older brother and a younger sister. We were dumbfounded when this mythological boogieman appeared in our village and demanded to see his former advisor. My father took him to our ancestor's grave.

"You would think that would be the end of it, but no. Geb raised my great great grandfather. He had long ago rotted away but—something—burst from the ground. Geb turned to my father and commanded he and all those of Osirion blood follow him. 'It's time,' Geb said, 'to come home.' What could we do? How could we protest? We had no idea what he was capable of. We were afraid, so we obeyed.

"Geb selected the youngest and brightest of us and began to teach us the art of necromancy. My brother couldn't understand. He had no gift for the arcane. Geb grew frustrated and one day blasted the flesh from my brother's bones. He raised his skeleton and sent it off to keep my ancestor company. My sister was doing little better. I tried to help her. In time Geb gave her to another. I never saw her again. There were perhaps three dozen of us, Geb's pupils. In time all were either killed and raised as undead or given as gifts to Geb's allies. Within a year only I remained."

"You must have been terrified."

"Yes. Thankfully, in time, Geb became busy with other matters. He gave me to one of his allies, a necromancer named Sekhem-khet. He was more patient than Geb. I spent years studying under him. But Geb wasn't done with me. One day he summoned me, interrogated me, and once he was confident in my abilities, he used me.

"This is how things went. Geb would send me to do his bidding. I would risk my life for him. I would return and resume my studies under Sekhem-khet; that is, until Geb had another task for me. During a particularly arduous task I was almost killed. I had to abandon my mission. I feared to tell Geb. I was afraid he would punish me for failing. But to hide the truth from him would be worse. To my surprise he took me to another of his allies. An Osirioni named Tcha-n-hebu and, as I would find out, he was a vampire.

"'Make him like you,' commanded Geb. 'I've invested too much time in him to let him get killed.'"

Kemnebi smiled. "Geb is practical, if nothing else. So, now you know how I met Geb, how I began my studies, and how I became a vampire. Of course, I've left out quite a lot, but—"

"Thank you," said Elana. "Why didn't you run away?" Kemnebi raised an eyebrow. "I mean, he sent you out, as you said, to risk your life for him. Why not run away? Why return?"

"I had seen others try it. Geb would send undead after them; shadows with eyes of fire. They were always drug back. Once back, it was worse than ever for them. Even if those who ran away died before Geb could get to them, he would recall their souls from the afterlife and punish them." Kemnebi shook his head. "There was no running away from Geb."

"How did you become chancellor?"

"Yes, that must be confusing to you. How did I change from a frightened youth, Geb's slave, into his confidant and the chancellor of his nation? It came about slowly. For a long time I studied necromancy out of fear. I learned necromancy not because I wanted to but because Geb wanted me to. Even as a vampire I was afraid of him.

"But in time I noticed he did not treat me like a slave but more as an equal. Don't misunderstand, Geb does not acknowledge any equal. Nor do I think he has an equal. But Geb trusted me. He valued my opinion. More and more I was counted amongst his closest allies. I was given tremendous responsibilities. I took over the role that my ancestor once held. I was powerful and influential. I liked how that felt.

"Yet it was something deeper than that. I began to understand how Geb thought. I understood his vision. I had lived well beyond my natural lifespan. I was many times more powerful than any mortal. I could scarcely be hurt. I had defeated death. I now had more in common with Geb and his undead relatives and allies than I had with any mortal, even those of my own blood.

"When one has power, wealth, and responsibility—when one makes decisions that affect other peoples' lives, when one can ruin a people or uplift them—a gulf grows between them and the common man. I understood society, and the individual's place in it, at a deeper level. I saw vast trends that are almost invisible to one who lives but a short time. Yes, I understood Geb. As much as anyone can understand a man like him. He knew I understood him. So, when he needed a chancellor, he picked me."

"A great honor."

"Yes."

"Are you the only chancellor there has ever been?"

"Yes."

"And yet," continued Elana, "Arazni?"

"Yes, Geb's Harlot Queen. But, at the risk of sounding rude, I would rather not talk about her. I'm more interested in you."

Elana blushed. "Me? I'm just a student."

"Saskia's believes in you."

"Yes, she's been a wonderful mentor." Elana shifted in her seat. "I'm not like you or even her. I'm not powerful, not yet. Although I hope one day to be a Blood Lord, that seems so far off, maybe even impossible."

"Not for you," said Kemnebi. "I understand that you are the best in your class. Trevedic has mentioned you. He says you are the fastest caster he's ever seen."

"Thank you for saying that. I try my best."

Kemnebi smiled. "When I began to study necromancy I wanted nothing more than to please Geb, really, to give him no reason to kill me. Fear is a powerful motivator, but perhaps not the best. Tell me, what is it you want from the study of necromancy? What motivates you?"

Elana blushed.

. . .

Sulah, Bones of Wood knelt, cupping the head of a flower in her palm, the stem between her fingers, and thought of her past. She was a ghoran, a plant-based life-form that reproduces itself by growing a seed in its abdomen. When an individual ghoran grows old it produces a seed, plants it, then dies. The next generation grows from this seed. This new ghoran was not a completely separate individual, nor was it the same as it had been before.

Sulah was from the Southern Fangwood, in Nirmathas. Before she could escape the Fangwood she was captured by sadistic fey and taken to Arlantia, a corrupted dryad who ruled the forest and who also worshipped Cyth-V'sug, the demon lord of disease, fungus, and rot.

Arlantia was intrigued by her new captive. She forced Sulah, under torture, to emit her seed. This the dryad planted in the diseased soil of her territory. She watered it with poison, curious what would grow. But the life force of the seed held true. The new Sulah was not as healthy as she would have been otherwise, but she was hardly the tribute to Cyth V'sug she was meant to be.

Arlantia was angered by this. She ordered more severe tortures, got Sulah to emit another seed, and planted this one in still fouler soil. Greater care was taken to corrupt the seed. It worked. The Sulah that grew from this seed was neither completely alive nor completely dead. She was full of rot, coated in fungus, but somehow still alive. This pleased Arlantia.

The change was not only physical. Cyth V'sug's corruption went deep. Sulah, who had once been a protector of the forest, now sought to destroy it. Arlantia welcomed this new Sulah to her wicked court.

But as time went on Sulah's body became more dead than alive. She worried her next seed would not grow. Some small sliver of self-love remained and she sought a cure. But she was a committed worshipper of Cyth V'sug. No cleric of a good god would cure her. Neither, she knew, would the demon lord she worshipped. No, she would need someone powerful, a god in their own right. She sought out Geb.

She was not able to meet Geb. He was not in Mechitar, like she hoped. She didn't know that he had retired to Geb's Rest to nurture his own corruption. She went to the Ebon Mausoleum and there met Trevedic Faull. He, along with Cassius Allius, determined that the new seed was lifeless. It seemed the Sulah before them would be the last—unless drastic measures were taken.

Sulah released her seed. It was planted, "nurtured" by necromantic magic and "watered" with various chemical concoctions. It "grew" but what came from the seed could not be rightly called a ghoran. It was a unique type of undead. A mixture of wickerwork, fungus, and necromantic energy.

The two Blood Lords were so proud of their creation they showed Sulah at a meeting in the Cinerarium. Arazni was so intrigued by Sulah that she asked the undead ghoran to join her clique. Many decades would pass before Arazni asked something else of Sulah. This is how the undead ghoran came to stand a bit upriver from Mechitar, waiting under a full moon.

She released the flower she held. It swayed then stilled, its white petals glowing in the moonlight. Sulah rose and peered into the darkness. She could not hear the approach of the giant bat, nor could she see it. She could only wait until the massive but silent form glided to a landing before her. She climbed onto the giant bat's shoulders, clung to its furry mantle, and held tight as the bat took off. Finally, decades after first trying, Sulah was going to see Geb.

. . .

Wamukota opened the door. He held a wand in one hand, keeping it hidden behind the partially opened door. Its tip, made of a large crystal, glowed, ready with a spell.

"Who are you?" he asked. "What do you want? Do you realize whose door you've been pounding on?"

"Mistress Rhianna," said the young man, speaking each syllable between sharp breaths. His face was flush. Wamukota gave the young man a moment to breathe. "She returned to her coffin. She—" Wamukota grabbed the young man by the shoulder and yanked him into from the street. He shut the door. He held the wand at his side but did not dismiss the readied spell.

"Go on."

Now that the messenger, who was one of Rhianna's thralls, was inside the Chancellor's private residence he lowered his voice. "She returned home and went straight to her coffin." He paused. "Not in physical form. There's more. Aedha left with her but did not return."

"Were you able speak to your mistress?"

The messenger shook his head. Wamukota dismissed the spell. He reached out and patted the messenger down with his free hand, searching for hidden weapons. When he was satisfied his fellow thrall was unarmed he eyed him with a mixture of suspicion and worry.

"Come with me."

. . .

"No, you didn't!" said Elana, laughing.

"I did."

"But she couldn't have meant it as—"

"With the benefit of hindsight, no," said Kemnebi, "but at the time—"

Elana reached out and gripped Kemnebi's bicep. She leaned her forehead against his shoulder.

"Oh, that poor woman." She laughed.

"You take her side?" asked Kemnebi, with mock injury.

"Master," interrupted Wamukota. He entered the living room and saw his master and Elana standing by a bookshelf. Kemnebi was holding a book in one hand, intent on re-shelving it. Elana was intimately close to him. When Wamukota entered she released her grip. Both turned. "A messenger has come from Rhianna's hunting lodge." Wamukota stepped aside. The messenger appeared. He bowed low to Kemnebi.

"What is it?"

"Chancellor," began the messenger, rising. "My mistress returned home and immediately went to her coffin."

"She was a cloud of gas," added Wamukota.

"Aedha was not with her," said the messenger. "Although," he was quick to add, "they left together."

Kemnebi shoved the book back in its slot. He approached the messenger, who couldn't help but recoil. "She returned? Just now?"

"Yes, Chancellor."

Kemnebi turned and looked at Elana. "They were on their way to speak to Nah-le-tah."

"The tomb giant?" asked Elana, crossing the room to stand next to Kemnebi.

"Yes. They should be speaking to him now."

"Something has happened," said Elana.

Kemnebi turned to the messenger. "Was she still in her coffin when you left?"

"Yes, Chancellor."

"Did you come straight here?"

"Yes, I rode my horse to exhaustion."

"Return and keep an eye on her," said Kemnebi. "Make sure her guards remain alert. Wamukota, go with him."

"Yes, Chancellor."

"I will come to the hunting lodge as soon as I can. Go." Both men turned and left. "We must retrace their steps," said Kemnebi, meaning the two vampires. "We must find Aedha."

"You think they were attacked?" asked Elana.

"I fear it."

"Who would be foolish enough to attack them?"

"That I must learn."

. . .

"Damn," said Kemnebi, kneeling in the avenue. He looked up and saw the twin towers of the Church of Epiphenomena in the distance. The street was deserted. He looked over his shoulder at Elana, who stood several feet back, her hands over her mouth.

"So much blood," she whispered through her fingers.

"Only Rhianna could spill this much blood." Kemnebi stood. "No corpses. No sign of Aedha. Damn it, I needed a corpse."

"To question?" asked Elana, stepping up but avoiding the congealing blood. She knew that there were necromantic spells that allowed the caster to speak with the dead.

"Yes."

The pair looked over the scene of the battle.

"So much blood should have drawn undead," said Elana. "Perhaps the bodies have been dragged away." She began to skirt the pool of blood, looking for drag marks. When she had rounded the pool she returned to Kemnebi's side. "There's a trail." She looked toward the twin black stone towers. The rose window, depicting the massive fly, being lit from behind, could be seen. Elana pointed. "That way." She looked at Kemnebi, but he was looking at something near the center of the pool. She followed his gaze. "What is it?"

"Ash," said Kemnebi. "I can smell it, taste it, even over the blood."

"Ash?"

"Aedha."

"But—"

"Look at the shape of it."

Elana looked. The ash, although trampled underfoot and washed partially away by blood, had a distinctively humanoid shape.

"Rhianna is a talented fighter," said Kemnebi. "She is a vampire. It would not be easy to defeat her in battle. Also," he motioned to the ash, "she would never allow that to happen if she could prevent it." He looked at Elana. "Someone knew what they were doing."

"They were attacked on purpose," concluded Elana.

Both Elana and Kemnebi stood a moment in contemplative silence. Elana reached out and gripped Kemnebi's bicep. "We shouldn't be here. It's not safe."

Kemnebi knelt and drug his fingers through the syrupy blood. "Perhaps this will be enough," he said, standing.

"Will their blood tell us anything?"

"Let's go to my office. I've a scroll there." He turned and began toward the Cinerarium. Elana once more gripped his arm. He turned to face her.

"Arazni?" She looked at the pool of blood.

"You think she did this?"

"Can you rule it out?"

Kemnebi looked at the pool of blood, to Elana, then to the Cinerarium. "I don't believe that, I won't. She may be angry but," he glanced again at the blood. "She wouldn't." He looked at Elana. "The blood will tell us something. It must." He sensed uneasiness in Elana. "I will go alone."

"Kemnebi, I—"

"Perhaps it is best if you weren't seen with me."

"But, I—" Tears began to well up in her eyes.

"Return to the Ebon Mausoleum," said Kemnebi. "You'll be safe there." He watched as Elana hurried toward the school. Earlier she had expressed a desire to be a Blood Lord. He wondered how she felt now.

. . .

Elana hurried to the nearest corner, turned, then turned back and gripped the corner of the building. She watched Kemnebi begin toward the Cinerarium. She waited until he was out of sight. She changed direction and ran.

A Bet and a Hedge, an Excursion, and Meeting Geb

Various locations, Mechitar and Geb's Rest, Geb, Gozran, 4711

"The blood led toward the church?" asked Saskia.

"Yes," said Elana. "It could have been a coincidence."

"No."

The two women were high in one of the few wizards towers in Mechitar. The cylindrical, stone towers, so beloved by wizards, were a rare sight in the city. Geb did not like them, preferring pyramids, as a result, few were ever built. Saskia's tower was recent, built long after Geb had abandoned Mechitar for his self-imposed exile, taking his architectural prohibitions with him.

Saskia stepped through the open door onto the balcony. The wind tossed her hair. She pulled it out of her face and looked to her right. In the distance she could see the twin towers of the Church of Epiphenomena. The rose window with its giant fly in stained glass was discernible even from this distance; a low, multicolored moon hung over the capital. The towers themselves could only be seen in shape, defined by the stars they blotted out.

Elana appeared in the doorway. "They can't have meant to let her escape."

Saskia stared at the church, then turned and looked toward the third of Mechitar that glowed like a phosphorescent algae on a black sea. Beyond that glow, the city faded into darkness. She was always struck by the oddness of Mechitar at night. She had never known a city like it.

Elana stepped in reverse to let Saskia back into the top-floor room. The night breeze, still retaining some of the day's warmth, drafted in behind her. Other than the two women there was one other occupant in the room. The undead was under Saskia's control but its need to destroy life was so strong that Elana's presence infuriated it. Those who were not schooled in necromancy might think it a skeleton not yet rid of its internal organs. The bloated, pulsing entrails clung to the mohrg's ribs and spine. Its esophagus surged upwards, reaching between the jaws, searching for living blood and tissue to satiate its depraved hunger.

Saskia reached out and took Elana's hands in her own. "It was a warning—to Kemnebi." Elana tilted her head. Saskia continued. "Aedha, poor elf, she was too weak to be a Blood Lord. Rhianna should never have demanded it. She doomed the poor girl." Saskia released Elana and went to a chair, but did not yet sit. "They couldn't kill anyone too close to Kemnebi: Aleksandr, Trevedic. He would never forgive that. It would mean war. But Aedha." Saskia shook her head.

"Rhianna?"

"Kemnebi has never been fond of her."

"Who?"

Saskia sat. Her familiar hopped through the open door of its cage and flew to the arm of the chair. Saskia extended her hand and the bird leapt onto her fingers. She lifted it to her lips and kissed the top of its head. "Shut the door, darling." Elana walked over and closed the door to the balcony. "I can tell you who it wasn't," said Saskia. "It wasn't Narcisse. He would not act in such a vulgar manner. It wasn't Sthaga. His ghouls would have lapped up every drop of blood." She glanced at Elana. "Nor would there have been any corpses to drag away."

Elana crossed the room and stood close to her mentor. "They were going to see Nah-le-tah."

"He would never be so bold." Saskia looked down at her familiar, petting its back and wings. "It was Latitia, or someone trying to make it look like it was Latitia."

Elana approached the chair and knelt, placing her hands on the arm. "A Blood Lord has been assassinated."

Saskia turned and looked into her protege's face. "It happens. But it hasn't for a while." She reached out and stroked Elana's hair. She smiled as she studied the younger woman's face. "Such a prize, so young, so attractive." Her look grew serious. "Are you comfortable staying close to him?"

"Kemnebi?"

"Yes." Saskia stopped petting her protege and resumed petting her familiar. "It would put you in harm's way. But," Saskia studied Elana's face, judging her response, "it offers a tremendous opportunity."

"You think he'll win?"

"Who can say?" asked Saskia. "But the power struggle has begun." She rose and walked to her familiar's cage. Elana rose and watched her mentor. Saskia held her hand up to the cage's entrance and the bird hopped in. Saskia shut the door and pulled the cloth over the cage. She spoke with her back to Elana. "He's learned much from Geb. He might come out on top. If he does," she turned to face Elana, "any who helped him would benefit."

"And if he doesn't," said Elana. "If he's destroyed. I'll be killed along with him." The two women looked into each other's eyes. "And all you will have lost is an assistant."

Saskia stepped forward and once more took Elana's hands into her own. "I would not sacrifice you."

"But you would put me in danger?"

"You were in danger the moment you entered Geb."

Elana smiled. "I'm a big girl. I can take care of myself."

"Yes, you can." Saskia smiled. Her smile faded. "No doubt, Rhianna felt the same." She glanced at the mohrg, thinking of her own efforts to preserve her safety; of which, it was only a small part. She looked back to Elana. "I won't force you. I won't choose for you. I will ask, stay close to him, for me, for yourself. Help him, in his time of need. Will you?"

"I will."

"Good," Saskia smiled. "I'll take you to him." She released Elana's hands and went to an armoire, intent on getting an enchanted cloak for added protection.

"I need to go by the Ebon Mausoleum," said Elana. "I need to gather some things." She started toward the door.

Saskia threw her cloak over her shoulders and spoke while fixing the clasp. "Send someone. The Chancellor has slaves."

Elana was at the door, which led into the stairwell, and began to pull it open. "I prefer—"

Saskia hurried to the door, placing one hand on it and the other on Elana's wrist. "Don't be foolish. You've been seen with him. You can't go anywhere alone. Don't you understand? Staying close to him is the only way you're safe."

A look of consternation crossed Elana's face. Her eyes darted, indicating she was rapidly cycling through options. She looked at Saskia. "Should you be seen escorting me to him?"

"I'm going to see Arazni."

"Why?"

Saskia smiled but there was wickedness in it. "In case she wins."

. . .

It took forty-eight hours of constant work by a dozen slaves to get the women's outfits together. The slaves, being alive—such delicate work could not be accomplished by undead—collapsed when the last thread was knotted, the last glittering star affixed. Araminta, a Carnival of Death, was in charge of costumes. It was her speciality.

Araminta was a changeling. Somewhere in her bloodline a hag had mated, become pregnant, and produced a living child. The stain of her foul blood had forever infected her descendants, with no loss over successive generations. This was evident in two ways. First, only the female offspring lived. Males were stillborn; the corpses grotesquely disfigured. Second, every child possessed mis-matched eyes. Araminta's left eye was the color of burnished silver, her right eye royal purple.

Three decades prior she had been killed by Lilith and brought back as a zombie lord. While the relationship was born from violence and violation, Araminta forgave Lilith, adapted to her new state, and flourished.

She had been Varisian in life, raised in a traveling caravan, a harrower, a layer of cards, a teller of fortunes. She could still hear the reverberations of Fate's puppet-strings. It was Arazni's great pleasure to receive a reading. Araminta amplified her cultural heritage, which was considered exotic in Geb. She threw fantastic parties and arranged elaborate carnivals in which Arazni and her clique were entertained and delighted.

The trip to the Ebon Mausoleum was Arazni's idea. The theme was Araminta's. She had a squad of skeletons carry the dresses, robes, and accessories from her workshop to the Cinerarium. There she entered Arazni's personal quarters and found her friends, all but Sulah and She-mah-hon. She dressed and delighted them. Arazni laughed when she beheld herself in her freestanding mirror. She looked at Lilith in the glass's reflection.

"Mother, I'm off for my first day at wizard's school. Aren't you proud?"

Lilith met Arazni's gaze in the glass. "I suspect you'll come home with a detention slip."

"Mother!"

The women laughed. They were dressed as stereotypical wizards might be; open-fronted robes adorned with magical script, stars, half moons, and lightning bolts of silver thread. They wore a gratuitous amount of magical accoutrements; brooches, rings, bracelets, gaudy necklaces. Everything was pushed well beyond good taste. They clanked when they walked. The hems of their skirts were too high. Their heels were too tall. The cuts of their blouses were too low. They considered themselves the "sexy" undead and they had no qualms about showing off. All but Lilith. Of all the outfits hers was the most restrained.

Arazni rushed to Araminta and threw her arms over her shoulders. "They won't know what to do with us." She laughed, throwing her head back. She turned and looked at Jasmine, the Dead Bride. "Finally, we shall get a proper fiancé for you."

Jasmine clasped her hands over her heart. "I'm loath to be out of my wedding dress but if I should finally win his heart." She lowered her head in mocked humility. Arazni released Araminta and went to Baya-Iza. On the way she passed Kimberly Silent Eyes. "And where, my pet, will you hide your poisoned daggers in this?" She plucked the puffed sleeve of her dress.

"I've three tucked away already."

"Ha! You scoundrel," said Arazni. "Baya, it's a scandal!" She grabbed the drow's bare arm and looked to Araminta. "Did you run out of fabric?" She looked at the drow. "If she was wearing anything less she would be ready for—"

Baya-Iza reached out and covered Arazni's mouth. "Don't say it." She chastised the Queen. "Or you'll ruin my luck." She lowered her hand. "I'm bringing home three students. Do you think there are three cute ones at the Ebon Mausoleum?"

"Three?" asked Moira. "You drow have never learned restraint."

Arazni studied Baya-Iza's skimpy outfit then turned to Araminta. "I see you know our dear drow better than we. You've dressed her perfectly, if she counts as dressed at all."

"Thank you, my Queen."

"Well, ladies," said Lilith. "I have no idea how we are to walk in these heels, but let us try."

"To the Ebon Mausoleum," commanded Arazni. "Go, go, you harlots!"

"Yes, our Harlot Queen!" cheered the women.

. . .

She-mah-hon stood like a sculpture at the base of the steps that led to the Cinerarium. Her legs were together, slightly bent at the knees, her torso twisted and bent backwards, one arm in the air, bent at the elbow, the other extending to the side. Her long near-white hair hung straight down. She looked straight up. She wore a skin-tight scarlet-colored leather body suit. Much of it was cut away to reveal her various piercings and body modifications. She was displaying herself. The group—who were arm-in-arm—stopped when they reached her.

"There's something new," said Jasmine, leaning forward to examine She-mah-hon. "Has to be."

"For shame," said Saskia. She looked to Araminta. "She doesn't match us. She's out of theme."

She-mah-hon broke her pose, looking at Saskia. A smile spread on her too-perfect face. She knelt and pulled a conical hat from behind her legs. It was the same color as her bodysuit but had the requisite stars, crescent moons, and lighting bolts in silver. She stood and plunked it on her head. The women looked at one another and burst out in laughter. They began toward the Ebon Mausoleum.

"It is a shame Sulah hasn't yet returned to us," said Moira. "What would you have done with her?" she asked, looking at Araminta.

"She would be the entanglement spell gone awry," answered Araminta.

"Shame on you," chastised Arazni.

Before long the women were walking the halls of the Ebon Mausoleum, their constant chatter, too-loud laughter, and mocking attempts at spellcasting, violating the solemn silence of the school. It took but moments before the entire campus learn of their presence. Serious study was impossible. Students came from cramped, darkened rooms to gawk. Instructors began to raise objection but when they saw Arazni they wisely played along with the farce. The women made a travesty of the library but the librarian, a wise old sage, did not even raise an eyebrow.

When the women were on the final hunt for cute students they ran into Eratosthenes. They sputtered to a halt before him, their ankles weak on their too-high heels. He looked them over, nodded to Lilith, who nodded back, then bowed before Arazni.

"Oh," said Arazni. "The head wizard bows to me, a mere student." She looked to Lilith. "And you thought I would get a detention."

"There's still time," quipped Lilith.

Eratosthenes rose. "We give no detentions here. To what do we owe the honor of your illustrious presence, my Queen?"

"Our feet hurt," whined Arazni. "Where, in this confusing maze of a school, is the student's lounge?"

Eratosthenes extended an arm, turned, and led the women to the most comfortably appointed room in the Ebon Mausoleum. Those few students who were attempting to study got up and left upon seeing who the new arrivals were. The women sat. Eratosthenes stood.

"Not all is business, Eratosthenes," said Saskia. "Can we not visit you and your students for pleasure?" The women giggled. A few glanced at Baya-Iza, who, despite no one noticing when or how she had acquired them, was seated at a couch with a handsome male student on either arm.

"Pleasure is a word seldom spoken here," said Eratosthenes.

Arazni smiled and motioned to Saskia. "And yet there is business." She looked at Eratosthenes. "I looked everywhere and did not see Trevedic. Is he on sabbatical?"

Eratosthenes did not immediately answer. He was contemplating the motivations behind the question and the ramifications that spawned from it. He looked toward the double doors that led into the hall. They slammed shut. He turned once more toward Arazni.

"Trevedic's status is insecure, his motivation muddled, and his final fate as yet undecided."

Arazni looked over the faces of her followers. She turned back to Eratosthenes. "Have the student's been complaining?"

"No."

"Has there been some issue, some—" She pursed her lips and left the question open.

"Chancellor Kemnebi put Trevedic in a difficult position," said Eratosthenes. "Until I am certain of Trevedic's loyalty his duties here have been suspended."

"Where is he now?" asked Arazni, her voice losing its playful irreverence.

"In his quarters."

"Here in the school?"

"Yes, below."

"See that he stays there."

"Yes, my Queen."

Arazni smiled. "It's funny you mention the Chancellor. He's been on my mind as of late." She studied Eratosthenes. "It's funny, too, you mention loyalty."

"My Queen, if I may anticipate your line of inquiry?" Arazni nodded. Eratosthenes continued. "You have my complete support. Furthermore, those I," he paused, "associate with," he meant the Whispering Way and Arazni knew it without having to be told, "fully support you. We always have, we always will."

"Always is a long time," said Arazni. "Much can change."

"Not as much as one might think."

Arazni rose. "We shall see." She stepped to Eratosthenes and reached out, cupping his cheek. She rose on her tips of her toes, her heels wobbling beneath her. She kissed Eratosthenes on the lips. He made no response. She pulled back and looked into his eyes. "I miss you," he said nothing. She released him, spun, and looked over her clique. "How is it Baya-Iza is the only one to find admirers? What are we? Hideous?" She waved her arms and her followers rose. She looked over her shoulder at Eratosthenes. "We're going to borrow a few of your students." She giggled. "We'll try not to break them." She glanced at She-mah-hon. "Although, I make no promises."

. . .

The bat was a living creature and therefore needed rest. It was not used to ferrying loads upon its back and was not well suited to the task. So it tired quicker than Sulah would have guessed. The bat's fatigue reminded her of the frailty of life, something she had forgotten. The giant bat did not take the straightest route from Mechitar to Geb's Rest, a trip of over two hundred miles. It flew parallel to Axan Wood and seemed to know which tree branches could support its weight and keep it in shadow.

Sulah did not stray far from the slumbering bat during the day. She was no more a fan of sunlight than it was, although she once could not go without. She did not hunt. She needed no sustenance. She meditated upon current events and imagined meeting Geb.

The giant bat flew west until it encountered the Shattered Range Mountains. It then flew north, skirting the range. While the bat clung to a cave ceiling, Sulah sat in the shadow of the entrance, observing the life of the natural world, a life she'd been forced to abandon. She remembered her years as a ranger in the Southern Fangwood. She replayed her capture by evil fey, who were tired of her interference. She recalled her first impression of Arlantia and all that came after. Her life was tragic and unbelievable, even to her.

When Arazni requested she travel to Geb's Rest she was honored but also stunned. She didn't know the Queen had such confidence in her. She realized that Arazni chose her, in part, because she knew more about the wilderness than any other Blood Lord.

The next night the bat left the range, turning east. Beneath its leathery wings the scrublands turned to grasslands. Even here, far from any major settlement, zombies worked the land. At night they stood watch, a field-full of scarecrows that only the cockiest of birds would alight upon.

Finally, the horizon was pierced by a broken triangle; Geb's abandoned pyramid. The bat descended sooner than Sulah expected. It landed and refused to go further. No living thing would go near Geb, not even one ensorcelled to act against its own interest. Sulah dismounted, settled her backpack on her shoulders, checked the swords at her belt, and began to walk. The bat, its magical compulsion fulfilled, lifted into the air like a shadow and disappeared.

Sulah walked amongst the massive, derelict stones, her twin swords in-hand. The area around the pyramid was unnaturally quiet. Not even crickets chirped. She studied every shadow, watched every gap amongst the littered stones, expecting danger that never came. As she approached the corner of the pyramid she saw a glow. She slowed, coming to a stop at the edge. She peered around the corner and saw him. He emitted as much light as a bonfire.

Geb was turned three-quarters away, staring off into the distance. She could just make out his profile, although looking into the light required her to squint. He was a ghost. Arazni told her what to expect, but the sight of him remained unnerving. His robes, twice as long as they would have been were he alive, flapped behind him as if he faced a strong wind. The same wind played with his long hair. It was a wind only he felt. He was no bigger than he had been in life but he floated six feet off the ground.

Sulah sheathed her swords and approached. She was—surprisingly—able to walk right up to him. He did not look at her. He did not acknowledge her at all. His gaze remained locked on something over the horizon.

"Master Geb?" Sulah kept her gaze down but when Geb did not acknowledge her she looked up at him. She was standing off to his side and studied him, taking in the features of a god, or the closest she would ever come to a god, until Pharasma judged her. She thought him handsome with a rectangular head, aristocratic features, a high brow, sculptural lips, and a broad chest, back, and shoulders. Of course, these were all planes of light, nothing more, but the man was still represented.

"Master Geb?" Sulah spoke a little louder. Still Geb did not respond. She walked around to face him, straining her neck to look up into his face. She had the notion to wave her arms to get his attention but thought that foolish. "Geb?" Still nothing. Sulah hadn't expected to be ignored and was momentarily at a loss. She decided she must continue, without having been formally acknowledged.

"Queen Arazni sent me." She paused, thinking perhaps the mention of Arazni's name would draw Geb's attention. Other than the soundless flapping of his ghostly robes there was nothing. She continued. "Chancellor Kemnebi has declared war on the undead of Geb." Again she paused. Geb made no response. "Chancellor Kemnebi has called for fewer undead. He says there are too many and that the living suffer." Still nothing. "Arazni has sent me to beg for your permission to destroy him—to kill Kemnebi." Geb offered no response. Sulah waited. She wondered if he had even heard her. "Geb?"

She was about to abandon her quest when Geb looked down at her. She had to turn away, so ferocious was his gaze.

"What are you?"

"What—I—my name is Sulah. I was sent by—"

Geb floated down. His robes shifted, now wrapping around Sulah. He lowered until his toes, he was barefoot, were six inches from the grass beneath him. He reached out and caressed the wicker that composed Sulah's face. The icy cold of his touch hurt her but she was unable to pull away. His hand moved down her body until it touched the dead seed in her abdomen.

He caressed the seed, feeling its contours. The pain Sulah felt was greater than any torture Arlantia had put to her. Geb reached *into* Sulah, cupping the seed. Although he was immaterial he dug the tips of his fingers behind the seed. Sulah screamed. With a pull, Geb popped the seed from Sulah's abdomen. She staggered backwards, feeling with both hands the void at the center of her being. She passed through Geb's ghostly robes, stumbling away from him. He paid her no mind, but studied the seed.

Sulah panicked. She could feel the necromantic magic that kept her together breaking up. She could feel her wooden bones cracking under their own weight. She didn't know what to do. She had the notion to grab her seed and put it back, but she knew it was too late. Besides, she couldn't take it from Geb. She fell to her knees, the wood of her thighs splintering. She reached toward Geb, intent on begging for his help, but her voice died within her. The necromantic magic dissipated. The fungus and rot at her core, the unwanted gift from Cyth V'sug, now overwhelmed her. She softened. She collapsed; now nothing more than a pile of rotten wood, covered with moss and mushrooms.

Geb turned the seed over in his hands. It was the size of a small pumpkin. He explored the necromantic energies within it and found them novel. This amused him. He at once discerned the purpose of the seed. He floated a few feet to the side of where he had stationed himself a thousand years prior. With a thought, a divot of dirt lifted. He knelt and placed the seed within the hole. The soil returned, covering it. He floated up and over, returning to his long-held post.

Patience and Faith

Various locations, Quantium, Nex, and Mechitar, Geb, Gozran, 4711

Ahrhune ag-Hashid sat in an office. He had been impatient on the journey from Aspenthar to Quantium but the winds in the sails were a comfort. He was making progress, that was something. He had arrived, but his impatience was worse. He felt his progress stall. As an old salt, he knew when the winds left the sails. He turned and looked out a window. Across a narrow, cobbled avenue was the Bandeshar. Armed guards paced the street.

He should be seated in the enormous, sprawling mansion and he knew it. He was so close and yet so far away. He ran his fingers over the jeweled scabbard of the scimitar. He could defeat any opponent, or at least had a chance, but he had no idea how to battle a bureaucracy.

A door opened and he turned. A short, rotund, middle-aged man entered. He had patches of long, thin hair, swept over the top of his head in an attempt to hide his increasing baldness. His nose was aquiline and on it was perched a pair of small, round-rimmed spectacles. He wore a robe of red and gold and slippers that curled up at the toes. His pudgy fingers were home to chunky gold rings. He was festooned like a court jester with ropes of gold and gaudy gems. He'd turned prodigality into an art. He paused in the doorway, glanced down at a sheet of parchment he held, then looked at Ahrhune.

"Yes, I agree," he said, but Ahrhune didn't think he was being spoken to. The man held the parchment over his shoulder. A feminine hand reached up and took it. The man entered, followed by two assistants, one a young woman, the other a young man. They were dressed like their boss, minus the gratuitous show of wealth. All three were human.

"The sail from Aspenthar?" asked the man, taking a seat behind the table that occupied the center of the room.

"Slow," said Ahrhune.

"Yes," said the man. He snapped his fingers and reached out. The young woman returned the parchment to him. "It says here that you are in a great hurry." The man did not look at the parchment, but held it for a moment as if it were a piece of evidence. He extended it and his assistant took it back.

"There is much to be done," said Ahrhune. He added, "To prepare."

"Prepare?" asked the balding official.

Ahrhune shifted in the chair. "I've thought it over." He glanced at the two assistants, then at the man. "An evacuation. It's the—"

"An evacuation of—" The man raised a bushy eyebrow.

"Quantium."

The man turned and looked at his two assistants. He smiled then turned back to Ahrhune. "Perhaps I should hear it from the beginning."

"A vision—from Sarenrae," began Ahrhune. "That's what it was. She told me—"

"Told?" interrupted the official. "You said 'vision.'"

"A dream."

"Ah, now it's a dream." The official glanced at his two assistants.

"Yes, a dream," continued Ahrhune. "A nightmare." He leaned forward, placing his hands on the table. "Quantium, overrun by the dead. I saw the corpses of your own people rise up, fill your streets, and slaughter those who remained. Quantium was surrounded by an army of dead so thick it spread to the horizon. Death hung above Quantium, wielding a blood-stained scythe. There was no escape." He shuddered, remembering the look of the dead. "There was something else." He paused. "I don't know who or what he was. He seemed a spirit. He could raise the fallen, those killed by the dead. When the living fell they stayed down but a moment, then this spirit-man raised them up and they killed those who, in life, they called their own. Your city fell. There were no survivors." He let the words hang in the air before continuing. "Sarenrae—"

"A nightmare," said the man. He glanced at his assistants, then at Ahrhune, "indeed."

"A prophecy," said Ahrhune, not realizing he was being mocked.

"The age of prophecy is no more," said the official. He clapped his hands. His rings, striking one another, gave off a dull thud. "And yet," he motioned to Ahrhune, "you, have received this nightmarish vision from your goddess." He stood and straightened his robes. "And this must be taken seriously. I will summarize your words in a report and see that it reaches the appropriate officials."

Ahrhune stood and was ready to argue his point, for he knew he had failed, but the official continued, turning to his assistants. "We've a room in the Battered Skull," he looked at Ahrhune, "despite the name it is the finest inn in Quantium." He looked at his female assistant. "See that our guest is properly housed." He looked at his male assistant. "Locate the soonest departure for Aspenthar and book passage." The official turned to Ahrhune. "Consider your quest completed." He motioned to his assistants. "These favors cost you nothing, repayment, for the favor you've done Nex." He turned and began from the room.

"Damn it," growled Ahrhune. "You don't—" But the official disappeared through the door, followed by his male assistant. The door shut behind them. Ahrhune slammed his fist on the table. He looked at the remaining assistant. She looked back, somewhat worried about his mood. "The Battered Skull, eh?"

"It's a nice inn," said the woman.

"How soon before I can speak to one of the Three and Nine?"

"Speak to—" The woman was at a loss for words.

"They need to know."

"I—I'm sure that," she motioned to the closed door, "ah, the report will—" She looked at Ahrhune. "Um." She emitted a nervous laugh and glanced at his scimitar.

. . .

Ahrhune sat in the common room of the Battered Skull, nursing a mug of spiced ale. "Damn it," he growled under his breath. A server set a plate of lamb chops and asparagus before him. The melting butter filled his nostrils with a pleasing aroma. He was reminded of the mansion he'd return to Prince Zinlo and of the life he'd lived for a brief two years. His appetite vanished. He stopped the server. "Is there a temple to Sarenrae here?"

"Of course," said the woman.

"Where?"

. . .

Ahrhune stormed down the steps of the temple dedicated to the goddess of healing, honesty, redemption, and the sun. He resisted the urge to turn and spit. He reminded himself to be humble, even though humility was the last emotion he was capable of at that moment. He'd begged for guidance, but Sarenrae gave none.

He turned and began to retrace his steps but stopped. He sniffed the air. He turned again and walked toward the docks. The smell of salt guided him. He found a sailor's dive and went in. He relaxed once he crossed the threshold; once the suspicious eyes of sailors were on him;

once he heard their whispered cant and their boisterous tall-talk.

He elbowed his way to the bar. "Grog and a room."

"No rooms," said the barkeep. "Beds."

"Got one in the corner?" asked Ahrhune.

The barkeep smiled, showing a gold tooth. "If you make it yours, it's yours."

. . .

Kemnebi was protected from the daylight, and from much else, inside a massive, enchanted sarcophagus. Wamukota snoozed in a chair next to his master, a wand set across his lap. The windowless chamber was lit by hundreds of candles, drying out the air. The smoke hung as a black cloud above them, pressing down from the high ceiling. Various wards were layered over the room but Elana, being inside of them when they were cast, could go out without triggering them. Of course, she could not get back in.

She rose from the bed and, carrying her shoes, tiptoed across the room toward the door. Before she reached it a form dropped from the smoke above and landed six feet away. The misshapen, humanoid undead rushed forward on its taloned hands, its legs kicking out behind it, and interposed itself between Elana and the exit. Its neck was elongated, its head, clearly once human, was more serpentine in form now; although, the impression could have come from the long, glistening fangs protruding from its mouth. A pestilent stench rose from its rotted flesh. It eyed Elana, a simple, aggressive intelligence struggled to decide her fate.

"Where are you going?"

Elana backed away from the vrykolakas and turned. Wamukota was standing, the wand alight with magic. He neither pointed it at her nor kept it lowered.

"I—lost track of time," blurted Elana.

Wamukota glanced at the vrykolakas, then back to Elana. "You could have gotten yourself killed. You should be in bed."

"I have an exam."

"A—what?"

"I should be in class. I have an exam."

Wamukota glanced at the sarcophagus and frowned. He looked at the vrykolakas and motioned with his head that it should move aside. The simpleminded undead struggled with the idea of not killing when it saw an opportunity, however, it was bound to obey Wamukota, by decree of Kemnebi, its true master. It reluctantly retreated.

"Don't attempt to return until nightfall. You'll be —"

"I know." Elana chuckled, a release of stress. "I'm late—I think. Gotta run." She labored to pull open the heavy door, slipped through the opening, then labored to pull it shut. Wamukota looked at the sarcophagus for a long time, hoping he had done the right thing. His master hadn't specifically forbidden his guest from leaving. He dismissed the readied spell, sat, and placed the wand across his lap. The vrykolakas climbed back up into the smoke.

. . .

Elana pushed open the door, ringing the bell above. Bhavya, a catfolk, was seated on a stool not far from the door. He wore wide-legged, richly patterned pants and a wide belt, but no shoes and no shirt. His open-front robe was folded in his lap, a curved dagger set atop it. A half-elven woman in a simple dress was combing and perfuming his silver and black hair. A gnome, her green and purple freshly braided hair hanging in two long plaits, was playing a xylophone, two pairs of small hammers held between the short fingers of both her hands. When the bell rang she stopped and looked.

"A shame," said Bhavya, "tomorrow—is in window—for sale—much coin." He rose and tucked his dagger into his belt. He slid on his robe. His groomer began to pack her combs and bottles into a leather satchel. The gnome set down the hammers and walked through an open door deeper into the pawn shop. She could be heard rummaging in the back.

Elana approached the counter. "I couldn't get away."

Xylia, the gnome, appeared and set a jewelry case on the counter. She looked up at Elana, smiled, then vanished. A moment later the hammers appeared to lift themselves and play the xylophone of their own accord.

"Much gratitude for Liza," said Bhavya.

The half elf nodded and left, the door ringing the bell again.

Bhavya pulled the jewelry case toward him and flipped it open. He spun it and pushed it toward Elana. "What amount—huh?—we agree?"

"One hundred," called the invisible gnome.

"Not I?" said Bhavya. "Is too much. I remember—ah—fifty." Xylia appeared. She set down the hammers and walked over to the counter.

"One hundred gold," she said, looking up at Elana and smiling. "I like your hair. Black, it's trendy." She looked at Bhavya. "I should do black."

"Not good for you—believe Bhavya—yes?"

Elana produced ten platinum coins from her purse and placed them on the counter. Bhavya reached out and with one claw spun each around. After toying with them for a moment he pulled each over the edge of the counter. Elana heard them drop into a metal box. She heard the box shut.

"I see again," said Bhavya, motioning to the jewelry case. "You—bad with money."

"Stop it," said Xylia.

"Next time—fifty. One hundred—too rich."

Elana pulled the earrings from the jewelry case and put them in her ear lobes. She pulled the necklace and clasped it around her neck. "I might. Will you hold them for thirty days?"

"If you do," said Xylia. "We'll give you the same terms."

"Thank you," said Elana. She began to turn away but Bhavya reached out and placed his hand lightly on hers. She looked at him.

"If you business," he said. He glanced at Xylia, who, once again vanished. Bhavya returned his green, feline eyes to Elana. "No partner—they is bad—no profit."

"Hush," said a disembodied voice.

Elana felt the invisible gnome squeeze her hand. She felt a small piece of parchment placed against her palm. She closed her fingers around it. When she got to the door she paused, holding it open. She looked at Bhavya. "You've got a beautiful coat."

"Is nice, yes?"

Elana smiled and left. When she was half a block from the pawn brokers she read the paper.

"The park in the living quarter. I'll make sure you aren't followed."

Elana tore the note into little pieces, dropping one piece every few feet as she made her way to the park.

. . .

A statue of Geb dominated the space, not leaving much room for grass, flowers, or benches. Elana sat and rest her chin in her palm, her fingers partially covering her mouth, the pendant on the necklace pinched between them, held close to her lips.

"Master Castelli?" she asked, her voice low. She looked around the park, watched the people in the streets, studied the few shadows she saw. She wondered if the gnome was close by or if she had returned to the shop. It took several minutes before she heard Master Castelli's voice emanate from the earrings.

"I had begun to worry. You missed our last scheduled communication."

"I couldn't get away."

"Nex is listening," said Master Castelli. It was code, letting Elana know that she was free to speak. If Master Castelli had said anything else—or nothing at all—it meant he was compromised and that she should divulge nothing of importance.

"Geb speaks," said Elana. It was her prescribed response, indicating to Master Castelli that she too was free from coercion. "So much has happened, Master, so much."

"Nex is certainly listening. Do tell."

. . .

Master Castelli waited as the Council of Three and Nine reviewed and debated the intelligence Elana had given him and that he had provided to them via a written report. He'd been summoned in a hurry, then told to wait. Hours passed and he had slipped into a light doze when the door opened. The sound of it woke him.

He had seen Iranez of the Orb from a distance. She now stood in the doorway, the pink-orange ioun stone of lightning glass that he'd crafted for her in orbit around her head. She stepped out into the anteroom and smiled at him.

Iranez appeared to be human, a Keleshite. Few knew if that's truly what she was. Her long, straight, black hair held a tint of red. Her skin was dark bronze. Her large, almond-shaped eyes had long lashes and chestnut colored irises. Her nose was straight and perfectly molded. Her lips were full, her teeth white and even. She possessed the kind of beauty that made those who looked at her self-conscious. She was like a goddess, and one cannot be truly at ease in the presence of a goddess.

Her dress was the height of fashion, long, sleek, and minimal; it hugged her curves and revealed too much. She wore just enough jewelry to dazzle the eye, but not so much it appeared she relied upon it to do so. She held a thin wand of beech in one hand, at the tip: a gold encrusted sapphire. She was a foot taller than Master Castelli, and she wasn't even wearing heels.

"Please," she said, stepping backwards into the room. Master Castelli rose and followed. The door shut of its own accord behind him. "Have you ever seen this room?" asked Iranez. Master Castelli had not. He took it in.

The room was situated at the heart of the Bandeshar. It had a fifteen foot high coffered ceiling made of citron wood and ivory supported by pillars of gold-filigreed ebony wood. A ten foot tall fireplace of white marble, which would have dominated most rooms, occupied the center of the opposite wall, looking regal but understated. A pair of carved doors sat on either side, also of citron, glowing with an inner hue. Paintings and tapestries occupied the walls. The walls themselves were papered in the most delicate and rarest of colored papers from Tian. Couches and chairs were set about the room, the pelts of magical beasts casually tossed over their backs, as if men hadn't died to procure them. Antique vases and tables were scattered about, each of which would have made an obscenely rich wedding dowry for even a nobleman's daughter.

Master Castelli's eyes settled on something that looked like a large skeletal armature made out of silver, filigreed with gold. Attached to the skeleton were glass containers filled with brightly colored fluids. A series of tubes connected these reservoirs to various pumps and actuators. It was attached to a wooden stand but held the promise of motion.

Iranez followed Master Castelli's gaze. "What do you make of it?"

Master Castelli motioned, "May I?" Iranez nodded. Master Castelli approached the silver-gold skeleton and examined it. "It's not magical."

"Surprisingly, no," said Iranez. She turned and spoke to an attendant who had entered, sending him away with the answer he sought.

"Borume," said Castelli. "Master alchemist of Oenopion."

"Well done," said Iranez. "Do you know Palovar?"

"I know of him," said Castelli, "Dunn Palovar, chief Fleshforger of Ecanus."

"Borume sends his consciousness into that," she motioned with her wand to the silver-gold skeleton. "Don't ask me how." She smiled, "Palovar sends his consciousness into a grotesque flesh golem, don't ask me why. Thankfully, it left the room. This is how they both manage to attend our little debates without leaving the comfort of their far flung outposts."

"I met Borume, briefly," said Master Castelli. "While I was in Oenopion. I attended a workshop. He spoke passionately about alchemy but didn't stick around to watch us fumble through the motions."

"I prefer brewing potions," said Iranez.

"Same."

"Well, Master Castelli," said Iranez, motioning that he should be seated. "You gave us quite a shock today. Kemnebi has called for fewer undead in Geb?"

"He has."

Iranez studied Master Castelli, evaluating him. "Tell me about our resources in Mechitar."

"Precious little to tell, I'm afraid."

"Mechitar is a heavy lift?" asked Iranez, meaning that the gathering of intelligence in the capital of Nex's long time enemy was difficult—at best.

"Yes, the Blood Lords are a most distrustful lot."

"And damn proficient at countering divination."

"I have an agent close to one of them," continued Master Castelli. "She has been taken into confidence by Saskia Kalff. A minor Blood Lord, but ambitious. Saskia is among those Queen Arazni keeps close."

"So our agent is getting information from Saskia Kalff?"

"Some, but," Master Castelli leaned forward. "Our agent has gotten close to Chancellor Kemnebi."

"Yes, I was surprised to read that."

"I was equally as surprised when I heard it. It's a level of access we could only previously dream of." Master Castelli sat back. "I've a few supporting agents near Elana, that's her name. Other than that—" He held out his hands.

"One agent and her support?"

"Sadly, that's all we have."

Iranez stood and began to walk the room. "Agrellus wanted to take you off the job. He said you weren't up to it." She glanced up at the ioun stone as it passed before her. "I argued to keep you on."

"Thank you."

"We're in a fragile state," said Iranez. "One agent—one way for information to get in or out." She looked at Master Castelli. "A damn fragile state."

"Geb is a," he modulated his voice, ensuring it was diplomatic, "difficult working environment. We lose most of what we put in."

"It's going to get more difficult. Is our agent capable?"

"I have absolute faith in her."

This did not seem to comfort Iranez. "The Council of Three and Nine has decided to support Chancellor Kemnebi. His desire to see fewer undead in Geb coincides with our own. However, we cannot be seen as interfering in Geb's internal politics. If Queen Arazni or the Blood Lords knew we were helping Kemnebi it would doom him all the quicker."

"Helping?"

"Yes." Iranez returned to her seat. When she sat her dress parted, revealing her long, shapely legs. Master Castelli was careful not to look. "I want you to do everything you can to help him," said Iranez. "You have the full support of the Council. Consider your resources unlimited. You've but to ask." Iranez allowed a few moments of silence to pass. She wanted her words to sink in. "Other than us, does he have allies?"

"The vampires support him. Other than that, I don't know. Our agent is certain that Queen Arazni is against him. Also, the Church of Urgathoa has made its displeasure known."

"Yes," said Iranez, "the attack. Yet another shock." She sighed. "It's unlikely they'll split down the middle. It's apt to be a one-sided battle."

"The Chancellor is quite powerful all on his own." Now Master Castelli paused. "Geb trusted him."

"Geb," said Iranez, laughing. "I forget he's still around. He's keeping an eye on the wasteland, from what I hear."

"He acts, when he's irritated enough."

"Will this irritate him?" asked Iranez.

"I can't say."

"Whomever Geb backs, wins." Iranez smiled. "If he backs no one," she tilted her head. "Well, Nex will back Kemnebi, perhaps that will even the odds."

"I would like to send more people down there," said Master Castelli. "I need more eyes and ears in Mechitar. I need capable people who know when to make a move and when to wait." Iranez nodded. "The problem is the living can't get close enough to anyone in power," said Master Castelli, "and if we try to employ undead—"

"They'll steal them from us and we'll be exposed." Finished Iranez.

"Yes."

Iranez rose. "From what you've told us this is internal. There's only so much we can do, but we must do it." She smiled. "Only not be seen doing it."

"Yes," said Master Castelli, who also rose, sensing that the meeting was coming to a close.

"Then again," said Iranez. "It's Geb. This might not be resolved for a hundred years."

"I've a feeling it will move at a more human pace."

"How old is our agent?" asked Iranez.

"She's young, bright, but young."

Iranez laughed. "At least we've got youth on our side."

All of One Mind

The Cinerarium, Mechitar, Geb, Desnus, 4711

Kemnebi sat at his writing desk, the chair turned so as to face the room. The shelf of candles behind him granted him a fiery halo. Wamukota had cleared the legal books and stepped out, taking Elana along. Aleksandr stood. Rhianna paced. Chevonde was reclined on the couch, balancing a skull in one palm.

A square-cut emerald was set in gold at the center of the skull's forehead. Glowing, green mist seeped from its eye sockets and mouth. Chevonde rotated the skull as he brought it to his lips. He whispered something into what would have been its ear, if it had flesh. The skull began to speak but Chevonde covered its mouth with his other hand, giggling at his own inopportune humor.

"Trevedic?" asked Kemnebi.

Aleksandr frowned. "I could not reach him by spell." Kemnebi looked up. "I sent a messenger to the Ebon Mausoleum."

Rhianna stopped pacing and looked at her former lover, then at Kemnebi. "Attacked, like me and Aedha."

"We've no cause to believe that," countered Aleksandr.

"What else could it be?" asked Rhianna. "He should have left that damned school as soon as you—" She motioned to Kemnebi but, in a rare moment of tact, didn't finish. She spun in frustration and resumed her pacing.

The group waited. Chevonde annoyed them with his skull-antics. In time there was a knock on the door.

"Enter," said Kemnebi.

Wamukota entered and approached. He glanced at Aleksandr but spoke to Kemnebi.

"The messenger has returned. Trevedic cannot leave the Ebon Mausoleum at this time."

"Cannot?" asked Aleksandr.

Wamukota looked at him but said nothing.

"Eratosthenes," said Aleksandr.

"He's dead—destroyed," growled Rhianna. "They betrayed him, those whispering bastards."

"It's dangerous to assume," began Aleksandr but he stopped when Kemnebi raised a hand.

"Thank you, Wamukota."

"Master," said Wamukota, bowing. He stood, turned, and left the room.

"Chevonde?" asked Kemnebi.

"Eh?" Chevonde had only partially been paying attention, as he was amusing himself with skull-juggling.

"You brought that thing," said Kemnebi. "Use it."

"Ah, yes," said Chevonde, sitting up. "Recourse to the divine." He cleared his throat and turned the skull to face the group. He held it in one hand, waving his other over it, dispersing the glowing mist. "We have lost our dear Trevedic," he said. "Tell us, Idaean Mother, oh, wise and powerful diviner, take us to his place and time, tell us what the Gods—"

"Chevonde!" yelled Rhianna.

Chevonde narrowed his eyes at Rhianna. "Where is Trevedic Faull?" He turned the skull to face him and kissed the emerald. He spun it to face the group once more. Such a volume of glowing, green mist began to pour from the eyes and mouth that Chevonde could not be seen. The flow of the mist returned to normal, the cloud dissipated, the jaw began to work. An eloquent, feminine voice issued forth.

"Interred in a great mausoleum, stone as dark as night."

"Damn it! I told you," said Rhianna to Aleksandr. "They hid his—"

"With two others, who yet live," finished the skull.

"He's locked in his quarters," said Aleksandr. He looked from Rhianna to Kemnebi. "At least they were thoughtful enough to provide him sustenance."

Kemnebi rose and walked to the door. He opened it and looked out. Across the grand hall stood a grave knight, guarding Arazni's door. It was already staring at Kemnebi's door directly opposite and did not look away. Kemnebi scanned the hall and, detecting nothing, shut the door and returned to his seat.

"Who knew," said Chevonde, "the life of an academic was so fraught with peril?"

"Now is no time for humor," said Aleksandr.

Chevonde leapt from the couch and rushed to Kemnebi—who was still in the process of seating himself—fell to his knees and, while clutching the skull in one hand, grabbed Kemnebi's knee with the other. "The prodigal son speaks the truth. Now is the time for action." Chevonde rose and turned to Rhianna. "We have been passive." He turned to Aleksandr. "We have given our opponents the time and space to do as they pleased." He held the skull at arm's length. "Oh, Cybele, drinker from Lythe's cup, rower on the Styx—do you not see Death before us? I beseech you: if we must fight to live, let us fight."

"For once," said Rhianna, "I agree with you."

"Khamati does as well," said Chevonde. He lowered the skull, tucking it under his arm, and turned to Kemnebi. "He's more than ready to take care of Hent for us."

"He's not powerful enough," said Aleksandr.

"You underestimate him," said Chevonde. "He's subtle—"

"Khamati? Subtle?" asked Aleksandr.

"Oh, yes," said Chevonde. "He's been collecting the pieces necessary for a big move. He wants to clear the board."

"Damn it, Chevonde," said Aleksandr. "This isn't a game."

"No," said Rhianna, taking Chevonde's arm in her own. "It's war." She looked from Aleksandr to Chevonde. "And he's right." She looked to Kemnebi. "The only way to win a war is to go on the offensive."

"Chancellor," said Aleksandr. "This is an emotional reaction. We must—"

Rhianna released Chevonde's arm and stepped to Aleksandr. "I've lost a lover! Now my other child is imprisoned. He's your friend, Aleksandr. Is your loyalty so shallow?"

Aleksandr controlled his anger. "He's safe, so long as we are cautious." He turned away from Rhianna and addressed Kemnebi. "As far as we know, Latitia acted on her own. Yes," he glanced at Rhianna, "they're all plotting against us. Hasn't that been the case for a millennium?" He looked at Kemnebi. "Only Latitia was impatient, rash. Hent wants to be chancellor. If she gets what she wants that will be the end of it. Kemnebi, there is only one way to resolve this. Give up your chancellorship. Appease Hent, peace will follow."

"You coward!" cried Rhianna.

"I'm not—"

Kemnebi raised his hands. "Everyone be seated." He waited until the emotions in the room had calmed before continuing. "Aedha is dead. Trevedic is being held, we presume, against his will." He looked at Aleksandr. "Part of what you say is true. Hent-er-Neheh wants to be chancellor. We cannot count on peace after."

"Once she gets what she wants," said Aleksandr, "why would she push further? There's naught to gain."

"She would be rid of an enemy," said Chevonde.

Aleksandr turned; they were seated side by side on the couch. Rhianna in a chair opposite Kemnebi, "it wouldn't be worth the risk." He looked at Kemnebi. "She would be stupid to go after you as soon as she got the chancellorship. She would expend too much of her power, leaving her weak. She'd be a tottering giant. Eratosthenes could topple her."

"Arazni would support her," said Chevonde. "And the Church."

"We are speaking now about things we cannot know," said Kemnebi. He motioned to Chevonde's mist-spilling skull, which Chevonde had set on the table. "Even Cybele can't divine the outcome. We know we're being isolated—attacked. First Aedha and Rhianna, then Trevedic. We know Latitia and Sthaga are our enemies. We know—"

"Kemnebi," interrupted Aleksandr. "Don't—"

"Let your Chancellor—your sire—speak," said Rhianna.

"Don't," continued Aleksandr, "make us fight a war we can't win."

Chevonde reached out and ran his hand down Aleksandr's back. "If I hadn't felt a spine just now I would believe—"

Aleksandr stood. "You're acting like fools! We've defeated death. We can't die. We have the power of patience, if only we'll use it." He waved his hand, indicating both Rhianna and Chevonde. "What are you two rushing toward? Destruction? Why?" He looked at Kemnebi. "To save face? Chancellor, there is only one way out of this."

"How did I ever love you?" asked Rhianna.

A tense silence settled over the room. Aleksandr sat.

"Aleksandr," said Kemnebi, "I rely on your wisdom. But you fail to see the ultimate outcome, the outcome for Geb itself. If Hent-er-Neheh is chancellor the living in Geb will disappear. Perhaps not in a year, or even ten, but surely they will go. Geb will be wholly a nation of undead." He held out his hands, "and when that day comes, Geb will be no more. It will collapse from within or be attacked from without, or both. The only way to save Geb is for me to remain as chancellor. I must reform Geb. The undead—we—must be the aristocracy. We cannot be both patrician and plebeian. A society—which is a living thing—composed of undead is a paradox, it will not work. No, Aleksandr, I must see this through to the end." He studied his child and was about to air a concern when Aleksandr, sensing Kemnebi's thoughts, spoke.

"Don't ask," he said. "You have my loyalty and always will. Even when I think you're wrong."

"Especially when you think he's wrong," added Chevonde, by way of making peace.

"Yes," said Aleksandr.

"Thank you," said Kemnebi. He brought his fingers together at his lips. "Alright, this is what we're going to do."

Four Meetings Under a New Moon

Various Locations, Axan Woods and Mechitar, Geb, Desnus, 4711

"You sleep with your sword?"

Rhianna opened her eyes. It is a trope that vampires sleep in coffins; although, many do, not by necessity, but for style. What is meant is that they do not sleep at all, for sleep is, despite the death-like disguise it adopts, a condition of life. When the sun rules the sky, vampires revert to corpses. They do not rest, as a living being would, they cease to be.

Rhianna did not sleep in a coffin. She slept in an enormous bed, nude, sprawled out, sans covers, lying on her stomach, her right arm draped over her sheathed sword, as it would a lover. When Aedha shared Rhianna's bed she occupied the sliver on the opposite side of the sword.

The room was at the center of Rhianna's hunting lodge in the Axan forest, north west of Mechitar. The room was windowless; the door barred, or so Rhianna assumed. Thus the presence of a visitor was surprising. What Rhianna had forgotten was that Aedha had always barred the door just before sunrise. It was a habit she would have to take up.

She rolled onto her side and scanned the darkness. She heard a piece of flint strike a rod of steel. An oiled wick took the spark, producing a flame. The glass door of the lantern was closed, a white-orange light issuing forth. A handsome human with angular features, long chestnut brown hair, and a short beard of the same, looked over Rhianna's nude form.

"A she-bitch, laid out for mating."

Rhianna rolled over, positioning herself to welcome him. The man did not miss that she gripped the handle of her sword and slid it closer. She smiled and motioned he should follow his inclination. When he did not she frowned.

"What's wrong, Nico, not in the mood?"

"Not for that." Nico nodded to Rhianna's sword.

Rhianna sat up, drawing her sword, and pointed the tip at Nico. "What are you doing in my room?"

"Making sure it's not a trap."

"Come now, aren't we friends?"

"Yes, you howl at the moon in our honor and we lap up blood in yours."

"What are you worried about?" asked Rhianna as she rose to get dressed. "Help me with my armor?"

Nico stepped closer and waited until Rhianna needed a hand. "We'll lose more than you."

"Who wants to live forever?" asked Rhianna, slipping into her cotton shirt and pants.

"Apparently you do, considering you're immortal."

Rhianna glanced over her shoulder at Nico. "I'm dead. Strap it tight, but not too tight, eh. I'll be charging around like a boar in heat."

"You're serious about this?"

"I only boast when I'm drunk," said Rhianna. "Or is that bragging?"

"You really think we'll walk into Urgathoa's church and kill everything there?"

Rhianna turned to face Nico. "If you're backing out on me," she smiled, "you'll never leave this room."

Nico frowned. "Who wants to live forever?"

Rhianna patted Nico on his cheek. "Good dog."

Nico reached up, grabbed Rhianna's wrist and threw her hand aside. "We hate being called that."

"Oh, Nico, such a sensitive boy." She looked him over. "For a werewolf." She turned. "Get the strap under my arm. Are they coming?"

"My entire clan."

"You said thirty, right?"

"Give or take."

Rhianna was now in her armor. She began to stretch, then step as if dodging blows, in order to test the fit. She stopped and looked at Nico. "A dozen of mine and three dozen of yours. Not a bad little war band."

"How many clerics?" asked Nico.

"Does it matter?"

Nico shrugged.

"Listen," said Rhianna, "you have to focus on the clerics. Swarm them. Make sure they can't cast. They can burn us to death or worse, command us. Your entire purpose for being there is to prevent that kind of shit." Nico nodded. "We'll take care of everything else then finish off the clerics." Rhianna picked up her sword and tied it around her waist. "The shadows?"

"They watched me enter."

"Won't they be shocked when a wave of wolf fur washes over them."

. . .

"You've something new," said Chevonde to himself. He was sneaking through Khamati's garden, spying on the mummy's preparations. Something that resembled a hunched-back wolf with a demonic bat's head was standing motionless by the gurgling pool. Chevonde had no idea what it was. It was mummified, with fresh linen, that's all he knew. He heard movement and realized he had been spotted. The mummified maftet was approaching. He stepped out onto the tiled path and smiled.

"Khamati?" he asked the half-lion, half-human, hawk-winged mummy. She did not answer but turned and escorted him to the patio by the pool. Also present, snug in the foliage beneath the date palms, was the mummified bulette.

After a few minutes, Khamati appeared on the winding garden path, a woman clinging to his arm. It wasn't until the pair left the partial cover of leaves that Chevonde realized the woman accompanying Khamati was actually a medusa; her eyes hidden behind a veil, her snake hair held back in a linen bag, which was tied in place. It was the motion beneath the linen and the accompanying hissing that informed Chevonde of her true nature.

"See, dear wife," said Khamati, "our guest is most punctual."

"Yes, dear husband," said the medusa. She studied Chevonde. "He is a Blood Lord?"

"A friend," said Khamati.

"A most honored friend," said Chevonde.

"Smart of you to take my advice," said Khamati.

"Husband?" asked the medusa.

Khamati turned to the medusa. "He came alone."

Chevonde smiled, "You offered to do all the heavy lifting." He motioned to the various mummified monsters. "Well, them."

"Not just them," said Khamati. Chevonde heard rustling in the shrubbery and flowers beneath the date palms. As he watched a half-dozen humans and half-elves approached. He knew at once they were vampires, but he had never seen any of them before. He turned to Khamati. "Do you think you and Kemnebi's little brood are the only vampires in Geb?"

"But," asked Chevonde, "why vampires?"

"Why not?" asked Khamati. "My kind are the pinnacle of undeath, to be certain, but vampires have their uses." The presence of unknown vampires made Chevonde suspicious, but it would be futile to oppose their inclusion. "Were you followed?"

"Someone has shadows watching all of us," said Chevonde.

"Arazni," said Khamati.

"Arazni? Why would she—"

"It is her prerogative," said Khamati. "Continue."

"I cut through the living quarter," said Chevonde, "where there's enough light to frighten even the most resilient shadow. Besides, they can't be all that intelligent. All it takes is a bit of cleverness to—"

"You succeeded," said Khamati. "If a shadow had followed you into my garden I would know. To demonstrate just how much of a friend you are, Marquis, I'm going to share a family secret with you. There is a system of tunnels that connects all of our pyramids. We'll be using them to sneak in." He pointed to the vampires, the bulette, the maftet, and the greater barghest, the bat-headed, wolf-like creature, "they will be joining us, as will my most beloved wife." He turned and began down the path toward his pyramidal home. "Come, Marquis, if all is to go as planned we must time matters perfectly."

. . .

"Thank you all for coming," said Kemnebi, speaking to his gathered staff, many of whom were undead, but not all. He had summoned them to Aleksandr's mansion. His pyramid, although large, did not have a room adequate for such a meeting, as so much of it was given over to books and magical apparatus. The Cinerarium would have been inappropriate and ill-advised. He gazed over the assembled faces, wondering which he could trust and which would work his plan. Of those he held closest, only Aleksandr was in attendance.

"As you may know," began Kemnebi, "there has been some disagreement amongst the Blood Lords. This was made public with the attack on Rhianna and Aedha, which resulted in the death of a Blood Lord." Some of his staff murmured. They had heard rumors, which were now confirmed. "I am the cause of this strife." Kemnebi glanced at Aleksandr, who stood nearby, then returned his gaze to his assembled staff.

"It is with a heavy heart that I will be announcing my resignation as chancellor of Geb." Kemnebi paused as the murmuring grew in volume. When it settled down he continued. "I will speak to Queen Arazni in three nights. I wanted to tell you first so that you will have time to prepare for a sudden transition. I doubt any of you will be in danger but certainly you are better judges of your individual situations than I." Kemnebi once again scanned the faces of his assembled staff. "I ask that you keep this information to yourselves. It would only endanger all of us to have my resignation publicly known before it is properly announced. You have three nights to do what you must. I thank you for your long and valuable service to Geb." Kemnebi bowed then motioned to Aleksandr, who took his place and began speaking.

While Aleksandr gave particulars, Kemnebi retired to an adjoining room and shut the door. Once alone he went to a table and lifted the lid to a glass jar. Inside was a half-rotted piece of flesh, drenched in necromantic magic. He picked it up and began to intone the words of a spell. When the spell was done he took on a foreign form, that belonging to the borrowed flesh, which, now that the spell was complete, dissolved in his hands. He stepped to the bed and disrobed. He took up a tattered robe of thick black cloth and pulled it over his head. He went to the door and listened.

When he heard the shuffling of feet and the lamentations of his more loyal staffers he partially opened the door. Aleksandr, who was keeping an eye on the door, nodded in acknowledgement. He spoke over the noise of the departing staff.

"Remember, it is of the utmost importance that this information not get out. Three nights are yours, if you discipline your tongues. Now, go—go while the night is young." He began to urge the stragglers out with gentle pushes. When no one was looking Kemnebi slipped out of the room and joined them. He paused for a second close to Aleksandr.

"Are you certain?"

"Word will spread as quickly as their feet can carry them."

"What if they *can* be trusted?" asked Kemnebi.

The cynical look on Aleksandr's face answered in place of speech.

. . .

Arazni's shadows, which are a type of incorporeal undead that are little more than their namesake, watched Aleksandr's mansion, having found easy hiding spots in the darkness of the new moon. There were five of them. Three had followed Kemnebi from his pyramid. Two were assigned to Aleksandr. Shadows are, like many undead, not particularly bright. Their minds are corrupted not only by death but by the necromantic energies that propel them. Their obsession with destroying life leaves little room for the higher functions of the intellect.

When forty-odd undead and living bodies exited the mansion the five shadows panicked at the feasibility of following their Queen's commands. How could they follow the comings and goings of Kemnebi, Aleksandr, and their associates and allies when they were so outnumbered? They fell back on their individual initiatives. These woeful springs left them bereft of ideas. They did their best. All five missed the black-robed ghoul who emerged last, turned toward the Church of Epiphenomena, and walked alone.

. . .

A pack of ghouls, carrying a pair of fresh corpses, emerged on the road ahead of Kemnebi. His first instinct was to pause and let them outdistance him. He thought about the opportunity they offered and their undoubted destination and instead jogged to join them. It was with such an opportune escort that he passed under the great, stained glass fly of the goddess of undeath.

Once inside he attempted to peel away from the ghouls but they had taken notice of him and, thinking he knew not where to go, grabbed him and carried him with. The ghouls carried him through the church, past the Blackmarrow Altar—an enchanted stack of skulls and bones as black as the walls that enclosed them—into the lair of the High Priest. Once inside, the ghouls joined their brethren, which must have numbered fifty or more, and these numbers were diminished, as many of Sthaga's ghouls were out robbing the graveyards of their bounty.

The cavernous room resembled a slaughterhouse more than a worshippers' sanctum. There were no pews, no furniture at all. There were nests, of sorts, made out of meat-picked bones and mold-encrusted grave-clothes.

A circle of statues on tall square bases, looming over the space like standing stones, all faced a central point. They were all statues of Geb, each of a different pose, but all set up as objects of veneration. This puzzled Kemnebi. Why would so many statues of Geb be in the Church of Epiphenomena, especially in the High Priest's personal domain?

While the statues puzzled Kemnebi he was grateful for them. He was able to hide behind one. At the center of the circle of statues was Sthaga. He was massive, twice as tall as Kemnebi and four times as broad. He was a mass of swirling necromantic energy with a vaguely human form from the waist up. His thick arms ended in long claws. Malevolence oozed from him like puss from an aggravated wound. His red, glowing eyes watched his brood as they tore corpses into grisly chunks and devoured them.

A few ghouls, their hunger not yet satiated, turned to leave, Kemnebi followed. Unlike his previous escort these did not care if he joined them, they, like vultures, bristle at competitive company. Once out of the room, he ducked behind a pew and watched them pass beneath the glittering eyes of Urgathoa's glass fly. He scanned the chapel for priests, saw a few who paid him no mind, then slinked off.

. . .

Rhianna leaned against the marble walls of the Church of Epiphenomena, looking over her war band. Those few who braved the night may have noticed an unusual amount of wolves making a bee-line through the city, but, as the residents of Mechitar have been conditioned to do, they minded their own business.

Rhianna heard the sounds of a heavy latch being thrown and turned to look at the door. A ghoul in a tattered robe of thick, dark cloth, his swollen face a purple-black mask of death, his blood-stained teeth fanged, his eyes bulging and discolored—but the keen intellect within familiar to her—pulled open the door.

. . .

Kemnebi made his way back to Sthaga's slaughterhouse. Once he entered he turned and clung to the walls. He turned again and made his way to the base of one of Geb's statues. From around the corner of its base he watched Sthaga and his ghouls. He dug into one of the pockets of the robe and produced a sunstone, a small bright-yellow stone that gave off both light and heat. He tore free a strip of his robe and dropped it at his feet. In a moment he would use a cantrip to set it alight. He would then have the two components necessary for a spell he never dreamed he would cast or even learn, so anathema was it to his kind. He only hoped he was outside of the burst radius, or, if not, that Geb would shield him.

. . .

Aleksandr stepped outside and cast a spell that allowed him to detect the presence of undead. He scanned the area and found nothing. The shadows had gone. He walked into the street and turned to look at the twin towers of the Church of Epiphenomena. The roofs of houses and pyramid-points blocked the rose window but the shape of the towers could be seen by the starlight they blotted out. He turned and walked the other direction, toward the Ebon Mausoleum.

. . .

Latitia sat on a throne too large for anyone but her, and possibly Nah-le-tah, dare he ever sit in it. Her throne was on a dais, raising her still higher above the room's miserable occupants. Several of her priests sat on the edge of this dais, chanting words of worship or reading Urgathoa's sacred text, *Serving Your Hunger*, in the dim light of the hall. The rest of the room was filled with the diseased, laid out on cots: lepers, plague victims, sufferers of syphilis, and those vile undead that nurture disease and rot. The stench in the room caused nausea. Rats, their balding coats lumpy with boils, scurried and fought viciously over scraps of food. The air was clouded by flies; their buzzing a hymn to Urgathoa.

Two unexpected but welcomed guest knelt before Latitia, their knees pressed painfully into the stone steps.

"Three nights?" She leaned forward, extended her scythe-like claw, positioning the tip under the chin of one of the visitors, and lifted his head. "And he steps down?"

"Yes, Mistress."

Latitia sat back, her claw slipping out from beneath the man's chin. She glanced at a nearby priestess, a woman so obviously sick with disease it was a wonder she still lived. She returned Latitia's smile. The Daughter of Urgathoa returned her gaze to her visitors.

"I wish he had more fight. I would like to kill him. I suppose I'll have to content myself with surrender." She laughed. "Bringing down a chancellor was easier than I thought." She waved her claw before her guests. "Why bring this to me?"

"With Kemnebi gone," said one of the pair, "what shall become of us?"

"We need protection," said the other.

"You wish to join the fold?" asked the diseased priestess, who, although neither visitor knew, had led the attack on Rhianna and Aedha. "To become one of us?"

"We believe," said one.

"We give ourselves to Urgathoa," said the other, "be praised."

Latitia laughed, savoring victory.

Then the door burst open.

Rhianna appeared, her gore-coated sword in one hand, the bloodless corpse of a priest—his neck sported twin puncture wounds—in the other. Rhianna tossed the priest aside, wiped the blood from her chin, looked to Latitia and smiled.

"Hey, cutie, wanna fight?"

As Rhianna spoke, werewolves bounded into the room.

. . .

"Uoser," said Khamati.

The younger mummy, who was at that moment escorting a small group of unexpected guests—staffers of the Chancellor—up to Hent-er-Neheh's chambers, spun and leveled his gilded ram-skull-topped staff at the darkness to his right. The emeralds that were its eyes began to glow with arcane power. Khamati stepped into the light.

Uoser pulled back his staff. "Khamati?" He studied his fellow mummy. Uoser hated Khamati. "What are you doing here?"

"A social visit."

"You never—"

"Never?" Khamati motioned to the group of staffers who nervously shifted, waiting to resume their quest. "I have chosen an inopportune moment to pay my respects to Hent-er-Neheh. She receives visitors?"

"News of Kemnebi," said Uoser.

"You mean Chancellor Kemnebi?" asked Khamati.

"Chancellor?" Uoser laughed. "Not for long."

"I play second to these," Khamati waved a dismissive hand toward Kemnebi's traitorous staffers, "toadies? So be it. I shall pay homage to he who is eldest among us."

Uoser once more began to lead Kemnebi's traitorous staff to his mistress.

"Uoser?" asked Khamati. "I too have news of the Chancellor. My visit is not entirely social. After you fulfill your duties," he waved to the staffers, "come see me."

"Can it wait?"

"Set aside your loathing for me, cousin. This is important. Our most supreme matriarch can spare you for a few minutes, can't she?"

"We'll see."

"I shall wait for you outside of Nakht-Neb-Tep-Nefer's chambers. Please, cousin, do not delay. My news is," Khamati smiled, "actionable, yet the window closes."

. . .

The door opened and a male priest—still recovering from a recent sword slash—stumbled in. He clutched his chest in a vain attempt to hold closed the gashes delivered by a wolf on two legs. He could not reach the ragged tears in his back, which bled profusely.

"We're under attack!"

His wounds overwhelmed him. He staggered forward, fell to his knees, and offered a quick prayer to Urgathoa that the ghouls would not devour his yet-living form—then passed out.

Kemnebi began the complicated litany that would bring forth the sun. He lit the cloth, offered the sunstone to the flame, then wove his hands, adding to the magical incantation. He glanced around the corner of the statue as he spoke the final words of the spell. He pointed to the center of the room, then dodged back behind the statue's base.

The birth of the sun in the High Priest's chamber was silent, like a super nova in the void of space. The room went from midnight darkness to midday bright. The statues of Geb cast harsh shadows against the walls. In one of these shadows Kemnebi crouched like a frightened child and screamed. His flesh cooked. His eyes watered tears of blood. The pain and fear he felt were beyond anything he had known—and he was in the shade.

The ghouls were vaporized. The hellish ball of light lasted but a moment. Darkness returned to the High Priest's domain. Kemnebi heard screaming, realized it was his own, and labored to calm himself. He was hurt, yes, but he had survived. He heard another lone, pained voice crying out in agony. He glanced around the statue's base.

Sthaga was writhing like a man dropped into a pool of acid. That he had survived was a testament to his power. The sunburst had burned holes through him. He appeared as tattered as Kemnebi's robe.

Kemnebi began to cast another spell. Sthaga, despite his injuries, realized he was not alone and began to search for the locus of his pain. Before he could spot Kemnebi the spell was complete. Its purpose? To gain control of Sthaga's mind. Kemnebi stepped out from behind the statue, pointed at Sthaga, and commanded that he obey.

Kemnebi reached into Sthaga's mind, intent on taking the reins, but he found something wholly unexpected there. He found Geb. He felt Geb's mind, the overwhelming will of that god-like necromancer. Kemnebi felt Geb turn his attention to him. He felt his former master's curiosity, amusement, and annoyance.

There was no way Kemnebi could wrestle control of Sthaga from Geb. He would not even try. He let the spell collapse. He had learned something profoundly disturbing. Geb controlled Sthaga. Geb controlled the High Priest of the Church of Epiphenomena and probably always had. Now Geb knew that Kemnebi knew. What would Geb do?

Kemnebi began to prepare another spell. He reckoned Sthaga would strike. At best, thought Kemnebi, he could destroy Sthaga. If Geb intervened—well, it was over, no spell would save him. But Sthaga, his screaming halted, the burns in his necromantic fabric slowly healing as Geb pumped magic into one of his more useful puppets, did nothing. He watched Kemnebi, rage in his glowing red eyes, but he did not advance.

Kemnebi, the spell's completion ready on his tongue, began to edge his way toward the door. Sthaga watched, but still did not act.

'You grant tacit agreement?' Thought Kemnebi. He did not finish the spell, but kept it in his memory. When he reached the door he paused and once more studied the hulking, swirling form of the dread wraith. He understood that there was no Sthaga. There was only Geb. The revelation was one he would have to meditate upon—after the civil war was over. He looked down and saw a priest lying unconsciously at his feet. He rolled the man over, gazed into his face, thought of killing him, then thought of Urgathoa and didn't.

Once out of Sthaga's chamber, Kemnebi let the undead anatomy spell fall away. Anyone he came across now would see him, Chancellor Kemnebi, a vampire lord not an unknown ghoul. Let there be no more subterfuge.

. . .

Aleksandr was not unknown in the Ebon Mausoleum—he often came to visit Trevedic—but he felt, as he walked the halls, that the students regarded him with mixed suspicion and shock. He watched them, listened to their hushed speech, and was ready for decisive action should the need arise.

He was on the look out for Eratosthenes. He hoped to avoid the elven lich. There were no open hostilities between Kemnebi and Eratosthenes so it followed Aleksandr should be safe, however, it was foolish to ignore the fact that Trevedic was likely being held prisoner and that Eratosthenes was either behind it or approved.

Aleksandr made his way beneath the Ebon Mausoleum without either being reproached by student or staff or running into Eratosthenes. He paused at the bottom of the stairs, listening. He stepped down a few more steps and looked out over the circular chamber. The doors were closed. He went to Trevedic's door and lightly knocked.

"Trevedic?" he asked with lowered voice.

"Aleksandr?" called Trevedic from within, his voice strained.

Aleksandr tested the door. There was no obvious lock or bar but it did not budge.

"Trevedic. Can you come out?"

"No."

"What happened?"

"Eratosthenes used an arcane lock," said Trevedic. "I cannot break it."

"Why did he—"

"Aleksandr. You must leave. It isn't safe here."

"I'm going to get you out."

"It's impossible."

"Turn to mist and seep between the—"

"I've tried," said Trevedic. "Aleksandr—"

"Yes."

"They're both dead."

"Who?"

"The chattel Eratosthenes put in here with me. The hunger—I drained them."

"Certainly he will give you more. He can't mean you to perish." As Aleksandr spoke he thought he heard a sound. He studied the doors and the steps up. He listened but heard nothing.

"I'm done for," said Trevedic. "Go, Aleksandr. Don't let them catch you here."

"Damn it, Trevedic. There has to be a way—"

One of the doors swung in. Ólchobar Yevan stepped out. He appeared to be on the cusp of liquefaction, his flesh, muscle, fat, and sinew sagged from his bones. His dark blue robes had the appearance of perpetual wetness. His face was a green mask of putrefaction, his eyes swollen and black. He saw Aleksandr and at once began a spell.

The beast within reacted faster than the lich's sluggish casting. Aleksandr turned into a bat and shot up the stairs. Ólchobar Yevan did not complete his spell. He stood for a moment, gazing at Trevedic's door, contemplating destroying the vampire who was proving to be a nuisance and distraction to his necromantic studies, but he thought better of it, turned, and went back to his room, shutting the door behind him.

. . .

A hall extended from the top of the stairs, lit by brass braziers. The walls were painted with scenes from ancient Osirion: wheat being gathered, animals slaughtered, a pyramid being erected, mourners wailing the death of a pharaoh.

At the end of the hall were a pair of bronze doors. Seated in gilded chairs on either side of the doors were two mummies. Standing before the doors was a semi-translucent humanoid form with a jackal's head. A bronze and wood shield rest against its thigh, a bronze sword gripped in one hand.

Khamati and Kalika, the medusa, arrived at the top of the stairs, advanced a few steps, and paused. The pharaonic guardian stepped forward. The two mummies turned their heads but did not yet rise. A ghostly image materialized before Khamati and the medusa. It was an image of Nakht-Neb-Tep-Nefer. The mummy wore a traditional mask of gold, inlaid with lapis lazuli and precious stones. It showed him as he had been thousands of years ago, a man in his prime, a man with commanding features.

"Khamati?"

"Yes, eldest among us?"

"Why have you come?"

"To send you to your god, ancient one."

When these words were spoken the vampires and mummified monsters, all of whom had been lying in wait on the stairs, rushed up, passed Khamati and the medusa, and advanced toward Nakht-Neb-Tep-Nefer's guards.

"I believed Groetus wished me to watch the end of times from the seat I currently occupy," said Nakht, "but if he wishes me to watch while seated at his right hand, so be it. But I won't make it easy for you."

By now the battle at the end of the hall had begun. Wings of pale blue light extended from the back of the pharaonic guardian. However, the wings were relatively useless. While they had the ability to drain life with a touch, none of the opponents it now faced had life to drain.

Kalika yanked off her veil and the linen sack holding back her serpents. She began to rush toward the battle but Khamati reached out and grabbed her arm. He turned his head. He did not possess eyes, it was true, but he wasn't certain that would save him from the petrifying gaze. The undead are immune to much that would slay a mortal. An undead would never bleed out or be killed by disease. But they can be petrified.

"Uoser."

Kalika remembered, turned, and went down the steps. Khamati glanced at the progress of the battle and watched as one of the vampires fell under the pharaonic guardian's blade and turn to mist. He knelt and drew a scroll from a case at his belt. The vampire flew over him and went down the stairs. Khamati rose and began to read from the scroll. He was a cleric of a god few knew. But that god still fed him magic. The contents of the scroll, a spell few can or would care to access, was a bane to casters.

. . .

Uoser, his mind aswirl with thoughts of the two unexpected visits and their ramifications, did not notice as he mounted the stairs to Nakht-Neb-Tep-Nefer's chambers that he could not hear his own footfalls. When he was two-thirds of the way up the stairs Khamati appeared at the top. He pointed his wand at Uoser and spoke, although Uoser heard nothing. A ray of scorching fire came from the wand, burning Uoser. The attack was so sudden and unexpected that Uoser was stunned into inaction. The pain soon shook him from his stupor.

He at once began a spell of his own and only then did he realize that he could not hear his own voice. The entire stairwell had been silenced by the spell on Khamati's scroll. The spell Uoser intended to cast would fail, for his words could not draw down the necessary magic in the zone of silence. He abandoned it. Just then Uoser felt a second source of pain, a dagger in the back. He spun and looked down—right into the eyes of a waiting medusa. His twisted pose was captured in stone.

Khamati walked down the down the steps, head bent, feeling along the wall. He waved at the medusa, indicating she should join the ongoing battle. She rushed up the stairs, touching his shoulder as she passed. Khamati "looked" at Uoser.

"I never liked you," he said to Uoser, of course, the sound was suppressed. He was three steps above his cousin. He extended his leg, placed his sandaled foot on Uoser's stone head, and kicked. Uoser tottered backwards. Khamati shoved more and Uoser tumbled down the stairs, breaking into chunks, his fall and subsequent shattering happening in complete silence. Khamati spun, took the stairs by two, and entered the hall. The doors at the other end were open. He could see the battle raging inside.

"Khamati!" shouted Nakht-Neb-Tep-Nefer above the din of violence.

. . .

Khamati knelt, holding the golden mask of Nakht. The ancient mummy had wounded his attacker, burning him with fire, in the same way Khamati had burned Uoser. But the will to live was weaker in Nakht than in Khamati, as was the will to power. If the god of end times was concerned at all with the fates of his worshippers he would have been amused at the outcome.

"Your wife," said Chevonde.

"A shame," said Khamati.

"We don't have enough to go after Hent," said Chevonde. "Everyone's been destroyed but us."

"A shame."

"Khamati!" The mummy looked up at the vampire. "What are we going to do now? He," Chevonde nodded to the golden mask, "was more powerful than we thought. We've failed. We have to—"

"Failed?" asked Khamati. He set the mask down and rose. "No, *we* have not failed."

"But—"

"*You* have failed," said Khamati. "I have succeeded." Khamati laughed, but his laugh ended abruptly. "Hent-er-Neheh!" Khamati nodded toward the open bronze doors. When Chevonde turned to look, Khamati slid a wooden stake from the sash at his waist and slammed it into Chevonde's back, just above the heart, but the stake did not enter.

Chevonde, feeling the impact, leapt away from Khamati. As he did so the mummy grabbed the vampire's shirt and tore it, revealing the elven chainmail beneath. An enchanted plate of steel, four inches square, had been attached to the chain shirt, just above the heart, on front and back, for added protection.

"Damn you, Khamati," growled Chevonde.

"I told you I would kill—"

Chevonde turned into a bat and retreated from the room. Khamati watched him race down the hall and disappear over the lip of the steps. He tucked the stake back into his sash, went to the fallen medusa, bent, and scooped up her dagger.

. . .

Hent-er-Neheh listened to what her guests had to say. She looked for Uoser, desiring him to escort Kemnebi's staff out, but he was not present. She had to do it herself. It was then that she went in search of her assistant. She did not find him in his quarters, nor hers, nor in the library, nor in the temple. The last place she could think to look was in her father's chambers.

She saw the broken pieces of stone on the stairs but did not immediately recognize her long-time assistant, the mummy she had come to treat like a son, for he was broken in such a way that defied quick recognition. The stone chunks and dust did alarm her. When she arrived at the top of the stairs she was coated in protective magics. (The silence spell had since expired.)

She could see the room at the other end through the open doors. She could see the corpses. It took her a few moments to recognize that Khamati was still "alive." She stood over him, her finger pointed down, its tip glowing with threatening magic.

"What have you done?"

Khamati, his legs and chest burnt, his torso laid bare by a gruesome gash, the bloodied dagger lying near, looked up at his aunt.

"One of Kemnebi's little blood suckers. Chevonde and a dozen of his kind."

Hent-er-Neheh looked over the corpses of the mummified monsters. She saw a shriveled husk that resembled a woman with serpents for hair. She saw her father's mask and his remains. She kept her spell poised.

"All I see here is betrayal."

"Ask Uoser," said Khamati. "I saw him escorting two visitors. It was I who wished to visit you with news of Kemnebi, but they were shown in first."

"What news do you have of Kemnebi?"

"He's stepping down in three nights. You are to be chancellor, I have no doubt. I came to celebrate. That is why I brought my household."

"And instead you stumbled into an ambush?"

"Yes."

"Where is Uoser?"

"I don't know. The last I saw he was leading others to you."

"You're telling me that the Marquis Chevonde Garron and a dozen vampires killed your pets, my father, his guards, and almost killed you?"

"They were well prepared."

"What's that?"

Khamati lifted his head to look at what Hent was pointing to with her other hand. He knew it was the corpse of the medusa, which had been drained of life by the pharaonic guardian's wings, but he feigned ignorance. He told Chevonde it was his wife and the medusa played along with the ruse, but she wasn't. She could not be linked to Khamati, at least not without the aid of magic.

Hent-er-Neheh let her spell dissipate. "You're a liar, Khamati."

"Aunt—"

"I know how you think. I know how you operate." She went to her father's remains and stood over them, looking down. "You've only weakened us."

"It wasn't—"

"It's only you, me, and Khufnu now." She glanced at Khamati, then back at her father's remains. "I will be Chancellor, yes. And we shall blame this attack of yours on

Kemnebi. Too bad we have little evidence to prove your claim. You could have at least—"

"I tried." Hent-er-Neheh looked at Khamati. "I tried to stake him, so we could show him to all of Geb."

"Tell me the truth, Khamati," said Hent-er-Neheh. "Is Uoser—"

"Yes."

"I should destroy you for that alone."

"You can mummify another young punk to serve you."

"No, Khamati, you shall serve me. Best to keep you close."

. . .

Howls, screams, and curses spilled forth from the chapel of the diseased, accentuated by the ringing of steel-on-steel. Kemnebi saw movement and readied a spell. A wolf, its gray fur wet with blood, limped from the doorway. It paused when it saw Kemnebi, its lustrous black eyes searching him, deciding on his potential for help or harm. It turned and limped away at a right angle, leaving a bloody smear on the wall. Kemnebi didn't know if it was a lycanthrope or a vampire. A flash of light from within the room drew his eyes and attention. He advanced, pausing in the archway.

The chapel, although large, was crowded. Sick beds had been overturned, their occupants scattered to the room's corners or lying in pools of their own blood. Severed limbs, still quivering with life, flopped like fish out of water. Blood sprayed from a multitude of springs. Many of the diseased had been put out of their misery by the werewolves; putrid bodies ruptured by tooth and claw. There were more corpses than standing combatants. The sight would have overwhelmed a lesser man, but Kemnebi had grown up in a world shaped by Geb. He had walked many a carpet of corpses.

Just as Nico had predicted, the werewolves had borne the brunt. They had already lost two-thirds of their number. Those that remained occupied those clerics that remained. Rhianna's vampires battled Latitia's undead. Kemnebi scanned the room, searching for Rhianna. He heard her laughter and followed the sound to the dais.

Latitia was standing before her throne, swinging her scythe-like claw in a wide arc. In this way she kept Rhianna and her vampires and werewolves from mounting the dais. Behind the protective circumference of Latitia's claw stood a group of clerics. They chanted spells, petitioned Urgathoa, and blasted searing beams of light from their palms, burning the flesh from their vampiric foes. However, one of their most devastating powers was neutralized: they could not channel negative energy for fear of hurting one another and healing their foes.

Kemnebi entered the room. A werewolf, clutching in its guts with one hand, swiping wildly with the other, emerged from the fray. A cleric retreated from the werewolf's advance, backing unknowingly into Kemnebi. He bumped into Kemnebi and hazarded a quick look over his shoulder. The werewolf, recognizing the Chancellor, hesitated.

In that moment of confusion Kemnebi reached out and grabbed the cleric by the shoulder. He called on the necromantic energy deep within his being and directed it into the cleric. The man shuddered, visibly blanched, then began to collapse. Kemnebi released his grip and the cleric fell to the side, drained of much of his life-force. The werewolf turned, blood sloshing from his wound, and sought out another to take to the grave with himself.

Kemnebi saw movement from an unexpected place, the ceiling. He looked up and raised his finger, ready to release a spell but he needn't, for it was one of his own, crawling along the ceiling like a spider. The vampire's eyes glowed red with bloodlust. It rushed forward and dropped down onto the dais behind Latitia, tackling a cleric, the pair rolling from the dais.

Kemnebi's arrival did not go unnoticed. A pair of clerics dispatched a werewolf with a pair of well placed strikes with their battle-scythes, the tips of the blades poking through the werewolf's back. When the beast fell the clerics saw Kemnebi. One rushed him, the other began to cast a spell.

The scythe came in a wide arc, sweeping low-to-high. Kemnebi dashed forward. The curved wooden haft of the weapon struck him in the hip. He locked eyes with the cleric with the intention of dominating him but the other cleric's spell interfered. A column of fire and divine magic materialized at the completion of the cleric's spell. Kemnebi could see nothing but flame and light. He threw himself in reverse, stumbling and falling out of the pillar. The fire and light disappeared. He was hurt but his inherent resistance to magic had taken much from the spell. Now his unnatural healing factor kicked in to repair the rest.

The scythe-wielding cleric advanced, his weapon posed to strike. Kemnebi got his feet under him and leapt backwards, high in the air. He clung to the wall above the door and there he began to cast.

The two clerics separated, advancing on Kemnebi's position from opposite angles. In this way they hoped to defeat any spell that required them to be close together for it to affect them both. But their stratagem, while wise, wasn't going to help them from the spreading fog bank that appeared beneath Kemnebi. The yellowish green vapors crowded out breathable air. The two clerics retreated, coughing and spitting up the poisonous fumes.

Kemnebi took a similar route to the vampire he saw when he first entered the room. He climbed the wall then pulled himself onto the ceiling, making his way toward the dais.

"The Chancellor!" screamed one of the two clerics he left behind. He looked and saw that both were pointing to him. He turned and saw that Latitia, her attention drawn, was gazing at him, malevolence in her eyes. Rhianna, not one to miss an opportunity, leapt onto the dais and advanced toward Latitia, who was forced to both turn her attention back to Rhianna and parry Rhianna's sword with her claw.

Kemnebi saw a wavering light below. He watched as a scythe made of divine light emerged from the poison cloud and raced toward him. He hastily worked to dispel it and did so before the scythe was able to strike him. He was preparing to drop to the floor and kill the two persistent clerics when he saw a few of the remaining werewolves leap at them. He resumed his ceiling crawling.

Latitia dropped her claw under Rhianna's guard but not in such a way that she could strike with the point; instead, she shoved Rhianna from the dais. Rhianna fell flat onto her back. The scythe-like claw, swung immediately after the push, swept over Rhianna's prone form, just missing. Rhianna smiled at the near miss then noticed Kemnebi clinging to the ceiling. She laughed, scooted backwards, out of the range of Latitia's claw, then stood.

"Hey, bitch!" yelled Rhianna. "Give up the high ground, will ya? You're making this hard."

Latitia growled and motioned that Rhianna should try to mount the dais once more.

Kemnebi dropped from the ceiling, landing behind the only remaining cleric on the dais. He reached out as if her were going to bear hug her, grabbed the her jaw in one hand, her shoulder in the other. She yelped in surprise and attempted to wrench herself free, but he was far stronger.

He yanked his arms wide. The cleric's head turned violently to her right. Her right shoulder turned violently to the left. The vertebrae in her neck were stripped like gears by the wrenching force. She dropped lifeless to Kemnebi's feet. Aedha's death was avenged.

"Latitia!" yelled Kemnebi.

The Daughter of Urgathoa, recognizing the hated voice that called her, spun. She scanned the dais and realized she was alone. She spun again and scanned the room, looking for allies, but those few clerics that remained were fighting for their own lives. She moved to stand beside her throne, positioning it between her and Kemnebi. Rhianna leapt onto the dais.

"Do you think the goddess of death will stand for this?" hissed Latitia.

"Let me kill her," begged Rhianna.

"You're fools!" Latitia laughed but it was hollow. "Don't you fear Geb?"

While Latitia was threatening, Kemnebi was casting. He reached into the spell pouch at his belt and pinched a bit sulfur between his thumb and forefinger. Once he had cast this into the air he went back into his spell pouch and found a pinch of powdered garlic. When this component had been added he said the final words and made the final motions of the spell. He pointed at Latitia.

No dazzling visual effects were summoned forth, no dramatic sounds, no alarming odors. Nothing at all seemed to happen. It took Rhianna a moment to realize that Latitia had succumbed to a spell. A halt in the incessant swaying and threatening of her claw indicated to Rhianna that her opponent had been paralyzed, held motionless and defenseless by Kemnebi's necromantic magic.

"Oh!" She laughed. "I'm going to enjoy this." Rhianna positioned her feet, leveled her sword, twisted her torso and with one wide, violent swing, decapitated Latitia. Her head leapt free, ectoplasm arcing from her neck in place of blood. Her head fell behind her, bounced on the edge of the dais, then rolled off and lodged itself in the gore and filth that carpeted her chapel.

"It's done," said Kemnebi.

"I'm taking her head," cried Rhianna. "Souvenir!" She laughed, jumped from the dais, and began to search for it. Kemnebi turned and looked over the room. The battle was not yet finished, but it was over.

A Queen Asserts Herself, an Office Shared, an Office Saved

The Cinerarium, Mechitar, Geb, Desnus, 4711

Arazni sat on the edge of her bed. Lilith was poised on her knees behind Arazni, perfuming and combing her hair. Saskia sat at Arazni's right hand, rubbing sesame oil into her skin. Moira, the Disowned, sat at Arazni's left, doing the same. Both Saskia and Moira were living beings, not undead. Their skin responded well to oil. Their soft, supple skin against her dry, dead flesh delighted Arazni. She hated being undead, being a lich. She never would have chosen such a fate for herself. It was torture. She did what she could to mimic life, to nurture its sensations and pleasures, as futile as her efforts were.

Baya-Iza, the drow necromancer, bent before Arazni, massaging the stitches and scars that crisscrossed her abdomen. Long ago, when Arazni was the favorite of Aroden, she was revered. Priests removed and preserved several of her organs. They became cherished artifacts and objects of veneration. She was stitched up with all due reverence but, being dead, she did not heal.

Although Arazni did not feel the absence, it bothered her. Nor did she feel the stitches, for they never pulled against her dead skin as such stitches do against living flesh, but she despised the sight of them. Baya-Iza, as a member of the violent dark elf culture, knew of an ointment that helped aid in the healing of cut flesh and the formation of scars. Female drow needed all the help they could get. Of course, the ointment was only an aid to living flesh, but Arazni demanded it be applied to her anyway.

The grave knights watched the bonding ritual without comprehension.

"Mother?"

"Soon, my Queen."

"Jasmine."

"Yes, Queen?" asked the Dead Bride.

"Peek out there."

Jasmine went to the door and opened it, peering out. She shut the door and went to Arazni. "They await you, Queen."

Arazni turned to Araminta, the changeling zombie lord. "Aren't you finished?"

"It hasn't been polished for years," said Araminta, laughing. "It looks like Hell—looked." She turned and held up the diamond tiara.

"Mother," said Arazni.

Lilith held out her hand. Araminta handed over the tiara. Lilith slid it into place and began to arrange Arazni's hair.

"Will you wear it?" asked Araminta, not referring to the tiara but to the dress she had hand-made for Arazni. Arazni smiled. Araminta bent and kissed Arazni on the cheek. "I'm so glad you like it. You know, I should have designed something with She-ma-hon's help long ago. It is understated, for her, anyway, but daring for any of us."

"It isn't too much, Mother?" asked Arazni.

"It says 'power,'" answered Lilith. "And warns of danger."

"Then it's perfect," said Baya-Iza.

Arazni stood. "Dress me." She held out her arms. "Where is She-ma-hon?"

"Flirting with Narcisse," said Jasmine.

"Disgusting," opined Moira. "Why would she do that?"

"He's moved up in the eyes of Urgathoa," said Kimberly Silent Eyes, who was leaning against the wall, cleaning her nails with the tip of a dagger. "Someone started a whisper campaign." She smirked. "Since Latitia and Sthaga were attacked in the Church of Epiphenomena it must certainly mean that Urgathoa was displeased with them. Why else would she have allowed it?"

"It follows," added Baya-Iza, who reached out to assist Araminta with the dress, "that since Nah-le-tah and Narcisse were not, the goddess must be pleased with them."

"The pieces move on the board," said Lilith, climbing down from the bed.

"Fuck the board," growled Arazni. "Fuck the pieces."

The dress was on. The top was leather, stained maroon and dark blue. It cupped Arazni's small breasts and shoved them up. Beneath was a scrollwork of gold piping. Small charms shaped like daggers hung from the piping, light glinting from them. The midriff was bare, showing Arazni's torso and her stitches and scars. Under any other circumstances she would not allow the Blood Lords to see these, but she wanted to remind them that she had a long and glorious history, that she had walked besides truly powerful men, and that she had vanquished many more foes than any of them had ever known. The stitches and scars said that and more. They shined with their coating of ointment.

The shoulders were large and elaborate. They resembled miniature wings made of dark blue feathers. Hidden amongst the feathers were two bird's skulls, sapphires glowing from within their sockets. The long, sweeping skirt was composed of layered fabric, deep purple and fiery orange. Gold chains swooped amongst the fabric, the links not rounded but pointed and sharp-edged. The belt was another golden chain. The belt buckle was the front half of a small human skull coated with gold.

Sapphires sat in its sockets as well. The back of the dress top was merely a few crisscrossing leather ties.

Arazni, who normally went barefoot, stepped into stiletto heels. She teetered briefly before steadying herself. "Don't touch it." She warned as Saskia reached for her staff. Arazni walked, uncertain at first on the heels, but gaining confidence as she went, across the room. "Geb made it you know?" She took up the staff. "If anyone but me even touches it." She looked at Saskia.

"Shall we proceed, Queen Arazni?" asked Lilith.

Arazni turned and stood erect, her chin high. "How do I look?"

"Like the ruler of a great nation," answered Lilith.

"Take you seats, my pets. Lilith, stay by the door. You will escort me to my throne."

. . .

The Blood Lords mingled and gossiped—rare indulgence sparked by recent drama. The drama of recent events provided the impetus. When the door to Arazni's personal chambers opened and the members of her clique emerged the Blood Lords found their seats. However, several seats remained empty, an ominous sight.

Lilith stood at the side of the door. The Blood Lords watched as three of Arazni's personal bodyguards emerged. The grave knights scanned the room, their cold eyes filled with malice. They made their way toward the throne. Arazni appeared in the doorway. She stepped out and paused. In one hand she held the staff that Geb had made, a powerful sign of his connection to her. She extended the other to Lilith, who took it and escorted her to Geb's throne. The remaining grave knights followed. The statue of Geb watched all.

Arazni sat. Lilith went to her own seat. Arazni turned to look at the closed door of Kemnebi's office. She smiled then looked back at the Blood Lords, her smile replaced with a countenance that was both regal and stern.

"Kemnebi, by his treacherous actions," began Arazni, "has disgraced his office. He has sacrificed Geb for his own personal gain. Needless to say, he is no longer chancellor to this great and powerful nation." She paused, thinking there would be murmurs, but silence reigned. "Not only has Kemnebi shown himself a traitor, so have his children. Witnesses have testified that Rhianna Ceinwen led the attack on Latitia, personally slaying her. An act of betrayal of not only Geb but of Urgathoa as well. Witnesses have testified that the Marquis Chevonde Garron led an attack on Geb's very own relatives, a cowardly ambush that resulted in the destruction of Nakht-Neb-Tep-Nefer." She motioned to Khamati. "Only with great personal sacrifice was this traitor forced to flee."

Khamati rose, bowed, then sat.

Arazni continued. "As of this moment we must consider Kemnebi and his children enemies of Geb. We must hunt down Rhianna and Chevonde and exact our revenge. I therefore decree that anyone who slays either of these traitorous criminal enemies, and can provide proof of their destruction, will take their place as a Blood Lord. If the slayer is already a Blood Lord they will earn my favor and," she glanced over her shoulder at the statue behind her, then turned back to the assembled group, "the favor of Geb."

Arazni sat straight, throwing her feathered shoulders back. "I now demand an oath of fealty from everyone who wishes to remain a Blood Lord. I call on all of you to publicly declare your loyalty to me and through me to Geb." She stood and held out her hand. Lilith was the first to rise and approach. She knelt before Arazni, took her hand, and kissed her fingers.

"I swear fealty to you and to Geb." She rose and returned to her seat.

Every other Blood Lord followed suit. Besides Kemnebi and his allies, and those Blood Lords who had been slain, only one other Blood Lord was missing; Sthaga. He never attended these meetings. His absence would not even be noted, except that he had been attacked and many were curious about his condition. Rumors were circulating that he had been destroyed. If he had been, countered those who heard such rumors, a new High Priest would be declared, and that hadn't happened.

The procession took some time, but Arazni delighted in it. She was almost giddy when the last pair of lips graced her fingers. She had to calm herself to continue.

"From this moment onwards," she said, looking to Hent-er-Neheh, who, expecting what was to come, struggled to hide her enthusiasm, "Hent-er-Neheh," Arazni now shifted her gaze to her former lover, "and Eratosthenes will share the office of chancellor."

It took every ounce of self control Hent-er-Neheh possessed not to scream aloud. Eratosthenes remained silent and unreadable. Arazni continued. "With two such minds to lead Geb this nation shall experience unprecedented times of greatness." She smiled, catching herself. "Times only eclipsed by those in which Geb himself ruled." Arazni saw that Eratosthenes was beginning to rise. She motioned that he should speak.

"You show great wisdom and also great initiative today, Queen Arazni."

"Thank you, Co-Chancellor."

"As my first act as Co-Chancellor may I suggest that not all of Kemnebi's children be condemned?" Arazni tilted her head and raised her eyebrows but allowed Eratosthenes to continue. "We have no evidence that Aleksandr Kovalenko has acted against Geb. Yes, he is

Kemnebi's creation, and so we must suspect him but," he paused, forming the argument in his mind, "with all of Kemnebi's allies banished from this assembly, the vampires in Geb will have none to speak for them. This will cause undue strife in a period already saturated with discord. May I suggest keeping Aleksandr as a Blood Lord? Let him speak for the vampires. Allow him to prove his loyalty." With this, Eratosthenes sat.

Arazni motioned to Hent-er-Neheh, who stood. She had calmed herself and in the intervening time between the announcement and this moment she had begun to work a plan to rid herself of Eratosthenes. She was able to speak without betraying her emotions. "I agree." She sat.

"Let this body know that I am capable of restraint even in times of anger. Also, let us make a good and lasting precedent, one of a Queen listening to her advisors. I restore Aleksandr Kovalenko to his office. He may remain a Blood Lord, but only if he swears as you have and only if he keeps his oath." She looked at Eratosthenes. "Perhaps the dearth of vampires now represented here will spur the ambitious to kill their own and take their seats."

Eratosthenes nodded.

Arazni stood. "I remind you all of the oaths you've sworn this day. I remind you also of the repercussions of breaking them. I will not tolerate another betrayal." She motioned to Lilith who rose and went to her, taking her arm, and leading her back to her quarters. The grave knights formed an escort for the pair. When the door to Arazni's chamber closed, the Blood Lords rose.

. . .

Once more Elana stood in the hall and judged the body language of the Blood Lords as they exited. Once more did Saskia rush to her, take her by the arm, and pull her close, whispering into her ear.

"Arazni has declared Kemnebi an enemy of Geb." The two women looked into each other's faces. Saskia pulled Elana down the hall, out of earshot of the other Blood Lords. "She has called for Rhianna and Chevonde to be hunted down and killed." Elana was so stunned she could not speak. Saskia continued. "Only Aleksandr is to be spared."

"Aleksandr? But—"

"He is to retain his station and title." Saskia watched the other Blood Lords as they exited. "Do you know where he is?"

"Aleksandr?" Saskia shook her head. Elana knew who she was enquiring about. "I—I'm not sure—but—"

"You don't have to tell me, child. But if you can get to him, do so."

"Do you intend that I should help him?" asked Elana. Saskia nodded. "But, it's over, isn't it? I mean—"

"Elana," said Saskia, "He's powerful, he was mentored by Geb. He's held the chancellorship forever," she laughed. "Do you think he'll simply it give up? You're close to him. You've learned something of his character. What do you think?"

"No, he won't."

"Then he'll act and in so doing he'll need help."

"Do you want him to win?" asked Elana.

"I want to be on the winning side," said Saskia. "Whichever side that is."

"But—I don't know what I can even do to help him. He's outnumbered, he'll be hunted, he—"

"He'll find a use for you," said Saskia. "Go now, and be careful."

News and Needs

Ebon Mausoleum, Mechitar, and Axan Wood, Geb, Desnus, 4711

"Don't speak," came a voice without a visible source. Elana had just stepped onto the avenue outside of the Cinerarium. It was Xylia, the gnome. "Go to the Ebon Mausoleum." Elana did not alter her pace. She showed no outward signs that she was being spoken to. She headed toward the school for necromancy. "You're being followed by two of Arazni's shadows." This alarmed Elana, but she had enough self-control to hide her reaction.

When she got to the Ebon Mausoleum she opened the door, paused, and turned to look behind her. Of course, as it was night, she could not see the shadows. She held the door long enough for Xylia to pass under her arm then entered.

"Well, well," said Stephanos, a bronze-skinned Garundi student with dark eyes and typical arrogance. "I thought you'd dropped out."

Elana smiled. "Were you all set on being valedictorian?"

"They don't bother with hollow distinctions here," said Stephanos, turning course to walk along side Elana. "Only real results."

"Is that how you comfort yourself?"

Stephanos smiled.

"Elana!" called another student, a Vudrani named Bina, short, energetic, and decidedly unlike a necromancer. Bina's good-humor disguised her ambition and persistent curiosity with the macabre. The young, living students at the Ebon Mausoleum formed a loose fraternity to stay sane. "Where have you been?"

"Carousing with Blood Lords, of course," answered Stephanos.

"That's right," said Bina. "You're barely one of us anymore. You're leaving us peons behind."

"Hardly," said Elana. "I'm—"

"This way," said Bina. "Kuthodari is in the library. She'll kill us if we interrupt her. Come on." The trio turned and headed toward the library. They found the Keleshite seated at a long table, hidden behind thick tomes. "Look who it is," called Bina.

Kuthodari sat back and crossed her arms. "If it isn't my long lost roommate. I thought you were a vampire."

"Why would I—"

"Come now," interrupted Stephanos. "We've heard the rumors."

Elana blushed.

"So they're true?" asked Bina. "You're dating the Chancellor?"

"I'm not dating anyone," pleaded Elana.

"Need I remind you," said Kuthodari, "this is a school for necromancy and we are necromancers, not air-headed socialites?" She narrowed her eyes at Bina.

"While I agree," said Stephanos, "we must consider that one of our own is dating Geb's Chancellor. This could prove beneficial for us. We now know someone who knows someone in the highest place possible."

"Conniving," said Kuthodari.

"What's he like?" asked Bina.

"Will all of you hush?" asked Elana. "I'm not dating anyone. I've been organizing Saskia's spell components and scribing scrolls for her. I've been bent over a desk this whole time."

Stephanos raised an eyebrow and looked at Kuthodari, who smirked, sharing his thoughts. She turned to Elana. "I hope you don't expect us to believe that."

"Damn it," whined Bina, "we want gossip. Have you two—" She tugged on Elana's sleeve and winked.

"Seriously, Bina?" asked Elana. "What have I missed? Tests? Spell trials? Where are we?"

"A pathetic attempt to divert our attention," said Stephanos.

"Oh, oh," said Bina. "We're learning the creepiest spell."

"And yet Bina falls for it," added Stephanos.

"No one's talking to you," said Bina. She looked back to Elana. "It allows you to take control of a skeleton, even a living person's. You can shake their bones inside of their own body." She shuddered. "It felt so horrible."

"Bina volunteered," said Kuthodari.

"Trevedic's been absent," said Stephanos.

"Absent?" asked Elana.

"Gurin took over his classes," said Kuthodari. "He refused to say a word as to why."

Elana feigned a yawn. "Ugh. I'm so tired. I need sleep."

"Romance keeping you up all night?" asked Stephanos.

"Scribing scrolls, I'm telling you," said Elana.

"The room's all yours," said Kuthodari. "I'm not leaving this seat until I've got animate dead perfected."

"You're already on animate dead?" asked Bina, shocked.

"Bina, teach me that spell you mentioned?" asked Elana.

"Yeah, yeah," Bina turned back to Kuthodari. "Animate dead! No way."

"Allow me to escort you home," offered Stephanos.

"What a gentleman."

The pair left the library and went to the students' quarters.

"I've heard other rumors," said Stephanos.

"I told you—"

"Not about that." He looked at Elana. "About a civil war."

"I don't—"

"I hope not," said Stephanos. "We all have our ambitions but we must realize that we cannot yet hold our own. If animate dead poses a challenge," he smiled, "the truly powerful undead are well beyond us. Be careful, Elana."

"I will."

. . .

"If only they knew," mumbled Elana when the door to her room was shut.

"It's better they don't," said Xylia. "Lock the door."

Elana began to cast the arcane lock spell. At the same time Xylia cast a spell of her own. After her spell's completion she became visible. "I don't detect any divination." She went to Kuthodari's bed and leapt up onto the edge. "The shadows didn't enter the school."

"Can we talk?" asked Elana.

"That's why I'm here. What went on in there?"

"Arazni dismissed Kemnebi. He's no longer chancellor."

"Who is?"

"Hent-er-Neheh and Eratosthenes."

The gnome smirked. "Oh, Arazni, you clever girl."

"She's called for Rhianna and Chevonde to be hunted down and slain."

Xylia thought about this news. "She didn't call for *all* of them to be hunted down?"

Elana shook her head. "Eratosthenes asked that Aleksandr not be dismissed but keep his status as Blood Lord." Xylia shot a questioning look. "Arazni agreed."

"Divide and conquer," said Xylia. "What about Kemnebi? Did Arazni call for his demise?"

"Not explicitly."

"Maybe she wants him for herself or maybe she figures it doesn't matter. He's out."

"Do you know where he is?"

"Axan Wood. Rhianna's hunting lodge. They're all there."

"I have to see him," said Elana.

Xylia studied Elana's face. "Be careful with that."

"What do you mean? Saskia wants—"

"'Saskia wants.'" Xylia chuckled. "Elana wants. But what you want isn't important. What Nex wants is important."

"Of course."

The two paused at noise in the hall. A group of students passed.

"We've got more resources," said Xylia.

"More agents?"

"For your own protection it's better you don't know specifics. We can do more, that's all that matters." She tilted her head, revealing Master Castelli's enchanted earrings. She pulled the necklace from under her collar. "From now on I'll do the talking. You're too visible." Elana nodded. Xylia jumped down from the bed and began to pace the small room. "The hunting lodge is well-protected; werewolves, vampires, some kind of bizarre undead with snake-like head—"

"I've seen it."

"Terrifying," said Xylia. "But we've got to get you out there." She looked at Elana and smiled. "Saskia said to stay close to him, didn't she?" Elana nodded. "She's playing both sides?" Again Elana nodded. "What a bitch."

"Can I get to him?"

"Wamukota can get you out there."

"Is he—"

"A Nexian spy?" asked Xylia. "Of course not. He's as loyal as he is addicted. But he's still in Mechitar and he knows how Kemnebi feels about you."

"How Kemnebi feels?"

"You've successfully seduced him, haven't you?"

"Um, I—yes, I suppose that's—"

"He's laying low, Wamukota, taking care of some last minute arrangements for his master, but we've got eyes on him."

"What's the plan?" asked Elana.

"The plan is to support Kemnebi. He doesn't know it, but he has the whole of Nex behind him. Take anything you need from here." She looked around the room. "Your student days are over."

. . .

"Wamukota?"

The Mwangi jumped and reached for the wand at his belt. Elana pulled back the hood of her cloak enough for him to see her face.

"You?"

"Take me out there." She pulled her hood down. With Xylia's help she had lost Arazni's shadows. Wamukota glanced around the midnight bazaar. He too wore his hood up. He paid the merchant, gathered up the spell components he'd purchased, grabbed Elana by the arm, and pulled her to the corner of the market.

"Out where? What are you—"

"Rhianna's hunting lodge."

"What makes you think—"

"Where else could they be?" asked Elana. "Katapesh?"

"You're too damn clever, girl. You're going to get yourself killed."

"Give me more credit than that, Wamukota. I found you."

"Bad luck."

"Wamukota—"

"Not so loud, girl."

"I need him," Elana insisted. "He needs me."

"Need? Oh, girl. You have no idea—"

"Take me to him, Wamukota, please."

"You're just some damn girl. You think—"

"Wamukota—please."

He sighed and studied Elana. "If he breaks my neck for this—" He shoved the spell components into her hands. "At least make yourself useful."

. . .

Elana rushed across the room and embraced Kemnebi. Her boldness startled them both, but his firm chest and strong arms comforted her. Rhianna looked at Aleksandr and smirked. Chevonde leaned against the mantle, gripping the stem of a glass of bloodwine, lost in thought.

"It was foolish of you to come," said Kemnebi. "But I'm glad you did."

"Throwing your lot in with the reckless ones, eh?" asked Rhianna.

Aleksandr approached Elana, who Kemnebi released. "Was there a meeting? I've heard—"

Elana nodded. Chevonde started paying attention. Aleksandr looked to Kemnebi then back to Elana. Elana looked into Kemnebi's eyes then looked away. "Arazni declared all of you—" She glanced at each vampire in turn, excluding Aleksandr. "Enemies of Geb." She looked at Kemnebi. "She stripped you of the chancellorship."

"Who did she give it to?" asked Aleksandr. "Henter-Neheh or Eratosthenes?"

"Both."

Aleksandr glanced at Kemnebi. "What else?"

Elana looked at Rhianna, then Chevonde. "She declared both of you traitors. She has called for your destruction. Whoever kills you takes your place as a Blood Lord."

Rhianna laughed. "Every rat in Mechitar's sewers will be sniffing around for us." She looked at Chevonde. "Where's your humor, Marquis?"

"A bit lacking at the moment, truly sorry."

"And me?" asked Aleksandr.

Elana turned to him. "Eratosthenes requested you remain a Blood Lord."

"What?" asked Aleksandr. He turned to Kemnebi. "I don't—"

"Did he give a reason?" asked Kemnebi.

"He wants Aleksandr to represent the vampires," said Elana. "Arazni said you would have to swear an oath of fealty to her."

"Ha!" Rhianna leapt from her chair. "I get a price on my head and you get to be head honcho." She walked over to Aleksandr and threw her arms around him. "Say, lover, can you pardon me?" She batted her eyes. "For old time's sake."

"I would if I could," said Aleksandr. Rhianna kissed his cheek and returned to her seat.

"What else?" asked Kemnebi.

"Saskia gives her support," said Elana.

For the first time since entering Elana looked around the room. She could only identify a few of the stuffed and mounted heads and pelts adorning the walls. She knew all of them belonged to the magical beasts that roamed the Axan Wood. The walls were wood paneled. A large cobblestone fireplace gave the room a rustic look; although, there was no fire. Instead, floating globes of magical light illuminated the room. There were numerous plush leather seats, small tables for supporting mugs of brandy mixed with blood, and a thick bear-hide rug in the middle of the room. Besides the trophies of the hunt there were a multitude of weapons mounted on the walls.

Rhianna reached out and patted the cushion of the chair next to her. Elana walked over and sat. "When are we going to make this girl a vampire?" asked Rhianna.

"First things first," said Aleksandr. He turned to Kemnebi. "Eratosthenes helped us more than he knows. With me still allowed in Mechitar we can do much."

"Why did he do it?" asked Chevonde.

"To keep the vampires in line," said Aleksandr.

"To keep an eye on you?" countered Chevonde. "And through you to catch our patriarch."

"Maybe," said Aleksandr. "But it doesn't matter." He turned to Kemnebi. "They can watch me, yes, but I can watch them too."

"We must make of this unexpected boon what we can," said Kemnebi. He began to pace, repeatedly stepping over the bear's permanently growling head. "Nah-le-tah and Narcisse are supportive, or, at the least, they owe us. We've helped them tremendously."

"Narcisse is already securing his position," said Aleksandr.

Kemnebi turned to Aleksandr. "Reach out to our kind. They have every reason to help us and none to shun us. Remind them how good un-life has been with one of their own as chancellor. If they want to keep enjoying such a blessed immortality they will do everything they can to return me to my post." Aleksandr nodded. Kemnebi looked to Rhianna then Chevonde. "The three of us will make clandestine trips into Mechitar, to strike here and there, drum up support, cause havoc, whatever we can do."

"Oh, happy day," said Rhianna, with a laugh. "Or should I say happy night?"

"We've got a price on our heads," reminded Chevonde.

"Where's your sense of adventure?" asked Rhianna. "Is that sadly lacking too?"

Chevonde did not answer.

"I would advise that the three of you stay as far away from Mechitar as possible," began Aleksandr. "But even I realize you can't simply hide out here."

"Elana," said Kemnebi. "Go to Saskia." He knelt before her, taking her hands into his. "We need an ally in Arazni's court. We need information. Do you understand?" Elana nodded.

"Is that wise?" asked Aleksandr. "She'll be in tremendous danger."

Kemnebi rose but kept hold of Elana's hand. He looked down at her when he spoke. "She can do it."

"Sire?" asked Aleksandr.

"We need her," said Kemnebi.

"I'll escort her back to the capital," said Aleksandr. "After all, I've got an oath to take."

"And break," added Rhianna.

Kemnebi nodded and everyone prepared to leave the room.

"Elana?" asked Kemnebi, indicating with a look she should remain. Everyone else left. Elana walked over and once more put herself in Kemnebi's arms. She looked up into his eyes as he spoke. "You don't have to help us. Go back to the Ebon Mausoleum. Be a student." Elana shook her head. "You're young, you're alive. You've so much time ahead of you. This is too risky."

"You said you needed me."

"I do. But," he kissed her forehead. "This is our mess, not yours. Don't risk your life for us."

"Kemnebi—" She needed a moment. "I—I'm falling—" But she couldn't say the words.

Kemnebi pressed her head into his chest. At that moment he wished he had a heartbeat. "Go with Aleksandr. He'll keep you safe. Once you're in the capital, stay close to Saskia."

"When will I see you again?"

"I don't know."

Elana looked up at him. "How will I find you?"

He looked down into her eyes. "I'll find you."

Storm Clouds Gather, a Light Shines Through

Various Locations, Mechitar, Geb, Sarenith, 4711

They met in the plains outside of Mechitar, under the protection of darkness, the fire from their torches mingling with the stars on the horizon. Not every priest or priestess loyal to Latitia stood with her when she fell, but the man speaking now had.

His name was Victi and he was proving to be a survivor. He survived a slash across his abdomen given by Rhianna's sword when Aedha was destroyed. He survived being mauled by werewolves when Latitia was destroyed. He even survived an encounter with Kemnebi when Sthaga came close to being destroyed, although he didn't know it.

He told those gathered what had happened in the Church of Epiphenomena. He spun the unbelievable tale of a Daughter of Urgathoa being killed in that goddess's very own sanctuary.

Not only did Victi enrage his fellow priest and priestesses against Rhianna and Kemnebi, he turned them against their own. After all, did Narcisse or Nah-le-tah rush to defend the church? Where were their followers? Why did they refrain from acting while those loyal to Latitia and Sthaga were destroyed?

Even now, rumors spread that Latitia had fallen from grace, otherwise, said this slanderous gossip, why would the goddess have allowed her destruction. It was obvious to those gathered that their faction, the faction of disease, had been intentionally weakened, both by Kemnebi and his allies, and by Narcisse and Nah-le-tah. This, argued Victi, was betrayal.

Together the faithful of the Pallid Princess swore an oath to get revenge.

. . .

They gathered on the roof of the eastern tower of the Church of Epiphenomena, eight vampires. There were others of their kind in Geb, in the villages, in the wilderness, in Yled, Geb's largest city, in Graydirge, that bizarre backwater of a town, but these were the remaining vampires in the capital and they thought themselves the only worth consulting. They had all flown there as bats and materialized as men and women. It amused them to meet there, although they seldom did.

Hu-pen Feng stood at the very edge of the flat roof, his slippered feet pointing out over the gulf below. He stood ram-rod straight with his arms clasped behind his back, yet swayed gently, as if the breeze alone kept him upright.

He came from Tian Xia, from a people so ancient they had buried multiple empires before the first was born on the Inner Sea. He had come as an acrobat, singer, and dancer, as part of a traveling troupe. He was a seducer as well, bringing the ancient art of lovemaking to the rough people on this side of Golarion. That's how he became a vampire, by seducing one, unknowingly.

He was dressed in the traditional style: dark brown, wide-legged pants that ended in tight cuffs at his ankles, black silk slippers, a long, loose dark blue tunic with equally long, loose sleeves, and a small red cap atop his head. His hair was long and braided. He had pasted a narrow strip of parchment on his forehead. Written on this parchment was a prayer in his native tongue. The parchment flapped in the wind.

Seated not far away, one leg dangling over the edge, was a middle-aged man with youth in his eyes—Pavel. He was lanky, his limbs loose, his body sinewy. He had pale skin and long brown hair pulled back. His features were ruggedly handsome but his smile was mischievous. His clothes were well-made but not flashy. He could never keep expensive clothes clean or free from damage, he was too physical, too impulsive too ill-mannered for finery.

A hundred years prior he had been the court jester to King Gaspodar of Cheliax. He had chuckled privately when the King went through his elaborate public rituals in preparation for the prophesied manifestation of Aroden. But Aroden died, and the Age of Prophecy became the Age of Lost Omens. After such a spectacular failure he left Cheliax and sought out an actual immortal, Geb. He glanced up at Hu-pen Feng, wondering what the odd piece of parchment was all about.

Standing nearby, and looking as shamefully seductive as always, was Tatyana. Her face was diamond shaped, her features sharp, her eyes too large and red. She possessed a dangerous attractiveness. She had been a tiefling in life, and her long, pointed tail was animated behind her. She wore an outfit that would be risqué in a brothel, nothing more than a few strips of black lace, really. There was more satin in her elbow-length gloves than fabric in the rest of her outfit. Over this she wore a sheer-cloth, open front robe, not for warmth—it would have failed spectacularly at that—but to tease. Her shoulder length hair blew into her eyes. She reached up and tucked it behind her curved horns.

A bald man with large black eyes and brown skin, a Garundi, stood close to Tatyana, but not staring at her, as might be expected. Instead he was peering out over Mechitar, the city in which he was born. If he had been alive he would have been thought dangerously thin. In undeath that hardly mattered. He wore only a simple, short, cotton robe tied at the waist with a length of hemp. He had nothing in his pockets, no jewelry, no worldly possessions at all save his robe. He was barefoot, his feet filthy. He was known to beg in the streets at night, which, to anyone familiar with Geb, was an alarming act. Of course, he need not worry.

He turned his eyes to another whose outfit could not be more in opposition. He wore a puffy coat of satin, two shades of green plus brown and white, with fur trim. He wore skin-tight breeches, each leg made of different garishly colored and patterned fabric. His low-heeled boots were made of bright green felt. His hat was huge, floppy, and feathered. His beard was long, black, and oiled. His eyebrows were dark and expressive. He had full red lips, dark eyes, a regal nose, and more arrogance than most vampires possessed. He extended his broadsword, the blade of which was five feet in length, and threatened to poke Hu-pen Feng in the rear with it.

"There was a sword swallower in my troupe," said Hu-pen Feng, without turning.

"Oh?" asked Marengo, who held his sword level but did not advance it.

"If I feel the tip of your blade," said Hu-pen Feng, "I shall demonstrate his technique," he turned and looked down past the strip of parchment at Marengo, "on you."

"What is that on your face, Hu?" asked Pavel, unable to contain his curiosity.

"We have more important questions to address," said Branca. She too was Garundi. She too was a native of Geb, like Jubair, the beggar. It was Branca who Kemnebi had surprised while she was feeding on a laborer. She had not forgotten that episode nor had she told anyone about it.

Much like she had worn the night Kemnebi caught her breaking the Dead Laws she was wearing a fashionable dress of gold-colored cloth adorned with jewels. She wore a small fortune worth of gold, silver, and precious stones. Her hair, despite being Garundi, was dark blonde, indicating her blood was not quite pure. Her eyes were dull gray. If Tatyana wasn't standing next to her, she would shine as a beauty and she was beautiful, only in a refined way, whereas Tatyana was pure sex. Branca turned to Ridwan, a Vudrani.

Ridwan was, in the absence of Kemnebi, the most authoritative amongst Geb's vampires. He had swarthy skin, dark eyes, dark hair, and wore his long beard in the style of his warrior-prince ancestors: as a series of long ringlets adorned with gold clasps. Of all eight only he wore armor, a full suit of enchanted leather. His scimitar was not as visually impressive as Marengo's broadsword, but it was equally as dangerous. He glanced at the two remaining vampires before speaking for the group.

They were siblings, half-elves, both, and stood embracing one another. Bayla was pressed against her brother's chest. She looked out over the group with large, light-blue eyes. Her long, straight hair was dark brown. She was freckled, with more of the light brown spots on her right cheek than her left. Her nose was small, her smile welcoming. She wore a dress of white cotton, a leather belt with a gold buckle, and leather sandals. Her wrist were adorned with gold bangles.

Danfrist, who was a foot taller than his sister, possessed a boyish charm. His shoulder-length blonde hair and his elven features made him stunningly beautiful. His teeth, other than his canines, were straight and white. His eyes were large and the same arresting blue as his sister's. The elven blood in him gave him the appearance of fragility, even innocence, yet most of the exposed flesh of his arms and hands—he wore leather pants and a short-sleeved cotton shirt—were covered with tattoos of black ink spelling out forbidden phrases that Tatyana's demonic ancestor would be well versed in.

"What are we to make of this?" asked Ridwan. "He has endangered us all with his foolishness."

"I was getting bored," said Pavel. "At least he shook things up."

"The Chancellor—" Began Branca, but Danfrist interrupted.

"Haven't you heard?"

Branca turned to face him.

Bayla continued her brother's thought. "Chancellor no more."

"There is a price on the heads of both Rhianna and Chevonde," said Marengo, who was lazily swinging his sword in wide arcs. Luckily the tower's dimensions were great enough to indulge him.

"If we wish to maintain our status and power," said Ridwan, "we must retain those seats."

"We could join Jubair in the streets," said Pavel, motioning to the beggar vampire, who bowed in appreciation.

"Filthy," said Branca.

"If I may?" asked Jubair. He motioned to Tatyana. "She will receive all the alms from the people, so, ah, revealing is her attire."

"I don't even have a beggar's bowl," said Tatyana. She acted as if she were searching for pockets. "And no where to keep the scarabs."

"Hu-pen?" asked Ridwan. "Speak."

Hu-pen Feng, who had returned to looking out over Mechitar, spoke without turning. The other vampires had to draw near to hear him. (Which meant Marengo finally had to rest his sword.) "Why do we stay?" asked Hu-pen. "This city is not for us."

"Do you think we should flee?" asked Branca.

"Flee?" Hu-pen reached up, tore free the parchment, and let the breeze lift it from his hand. He turned and faced his brethren, now balancing on his toes. "This is a place of death. This is a place where corpses rule."

"Aren't we corpses?" asked Tatyana.

"We are predators," said Hu-pen. "And yet we do not hunt. Our fare is bred in pens and presented to us, such rich viands for our table." He looked over his shoulder then back to the assembled vampires. "I did not hear Kemnebi's speech but I've thought his thoughts. This is a dead place. We do not belong in a place of death, but of life."

"Yled?" asked Marengo.

Branca scoffed.

"There is much to sustain us there," said Danfrist.

"Bother," said Bayla.

"Yes?"

She shook her head.

"Leaving Mechitar," said Ridwan, "would be admitting defeat."

"Besides," added Branca, "there are too many damn priests there—worse than here."

"Tell me sister, why not Yled?"

"Don't you remember those vampires?" asked Bayla. "They're so—weird."

"Have you met the ones in Graydirge?" asked Marengo. He shuddered at the thought of them.

"Hu-pen," said Pavel. "Yled?"

"To change one city in Geb for another," said Hu-pen, "would solve nothing. Forget not that we prey on life. We are sustained by life. So, I ask again, why do we stay in a land of the dead?"

"Because here," Ridwan pointed to the city beneath his feet, "we have power. More power than we could have anywhere else."

"And we aren't hunted," added Branca.

"We will never again be so powerful," said Pavel, who stood. "Hent-er-Neheh, Eratosthenes, Queen Arazni." He shook his head. "Even if we were to keep two seats among sixty, they will do us little good."

"I have never surrendered anything in my life, or undeath," growled Ridwan. "My ancestors raised armies, went to war, decided the fates of multitudes, and now I carry on their great tradition, and shall do so until this world turns cold."

"We won't just have two seats," said Branca. "Don't forget Aleksandr. He is still powerful, still influential. We can build on that."

"I'm bored," said Pavel. He looked at Hu-pen Feng. "You have a point. All the fun's gone out of immortality."

"I wasn't thinking of amusement," said Hu-pen. "But, yes, the beast in us grows fat and lazy."

"Go then, if Geb bores you," said Ridwan. "Those of us who are serious," he glanced at Branca, "will do what we must to maintain our exalted positions in Geb. We must kill Rhianna and Chevonde. We must take their seats. We must join with Aleksandr." He looked over the assembled group. "Who will fight?" He looked at Hu-pen Feng and Pavel. "And who will flee?"

"A fine speech," said Danfrist. Ridwan spun to face him. Danfrist was not perturbed by Ridwan's angry stare. "It would be suicide to attempt to kill Rhianna. She's too strong, even for you."

"And Chevonde's too cute to kill," said Bayla.

"Sister?"

"Well, he is."

"So you'll flee?" asked Ridwan. "You consort with demons but you are afraid of Rhianna?"

"Patience," said Jabair. "There is a way to things." The vampires looked at him. "What I need," he waved his hand to encompass all around him, "comes to me, in time." He smiled. "All that is asked of me is patience."

"What he means," said Marengo, "is we must let this little tiff play out. Might there be a better opportunity in the future?"

"After all," said Tatyana, "if Kemnebi comes out on top, we'll have all the power we'd ever want."

"You're saying we should help him?" asked Branca.

"No," said Marengo, "we should," he smiled at Jabair, "be patient."

"Cowards, the lot of you," growled Ridwan. "You want to flee," he waved a dismissive hand at Hu-pen and Pavel, "you want to wait," he waved a dismissive hand at Marengo and the two half-elves, "when what is called for is courage." He balled his hand into a fist. "Courage and ruthless action."

"You think too highly of yourself, Ridwan," said Danfrist. "Kemnebi, Rhianna, Aleksandr, even Chevonde and Trevedic are where they are because they're powerful."

"And where are they?" asked Ridwan. "Exiled, with prices on their heads."

"What good is immortality," asked Hu-pen, "if it is filled with rash action?" He gazed out once more over Mechitar. "Do as you wish," he said. "As for me," he held out his hand, "I feel an ill wind blowing. Perhaps I shall return to my homeland."

"Care for company along the way?" asked Pavel. "I can earn a living by juggling knives. You can do back flips."

"A lot of cowards you are," growled Ridwan, but the bravado had gone from his voice.

. . .

Khamati leaned in close to his cousin. "Why not hunt him?"

Khufnu glanced at Khamati, but did not answer.

"Why not make him your prey?"

"Hent-er-Neheh," said Khufnu, "has not asked—"

"I'm asking, cousin."

Khufnu was a loner. He was a Blood Lord, yes, and he was a distant relative of Geb's, but he didn't care for politics, nor did he care for power. He was a follower of Shax, the demon lord of sadistic murder. Khufnu stalked the entire eastern seaboard, from Mechitar to Sothis, torturing and killing.

"With Aleksandr allowed in Mechitar," said Khamati, "with him as a Blood Lord, our position is insecure. He'll thank Eratosthenes for having saved his hide and he'll undermine Hent-er-Neheh." Again Khufnu studied his fellow mummy, but said nothing. "He must be destroyed."

"I don't—"

"If Hent-er-Neheh demanded it?"

Khufnu nodded.

Khamati rose and walked away, turning his back on Khufnu in frustration. He spun to face him. "She mummified you, her and Nakht. You owe them both."

Khufnu watched his cousin, but remained silent.

"What is it?" asked Khamati. "Why not make him one of your many victims? What's stopping you? Fear?"

"I—I don't choose my victims."

"What do you— Who does?"

Khufnu hesitated.

"Well?" demanded Khamati.

"Shax—shows them to me."

Khamati once more returned to his seat, pulling it even closer to Khufnu. "Damn it, make an exception. Kill Aleksandr. Rob Eratosthenes of his puppet. Rob Kemnebi of his conduit into Mechitar. Silence the voice of the vampires. Khufnu, cousin, do this for us, for Geb and those most loyal to him. You're a killer—kill Aleksandr."

. . .

Arazni sat in Geb's throne. Hent-er-Neheh stood at her right hand, Eratosthenes at her left. Aleksandr knelt at her feet. The grave knights surrounded them. The statue of Geb watched all.

"Where is he, Aleksandr?" asked Hent-er-Neheh.

"I've lost contact with him."

"When was the last time you saw or spoke to him?" asked Eratosthenes.

"We met at my mansion, with our staff. That was the last time."

Arazni, who was seated with her legs under her, shifted and extended her foot, raising Aleksandr's chin with her toes. "Is he at Rhianna's hunting lodge?"

"Forgive me, Queen, I don't know."

Arazni withdrew her foot and looked at Eratosthenes. He knew the unspoken question and answered it.

"We have had no luck with our divinations. He is well shielded."

Arazni turned to look at Hent-er-Neheh, who merely shook her head. Arazni turned back to Aleksandr. "Maybe I'll torture you," she said. "The undead can be tortured." She chuckled. "Ask Trevedic. I hear he is suffering terrible withdraws." She glanced at Eratosthenes, who gave no visible response. She looked back at Aleksandr. "You swore an oath just now. You must decide where your loyalties lie."

"I'm loyal to you, Queen, and to Geb."

"Then tell me where he is."

"Queen," Aleksandr glanced up at her, then to Eratosthenes, then back to the floor. "I don't think he trusts me anymore."

"Why not?" asked Hent-er-Neheh.

Aleksandr glanced at her. "I advised him not to embark on this path. I begged him to resign. I begged him not to attack, but to withdraw."

"His words have the ring of truth," said Eratosthenes.

"After he left he went to the Church of Epiphenomena," said Aleksandr. "We know what happened next."

"Where did you go?" asked Eratosthenes, although he already knew the answer.

Aleksandr glanced at him. "I went to the Ebon Mausoleum, to free Trevedic."

"Where you able to?" asked Arazni, although she too knew the answer. Eratosthenes had informed her.

"No, Queen, I failed."

"Rhianna and your sire attacked Latitia," said Hent-er-Neheh, "Chevonde attacked myself and my father. You alone refrained?"

"I was willing to attempt to free Trevedic," said Aleksandr. "As for attacking a fellow Blood Lord—" He shook his head.

"Did you know of the planned attacks?" asked Hent-er-Neheh.

Aleksandr paused before answering. "Yes."

"Destroy him, Queen," said Hent-er-Neheh. "He cannot be trusted."

"His loyalty *was* conflicted," said Eratosthenes. "Now it is fixed upon you, Queen Arazni."

"Still, I think I'll torture him," said Arazni.

"If your Highness wishes," said Eratosthenes, "I can see to it."

"Poor Aleksandr," Arazni purred, smirking. "Do you wish you were with him, your sire?"

"My place is as a Blood Lord," said Aleksandr, "in service to Geb."

"Arazni—Queen," said Hent-er-Neheh, "he's lying to you. He can't be trusted."

Arazni once more reached out with her foot and lifted Aleksandr's chin. She studied his face. "Eratosthenes will learn the truth." She pushed against his cheek with her toes, turning his head to the side.

. . .

"Can't you get it out of him?" asked Noreen Paisely, the Llorona, of Moira, Aleksandr's former lover. The "it" was the location of Rhianna and Chevonde, the two hunted former Blood Lords.

"I haven't talked to him in a romantic sense in years," said Moira.

"He's in need of a friend," said Lilith. "Someone to whom he can unburden his heart."

Moira shrugged her shoulders. "I can try."

"I've the perfect dress for a seduction," said Araminta.

"Why are we bothering with seduction?" asked Kimberly Silent Eyes. "Why not just kill him?"

"He's a Blood Lord," said Lilith. "Besides, we don't want him dead, not yet. We want Rhianna and Chevonde dead."

"And Kemnebi," said Baya-Iza.

"Arazni did not call for that," said Lilith.

"Why not?" asked Saskia. "Why just Rhianna and Chevonde?"

"I've wondered that myself," said Lilith.

"You haven't asked her?" asked Saskia.

"No, I've been—delicate—with her," said Lilith. "These are difficult times and we all know how emotional she can get."

"Why didn't she make you chancellor, Mother?" asked Jasmine, the Dead Bride.

"She must keep Hent-er-Neheh and Eratosthenes close."

"She should have made you chancellor," said Jasmine.

"We need not worry about our own power," said Lilith. "With Arazni as queen we are assured great influence. But," she added, "killing Rhianna and Chevonde would please her and show the other Blood Lords that we are not mere hangers-on, but a force to be reckoned with." She looked over the assembled women. "We must consider this, the balance of power has changed. Every Blood Lord is going to act to increase their own power. We too must act. We may lack the raw arcane might of the Whispering Way, or the divine magic of the worshippers of Urgathoa, but we have our own ways. If we can draw Aleksandr to us we can, through him, draw Rhianna and Chevonde into our hands."

"Then we kill them," said Kimberly Silent Eyes.

"Yes," said Lilith.

Saskia thought much of the conversation, but said little. She did not want to increase the power of anyone but herself and she had her own way of doing that.

. . .

"Well," said Narcisse, looking around Latitia's chapel. "Nothing a good scrubbing won't fix."

"We *have* scrubbed it," said Nah-le-tah. He was seated in Latitia's throne. It was a bit too narrow for him, he being a tomb giant, thirteen feet in height and nearly four feet wide at the hips, but he appreciated the still more elevated vantage point.

"I presume you aren't going to let them rot?" Narcisse motioned to the corpses left behind by Rhianna and Kemnebi.

"I have ideas."

Narcisse stepped amongst the corpses until he found a cot. He turned it upright, dragged it close to the dais, set it down then sat. The two were alone in the chapel. "You've got allies, is what you have," said Narcisse. He rubbed his neck, as he was craning it to look up at his fellow priest. "You were sponsored for your Lordship by Eratosthenes, seconded by Aleksandr, and approved by Arazni."

"Your story is much the same," said Nah-le-tah.

Narcisse crinkled his nose. "The smell in here is, ah, unpleasant." Narcisse waved a hand before his face, to no effect. "The church is ours, you know?"

"I hesitate to make such a claim when Sthaga retains the title of High Priest."

"There's something not quite right about our High Priest," said Narcisse.

"Perhaps it is his hatred for life that troubles you?"

Narcisse waved his hand. "That?" He chuckled. "I'm used to that. No, the little scuffle in his chapel was—peculiar. Wouldn't you agree?"

"In that he survived?"

"In that he didn't fight back."

"How do you know he didn't fight back?" asked Nah-le-tah.

"Ah, that?" Narcisse chuckled. "Divine providence."

"You were spying on him?"

"Spying has such a negative connotation," said Narcisse. "I was concerned about the welfare of our High Priest, as are you, I'm sure."

"Are you equally concerned about my welfare?" asked Nah-le-tah.

Narcisse smiled. "What are we to make of matters, eh? Kemnebi is out. The church itself is weakened, although we have benefitted. Hent-er-Neheh and Eratosthenes are strengthened. Which side are we to choose?"

"We swore an oath—"

Narcisse waved a dismissive hand. "A ridiculous gimmick." He rose but stood in place, shifting his weight between his feet. "It's not over, you know? Kemnebi will certainly strike back."

"What you're talking about is treasonous."

"What I'm talking about are opportunities."

"To do what?" asked Nah-le-tah.

"To increase our power still further."

"By—"

"By facilitating a more complete conclusion to matters."

"You talk like a politician," complained Nah-le-tah.

"I am a politician." Narcisse laughed. He eyed the cot, tempted to sit despite his aching knees, but it offered little comfort. He chose to test his knees a bit further and turned back to his fellow priest. "It's silly, isn't it, that a nation of undead is ruled by—"

"Undead?"

"No, by anyone other than a priest of the Goddess of Undeath."

"Is that what—"

"No, neither of us can rise to that challenge as of now. We need to bide our time, grow our resources, and replace our own High Priest."

"That—is certainly treasonous," said Nah-le-tah.

Narcisse laughed. "Opportunities, my tall friend. We do not benefit if things settle down, if our former Chancellor and his associates fade quietly into the dawn light. Arazni pays lip service to our glorious goddess. Eratosthenes and Hent-er-Neheh don't even do that. A congregation of ghouls is certainly powerful but hardly useful in a social sense. We need to change the direction of the Church. We need to reach out to the, what did Kemnebi call them, the plebeians, the common man in the street. The living fear the dead. Why? Urgathoa can show them a better way."

"Your words echo those of our disgraced Chancellor."

"Was he entirely wrong?" asked Narcisse. "He wanted to protect the living in Geb, to coddle them. What I want to do is co-opt them, bring them into the church. Show them a path out of fear and submission, toward power and everlasting grace. They live in Geb. They should embrace the opportunity fate gave them."

"I never knew you to be a visionary, Narcisse."

"Kemnebi inspired me."

"Do you wish to repay him with your support?"

"Not explicitly, no. What I want is to give us—you and me—room to maneuver. The longer this conflict goes on, the more those above us spend their energy fighting one another, the more room we have and the more time." The two priest of Urgathoa studied one another. "It would be better if we combined our efforts."

"What of Sthaga?" asked Nah-le-tah.

"He can safely be ignored." Narcisse sat on the cot but, enthused by his coming speech, rose again. "My vision is of a church divided as such: you handle the dead, to me," he touched his chest, "the living. And until we can arrive at that glorious state—"

Nah-le-tah smiled, beginning to see the vision, "we ensure that those who would oppose us are otherwise occupied."

"Now who sounds like a politician?"

"You inspire me."

. . .

Aleksandr followed Eratosthenes, feeling much like a whipped puppy following its master. He hadn't felt like that since he was a child, following his father after being scolded. He did not enjoy the feeling nor did he enjoy the prospect of torture. He knew Trevedic was still locked away in his room. He wondered what condition his friend was in and thought of asking Eratosthenes, but he feared the answer.

Eratosthenes did not actually walk, but floated a few inches above the cobbled streets of Mechitar. Much to Aleksandr's surprise he turned from the street that led to the Ebon Mausoleum onto a street Aleksandr was quite familiar with, for he lived on it. When Eratosthenes stopped before Aleksandr's doorstep Aleksandr was confused. He walked up to Eratosthenes and studied the elven lich.

Eratosthenes turned but looked past Aleksandr. "Return to your Queen," he said to the shadows that had been following him and Aleksandr. "Tell her I took him into the Ebon Mausoleum, where you cannot follow. Tell her you heard his screams through the walls."

Aleksandr looked for the shadows but did not see them. He looked back to Eratosthenes. The lich was quiet for a moment, his attention directed at the retreating shadows. Once he was certain they were gone he turned to face the way he had been floating. This put him profile to Aleksandr.

"Torture you?" He turned and looked at Aleksandr. "How stupid."

Aleksandr watched him float down the street. He looked at the door to his mansion, looked again at Eratosthenes, then hurried into the safety of his home.

Three Nights, One Day

Various Locations, Yled, Mechitar, and the Axan Wood, Geb, Erastus, 4711

First night.

Mechitar was Geb's capital but it was not that nation's largest city, not even by half. That honor belonged to Yled, a sprawling city at Geb's northern border. The city had begun its life as a military outpost and it retained the feeling of an overgrown camp; with haphazardly organized streets, practical, plain structures, and a distinct lack of frills.

Yled had both more undead than Mechitar *and* more living. It was the type of undead that made all the difference, for Yled was home to the majority of Geb's undead army. The city was full to overflowing with the lesser types of undead: skeletons, zombies, ghouls, wights, wraiths, and so on.

Unlike Mechitar, the elites in Yled were predominantly alive. They were necromancers, scholars, bone-workers, and the assorted priests of a half-dozen gods and demon lords, with Nethys, Urgathoa, and Zon-Kuthon drawing the majority of the faithful. Craftsmen and merchants filled out the city; paper makers, book binders, blacksmiths, herbalist, and on and on.

There were no pyramids in Yled. Geb himself took little interest in the architecture of that city, excepting one feature—the Bonewall. He created the vast, encircling wall of bleached bones when Nex—his rival wizard-king—was still just few hundred miles to the north. With a command, the Bonewall would become animate. Geb would not settle for mere defense. Even his walls must attack.

The only other architectural feature that stood out was the Mortuarium. This tower was erected not by Geb but by his most trusted and powerful fellow necromancers. At one time it had been a straight, shimmering black finger pointed in defiance at Heaven above. The builders of this school for necromancy had intended for Nex to see it from Quantium, so great was its height. Never mind that Nex himself had built a tower a mile high in Absalom, so his idea of a tall tower was many degrees greater than theirs.

Still, Nex could not rightly allow the shimmering tower to remain as it was, nor did he feel like erasing it from the surface of Golarion. Instead, as part of a larger attack on Geb, he caused the tower to gnarl itself like a branch grown into a confined space. The tower remained mercifully usable—Nex didn't want them to tear it down—it also remained a testament to his power. He'd turned their arrogant finger into a twisted claw and he'd thumbed their noses with it.

It was raining that night in Geb. The maze-like streets of Yled were wet and reflected the moon above. Mechitar is a city of extremes at night, a pool of light surrounded by a frightening darkness. Yled is neither well-lit nor intentionally dark. The living control the city, use its streets, stores, and homes. The undead soldiers have no need of recreation, nor even of quarters. The majority of Geb's undead army, the skeletons and zombies, stand, night and day, year after year, on the parade grounds. Tens of thousands of necromantic statues staring north, waiting for a command to spill across the Mana Waste, to overrun Nex.

The living don't fear the dead as much in Yled as they do in the capital. Since the majority of the living in Yled have some knowledge of necromancy, and the majority of undead were of the weaker variety, the necromancers and priests went about their business, even at night. This was why Khufnu liked Yled. So long as he hid his linen wrapping he could blend in with the living, watch them, listen to them, stalk them. And, if he was lucky, Shax would single one out.

It was always a revelation when a victim was presented to him. Once he had been waiting in the shadows of a market stall and a woman reached for a piece of fruit. It was her wrist, the shape of the bones under the flesh, the elegant proportions, the vein that ran down the back, raising up the skin. He had a vision of peeling back the skin without breaking the vein. He had a vision of seeing the bones beneath the muscle and tendon. That is how Shax had revealed that particular victim. It was up to Khufnu to make the vision real—and he had.

Sometimes months passed before the swan-headed demon lord could be bothered with yet another serial killer hungering for a victim. He had his own prey to hunt. Khufnu was never impatient. He was always filled with a delightful anticipation. He was fascinated with the living, fascinated with their anatomy, with their ability to feel, to scream. While he stalked he fantasized. He heard begging and whimpering, he saw bodies twist in agony, he saw the light fade from his victim's eyes. One thing he never imagined was that he was being stalked, but he was.

He wasn't being stalked by one of his own, a thrill-seeking killer. He wasn't being stalked by an undead, a necromancer bent on control, or a priest desiring a shiny new trophy with which to please his god. He was being stalked by a team of professional killers. A team that knew him well, had studied his methods, his habits, his weaknesses. They were from Nex and they had come with fire, for old linen burned quite well.

Khufnu paused and looked up at the Mortuarium. The agonized architecture reminded him of his own sick pursuit. How many times had he seen an arm so twisted in agony? He turned and headed toward the outskirts of Yled. He had a small, nondescript house with a large dungeon beneath filled with the tools of torture. He waited out the day there, pondering his craft, or reading about those who practiced it and their disturbing discoveries. Sometimes he spent an entire day simply gazing at the implements of torture in his possession, admiring them, remembering what he had done with them.

As he approached his home in Yled he began to slip into a waking revelry, one filled with the delightful—to him—images of suffering. He turned a corner and saw a trio of dark-clad people fan out. He saw little flashes of light and looked more carefully at them. The dark-clad strangers each had bows, the heads of the arrows alight with flame. Before Khufnu could react the archers fired. A trio of flaming arrows slammed into Khufnu's chest. His robes and linen wrapping burst into flame. The archers drew more arrows. As soon as the arrows were notched the tips began to glow with fire.

Khufnu pulled a long dagger from beneath his robes and judged the distance between him and the archers. He glanced at the door to his house and judged the distance between himself and it. His calculations were interrupted by the fire blossoming on his chest. He slapped his chest with one hand and began to run, deciding on the safety of his home.

Two more darkly dressed figures appeared from around the corner of an adjacent home. They held glass bottles and when they saw Khufnu they threw them at the ground ahead of him. The alchemical fire splashed onto his legs and, now that it was exposed to air, burst into flame. Still, he ran. Two of the arrows slammed into him, one in the arm, one in the neck. The third whizzed by like a shooting star.

The fire now fully consumed Khufnu. The light of it filled the street and colored the house-fronts nearby. The two men reached for more bottles of alchemical fire. The three archers reached for a third volley. Khufnu reached his door and yanked on the pull, breaking it free from the door, which didn't budge. The door was locked with magic. For a moment he stared at the door, dumbfounded. Painted on its surface was a skull, its mouth gagged. He did not know that this was the symbol of the Whispering Way. He did not know how it had gotten on his door or why. The pain of the fire reminded him of the danger he was in. He dropped the door pull, turned, and rushed toward the archers, which he could barely see through the flames.

The final member of the Nexian team stepped out from the corner of Khufnu's house. She was finishing a spell and when it was done three beams of fire launched from her hand. One beam narrowly missed Khufnu, just singing his left thigh. The other two struck him, one in the stomach, the other in the groin.

Khufnu staggered and fell to one knee. The blade tumbled from his hand. He tried to pat out the fire but it was hopeless. He was being eaten up by it. But he was powerful. The necromantic magic within him would not so easily succumb, not even to flame. He got his feet under him and rose, pulling the flaming robe from him and tossing it aside. Now his attackers could see him and even though he was still aflame the despair that accompanied his awesome transformation into a mummy shone through. It paralyzed one of the archers and one of the vial-throwing men with fear.

Even though he had discarded the burning mantle the alchemical fire climbed up his legs, the burning arrows lit the linen wrappings around his torso. The flames once more obscured his vision. He rushed forward, swinging wildly for the archers. But he could not see them and although his burning fists whooshed through the air they hit nothing. The archers were ten feet back, preparing to fire point-blank.

As Khufnu staggered forward, arms flailing, the archers—the two whom had resisted the fear-inducing power of his necromantic curse—released their enchanted arrows. Once again the flaming shafts slammed into his chest. The archers hastily pulled yet another round of arrows. They needn't have bothered. Khufnu collapsed and lay silent and motionless in the street. Only the fire crackled.

The archers shot anyway, sinking their arrows into Khufnu's still form. Those who weren't paralyzed by fear grabbed those who were and ran. As the two men ran past Khufnu, they threw more glass bottles at the cobblestones, shattering the glass, spreading the burning solution over Khufnu and the pavement around him. The wizard who had cast the scorching ray spell jogged close to Khufnu, paused, and studied the dark mass at the heart of the fire. Certain he was ash, she bolted after the others. In twenty minutes they would be out of the city and on their way back to Mechitar.

The alchemical fire continued to burn. By dawn there would be little left of the demon-worshipping, serial-killing mummy. There would be no new victims shown to him by Shax, for Khufnu himself had met a grisly fate.

. . .

Lilith stood in the doorway to Arazni's personal chambers in the Cinerarium, watching her Queen. Two grave knights stood just within the door, watching Lilith. She was so used to their malevolent gazes she paid them no mind.

Arazni had piled her pillows up on the floor and covered them with a blanket. She'd modeled this pile of fabric and cushioning into something like a mountain. She was on her knees next to it, a wooden doll in each hand.

One of the dolls was dressed like a wizard, the other like a warrior. Arazni was so absorbed in her role-play that she didn't notice Lilith's presence. Lilith shut the door, walked to Arazni's side, and knelt.

"What do we have here," Lilith asked, "my Queen?"

Arazni looked up and smiled. She held up the wizard doll and said, "Aroden." She held up the warrior doll and said, "Warlord Voradni Voon." She nodded to the covered pillows. "Aroden has just created the Isle of Kortos."

"Who is Voradni Voon?" asked Lilith.

"A bad man," said Arazni, her brow furrowing.

"Why?"

"He's mean."

"To Aroden?"

"Yes, he attacked Aroden." Arazni pouted but it turned into a smile. "But Aroden defeated him." She looked at Lilith. "Do you want to play, Mother?"

Lilith stood. "Not now, Queen. Come, let's sit. I'll comb your hair."

"Yay!" Arazni set down her wooden dolls, jumped to her feet, and rushed to the bed. She sat with her hands on her thighs.

Lilith walked around the bed. She found the brush on the bedside table. She climbed onto her knees, scooted to Arazni, and began to brush her hair. "Moira just left."

"Where'd she go?"

"To see Aleksandr."

"Mother."

"Yes, Queen?"

"I don't like him."

"I know."

"Why should Moira go?"

"To seduce him," said Lilith. "To turn him against Kemnebi. Or, if that isn't possible, to learn what she can, so she can tell us."

"Kemnebi?" asked Arazni. Her voice was hollow, as if the name held no meaning for her.

"You remember Kemnebi, don't you?"

"Aroden," said Arazni. "I remember Aroden."

"That was a long time ago."

"Why do they stare at us like that, Mother?" Arazni pointed to the grave knights before them.

"To make sure we're safe."

"Are we safe, Mother?"

"When Kemnebi is gone, we will be safe."

"Is he like Voradni Voon?"

"Yes," said Lilith.

"Will he attack us?"

"He might."

Arazni was silent. Minutes passed in which Lilith combed her hair.

"When will Geb be back?" asked Arazni.

"Soon."

"Where did he go?"

"He's checking on his people," said Lilith. "Making sure everyone's safe."

"Mother," said Arazni, her voice barely a whisper.

"Yes?"

"I think I'm dead."

Lilith did not respond.

Arazni half turned and grabbed Lilith's wrist. "I think I died, Mother, and this is Hell."

"No, Queen." Lilith gently turned Arazni forward and resumed combing her hair. "Don't think such thoughts."

Again there were several minutes of silence. Arazni shuddered and stood, wrapping her arms around herself.

"What did you say about Moira?" she asked, not looking at Lilith.

"She went to Aleksandr."

"Good," said Arazni, her voice losing its child-like pitch. "When she returns bring her to me."

"Yes, Queen."

Arazni looked down at the pile of pillows and the blanket covering them. She studied her childish construction, a look of dismay on her face. "I want to be alone now."

. . .

"You'll lose a finger that way," warned Chevonde.

Khamati, who was kneeling by the garden pool, allowing the blue-shelled crabs to gnaw on his fingertips, in one motion, spun, rose, and pulled the dagger from his belt. He began a spell but when he realized Chevonde was casually leaning against the trunk of a date palm, he stopped. He gathered his emotions, sheathed his dagger, and smiled.

"Marquis."

Chevonde shoved himself from the date palm. "Want to try again?"

Khamati laughed.

"As I see it," said Chevonde, "she's the only one left in your way."

"I underestimated you, Marquis."

"I know." Chevonde smiled. "Well?"

Khamati walked to the patio, motioning that his unexpected guest should sit. Chevonde did so, as did Khamati. The mummified lamia appeared from the shadows, a look of alarm on her face, her kukri in-hand.

Khamati waved that she should stand down and she did so. He thought for a moment.

"I expended a great deal of my resources in the last effort."

"Down a few pets, are we?"

"Yes."

"Your wife?" asked Chevonde.

"It's the life of a bachelor for me."

"A shame. Shall I be going?"

"No, let me think a moment." The two men sat in silence. "A surprise attack now would be completely unexpected," said Khamati. "And, with circumstances changed, a new opportunity presents itself." He "looked" at Chevonde, his empty sockets filled with shadow. "If we make it look like Eratosthenes was behind the attack, even if we failed, her attention would be directed to a mutual enemy."

"I'm learning that that's one of your tricks."

"It works," said Khamati. "Now, how to make it look like Eratosthenes is behind—"

"Kemnebi can do that."

Khamati studied Chevonde. "Would he be willing to play an active role in—"

Chevonde nodded.

"Well, that changes things." Khamati glanced the direction of Hent-er-Neheh's pyramid, although it could not be seen through the leaves of the palms. "I'm almost afraid to see those two battle." He looked at Chevonde. "Two nights. Meet here in two nights. I need time to prepare."

Chevonde rose. Khamati rose.

"I don't trust you," said Chevonde. "But I trust your hunger."

. . .

It stood twelve feet in height and weighed five thousand pounds. Its head almost touched the ceiling. It was solid iron, enough iron to outfight an army in chainmail shirts. It crushed the rug beneath its feet. An iron golem. It stood in Kemnebi's living room.

Spellcasters hate golems, unless they control them. They hate golems because golems are immune to magic, for the most part. This golem was on loan. Queen Arazni had requested the owner lend it to her for use against Kemnebi. The price was steep, the golem's creator charged by the day, but the treasury of a nation like Geb could shoulder the burden with little effort.

It was not the only golem watching for Kemnebi. A weaker type, on loan from the army in Yled, was positioned outside. It was shorter by four feet, weighed a tenth of the iron golem's total, and had been assembled from body parts stitched together: a flesh golem. It too was largely immune to magic. It walked a circuit around Kemnebi's pyramidal home. It was accompanied by two dozen shadows whose blacked-out eyes covered every conceivable angle of approach.

Despite all this a thief had made her way into Kemnebi's home. She crouched in the darkness, gazing—she could see perfectly well—at the golem's back. She craned her neck, searching for the cabinet. Elana's report told of an ancient medallion. The thief looked again at the golem. The medallion, if it was still in the cabinet, was a few feet from the iron monstrosity. It could swing out with its arm and crush the cabinet like a giant crushes a bug.

The thief rose, took one step, and paused. The golem was oblivious to her presence. She took another step and paused, then another. A dozen such steps positioned her just behind the golem. She turned, took three more steps and knelt. She reached out, a glass vial in her hand. She uncorked it, tilted it, and oiled the hinges on the cabinet's door. She re-corked the bottle and tucked it into a pocket. As she did this she looked over her shoulder at the golem.

She turned back to the cabinet and tested the door, opening it a few centimeters. No sound came. She slowly opened the door. It took a full minute to pull it open, so slowly did she pull. She controlled her breathing—long, deep breaths. Her body was relaxed. Her mind focused. She studied the contents of the cabinet. The medallion was on a shelf, lying on what must have been a felt bag. She was pleased to see it didn't have a chain. That would have complicated things.

She mentally rehearsed pulling the medallion from the cabinet. She tried to imagine which items she was likely to knock over. She imagined knocking something over. She imagined the golem reacting and her reaction to it. She glanced over her shoulder. The golem was motionless, a ridiculous statue stationed in the middle of a living room. She hoped it hadn't been ordered to turn around every half hour. If so, but she didn't follow that line of thought.

She rehearsed picking up the medallion once more, then reached into the cabinet. She drew out the medallion without making a sound. She tucked it into an empty pouch on her belt. She rose. Her knee popped. She froze and listened. To her the sound of her knee popping was echoing around the room. She controlled her breathing. She relaxed her muscles. She looked once more at the golem. It hadn't moved.

The thief turned and took a single step. She followed the same route across the living room that had led her to the cabinet. Once she was out of the living room she moved quickly. She made her way out of Kemnebi's pyramid the same way she'd gotten in. Of course, no one saw or heard her, no golems, no shadows, no one.

. . .

A wolf scratched its side with its hind leg, kicking like a rabbit. It sniffed the air. It lifted a front paw and licked the back of it. It settled down and watched Aleksandr's house. It wasn't the only watcher. Arazni had stationed three shadows outside. The wolf, Rhianna in wolf form, knew all about the shadows. She knew where they were. But they hadn't noticed her, so intently were they watching Aleksandr's home.

'Can that bastard be trusted?' Rhianna asked herself. She wasn't sure. That's why she was watching. But she was more worried than suspicious. She knew Aleksandr was in a dangerous spot. She still loved him and wanted to keep an eye on him. But, she told herself, if he betrayed them she wouldn't hesitate to destroy him. Her paw itched again and she gnawed it, her eyes on the mansion's front door.

She stopped gnawing her paw when she saw Moira, the Disowned, walking casually down the street. Moira turned and went to Aleksandr's door, knocked, and waited. Rhianna turned her ears toward the door. After a few minutes one of Aleksandr's servants opened the door and let Moira in. 'I don't like that.' Thought Rhianna.

. . .

"Forgive me," said Aleksandr. He had kept Moira waiting. "I wasn't expecting company."

Moira stood, walked to Aleksandr, and embraced him. He did not embrace her back but she didn't seem to notice. She hugged him a bit longer than was appropriate for the circumstances. When she parted she looked up into his face.

"I'm the one who should beg forgiveness."

Aleksandr motioned to the chairs nearby. They sat.

"Moira, things are a bit hectic. I—"

"I've been so worried about you," said Moira. "I heard you were tortured."

"Ah, yes, that, well—"

"It must have been horrible."

"Horrible? Yes," Aleksandr forced a laugh. "It *was* torture."

"So much has happened," said Moira. "So much, so fast."

"Yes."

"But you're still here." Moira smiled. "I knew you'd survive. You were always so smart about—politics."

"I went to a good school."

"Huh?"

"Cheliax."

"Oh, yes, that." Moira laughed. "You must be asking yourself why I'm here."

"The thought had crossed my mind."

"What happened before, you know, I didn't want that for us."

"Arazni?"

"Yes, what she did to us."

"The angel of death takes our dreams away."

"Huh?"

Aleksandr rubbed his forehead with his thumb and forefinger. "Moira, I—"

"Me too," said Moira. Of course, she had misunderstood him. He was trying to get rid of her, but she thought he was trying to express the inexpressible. "How is Kemnebi?"

"I can't say."

"Can't?" asked Moira. "Or won't?"

"I swore an oath to Queen Arazni. I'm focused on Geb, on Geb's future, not Geb's past."

"But he's out there, somewhere, isn't he?"

"Must be."

"Aren't you curious?"

"Curious?"

"About what's happened to him."

"I know what happened."

"I mean," Moira searched for the right words. "He was chancellor now he's—"

Aleksandr stood. "Moira, forgive me, please, but there is much I must attend—"

"Yes, of course." Moira stood. Once more she went to Aleksandr and wrapped her arms around him. "I used to believe this was my home, here," she looked up at him, "in your arms. Aleksandr, hold me."

"Moira—"

"Why won't you? Do you hate me?"

Aleksandr didn't answer, nor did he put his arms around her. She returned her head to his chest.

"I don't blame you if you do."

"Perhaps another time, Moira—"

"But beneath your hate," she looked up at him, "under your wounds, don't you retain some feelings for me?"

Aleksandr looked down into her face, his own face betraying no emotion.

"You're still so beautiful to me," said Moira. She rose up on her toes and kissed him. She pressed her tongue against his lips, but he recoiled.

"Moira."

She released him and composed herself. "Maybe we could—" She studied his face.

"When this is over," said Aleksandr, "let us speak. Perhaps we can find—"

"When what's over?"

"This," he paused, searching, "upheaval. This battle for supremacy."

"It *is* over, Aleksandr. You swore an oath—"

"Yes, of course, I meant—" He held out his hands. "It was good to see you again, Moira. If I wasn't so—" He chuckled. "I hope you'll return when my head is clear."

"Do you want to see me again, Aleksandr?"

Aleksandr faked a smile. He moved, ushering Moira to the door. She paused, rose up on her toes once more, and pecked him on his cheek.

"Maybe next time you'll kiss me back."

. . .

Hent-er-Neheh heard the scrape of linen-wrapped hands on stone and smiled to herself. She turned her head to the side and peered down the long, brazier-lit hall. Khamati could be seen at the far end, sliding forward on his belly like the serpent he was. He slithered the entire length, lying on his belly, pressing his forehead to the floor, when he reached her.

"What do you want, Khamati?"

"I have news—"

"Did your little eyes and ears out in the streets of Mechitar pick up some juicy bit of gossip?"

"No," said Khamati, breathing in the grit of the floor. "May I lift my face from the—"

"No. I like you like that—humble. Now tell me what you came to tell me."

"The Marquis Chevonde Garron came to my garden."

"Just now?" asked Hent-er-Neheh.

"Just now."

"You are unhurt?"

"He didn't want revenge."

"What did he want?"

"To kill you," said Khamati.

"Lift your head and say that again."

"To kill you."

"Why did he come to *you*, Khamati?"

Khamati smiled. "We can lay a trap for him—and Kemnebi."

"You may stand, nephew."

Khamati rose and dusted himself off. Hent-er-Neheh watched him.

"Kemnebi?" she asked.

"Chevonde promised to bring him. I guess he wants to kill you himself."

"What did you tell him?"

"I told him to come back in two nights—and to bring Kemnebi."

Hent-er-Neheh thought for a moment. "Do you think he's serious?"

"He's just crazy enough to do it."

"It's so unlike Kemnebi. He's patient, careful."

"That's what makes it such a good plan. It's unexpected."

Hent-er-Neheh studied her nephew but thought of Kemnebi.

"Unexpected, yes" she repeated. "You betrayed him once, nephew. Why would they trust you?"

"He doesn't trust me. He said so himself."

"Then why—"

"They're desperate and they know I'm—"

Hent-er-Neheh laughed. "They know you're," she waved her hand, "how you are."

"Yes."

"So we lay a trap for them?" She stood. "And I kill him." She looked at Khamati. "When I bring Kemnebi's head to Arazni she'll make me sole chancellor. I'll demand it."

"In two nights," Khamati smiled, "you'll get what you've longed for."

"And you, dear nephew, will have redeemed yourself."

. . .

Rhianna and Arazni's shadows watched Moira exit Aleksandr's mansion. The human necromancer, the exile from Galt, the exile from her own family, smiled to herself, turned, and walked the way she'd come.

Rhianna, so intent on taking out an enemy, momentarily forgot about Arazni's shadows. She turned, jogged to the next street over, and began to parallel Moira, spotting her between buildings.

One of Arazni's shadows, having been commanded to follow anyone who left Aleksandr's mansion, floated in the darkness mere yards behind Moira, unseen and unheard.

. . .

Chevonde did not particularly enjoy traveling as a wolf. It did, however, make tromping through the Axan Woods easier. He could have been a bat, but he liked that even less. As a bat he struggled to resist the impulse to eat bugs. The taste they left in his mouth was atrocious. Also, he was paranoid about owls, although he need not be.

He sniffed until he picked up Kemnebi's scent. He followed it to a dense patch of trees and bushes interspersed with boulders. At the center of this overgrowth was a small clearing. He nosed his way to it. Once in, he saw the glowing eyes of another wolf. He approached and both turned into men.

"I went to Khamati."

"What?" asked Kemnebi.

"I proposed that we kill Hent-er-Neheh."

Kemnebi studied Chevonde. "I didn't ask you to —"

"He said he would help us."

"Us?"

"Don't you want to kill her?"

"Yes, no, I never—"

"We must kill her."

Kemnebi shook his head. "Look at us. All I wanted to do was reform Geb. Now—"

"You can reform Geb when you rule it."

Kemnebi did not speak.

"We can't live as wolves," said Chevonde, "getting our blood from deer and wild boar. We can't hide in Rhianna's hunting lodge. She has a fine collection of hearty men and women who willingly offer us their necks, believing it a primal game, but we will consume them before we know it. When was the last time you fed?"

"When I first awoke," said Kemnebi. "I called a pack of wolves and drained—"

"And?"

"Horrible."

"Still hungry?"

Kemnebi did not answer.

"How many wolves does the Axan hold?" asked Chevonde. "How long before we're reduced to draining rats dry?"

Kemnebi watched the other vampire speak, but maintained silence.

"The only path forward is to kill Hent-er-Neheh, kill Eratosthenes, kill Arazni if we must, and take over. That begins with Khamati."

Kemnebi sighed. "He can't be trusted."

"Trust his lust for power."

"He'll betray us."

"Not this time," argued Chevonde. "Not if you're there. Not if you promise to kill Hent for him."

"Aleksandr begged me not to start a war we couldn't win," said Kemnebi. "I told him I must." He looked at Chevonde. "Cybele?"

"At Rhianna's. Shall I fetch her?"

Kemnebi nodded.

Chevonde changed shape, becoming a wolf, and found his way from the secluded spot. Kemnebi too changed into a wolf. He curled up in a natural divot in the earth, lowered his head between his paws, and contemplated the repercussions that stemmed from Chevonde's unexpected actions. He could not bring himself to think about the mistakes he had made and *their* repercussions.

. . .

Why Arazni persisted on using shadows mystified Aleksandr. They were too easy to elude. He wondered if perhaps she meant them as a distraction, something for him and his allies to focus on while remaining ignorant of the real danger.

He cracked a window on the second floor, in one of his many guest rooms. He went to his study and concluded some business, signing papers and paying bills, handing them off to his staff. That mundane work must still be done. If he were to survive he must see to his wealth. When he was finished he assumed gaseous form and slipped out the partially opened window. He rode the breeze from the Obari Ocean inland until he was out of Mechitar.

He changed into a bat, banked to his right, and flew to the Axan Wood. He found Kemnebi as Chevonde had left him, his chin between his paws. When Aleksandr entered the hidden clearing both men turned into their true forms.

"It's done, I took her oath."

Kemnebi nodded.

"She ordered me tortured, to determine if I retained any loyalty to you."

Kemnebi's eyes widened.

"Eratosthenes was to do it." Aleksandr shook his head. "He didn't."

"It wasn't to his advantage."

Aleksandr looked around at the confined space. "Why here? Rhianna's lodge is well defended." When Kemnebi didn't answer, Aleksandr continued. "Moira came around. It was obvious. I don't know if Arazni put her up to it or she thought of it herself."

"Can you reverse it?" asked Kemnebi. "Seduce her?"

"Of course. Who knows what it will be worth, but it's something. Where is Rhianna, Chevonde?"

Kemnebi did not answer.

"Sire? What is it?"

"Go from me, I wish to be alone."

"Do you plan on staying here?"

"Go, Aleksandr."

Aleksandr nodded and turned, preparing to resume his bat form, when he heard a rustling. He began a spell but Kemnebi stepped up and grabbed his shoulder, stopping him. Chevonde, as a wolf, came into the clearing. He sniffed at Aleksandr then turned into a man.

"Your timing is impeccable," he said to Aleksandr. "I have just returned from Rhianna's with Cybele." Aleksandr turned and looked at Kemnebi.

"Shall I go?" he asked, accusation in his tone.

Kemnebi shook his head and looked away.

"Why would you go?" asked Chevonde. He held the bejeweled skull before him.

"Oh, Cybele, drinker from the cup of Lythe, rower on the river Styx, do you not see Death before us?" He smiled and winked at Aleksandr, who looked back and forth between Chevonde and Kemnebi. "We seek the heart of Hent-er-Neheh. We seek to drive a dagger in it. Will Khamati lead us—"

Aleksandr reached out and plucked the skull from Chevonde's hands. "What?" He turned and looked at Kemnebi. "Are you serious?" Despite being pulled from its owner's grasp the skull began to spill its customary green mist. "Sire, do you want to kill Hent?"

"Of course," answered Chevonde.

"Aleksandr, I—we—" Mumbled Kemnebi.

Aleksandr spun to face Chevonde. "You put him up this, didn't you?"

"It's the next step," said Chevonde, reaching for Cybele. Aleksandr moved the mist-spilling skull out of Chevonde's reach.

"Sire, this is folly. Hent-er-Neheh is more powerful than ever."

"She's weaker," said Chevonde. "She's lost two of her own. Khamati will—"

Cybele interrupted. "Great is his ambition," she said, speaking of Khamati. "Great also is his cowardice. Steady are his words and actions, guided by both a bright and a dark star. Khamati leads all to a place of death."

Aleksandr threw the skull from him, with Chevonde barely catching it.

"A place of death. Hear that?"

"Hent-er-Neheh's death," said Chevonde.

"Your death!" yelled Aleksandr, pointing to Chevonde. He turned his finger to Kemnebi. "Your death."

"Have you forgotten that we're at war?" asked Chevonde.

"What would you have us do?" asked Kemnebi.

"Pause, regroup, think, plan. Let Hent-er-Neheh and Eratosthenes overstep their authority. Give them time to make enemies. Let them tug on the rod of rulership and weaken one another. Let them forget us. Then we can strike."

"A century from now?" asked Chevonde.

"If it takes that long, yes."

"In a hundred years," said Kemnebi. "There won't be enough of Geb left to fight over."

"Sire," said Aleksandr, pleading, "you can't honestly believe that Khamati would help you kill Hent-er-Neheh."

"Why not?" asked Chevonde.

Aleksandr turned to him. "It would leave only him and Khufnu. The only reason he can act as he does is because his aunt protects him. She acts as a check on all those who would destroy Khamati and incur her wrath." He turned to Kemnebi. "With her gone Khamati wouldn't survive. He would piss someone off, one of the liches, and he would be destroyed."

"Why is that our problem?" asked Chevonde.

"Khamati may be an ambitious coward but he's not stupid. He knows he needs Hent-er-Neheh. He's not going to help you destroy her. He's going to help *her* destroy you."

"It's worth the risk," said Chevonde. "If Khamati tries to turn on us we'll get out of there, like I did before."

"You would tempt fate twice?" asked Aleksandr.

"Please, my children, do not argue," said Kemnebi. He looked at Chevonde. "Aleksandr is right. So is Cybele. Khamati will betray us. We have to think of something else."

"We have to wait until—" Began Aleksandr.

Kemnebi spun to face his child. "We can't wait."

. . .

Moira was a block from her home when she heard the sounds of movement—quick movement—behind her. She spun and saw a large wolf, its fangs bared, rushing toward her. Despite its form she guessed correctly that it was not an actual wolf, but a vampire in that form. She began a spell that would halt her attacker in her tracks.

Her spell went off just as Rhianna leapt into the air. Rhianna slammed into Moira, knocking her onto her back. The spell did not work, Rhianna was too powerful. She stood on Moira's chest, growling into the necromancer's face.

Spellcasters, which is what Moira was, find it difficult to cast spells when a hundred and twenty pound, angry canine is standing on their chest. The best Moira could do was to try to roll to the side, get Rhianna off of her, and at the same time shield her face from any potential bite. However, Rhianna didn't go for Moira's face, she went for her throat.

The two tussled, Moira trying to fight off Rhianna, who now had a death grip on her throat. But the fight was lopsided. Rhianna was better equipped and far more experienced for that kind of fight. She sank her fangs into Moira's throat. She bit down hard and pulled. Moira could not cast. Moira could not dislodge the fangs from her neck.

When Moira was dead, Rhianna dragged her corpse into an alleyway. She left, licking Moira's blood from her fur, and went back to Aleksandr's mansion.

The shadow had seen everything but it did not truly comprehend the repercussions of what it had seen, otherwise it would have reported the murder immediately. Instead it flew back to its post outside of Alexander's mansion. It would report when it was summoned and told to report.

...

The next night.

Chevonde had never set foot in the Ebon Mausoleum. He had the distinct look of someone who didn't know his way around. He was easily spotted, made his enquiries, and was led to an empty classroom and told to wait.

He found the classroom delightful, for it was not truly empty. It was filled with the artifacts of necromancy; skulls, bones, grave-goods, all manner of gruesome spell components, and a healthy dose of macabre art to inspire learning. He was examining a tapestry when Eratosthenes entered.

"Ah, Co-Chancellor," said Chevonde, turning. Eratosthenes floated into the classroom. The door closed behind him. Chevonde approached and paused, expecting Eratosthenes to say something. Eratosthenes said nothing. Chevonde cleared his throat and continued. "How does it feel to be Co-Chancellor?" He emphasized the "co."

"Are you aware," said Eratosthenes, "that Queen Arazni, has called for your destruction?"

"Oh, yes, that." Chevonde waved a hand.

"Yet you walk into my school as if you were assured safety."

"Well, I figured by dropping your name no one would dare destroy me."

"What do you want?"

"It's not so much what I want," said Chevonde, "it's what I can give you."

Eratosthenes did not ask what that was.

Chevonde needed no prompting. "The chancellorship—all to yourself." When Eratosthenes did not speak, Chevonde continued. "How would you like to destroy Hent-er-Neheh?" He smiled. "I know where she'll be, what she'll be doing, and who she'll be with tomorrow night. She'll be waiting for me and Kemnebi to attack her, only we aren't going to."

"I fail to see how this is relevant to me."

"Because when she realizes we aren't coming she'll disband her little war party. That's when you will attack her. You see, she's laying a trap, you can turn that trap into an ambush."

A few moments of tense silence passed before Eratosthenes spoke. "Flee Mechitar, flee Geb, and never come back." With that Eratosthenes turned, the door opened, obeying his silent command, and he floated from the room.

Chevonde found his own way out.

. . .

Arazni was seated at the desk in Kemnebi's office inside the Cinerarium; her grave knights standing guard, one at the door, the others by the desk. Lilith, who had first went into Arazni's quarters and who was shocked not to find her there now made her way into Kemnebi's office. She had never seen it before. She was not only surprised to see Arazni seated at his desk, but to see a shelf-full of candles lit above her.

"Queen?"

"He kept candles," said Arazni. "Aren't vampires supposed to be afraid of fire?"

Lilith stepped up and looked at the candles. She looked down at Arazni. Arazni turned in his chair and motioned to a nearby bookshelf. "His law books." She motioned to the couch nearby and Lilith sat. "I've never wondered how anyone else thought, what their thought process was, until now." She looked at the couch. "Did he feed there? His victims draped over his thighs, held in his arms like a lover?" She glanced at Lilith. "Did he feed his blood thralls there, sitting as you're sitting this very moment, they kneeling at his feet?" She gazed out over the office. "He threw all this away. Why?"

"He said—"

Arazni looked at Lilith. "What he said made no sense." She reached out and ran her palm over the top of his desk. "Moira?"

"That's why I came, my Queen." Arazni looked at Lilith. "She can't be found."

"Can't be found?" asked Arazni.

"She's not at home," said Lilith. "None of the other Blood Lords have seen her. She's not at the Ebon Mausoleum or the Cathedral of Epiphenomena. She's gone."

"Get Aleksandr here. I want him on his knees!" screamed Arazni, but she caught herself. "No, not yet. First —" She concentrated, sending a mental command to the shadows watching his mansion. "Come, Mother," she said, and left Kemnebi's offices for her own chambers. In ten minutes the three shadows were hovering before her.

"Did you see Moira enter Aleksandr's house?" Arazni asked the shadows. They could not speak, having no anatomy, but they broadcast their thoughts, which she received. "Did you see her leave?" Again she received the answer. "Was Aleksandr with her? Has he left? Where did Moira go?" Arazni listened, her expression changing from annoyance to rage, as one of her shadows explained what it had seen.

She turned to Lilith, anger apparent on her face. "She's dead!"

"Queen?"

"Moira, killed by a fucking wolf!" Arazni turned and faced the three shadows. "Damn these worthless things!" She began to cast a spell. Her grave knights did not interfere, nor did Lilith. The shadow who had witnessed Moira's death, and who had not reported it until now, not being intelligent enough to realize it was in danger, waited before its executioner.

Five orbs of blue-white magic grew from the tips of Arazni's fingers. She pointed at the shadow and the orbs shot off, now resembling mini-comets. They made fantastic turns, not shooting straight, but arcing wildly, before slamming into the shadow. It broke up into myriad pieces before disappearing completely. "You two, return to Aleksandr's mansion. Follow anyone who leaves. And if anyone should kill them, report it immediately!"

"Moira's dead?" asked Lilith. "Not a wolf. It must have been a vampire."

"Rhianna! It was Rhianna." Arazni began to pace. "What am I doing anyway? Waiting? Watching? What a fool I've been!" She turned to one of her grave knights. "Go to Aleksandr's house and kill him." The grave knight turned and began to walk toward the door. She looked over the remaining four. "Go to Rhianna's hunting lodge and kill everything you find there." The four grave knights began to follow the first. "Wait!" screamed Arazni. The grave knights turned to face her. Lilith watched as Arazni calmed, then smiled. "She's still there, that flea-ridden dog, watching her former love." She walked to her bed and sat. She looked at Lilith. "I've been a weak fool, Mother."

"Queen, you've been cautious—"

"No." Arazni laughed. "I should have struck him down right there, in that meeting. What did I do instead? I begged Geb to let me act." She rose. "I let Kemnebi gather his allies. I let him act against me." She shook her head. "Not any more, Mother."

"What are you going to do, Queen?"

"I'm going to capture Rhianna and execute her—with you. I want everyone in Mechitar to see her die."

"What about Aleksandr? What about—"

"Rhianna first." Arazni smiled. "Once Aleksandr sees her die he'll know better than to raise his hand against me." She looked at Lilith. "As for Kemnebi. Let him come." She thought for a moment. "We must prepare, Mother. We can't let her slip through our fingers."

"What if she isn't watching him? What if—"

"She's there. I can *feel* her in my city."

. . .

The following day.

Those who are obsessed with the dark art of necromancy rarely follow the bright, colorful school of illusion. They see no use for mesmerizing their victims when they could wither their limbs or make them rot from the inside out. Why trick someone with a spell of light and sound when you could simply kill them and raise their corpse to serve you?

It is because necromancers think so little of illusionist that they discount what the school of illusion magic can do. Illusion is the school of altering perception, or of making honest perception impossible.

Few students or teachers in the Ebon Mausoleum are awake during the day. The undead prefer to be active at night, under the cover of darkness, and the living students have acclimated to this nocturnal existence. During the daylight hours the halls of Ebon Mausoleum are empty and silent. By all appearances they remained that way, thanks to the school of illusion.

The Nexian hit squad made their way through the Ebon Mausoleum, unseen and unheard, found the staircase that led to the chambers beneath the school, dispelled the wards and magical traps that protected those below, and went down, pausing on the stairs. Here they listened, for liches did not sleep, and they had no intention of running across one of those. It was a lich-in-the-making that they sought.

They heard nothing and advanced. Once in the circular chamber they paused again, wary of spells that had eluded them, or of undead that lay in wait. But liches are arrogant, especially the liches of the Whispering Way. They never imagined that anyone would dare to violate their chamber. Their arrogance was yet another weakness.

The Nexians fanned out, listening at every door. One of them read from a scroll, her voice hushed. When the spell was completed she pressed her forehead against the nearest door, peering inside with the aid of a clairvoyance spell. She had to repeat this process for every door, using multiple scrolls. What she saw in Trevedic's room alarmed her but she had to dismiss the disturbing vision in order to continue.

This was nerve-wracking for the Nexians. Not only did it take time, it left them exposed. They were invisible, yes, but they were making noise and, what was worse, some undead could sense the living. Liches had this ability. But they had to be looking. If they were bent over their books or completing some complicated ritual they may not notice the six living beings just outside their doors. But then again, they just might. It was an incredible risk, but the Nexians were prepared to take it, and had.

Finally, they located Dagillus, the one they sought. The wizard using clairvoyance turned her "eye" within the room. Dagillus was lying in a stone slap made somewhat more comfortable with thick furs. He slept on his back, furs pulled to his chin. A torch, fed not by resin, but by magic, filled the small room with soft light, just enough to see by. There were no undead guards. Dagillus was alone.

The Nexian wizard allowed the clairvoyance spell to end. She whispered and the team assembled outside of Dagillus's door, feeling for one another to know how each was positioned. The wizard cast another spell, this one from memory. Again, she kept her voice as quiet as she could. The spell revealed that Dagillus's door was enchanted with protective runes. These she dispelled.

When this was done another of the team approached the door, knelt, and produced a black leather wallet. None saw the wallet open nor the pick and tension rod being pulled. These too were invisible. However, they all saw the lock turn and the door being pushed open. The pick, tension rod, and leather wallet were put away.

Dagillus's room was too small to admit the entire team. The lock-picker and the leader—the wizard who had risked them all with her whispered casting—remained in the circular chamber. The other team members, two women and two men, stepped into the room. They shut the door.

With a whispered command the fur blanket was yanked off of Dagillus. One of the men grabbed his ankles and held them tight. In doing so he seemed to materialize out of thin air. The two women threw themselves over Dagillus, pinning his arms—two bodies leaping out from nothing to become visible as they flopped against him. The remaining man pressed down on Dagillus's forehead, keeping it stationary. He too, his invisibility spell ended by his aggressive action, was now visible. With the other hand he drew a razor-sharp blade over Dagillus's throat. But something went terribly wrong. The edge of the blade skated across Dagillus's flesh as if it were stone. Dagillus opened his eyes and, his mouth not being covered, screamed.

The two Nexians in the circular chamber heard the scream even through the closed door. The wizard immediately began to cast a spell, the thief produced a short sword and a dagger and prepared to defend the wizard. They prayed that the team would emerge from the room and that they could run from the Ebon Mausoleum. When another of the doors opened they knew that wasn't going to happen.

Cassius Allius, always alert to the danger loud noises posed to his delicate experiments, opened his door and looked out. He was ready to scold whomever had pierced the quiet with their scream but he saw no one. Even though he didn't see the Nexians with his eyes, he sensed them. He reached down to his belt, yanked free a glass bottle, and tossed it across the chamber. The Nexian finished her spell just as the bottle broke against the wall behind her. She and her teammate found themselves in both an anti-magic field—the result of the spell—and a bank of yellowish green vapors.

The spell suppressed the poisonous effects of the vapors, something Cassius immediately noticed. The screaming still came from behind the closed door to Dagillus's room. Inside he was struggling to free himself from his attackers. His stone-like skin, the result of a spell he cast upon himself each night before he slept, had kept their blades from hurting him, but he was still pinned. His spell, now inside of the anti-magic field, was gone, but he had fought hard enough to free an arm and grab the wrist of the knife's controller.

Another door opened and Ólchobar Yevan appeared. He looked to Cassius, looked to the growing cloud of poison, and sensed the two life forces within. He also saw them. The anti-magic field had cancelled their invisibility spell. Cassius saw them, too, and both liches knew the two strangers were unwelcome company.

"They're suppressing magic," warned Cassius.

Ólchobar nodded and began to advance toward the two Nexians. Even though they were practiced agents, and had faced dangerous foes in the past, the sight of two liches unnerved them both. They knew they were in dire straights. A lich relies primarily on his or her magic but they were far from neutered without it. They could paralyze with a touch. The Nexian wizard, her magic now useless, drew her dagger with one hand and banged on the door behind her with the other.

"We have to get out of here!" she screamed.

"He's still alive," said the man attempting to slit Dagillus's throat.

"Abort! Damn it! Abort!" screamed the Nexian wizard.

. . .

"Who are you?" asked Eratosthenes.

The Nexian wizard's corpse was lying in the center of the circular chamber, surrounded by the liches of the Whispering Way, and Dagillus, their intended victim. The corpses of the others lay scattered about. The liches had paralyzed them and used their own weapons to slit their throats. They didn't need to keep them alive to question them. In fact, they preferred they be dead.

"Brook Lethbridge," said the corpse, its voice pained.

"Who sent you?"

In halting words, as if fighting not to answer, the corpse said, "Iranez of the Orb."

The liches looked at one another.

"Nex?" asked Dagillus. He was still in his night robe and was unconsciously touching his throat. He hadn't felt the blade, or really even the grip of those who held him, until his spell was cancelled. All at once he felt everything and he knew he was in danger. He tried not to show his shock. Nor did he dare to imagine what his fellow Whispering Way adherents would have done with his corpse.

"Why did Iranez of the Orb send you to assassinate Dagillus?" asked Eratosthenes.

"To sow discord within Geb."

"Where did you get this medallion?" asked Eratosthenes.

"Stolen," said the corpse, "from Kemnebi's home."

"Did you intend to plant this medallion on Dagillus's corpse?"

"Yes."

"Why?" asked Eratosthenes.

"To sow discord within Geb."

Masgava, who was currently examining the medallion, handed it to Ashoka. He spoke to the group. "From ancient Osirion. The cult birthed by Geb and his relatives—the mummies."

"Pathetic," said Ashoka, who handed the medallion to Neacal Aodhan. "Does Iranez believe we would fall for such a ruse?"

"Are there other agents from Nex within Geb?" asked Eratosthenes.

The corpse made a choking sound but did not answer.

"She fights," said Ólchobar. "There must be other agents."

Eratosthenes repeated the question. Again, the corpse held back the answer.

"There are five other corpses to question," said Masgava. "Will they all be as strong?"

. . .

That night.

Khamati sat by the gurgling pool in his garden, trying not to look into the darkness to his right. Seated in the shadows under the date palms was his aunt, Hent-er-Neheh. She was seated between the twin Taotiehs, brought from her pyramidal home. These were not the only help-mates she had brought. An emaciated mummy with a crocodile's head stood nearby.

Both Hent-er-Neheh and Khamati had emptied their private stores of magical items and artifacts in order to prepare themselves for the battle with Kemnebi, Chevonde, and whomever else would show up. They were in full power. But they were passive, waiting, and they hated that.

Neither spoke. Khamati watched the leaves and flowers of his garden move on the breeze. He studied his mummified pets. Anything to keep his mind from his aunt's impatience; which, he could feel coming off of her like steam. The hours passed. The moon traveled in its arc across the heavens, shining through the palm leaves above.

"Master?" Came a whispered voice. It was communicated across Mechitar via spell, reaching Khamati's ear. "No sign of them."

"Nephew?"

"There's still time," said Khamati.

"Wasted time," said Hent-er-Neheh.

Khamati tensed as her footsteps neared. She appeared at the edge of the clearing. "I do not fault you, nephew." Hent-er-Neheh began across the clearing toward Khamati's home. She would take the tunnel beneath to her own. Her Taotiehs followed, as did the cursed king, the crocodile-headed mummy.

"Damn you, Chevonde," Khamati growled under his breath.

. . .

A servant was waiting for her return. He was a type of intelligent skeleton, with a modicum of freewill. When Hent-er-Neheh climbed the stairs he met her at the top, bowing deeply. "A visitor, Chancellor."

"I'm in no mood for—"

The skeleton rose. "A devil."

Hent-er-Neheh paused and studied her servant.

The skeleton made an approximation with his hands. "A small one."

The imp, a devil that would look quite fearsome, if weren't the size of a cat standing on its hind legs, was perched on the arm of one of the chairs at the end of the hall. When Hent-er-Neheh approached it bowed.

"Your master?" asked Hent-er-Neheh.

"Ulrich Grigson," answered the imp, "of Yled, is my master."

Hent-er-Neheh tried to place the name but couldn't. "What can I do for Ulrich Grigson?"

"My master asks nothing, Chancellor," said the imp, who was the wizard's familiar. "He only wishes you to be apprised of the destruction of the Blood Lord Khufnu. He is a relative of yours, my master believes."

"What?"

"Some burnt remains were found in Yled. An investigation, led by my master, who is authorized to carry out such duties, revealed the remains to belong to Khufnu."

Hent-er-Neheh passed the imp and sat.

"My master regrets that such a tragedy has occurred. He sends his condolences."

Hent-er-Neheh studied the imp. "What happened?"

"There were no witnesses," said the imp. "However, there is ample evidence that he was attacked. He was shot with arrows and exposed to magical and mundane fire. My master endeavors to learn more and is doing so now, or else he would have come in person."

"Is that all?"

The imp searched the mummy's face, curious about her and her response. "There was a mark painted on the door of a nearby house. The house is being investigated."

"What kind of mark?" asked Hent-er-Neheh.

"A skull whose mouth is gagged."

"Damn it!" cried Hent-er-Neheh. The imp, used to violent outburst, watched but otherwise did not react.

"My master enquires if this symbol has any meaning to you. Any information the Chancellor wishes to supply will undoubtedly aid his investigation."

Hent-er-Neheh looked at the imp. "No."

"If I may be of any further service, Chancellor?"

"Return to your master and tell him to keep me apprised."

"Yes, Chancellor." The imp bowed then launched itself from the chair's arm. He flew down the hall, his wings beating rapidly.

"Damn you, Eratosthenes," growled Hent-er-Neheh. "Damn you to Hell."

Going Away

Mechitar, Geb, Erastus, 4711

Arazni was lying on Kemnebi's couch, balancing an enchanted wand on the tip of one finger.

"Will it work, Mother?" She looked from the wand to Lilith, who stood at Kemnebi's desk, looking down at an open spell book.

In theory, yes, but your phylactery's still a question."

"Tell me why it will fail, Mother."

Lilith looked to Arazni. "I can't predict exactly how the anchoring to your phylactery will interfere."

Arazni examined her other hand, holding it aloft. She hated the color of her flesh. She turned it, examining the scars. For a moment she saw her hand as it had been long ago, whole, filled with the warm hues of life. She saw her hand held in Aroden's. She clenched her hand into a fist, banishing those useless and painful images. "If I can animate this broken vessel—" She unclenched her fist and lowered her hand to her side. "What else, Mother?"

"If her will is strong, she may resist—"

"She's a petulant child," Arazni sneered. "She's not as strong as I am."

"Of that I have no doubt."

"Besides, her will can be weakened." Arazni looked to Lilith, winked and smiled, then turned her attention back to her still precariously balanced wand. "Will it work, Mother?"

"Yes, Queen."

"What's it going to feel like, I wonder?"

"For you or her?"

Arazni laughed. She rose, grabbing her wand before it tumbled from her fingertip. She walked to

Kemnebi's desk chair, bent, flipped it onto its back and snapped off one of the legs. She tossed the leg to the nearest grave knight. "Sharpen it," she commanded. "Mother?" Lilith turned to Arazni. "I want you to stake me," she pointed to her chest, above her heart. "Here." Lilith nodded. Arazni threw her arms around Lilith's neck and rested her head on Lilith's shoulder. "Oh, Mother."

"Yes, Queen?"

"Do you think he'll be watching?"

"Who?"

"Geb."

"Geb sees all, Queen."

"I want him to be proud of me," said Arazni.

"He is."

. . .

The Ulfen grave knight walked alone down the avenue until he could see Aleksandr's mansion. He stopped, standing in the middle of the street, scanning the darkness. A slight breeze blew his long hair about the fur on his shoulders. He detected movement and saw the moon's light reflected in a pair of eyes low to the ground. He carried his claymore over his shoulder, the blade partially buried in the fur of his cloak. He watched the eyes watching him. Once he was certain he was seen he continued, stopping before Aleksandr's door. He stood there, facing Aleksandr's door, his back turned to the wolf that watched him.

. . .

Rhianna watched the grave knight. She recognized him. She knew the grave knights never left Arazni's side, unless she sent them to accomplish a particular task, and that was rare. She wondered if the grave knight had been sent to kill Aleksandr. She, the Queen, no doubt knew Moira was dead. For a moment Rhianna panicked, thinking that Arazni had blamed Aleksandr and was now intent on revenge.

She was so intent on the grave knight that she failed to notice the fog that crept into her hiding place. The fog seeped into her nose and mouth. It was odorless and tasteless but not without harm. It began to seep into her brain, too, fogging her mind. She felt her focus weaken, her mind blank, and shook her head to clear it. She returned her gaze to the grave knight. 'Why are you just standing there?'

Rhianna heard movement behind her and turned. She saw a second grave knight step out into the open, sword and shield at the ready, staring at her. She at once changed into her human form and drew her sword. She glanced at the Ulfen grave knight. He was still facing the door to Aleksandr's mansion but a third grave knight now stepped into view between the Ulfen and her.

Her first instinct was to fight. But three grave knights? She was confident, maybe even arrogant, but she wasn't foolish. But, despite the danger of the situation, her instincts were dulled. She was having trouble thinking. The fog that surrounded her had thoroughly penetrated her mind. She couldn't seem to focus.

She heard a spell's chant and spun. The grave knight was now blocking another with his shield. Rhianna recognized the caster—Lilith. She had heard the spell before, and recently, but her addled mind couldn't place it. Still, she knew she was in danger.

First three grave knights and now a lich.

. . .

Further down the street, hundreds of feet from Rhianna, but still able to see her, Arazni was casting a spell. Two of her grave knights stood next to her, guarding her. Arazni had been casting the rather involved spell since the Ulfen had caught Rhianna's attention. So long as

Rhianna didn't break line of sight the spell would complete.

The problem was Rhianna's ability to turn into gas and become both insubstantial and nearly impossible to see. Arazni had thought of a solution. First, the mind fog, to slow Rhianna's reactions, to dull her honed warrior's instinct. Lilith had cast that. Now came the master stroke. A crystal rested in Arazni's right palm. As she cast her spell, light gathered inside the crystal. Arazni knew what the light was. It took all of her self-control not to laugh, for she realized the spell was working.

. . .

Rhianna knew standing to fight was suicide. She feigned a charge at Lilith in the hopes of upsetting her spell. It didn't work. The spell went off. Rhianna felt a necromantic force grip her. Lilith's spell was simple but effective. It halted undead in their tracks, paralyzed them, locking them in the grip of necromantic energy. Kemnebi had used the same spell to paralyze Latitia. Rhianna gleefully beheaded the Daughter of Urgathoa. Now the same spell threatened to paralyze her.

Rhianna had shrugged off such a spell before. But this spell was cast by a powerful lich. Add to that the magical fog that slowed her mind and weakened her will and the spell was that much harder to repel. Rhianna thought of Aedha's death. She thought of the danger Aleksandr was certainly in should she fail to resist. These were the two most powerful emotional anchors at her command, and with her emotions so riled up she fought off the spell. Little did she know that the spell itself was a feint. If it worked, so much the better, but it wasn't the main attack. That had already begun.

Rhianna spun away from Lilith and turned her focus to changing her form, but something was wrong. She felt weak. She felt disembodied, as if she had not only lost command of her thoughts but of her limbs as well. She heard her sword rap against the cobblestones at her feet and looked down in amazement. She felt light, airy, as if she were turning to mist, but when she looked at her hands nothing had changed.

She looked up and saw something beyond her experience. It appeared that the entire world was becoming encased in rose-hued crystal. She tried to will herself to become a cloud of gas, to flee, but nothing happened. Instead the rose-hued crystal became more and more solid. It began to enclose her, blotting out the moon and stars, then the buildings in the distance. The rose-hued wall rushed toward her.

As Rhianna watched in horror all of Mechitar, all of existence, was swallowed by the rose-hued crystal. Soon it was all she could see. She tried to bend down and scoop up her sword but when she did she realized she didn't have a body to command. There was no sword, no hand. There was only the rose-hued semi-transparent walls that surrounded her. It was as if she were a bug encased in amber.

. . .

Lilith knew the halt undead spell had failed. Rhianna spun and began the other way. Then she stopped. Her sword fell from her hand. She looked at her hand then at her sword. She turned and glanced behind her, turned again and looked away at the horizon. She raised her hands, as if shielding her face against something rushing at her. Then she dropped her arms and stood still. Finally she turned to face Lilith.

"It worked!" Arazni, who was now inhabiting Rhianna's body, laughed.

Lilith and the two grave knights approached. The Ulfen stayed outside of Aleksandr's door. "Is she—"

"Her soul is trapped," said Arazni. She looked over her captive form. "Her body is mine." She looked up at Lilith. "Oh, I wish I could command her powers; turn into a wolf or a bat. Oh, I wish I could feast on blood and make love like she does." Her laughing stopped. "I suppose I'll have to accept a stake in the heart."

"Here?" asked Lilith.

"No, Mother, in Kemnebi's office. It's more poetic that way. Come." She spun and jogged off. "She's muscular. I like it." She stopped. "Pick up her sword." She commanded to the grave knight closest to it. "I'm going to run home." She turned to her grave knights. "See if you can keep up." With that she bolted off. Her grave knights rushed to keep up. The one carrying her empty body—empty as a result of the spell—lagging far behind.

. . .

"Look, Mother," commanded Arazni. She was doing a hand stand. "She's so strong, so balanced." She dropped her feet and stood. "Oh, to have a physique like this."

"The spell won't last forever, Queen."

"If only one of those students from the Ebon Mausoleum were here," said Arazni. "What I would do to him."

"Queen."

"Yes, you're right," said Arazni. She went to the grave knight who held Rhianna's crystal prison. She looked into the crystal as it sat in the knight's palm. "Can you see her in there, Mother?"

"I see light."

"That's her." Arazni laughed. "Do you see your body, little vampire soul? Do you realize what I've done to you? It's called the magic jar spell. Us liches know all about it." She looked to Lilith. "Mother, this is glorious!" Arazni spun, waving her arms over her head. She stopped, her expression serious. "It's time, Mother. I want to feel it go in." She reached up and tapped her chest. She turned to one of her grave knights. "Get this armor off of me."

Once the armor was off, Arazni went to Lilith. "Mother," she said, emotion evident in her voice. She reached down and took Lilith's wrist in her hands. She lifted it until the stake Lilith held was over her heart, the point pressing into her—Rhianna's—flesh. She stared for a long time at the stake.

"Can you do it, Mother? Can you drive this stake into my heart?"

"Queen, it isn't—" Lilith stopped speaking because Arazni had started to cry tears of blood.

"They can cry, Mother," said Arazni, reaching up and wiping a tear from her—Rhianna's—cheek. "Just like me."

Lilith started to pull her hand back in preparation for staking Rhianna but Arazni held onto her wrist with emotion-fueled strength.

"Mother, when I die—"

"You aren't going to die—"

"When I die," continued Arazni, "I'll go before her again."

"Who—"

"She'll judge me." Arazni stared into Lilith's eyes but she was seeing something else. She was seeing Pharasma in her celestial throne. She had seen her before, had been judged and found worthy. But she knew the second judgment would be harsh, unforgiving. "I have to kill him," she said, her voice a whisper. "I have to kill Kemnebi. He wants to kill me. If he kills me—" Her eyes flashed. "Mother!"

"Queen?"

"He can't kill me! Mother! He can't—"

Arazni was growing wild. She gripped Lilith's wrist with all of Rhianna's borrowed strength.

"Mother, I can't go—I have to live forever. I can never—"

Lilith yanked her hand free, pulled it back, then slammed the wooden stake into Rhianna's unprotected heart. Rhianna froze, falling backward into a grave knight's arms. The grave knight laid her on the floor. She was a stiff as the wooden stake that pierced her heart.

Arazni, whose body was lying on the couch, gasped and sat upright. She looked down while at the same time bringing her hands up to her chest, just over her heart. She felt her chest as if she expected a stake to protrude from it. She turned and looked at Lilith, a questioning, hurt expression on her face. She realized her emotions were wrong and looked down at Rhianna's paralyzed form. She leapt up from the couch and grabbed the crystal from the grave knight's palm. She studied it and looked up at Lilith.

"The light's gone."

"Her soul has returned to her body."

Arazni studied Rhianna. She walked to her and knelt, reaching out to comb the hair from Rhianna's eyes. "It's almost a shame to destroy something so fine."

"How are you going to do it, Queen?"

Arazni bent over Rhianna. She brought her own face close to the vampire's, looking into Rhianna's eyes, which were stuck open, seeing all, unable to look away. Arazni whispered, speaking to Rhianna. "We're going to watch the sun rise together." She bent lower and kissed Rhianna on the lips. "I loved being you. But now I have to destroy you." She looked at Lilith, a mischievous grin spreading on her face. "Get Araminta. Get me the Carnival of Death." She laughed. "We're going to throw a hell of a bash for our guest." She looked back down at Rhianna, sudden, unexpected tears falling from her cheeks to Rhianna's. Her salted tears of water mixing with Rhianna's tears of blood. Her voice spoke of sadness and loss. "A going away party. Going away forever."

Powerless

Various locations, Mechitar, Geb, Erastus, 4711

Elana was in the midnight bazaar, searching for onyx. A spell used to create undead required onyx as one of its spell components. With so many necromancers in Geb craving onyx, it was a pain to find. It was one of Saskia's errands, given to her assistant to run. It was ill-timed, but Saskia was thinking of her own protection. One mohrg wasn't going to be enough.

Elana felt a tug on one finger and glanced down but saw nothing. The tug continued and she allowed herself to be led. The door to the pawn shop seemed to unlock and open itself. Elana stepped in and the door shut. Xylia appeared. She hurried to the back room, Elana following.

"It's over."

Over?" Elana asked. "What do you mean?"

Xylia began to dig through cabinet drawers, gathering hidden valuables from false bottoms. "We tried to assassinate Dagillus." She looked at Elana. "It wasn't my idea. It came from on high." She slammed a drawer. "It was a damn stupid—" She stopped and looked at Elana. "We lost—" She looked as if she were going to cry but she stopped her emotions from overwhelming her. "The entire team."

"Dagillus killed—"

"The liches." Xylia went to another hiding spot and began to dig through bolts of fabric, pulling scrolls from them, tossing the scrolls into a pile. "They know all about us, they have to." She looked at Elana. "You're probably compromised. We all are."

"What does—"

"Back to Nex. We'll all take different routes, some overland, some by sea. You'll—"

Elana rushed to the gnome and grabbed her shoulder. "Back to Nex?"

"Yes."

"I can't."

Xylia studied Elana. "What do you mean you can't? It's over. The Whispering Way—"

"Kemnebi needs me."

"Kemnebi needs—" Xylia shook her head. "Do you hear what you're saying?"

"He needs me and I need him."

"Damn it, I told you—" Xylia bent her head and sighed. "We've been ordered to pull out of Geb." She looked at Elana. "All of us. It's over, don't you understand? Kemnebi lost."

"No, he's—"

Xylia reached up and knocked Elana's hand from her shoulder. "You're a damn fool! Where is he? Out in the Axan? What's he going to do out there? Huh? Drain the rabbits dry?"

"He—"

"What? He what?"

"He has a plan," said Elana.

"So did we," said Xylia. "So does every one." She resumed her search. "Our new plan is to get out of here before we get ourselves killed and raised as undead."

"I'm staying."

"Like hell you are!"

"I'm going to Kemnebi. He—"

"I have tactical command," growled Xylia. "I say you return to Nex and that's what you're going to do. Understand?"

"Give me the earrings and necklace," said Elana. "I want to talk to Master Castelli."

"It's too dangerous," said Xylia. "The liches are looking for us."

"I have a mission," said Elana, kneeling so she was face-to-face with the much shorter gnome. "It's not too late."

"He's fresh out of friends," said Xylia.

"It's not over." Elana said. "There is so much he can do now. He's free of restraints. Don't you see? He can act. He's got Aleksandr in the city. He's got Rhianna. He's got —" Elana read Xylia's expression. "What?"

"Rhianna—" Xylia shook her head.

"What?"

"She's done."

"What do you mean she's done? What are you talking about?"

"Arazni, Lilith, the grave knights—they got her, outside of Aleksandr's. We were watching."

"What? They—"

Xylia put her hands on Elana's shoulders. "That's what I'm trying to tell you. It's over. Now, listen, there is a skiff just north of the harbor. It's going to take you out. You didn't screw up your mission. It's not your fault. But the —"

Elana stood. "My mission isn't over."

"Yes it is."

Elana started toward the door. "I've got to tell Kemnebi about Rhianna."

"Elana," said Xylia. She sighed and reached up to take off the enchanted earrings. "Damn stubborn—you're going to need these."

Elana stepped up and held out her hand. Xylia placed the earrings and the necklace in her open palm. "You're brave or stupid or both."

"I'm in love." Elana felt tears well up in her eyes. She hadn't said the words out loud until now but she knew. She'd been in love since Saskia dragged her to him.

Xylia chuckled. "Love is it? So it's both." She closed Elana's fingers around the jewelry. "It's suicide, you know?"

"I've got powerful friends."

"Saskia? Kemnebi?"

Elana nodded.

Xylia glanced at the pile of mundane and enchanted goods. "I'll get you a big bag to put all that crap in."

"Thank you, Xylia."

"Shit lot of good it's going to do you against the Whispering Way."

"I'm not saying thank you for that." The two spies looked at one another. "Thank you for letting me stay."

"Officially speaking—you disobeyed a direct order from your superior." Xylia smiled, but it was edged with sadness. "Unofficially, I hope he's worth it."

"He is."

"He's a damn vampire," said Xylia. "Don't forget that."

"I won't."

Xylia found a shoulder bag and began to stuff the scrolls and other items into it. She lifted the strap. Elana bent and Xylia placed it over her shoulder. "You'd better get back to one of them, Saskia or Kemnebi, and stay close."

Elana nodded and rose. She started to leave but paused. "Oh, do you have any onyxes around here? For the create undead—"

"Get the hell out of here."

"Right."

"Elana, wait," called Xylia. Elana turned. Xylia stepped to her, taking a ring from her finger. She held it out. Elana extended her hand and Xylia slipped the ring onto her pinkie finger. "To foil scrying." She looked up into Elana's eyes. "You'll be out in the cold. Do you know what that means?" Elana nodded. "Damn it," said Xylia, "if he doesn't love you back—" Elana smiled, opened the door, and disappeared into Mechitar's darkness.

. . .

Elana was running to Saskia's tower when a cloaked figure stepped out before her, wand at the ready. She slid to a halt and was about to begin casting when the figure reached up and yanked back the hood.

"Wamukota?"

"Can you be trusted?"

"What are you—" Elana studied the blood thrall's face, reading his emotions. He was distraught. "Yes." She walked to him and placed a hand on his wrist to gently lower the wand. "Why did you ask me that?"

Wamukota glanced behind him, at Saskia's tower. He turned to Elana. "They grabbed Rhianna."

"How did you—"

"Word has gone out. There is to be an execution at dawn." He lowered his wand, letting the magic fade. "Everyone is talking about it. Every intelligent undead in Mechitar has been ordered to attend." He looked toward the Cinerarium. "They're throwing a damn party as we speak." He looked at Elana. "I'm surprised you aren't there."

"I didn't know. I was out—"

Wamukota pulled his hood back up. "He doesn't know yet—about Rhianna."

"Kemnebi?"

"Yes," said Wamukota, "at least, I doubt he knows. Unless Aleksandr or Chevonde has gotten word to him."

"What are you doing in Mechitar?"

"Looking for you."

"Why?" asked Elana.

"Kemnebi is worried. He sent me." He glanced at Saskia's tower. "He said you might be here."

"They're going to execute Rhianna?"

Wamukota glanced at the moon. "In a couple of hours." He looked at Elana from under his hood. "By the river." He nodded that way. "They're building a platform."

"Can we stop it?"

Wamukota scoffed. "I hope no one tells him until it's over. Otherwise, he might try. It will be the death of them both."

"The party. Can't we crash the party? Rescue her?"

Wamukota shook his head.

"We have to do something!"

"What, girl? What could *we* do?"

"With Kemnebi, Chevonde, and all those warriors at the lodge. We—" Elana began to cry.

"No, there's nothing we can do now." Wamukota reached out and put his arm around Elana. "Come on, we can't just stand here until dawn. It isn't safe."

"Where—"

"Aleksandr will know what to do."

. . .

Aleksandr looked shocked when Wamukota and Elana entered his study, even though one of his trusted staff led them in and was about to announce them. Tension and emotion were clear on Aleksandr's face. He rose and met them as they crossed the room.

He wasn't alone, two other vampires were present, Ridwan and Branca. They'd been alarmed upon hearing of Rhianna's pending execution. Of course, they weren't expected to attend. Arazni did not expect them to witness the sunrise. What they worried about was what Rhianna's execution meant. They feared it was open season on their kind. They'd come to Aleksandr to seek his advice.

Neither Ridwan nor Branca recognized Wamukota or Elana. They studied the new comers. Aleksandr did not introduce them. He turned to his fellow vampires.

"This too shall pass," he said. "Continue on as you have been—"

"Will we be next?" asked Branca.

"No," said Aleksandr. "Queen Arazni is not angry with all the vampires under her rule," he glanced at Wamukota, "only some of them." He went to the two vampires, taking them by their arms and leading them to the door, "see to your personal security, as always." He looked into their faces. "And hunt carefully."

"Who shall get her seat?" asked Ridwan.

"I cannot say," answered Aleksandr. "Please, the dawn approaches and there is much still to be done." He nodded to his staff, who led the two vampires out. Once they were gone and the door was shut he turned to Wamukota and Elana.

"You know?" asked Wamukota.

Aleksandr nodded. He took both by the arm and led them to chairs. He resumed his seat.

"Have you told him?" Wamukota asked.

Aleksandr glanced up but looked down and shook his head.

"Why not?" asked Elana.

"He would try to—"

"Save her," finished Wamukota.

"Yes," said Aleksandr.

"Are you just going to let her die?" asked Elana.

"I'm trying to think of something." Aleksandr rose and began to pace his study. "Some way to get her out of there or stop the—" He fell silent. "But I haven't been able to think of anything."

Elana leaned forward. "I know you both think he'll overreact but we have to tell him." She looked at Aleksandr, who was looking at her. "Maybe he can think of something."

Aleksandr sat. "Dawn is in a little over two hours. It takes about twenty five minutes to fly to Rhianna's lodge. I could contact him via spell but he would have to fly here, unless he can transport by spell. He doesn't often keep such spells in his memory; although, he might have a scroll for teleportation. At any rate, we would have to fight our way to Rhianna, free her, fight our way out, and get to the safety of our coffins before dawn." He held out his hands. "Even if we could do all that, they, Arazni, Lilith, Eratosthenes, Hent-er-Neheh, and all the rest, don't have to sleep during the day. They could search for us, probably find us, and destroy us. We're helpless during the day."

"But—" Protested Elana.

"It isn't cowardice, it's—" Aleksandr looked at Wamukota. "You know him better even than I do. What—"

"There isn't— You don't even have time to move your coffins to safer ground and secure them," said Wamukota. "It would be suicide."

"He might destroy you for not telling him," said Aleksandr.

"He might," agreed Wamukota. "Better me than him."

"Where is Chevonde?" asked Elana.

I tried a spell," Aleksandr said, shaking his head, "but got no response."

"Do you think he's been captured too?" asked Elana.

Frustration was clear on his face when Aleksandr answered. "I don't know."

"Are we safe here?" asked Wamukota.

Aleksandr looked at him. "I don't know."

. . .

None of the other musicians noticed when Chevonde lost the beat. Nor did they notice when he stopped playing entirely. They were far too nervous, surrounded, as they were, by the assembled Blood Lords of Geb.

The Cinerarium was experiencing a first, a masquerade ball. The grand hall, Arazni's quarters, and Kemnebi's offices had been transformed in short order by Araminta and her overworked crew. The furniture had been removed—stashed in a lower hall. Hastily assembled decorations had been put in place, mood lighting designed, and musicians roused from their beds by unexpected—and most definitely unwelcome—visitors. Chevonde, a musician himself, saw a way in.

He cut his hair short, put rouge on his hands and neck to hide his pale skin, donned a mask and a suitable outfit, and tagged along. Now he watched in horror as Rhianna, the guest of honor, was revealed. She had been covered in a cloth, carried in by skeletal servants, and positioned before the statue of Geb. The tenting of the cloth was alarming to Chevonde, since he knew what caused it. Arazni said a few words then yanked the covering free. That's when Chevonde's fingers fell dead on his instrument's strings.

Rhianna leaned against the statue, propped by one of Geb's stone arms. Her eyes were wide open. Her cotton under shirt was partially ripped, revealing the curvature of her breasts. A wooden stake pierced her heart, the tip protruding from her back. There was a mere trickle of blood, which had dried. She looked no different than she had at any other time Chevonde had seen her, but everything was wrong.

Rhianna was physical, she was a fighter, she had a physical presence, a promise of movement, of action. That was gone, utterly gone and its absence was unnerving. Her expression was calm but her eyes spoke sheer panic.

After Rhianna was revealed, Arazni invited her Co-Chancellors to step closer and make their observations. The trio surrounded Rhianna's paralyzed form, chatting. Chevonde had no idea that Hent-er-Neheh was barely able to control her rage, thinking, as she did, that the elven lich standing next to her caused the destruction of Khufnu. He had no idea that Eratosthenes held a secret knowledge about Nexian spies in the capital, knowledge he had not shared—and did not intend to share—with either of the two women he spoke with. Chevonde did not know these things and even if he had, he would not care. The sight of Rhianna frightened him. He hadn't experienced fright in a long time.

Once the trio broke up other Blood Lords began a lazy procession to view the guest of honor, make snide comments, and to otherwise gloat and gossip. Rhianna was guarded by two grave knights, who carefully watched those who approached her. They didn't want anyone yanking out the stake.

Time passed, the ball progressed. Some of the less self-conscious—living—Blood Lords attempted to dance. Others stood, silently watching the festivities, waiting for dawn. The musicians took a break and Chevonde approached Rhianna, waiting in line for his opportunity to see Arazni's prize catch.

When he finally made his way to her, emotion nearly overtook him. He could see the fear in her eyes. He'd never known Rhianna to fear anything. The emotions he felt overrode his caution. He moved to yank the stake free, but a grave knight intercepted his half-raised hand. Chevonde caught himself and lifted his hand higher, dodging the grave knight's interception. He caressed Rhianna cheek. The grave knight reached up and grabbed his wrist, but did not move it.

"So beautiful, so pure." The grave knight did not answer but that was fine, Chevonde wasn't speaking to him. "Rhianna—" He didn't have the words to match such a moment, and even if he did, he couldn't say them aloud, not without dooming himself. He looked into Rhianna's eyes, trying to see past her fear and pain. "Be comforted, great hunter, it will all be over soon." He began to pull his hand back. The grave knight held on still, guiding Chevonde's hand until it was clear of the stake.

"What of Chevonde?" He heard someone ask. He turned away from Rhianna and drifted toward the conversation. Arazni answered. "He's next." She laughed. "Don't they all deserve to see the sun one last time before leaving Geb?" Those around the Queen laughed. Chevonde looked at Rhianna, then looked at the grave knights guarding her. He turned and studied the room, noting the Blood Lords, noting Arazni and the Co-Chancellors. He even saw the diplomats from Nemret Noktoria, their hideousness barely hidden by their masks.

Another Blood Lord wished to gawk and he stepped aside, still looking at Rhianna, staring at the stake in her heart. He knew he could pull it free before the grave knights could stop him. He knew that he and Rhianna would immediately change shape and try to escape. What he didn't know was if they could. He glanced once more at Arazni, Eratosthenes, and Hent-er-Neheh who, not counting Geb and Kemnebi, were the most powerful necromancers in Geb. He thought of the construction and layout of the Cinerarium. There were no windows and few doors. He thought of all of Geb aligned against them. He thought of Kemnebi hiding amongst the boulders and brambles in the Axan Wood. He thought of his pleasure barge in the harbor in Katapesh and those mysterious Pactmasters whose tacit blessing of his residency in their city had provided more security than he had realized and—after all this—he made up his mind.

He looked at Rhianna once more and mouthed the word, "Goodbye."

To See the Dawn

By the Axanir River, Mechitar, Geb, Erastus, 4711

It amazed Arazni just how many intelligent undead there were in Mechitar. She had never seen them assembled in one place, as they were now. This crowd excluded free-willed undead too violent to endure an execution calmly. These undead were disciplined—as much as they can be—by the Whispering Way. They existed on the periphery of so-called polite society. Nor were there those undead who were sensitive to light, such as wraiths and vampires, in attendance—except one.

What extended out at Arazni's feet, as she walked the hastily erected elevated wooden platform from the Cinerarium's steps to the clay-heavy shore of the Axanir River, was a thick ribbon of devourers, ghouls, liches, mohrgs, mummies, mummy lords, skeletal champions, wights, zombie lords, and on and on. Unexpected attendees joined: devils, hags, kytons—no doubt She-mahhon's guests—oni, rakshasas, and towering tomb giants at the rear. There were, of course, plenty of necromancers and priests. All the living in attendance had some command over necromancy. Those who did not wisely stayed away.

Arazni led a progression that included her grave knights, her Co-Chancellors, and her entire coterie. She did not actually lead it, two of her grave knights did. They held in their arms Rhianna's stiff form. Those in her coterie all carried torches. Many in the crowd held torches as well, giving the dark ribbon the appearance of a galaxy seen on edge.

Arazni was overwhelmed by emotion. She was triumphant. Now, after being his virtual slave, she truly understood how Geb felt. She knew what mastery felt like. All of those powerful beings were obeying her. She'd commanded their presence and they'd come. Now she was going to show them power. She was going to kill a feared vampire, once a Blood Lord, right before their eyes.

She knew that almost all of the undead present despised daylight. She knew that, along with Rhianna, she was forcing them to watch the sunrise. Such acknowledgement of her power was intoxicating. She even wobbled for a moment while thinking about it. Eratosthenes, who walked behind her, reached out and steadied her. She did not turn to acknowledge him, nor did he expect her to. He had done a quiet service. As her co-chancellor, that was his role.

The elevated walkway terminated at the juncture of the Axanir and the Obari. It led to a stage and before this stage gathered the undead of Mechitar. They formed a wedge of death hemmed in by life-giving water. A single plank of wood stood erect at the center of this stage, facing east. The grave knights carrying Rhianna stood her against this plank. The paralyzed vampire stared out over the Obari Ocean, awaiting a sight she thought she would never see again.

Eratosthenes and Hent-er-Neheh stood beside and slightly behind Rhianna. Arazni's coterie fanned out behind them, Lilith in the fore. Arazni herself went to the front edge of the stage and looked out over the audience. She did not speak, although she had intended to deliver a speech. Instead she studied them, fascinated, enchanted, and made dumb by their eyes which stared up at her in fear and admiration. She felt not the passing of time, heard no sounds, but seemed only a sponge that soaked up the world that—at that moment—she commanded.

The spell of her power was not broken until she saw a glow in her peripheral vision. She looked and saw the thinnest sliver of light over the undulating line of the Obari. She studied this silvery, wobbling line for a moment then turned to the audience. Behold"—she extended her arm—"the sun!" She stepped close to Rhianna, watching her.

As the sun's light bent over the horizon and began to illuminate the captive vampire her skin began to smolder. Arazni stared into Rhianna's eyes and drank in her terror. This deepened her intoxication. She leaned into Rhianna, "Yes, yes," she whispered. She gripped the stake with a steady hand.

The sun climbed much faster than she had expected. Within minutes the silver line turned to gold. What was hazy and unformed became solid, crisp, and hard. The Obari lit up with kaleidoscopic reflections, the sun's light bouncing from its waves. The orb of the sun broke the horizon, rising like a chariot of fire. Rhianna's hair began to smoke. Her skin began to turn red and blister. Tiny flames came to life and danced over her body before winking out.

Arazni could feel the heat pouring from Rhianna's body. She could smell her flesh cooking. She glanced and saw that her hair was curling, burning away. Boils burst, pus oozing free. She kept her eyes on Rhianna as she yanked the stake free and leapt back.

Rhianna screamed, raising her hands to shield her eyes from the sun. She burst into flames and frantically began to beat her palms against the fire. She turned and tried to leap onto Arazni but her legs, being eaten away by the sun's rays, broke beneath her. She fell onto her knees and reached out, looking at Arazni.

Arazni knelt and reached out, her fingers inches from Rhianna's. Rhianna tried to speak but the sun had burned holes through her body, through her lungs, and she held no air with which to speak. She was black now, her flesh becoming like charcoal. Her hair burned away. The fine musculature, which Arazni had so enjoyed, was disappearing, fueling the fires of her destruction.

Arazni watched every moment. She wanted to memorize every sensation, thought, and emotion. She wanted to cherish these moments for all of eternity. They were far too few for her liking. Rhianna was gone in seconds. She fell onto her stomach and lay motionless, sizzling and popping. After this, all that remained was a burnt husk. Even this disintegrated under the sun's powerful light. A minute after the sun first broke the horizon Rhianna was nothing but ash. A breeze blew in from the Obari and she was gone.

Arazni rose, still holding the stake—a sharpened leg from Kemnebi's office chair—in one hand. She grew weak in the knees and Lilith rushed to her. Arazni fell into her arms. "Did you see, Mother—see the bad woman burn?"

"Yes, Queen."

"I did that."

. . .

Wamukota and Elana held each other, shocked, dismayed, and horrified. The avenue sloped to the Axanir, offering a clear view of Rhianna's death. They watched the actors on stage, though from their distance, Arazni and the rest looked like marionettes in a nightmarish play.

Elana wept and turned away from the grisly sight. She buried her head in Wamukota's chest. Wamukota, his innocence having been long ago lost, was able to rouse his stoicism. He didn't speak. He could think of nothing meaningful to say, besides, he was afraid his voice would crack under the strain of emotion. Instead he directed Elana to Aleksandr's mansion. The shadows, who had watched them enter hours prior, and who had escorted them to their vantage point, had been driven away by the sun. Would the shadows tell Arazni, wondered Wamukota.

If so, it would be yet another victory for Geb's Harlot Queen, another defeat for Geb's former chancellor.

A Falling Out

Rhianna's Hunting Lodge, the Axan Wood, Geb, Erastus, 4711

Aleksandr woke them just after sunset. He did not speak, but merely shook them. A servant brought food. The pair ate in silence, Aleksandr seated nearby, his chin on his fist, staring at the wall, lost in thought.

"I will leave first," he said, "to draw Arazni's shadows." He looked at Wamukota. "You two leave after. I'll meet you at the edge of the Axan Wood. There are horses outside, saddled and ready."

"Kemnebi?" asked Wamukota.

"At Rhianna's hunting lodge." He looked at Elana. "I want him to hear it from me." Elana nodded. Aleksandr rose and left the room. A few minutes later the same servant who brought in the food returned to collect the empty plates and cups. He spoke without lifting his eyes from his work.

"The Master has left."

. . .

The room's trophies—pelts, mounted heads, polished weapons—now stood as sad reminders. Aleksandr stood at one end of the bear fur rug, Wamukota and Elana behind him. Kemnebi sat in a chair by the roaring fire, bent over a book. He finished reviewing the spell he needed and looked up. He at once saw that something was wrong and set the book aside. Aleksandr approached but hesitated.

"Tell me."

"Rhianna—" Aleksandr suffered a moment of weakness and could not continue. Kemnebi stood and gripped his child's shoulders. Aleksandr looked into his sire's face. "She was—executed." The words struck

Kemnebi like a blow to the chest. He fell back into the chair. Wamukota rushed across the room and knelt next to Kemnebi. Elana too came forward.

"What happened?" asked Kemnebi.

"Arazni captured her," said Aleksandr. "She staked her and this morning—" He struggled but finally said the words. "This morning Rhianna was placed before the sun."

Kemnebi began to tremble but not with grief, with rage. The beast within him rushed to the surface, transmogrifying his features, making them feral. He leapt from the chair, growling without knowing it, clenching his fists. His nails bit into his palms, blood dripped. The show of unbridled power frightened both Wamukota and Elana, who fell away from him.

Aleksandr had seen his sire like this only once before, when he killed Leah in a fit of rage. He knew that Kemnebi wasn't completely in control of himself at that moment. He knew that both Wamukota and Elana were in danger, as was everyone in Rhianna's hunting lodge. He unleashed his inner beast, lunging at Kemnebi to seize his arms. What followed took only seconds but the two beast warred, the one attempting to rein in the other. The weaker beast tried to cow the stronger. It worked, but only partially.

Kemnebi, now realizing what had happened, and mixing guilt and shame with his anger, turned away, pulling himself from Aleksandr's grasp. He went to the fire and stared at the flames.

"How could I have let this happen?"

"Sire, there was nothing—nothing we could do."

"I was a fool," growled Kemnebi. "I thought the Blood Lords would listen." He turned and looked at Aleksandr. "I thought they would understand that I was trying to save Geb. I believed them capable of looking past their own petty needs to realize that without the living in Geb they would perish." He stepped forward. "I went about this all wrong."

"Sire?"

"I will do now what I should have done in the beginning." He turned and went to the wall, plucking a sword from its pegs. "I will destroy them."

Aleksandr went to Kemnebi's side. "Who? Arazni? Eratosthenes? Hent-er-Neheh?"

Kemnebi turned and looked at his child. "Yes, all of them. Every Blood Lord, if I must. I'll destroy the Whispering Way. I'll tear down the Church of Epiphenomena. I'll do whatever it takes."

"What are you saying?"

"Kemnebi?" asked Elana.

"Master?" asked Wamukota. "You can't be serious."

Kemnebi looked the three over. "You're afraid, all of you. I can smell it." He spun and went once more to the fire, holding the sword out to reflect the dance of the flames. "I'm not afraid of any of them. I'll destroy them. I'll make them pay for Rhianna, for Aedha, for Trevedic." He spun to face Aleksandr. "I shouldn't have listened to you."

Aleksandr stared back. "You should listen to yourself, now. What you're saying is madness."

"No!" screamed Kemnebi. Again the beast showed. Wamukota and Elana were repelled. They rushed to the door, Wamukota opened it, and both ran through. "They killed her!" screamed Kemnebi. "They showed her the sun!" He stomped to Aleksandr. "All because we were careful, because we tried reason," he spun and slashed the air with the sword. "But they aren't reasonable. They're animals!" He turned back to Aleksandr. "So I will put them down, like the rabid dogs they are."

You've gone too far!" Aleksandr yelled. "You didn't try reason, you gave an ultimatum. You expected them to change thousands of years of tradition, of their way of doing things, all because you said so."

"I was their chancellor!"

"You were a fool!"

Kemnebi brought the sword up, menacing his own child. The beast was full in his face, in his thoughts.

"Are you going to kill me?" asked Aleksandr. "Like you did Leah?" At once the beast retreated. The sword lowered, as did Kemnebi's gaze. "And why did you kill her?"

Kemnebi turned to the fire. "Don't speak of that."

"Because she defied you?"

"Please, I beg you."

"Because she questioned your judgment, like I am now."

Kemnebi turned back to face Aleksandr. "She humiliated me in front of the assembled Blood Lords!"

"And for that she died, killed by the one who made her." Aleksandr shook his head. "All because she didn't obey. Now Aedha is gone, Rhianna is dead, why? Because they *did* obey. And Trevedic? You commanded he do the impossible. Did you honestly believe he could convince the Whispering Way of your vision?"

"If Geb is to survive—"

"You sent him to his death!"

"Aleksandr, don't condemn me," begged Kemnebi. "Don't betray me."

"You betrayed yourself. You betrayed all of us, every vampire in Geb."

"I was trying to save you!"

Aleksandr shook his head. "You failed."

The beast, having endured enough, lashed out. Quicker than the eye could see Kemnebi charged Aleksandr and swiped at his face, not with the sword, but with his claws. Only a vampire's reflexes spared Aleksandr from death. He was knocked back, moving with the blow, his cheek torn by ragged claw marks. He reached up and felt the wounds. He pulled his hand back, blood on his fingers.

"You've gone mad!"

Kemnebi loomed, growling, wrestling his emotions and the beast. Aleksandr rose, ready to leap away. But Kemnebi did not attack him a second time. For a moment it seemed as if Aleksandr wanted to speak but instead he stared at his sire, his emotions conflicted. He backed out of the room, pausing at the door. Kemnebi did not look at him. He was staring at where Aleksandr had fallen. Without a word, Aleksandr turned and left.

. . .

Kemnebi sat before the charred remains of the fire. Only the embers gave light. Elana entered and approached, kneeling next to the chair. She took one of his hands into hers and studied his face.

"Please ask Aleksandr to come speak with me," said Kemnebi.

"He's gone."

Kemnebi turned and looked at Elana. He studied her face for a moment then looked back to the remains of the fire.

"There is much we need to do. Have one of Rhianna's children—"

"They left, all of them." Kemnebi glanced at her. Elana continued. "They took their coffins."

"The hunters, her thralls?"

"Gone."

Kemnebi looked back to the cooling embers. “Wamukota?”

“He’s here. It’s just the three of us and—”

“We have little protection," said Kemnebi. He looked at the mounted heads, which were made even more horrific in the gloom. “I’ll make another vrykolakas. I wish I knew how to contact the werewolves.”

“Should we stay here, even with those—things? Shouldn’t we go to the clearing?”

“We?” He looked at Elana. “You and Wamukota—” He fell silent.

“Kemnebi?”

“Aren’t you missing class?”

“I’m not a student anymore.” Kemnebi looked at her. She squeezed his hand. “You need me.”

“I struck him—Aleksandr.”

“I know.”

“If I lose my temper again—if you’re close to me—”

“He shouldn’t have said—”

Kemnebi looked at the cooling embers. “I always asked him to speak honestly, not to hold anything from me, not to spare my feelings.” He paused, replaying the past. “I asked the same of Leah.”

“You’re only human.”

Kemnebi looked at her. “No, I’m not.”

“I meant—”

Kemnebi stood. Elana stood too, but his hand slipped from hers. “There is something I must do.”

“What?”

He didn’t look at her as he spoke. “You can’t come with me, neither you nor Wamukota. I must do this alone.” He turned to her, taking her hands. “You and Wamukota can stay here until I return. It will take a few hours to make the new vrykolakas, then I must leave. Do you have your spell books?"

Elana glanced at the shoulder bag. "I have everything."

"Stay here. There is food enough—"

"How long?"

"Fetch Wamukota. He needs to feed."

Elana nodded and began to leave but before turning from Kemnebi she rose up onto her toes and kissed him. He did not return her kiss and she turned from him, dejected. He grabbed her, pulled her close, and kissed her passionately.

. . .

"Wamukota," said Kemnebi, after his thrall had fed. "If I do not return by dawn," he studied the other man's face. "Go to Aleksandr and pledge your loyalty to him. He will take you on, feed you, and keep you safe. Take Elana with you and ask Aleksandr to get her out of Geb. She's not safe here."

"Master?"

"What I need to do—"

Wamukota grabbed Kemnebi by the arms, looked into his face, then hugged him and held him tight. "Master! Do not do this thing!"

"I must."

A Meeting with Death

The Ebon Mausoleum, Mechitar, Geb, Erastus, 4711

Bats were common familiars among necromancers, so one flapping silently through the Ebon Mausoleum's halls drew no notice. The bat angled down the steps, going below the school proper, flapped to a stop, then transformed into a man.

Kemnebi stood at the edge of the circular, door-lined room that made up the central hub of the Whispering Way's domicile beneath the Ebon Mausoleum. He had never set foot here. He had never wanted to, even as chancellor. He could feel their power. He could feel the reverberations of their intense necromantic energies ebbing from behind the closed doors. He wondered if they could feel him, an enemy in their space. He could not feel Trevedic and that troubled him.

He heard a rustling of cloth and looked across the room. An open archway led to stairs that led to a chamber still lower. As he watched, Eratosthenes floated up the stairs in an effortless glide. The elven lich, now co-chancellor, entered the room and stopped. He held a staff in one hand, the tip glowing with potent arcane energy.

A door opened and Ólchobar Yevan stepped out. The door shut behind him. He looked at Kemnebi, his putrid eyes yellow in his ghastly, green face. Another door opened and Masgava stepped out. He too looked at Kemnebi. No one had yet spoken. Another door opened and Neacal Aodhan stepped out. He looked over his fellow liches, his eyes resting on Eratosthenes for a moment, then he too looked at Kemnebi. Yet another door opened and Ashoka joined his fellow liches. They all studied their unexpected visitor.

"I've come for Trevedic."

Eratosthenes tilted his staff a few degrees, indicating one of the three doors yet to open. With a thought he dispelled the arcane lock he had placed on the door. Ólchobar Yevan turned, the door behind him opening, and returned to his quarters. The rest of the liches did likewise.

Kemnebi stepped to the door of Trevedic's room and paused, his hand on the pull. Long ago his own sire had warned him never to go without blood. "It is worse than death." Kemnebi had never experienced a prolonged period without fresh blood. He had never seen a vampire who had. He assumed they perished, but he didn't know. He didn't want to know.

He pulled the door open. The stench of two rotting corpses on the floor overwhelmed him. He held his breath, stepping over them. A cloud of flies rose from the bodies at the disturbance but settled back on them to feed. Kemnebi went to the narrow bed, the only furniture in the room, other than a small desk and an uncomfortable looking wooden chair. Trevedic was lying on his side, curled like a child, his hands on his throat, as if he had died by self-strangulation. He wore only pants. He had ripped his shirt free. His chest was covered with self-inflicted claw marks.

His flesh was translucent, pulled taut over bones and muscles. He was dehydrated but not of water, of blood. His eyes were closed but his mouth was open. His tongue was swollen, sticking out of his mouth, firm, fat, and purple. His fangs were down. His gums had pulled back from his teeth, leaving thin gaps.

Kemnebi reached under Trevedic and lifted him. He had almost no weight. Kemnebi turned and edged his way through the open door, careful not to step on the corpses that Trevedic had drained dry. He entered the circular chamber and paused.

Only Eratosthenes remained. The other liches had returned to their studies. Their closed doors stared like accusing eyes. Kemnebi held Trevedic out, showing him to Eratosthenes like one shows a damning piece of evidence, but Eratosthenes had no guilt or shame. His face remained inscrutable.

Kemnebi turned and began up the stairs. Now his presence drew attention. Students lined the halls, watching their former chancellor carry their former—almost unrecognizable—instructor from the school. Trevedic's fellow instructors studied him, a mix of self-righteousness and fear on their faces. None dared confront Kemnebi. None spoke to him. None accused him. They could do nothing but watch. His majesty and the tragedy of the situation held them in silent awe.

Once he was out on the avenue before the Ebon Mausoleum he cast a spell and took flight. He headed out over the Obari until Mechitar was a mere smudge of light sunk in darkness, then banked left and headed to the Axan Wood.

. . .

The vrykolakas emerged from the darkness when Kemnebi landed outside of Rhianna's hunting lodge. The humanoid undead crawled on all fours, approaching its creator like a faithful hound. It sniffed Trevedic and growled. Kemnebi ignored it and entered the lodge. The second vrykolakas rushed toward him then stopped.

"Elana?" called Kemnebi. He heard her coming but warned her to stay away. He didn't want her to see Trevedic in his current state. He heard her footsteps pause. He felt her desire to approach. He was thankful she didn't. "Wamukota?"

"Master?"

"Attend me."

. . .

Kemnebi knelt and laid Trevedic on the bear fur rug. He bit open the vein in his wrist and placed it against Trevedic's lips. The blood spilled into his mouth, coating his tongue, gums, and teeth, but Trevedic made no response. Kemnebi tilted Trevedic's head so that gravity would carry the blood down his throat.

Master!" Wamukota cried, dropping to his knees beside Trevedic.

"He's—"

"Master! You went to—" Wamukota was in disbelief.

"He's in some kind of torpor," said Kemnebi. "I don't know if this will bring him back."

"A spell?"

Kemnebi looked at his thrall. "Divine magic, perhaps." He looked at Trevedic. "I should have taken him to Narcisse."

"Shall I go get him?"

"No." Kemnebi's blood filled Trevedic's mouth and spilled onto the pelt. Kemnebi let his wrist mend. He reached out and gripped Wamukota's shoulder. "Look at him." Wamukota looked down at Trevedic. "Now you see what we truly are." Wamukota looked back at Kemnebi. "You must leave me, faithful friend."

"Master?"

Kemnebi looked down at Trevedic. He removed his hand from Wamukota's shoulder and wiped the blood from Trevedic's face. "I want you to take him to Katapesh." Kemnebi looked up at Wamukota. "Take him to Chevonde."

"Is he—"

"If he's smart, he's left Geb." Kemnebi looked once more at Trevedic. "He could be at his mansion or on his barge. I trust you to find him."

"But Master, how can I—"

"Survive without my blood?"

"Yes."

"I will fill vessels enough with my blood to get you to Katapesh. Once there you must devote yourself to Chevonde."

"Master, I serve you."

"You *have* served me, and faithfully, Wamukota. But you can serve me no longer."

"Let me take him and return to you."

"No. Once you leave Geb you must never return."

"I don't care if I die, Master. I want—"

"I care, Wamukota."

"Master, what if Chevonde isn't in Katapesh? What if I can't find him? Can you fill bottles enough for that?"

"I—"

"Embrace me, Master. Give me the dark gift."

"No! Wamukota, you've seen what we can become. You've seen me kill in rage, that is the beast within me." He looked at Trevedic. "Now you see how we can suffer. How can you ask me for this?"

"It's the only way I can keep him safe."

"Wamukota. No!" Kemnebi stood and turned away.

Wamukota remained by Trevedic, looking at him. He looked at Kemnebi. "We've no choice, Master. Neither of us."

"I won't damn you for eternity."

"Let me worry about the state of my soul," said Wamukota. Kemnebi turned. Wamukota looked at him not as one beholden, but as one equally damned. "The dark gift, Kemnebi." Wamukota glanced at Trevedic. "Or he and I both die."

"You don't know what you ask!"

"Where is Chevonde?"

Kemnebi shook his head.

"Yet you send me to him so I may be safe? I accept this charge you give me. I will search for Chevonde. I will keep Trevedic safe and restore him, if it is possible. But I cannot do it as I am now. You know I speak the truth."

"It is no dark gift, Wamukota. It's a curse."

"It matters not. It is the only way left to us."

"You would embrace death to prevent death?" asked Kemnebi.

"Yes."

Only Lovers Remain

Rhianna's Hunting Lodge, Axan Wood, Geb, Erastus, 4711

Kemnebi stood looking out of a window. Wamukota loaded an old wagon with two coffins, covered them with tarps, and hitched it to the horses he and Elana rode to the lodge. Then he headed toward Mechitar.

Kemnebi heard Elana enter and approach. He spoke without looking at her. "I wrote a letter begging Narcisse to do what he could for Trevedic and gave it to Wamukota." Elana came up, wrapped her arms around Kemnebi's shoulders, and placed her cheek against his back. "If Narcisse cannot help, or if it is too dangerous to approach him, I wrote a second letter—to Aleksandr, begging forgiveness." Kemnebi reached up and touched Elana's elbow. He bent his head and kissed her hand. "Aleksandr would never deny Trevedic aid. Either way, I ordered Wamukota to book passage to Katapesh. With any luck they'll be on the Obari this time tomorrow."

"Do you think Chevonde is there?"

"He may not be there yet, but he will be. If I were him I would think no more of Geb."

"Kemnebi?"

Kemnebi turned and embraced Elana, looking down into her eyes.

"Why didn't *you* go?" she asked. Kemnebi raised an eyebrow. "Why stay? Why not join Chevonde?"

Kemnebi thought for a moment then drew a deep breath, ready to explain his thoughts and feelings. Elana stopped him by lifting up on her toes and kissing him.

"Lie with me, Kemnebi," she said. She kissed him again. "Hold me and open your heart to me."

Kemnebi nodded and they made their way to Rhianna's bedroom. The vrykolakas watched them, then moved to follow. With a thought Kemnebi ordered them to remain outside of the room, then shut the door.

When he turned he saw Elana before him. He cast a cantrip, conjuring four wavering, warm lights that floated to the room's corners. Elana reached up and pulled down the right shoulder strap of her dress. She held the bodice in place then pulled down the left shoulder strap. She looked into Kemnebi's eyes then let her dress fall to the floor at her feet.

Kemnebi stayed still, taking in her naked form. She stepped to him, put her arms around his neck, then pulled his mouth to hers. "Make love to me," she whispered between kisses.

. . .

Elana was half-dozing when Kemnebi began to speak. She roused herself, snuggled close to him, and listened. They were in Rhianna's massive bed, a sheet pulled over them, the four lights coloring their faces in warm hues.

"What have I known?" he asked. "I've known the jungle, as a child, but that was so long ago it barely registers as a memory. Then I knew Geb, the man, and Geb, the nation. My entire being, my identity, is defined by these two Gebs.

"Long ago, when Geb sent me to do his bidding, I visited distant lands. I experienced snow for the first time and I thought it was a spell cast by someone powerful I couldn't see for a purpose I couldn't discern. How silly." They both chuckled. "That only tells you how paranoid I was then. One must cultivate paranoia to survive in Geb's court." Kemnebi sighed. "And now? I could travel the world, even go to other planes. Could I make my way to the gates of Heaven? The gates of Hell? Magic provides a way. I could roam forever—tireless, timeless. I could see different stars, know different heavens." He reached over and caressed Elana. "I could take you with me. I have wealth enough, hidden away, and arcane knowledge enough to overcome nearly any obstacle. So why? Why do I stay?"

Elana pulled his hand to her lips and kissed it before returning it to her body.

"I have helped rule Geb for so long," said Kemnebi. "It's all I know. I can't turn my back on Geb." Elana didn't speak, but squeezed him so he knew she was listening. "I never once felt responsible for the living in Geb. Saying that sounds heartless, but I didn't pay them much mind. But in time I began to understand how a society functions, an economy functions, what people do, what they need. I understood that although Geb was a nation of undead it needed the living. I began to think about protecting them, nurturing them, not for their sake but for ours."

"Less violent undead."

"Yes. There must be enough living in Geb to support the dead. Once the scales tip, they will swing wildly and Geb will crumble. Despite my failures, they still need to be protected, not for their sake, but for ours." He sighed. "Aleksandr is right. We must bide our time, rebuild our resources, let Eratosthenes and Hent-er-Neheh battle each other for control, overextend, weaken themselves, then, in a hundred years," he chuckled, "I can try again. "For now, I must work covertly to undermine them," he smiled, "and protect the living."

"You said that in a hundred years there wouldn't be enough left to fight for."

"I've been wrong about much," said Kemnebi. "Hopefully I'm wrong about that." He fell silent and spent several minutes lost in thought. He paused, noticing Elana's fight to stay awake. He held her and kissed her forehead. "Sleep. When you wake, I'll be as if dead, but don't be alarmed." Elana wasn't listening, she was snoring softly. Kemnebi kissed her then looked at the ceiling and began to consider alternate futures.

The Spell Scarred

The Spellscar Desert, the Mana Waste, Arodus, 4711

Ilyx sat on a low ridge, a woven cloth map laid across his lap, looking out over the Spellscar. The map had once, a few thousand years prior, belonged to a commander in Nex's army. The only reason the fabric held was due to enchantment, but even magic frays in time. The map showed a series of storage depots. Ilyx had already found two. Mutated Spellscar inhabitants had looted them long ago, or Calikangs destroyed the enchanted items to free their magic back to the land.

Ilyx thought for a moment about the mutants and the Calikangs. He knew both intimately. Long ago, before Geb and Nex warred, the land between their nations was inhabited by nomadic tribes and frontier settlers. These unfortunates were trapped between two wizard-kings and became, along with the land itself, their victims.

The Spellscar, like all the Mana Waste, had been blasted by world-rending magic. This transformed the rocky plains into a mishmash of unnatural features; multicolored sands which seeped various types of magical energy, from electricity to acid, furrows filled with a magical slurry that vaporized anything that touch it, plants that drank not water but which soaked magic from the soil, turning them into multi-colored, surreal sculptures that occasionally attained an angry sentience.

Not just the land suffered. The weather too was made unnatural. Whenever a storm moved over the Mana Waste it changed. The howling in the wind wasn't mere noise. The rain didn't splash—it bit like razors hurled by an angry god. When lightning struck it did not do so randomly, but with a base intelligence that sought to destroy. During the day the air was made scorching, at night the cold was unbearable. The Mana Waste took every malicious aspect of nature, amplified it, and gave it a home.

That such an environment existed troubled the Calikangs. They were once the willing servants of Nex. They are towering, six-armed, magical humanoids. Few know that their faces are handsome, if rugged, for they often wear elaborate helmets. These helmets do not cover their mouths, however, for Calikangs can breathe out, as a form of attack, many different types of energy, from cold wind to fire. Their armor is elaborate, studded with gems and decorated with magical symbols. They wield massive falchions.

When Nex turned his back on Golarion and entered his Refuge the Calikangs fled from Nex, so troubled were they by his absence. They felt responsible for the destruction wrought by their master and took it upon themselves to repair what he and Geb had done. Thus they roam the Mana Waste, especially the Spellscar Desert. They devote their long lives to the monumental—perhaps impossible—task of repairing the land.

Ilyx avoided them. First, they were ten feet taller than he and the gnome feared being trampled. Second, they were almost impossible to converse with. The Calikangs believed that even the gods could fail and this belief so troubled them that they obsessed over it. Ilyx didn't much care if the gods could fail or not. He was curious about the reality that confronted him. As a source of knowledge and conversation the Calikangs were lacking. Finally, the Calikangs were devoted to destroying magical items in order to free the magic within, believing it to be trapped. Ilyx happened to find what little magic he had trapped to be rather useful.

Ilyx's keen eyes saw movement on the plain below. He raised his rifle out of reflexive caution, but the movement was too far away to be a threat. It took him a moment to recognize what it was. A group of mutated gnolls were hunting. They stalked unseen prey, gathered in a loose group, carrying crudely made weapons. He could not detect their mutations at such a distance, but he could imagine them. The wild magic of the Spellscar penetrated the womb, altering the embryo within. Some had crippled arms, some were born eyeless, some deaf, some were born without minds—but these seldom lived long.

Not all were debilitated, or only debilitated. Some moved with unnatural celerity. Some possessed supernatural healing powers, with wounds closing in seconds. Some were resistant to magic, some could command it with but a thought. He avoided the mutants as assiduously as he avoided the Calikangs, but for a more personal reason.

Ilyx watched the gnolls lumber across the plain. In time they moved beyond his vision. He checked the map once more, judged the distance, rolled the map up and tucked it away. He shouldered his rifle and looked to the sky, judging the remaining light. He preferred to approach the cache of Nexian supplies under the cover of darkness. If the map was accurate, he would do so. He only hoped it hadn't yet been discovered. If it hadn't, he hoped it wasn't guarded.

. . .

Ilyx approached the faintly glowing, roughly-carved obelisk with his rifle held at his hip. He paused on a rise overlooking the stone and studied it and its surroundings. The glow came from a spiral engraved on one side of the obelisk. The stone itself was eight feet tall and sat at the bottom of a shallow valley. It couldn't be seen unless one crested the ridge. A few loose boulders were scattered about. Patches of scraggly grass bent in the breeze. A thin creek carved a rut at the bottom of the valley, passing before the obelisk.

Ilyx reached up and pulled his fur cloak tighter around him. He listened but heard nothing but the dull chatter of insects. He stepped over the ridge into the valley and made his way to the obelisk. Once at its foot he began to examine it. If the map was accurate he had found a hidden cache. It didn't seem to have been disturbed. He allowed himself to get excited.

The deep gnome wasn't the only intelligence in the valley. A black fog blanketed the bottom. It was spread thin, only a few inches deep, and thus had escaped notice. But it felt Ilyx. It pulled away from him, gathering some distance away. It was not properly a fog. It was not only air and moisture. Nor was it native to Golarion. It had been summoned, thousands of years ago, by Nex. It was a native of the elemental plane of air. On that plane it was a ruthless hunter. It was called a mihstu. Nex had brought this immortal being to Golarion to battle the minions of Geb. Now it stalked the Spellscar, an unnatural hunter in an unnatural ecosystem.

It floated toward Ilyx, silent and unseen. It reached out with a tentacle of moisture, reaching for its prey, but did not yet strike. It moved until it was almost touching Ilyx and paused, savoring the moment. Ilyx, who had been crouching at the base of the obelisk, now stood. He looked up at the glowing spiral, still unaware of the threat behind him. The mihstu floated forward, capturing Ilyx in its deadly embrace.

. . .

Ilyx felt warmth where there had been cold. He felt moisture where there had been none. He turned and leveled his rifle but his foe was all around, pressing into him, suffocating him. He fired the rifle. The bullet tore a hole in the fog but it quickly filled. Ilyx dropped his rifle and grabbed at his belt.

He felt tears come to his eyes but instead of falling to his cheeks they leapt from his face and joined the fog around him. Blood ran in his nose, and like his tears, the droplets leapt free. He even felt urine forced from him.

He ripped open one of the leather bags on his belt and yanked free the bottle of air that Master Castelli had crafted for him. He pulled the cork and held it. He put the bottle of air to his lips and sucked. He staggered forward, desperate to get out of the fluid-draining fog. But the mihstu stayed with him.

More tears, more blood, more fluids necessary for life were being drained by the fog. That was how the mihstu toyed with its prey. Ilyx felt his strength ebbing fast. He tried to run but he grew exhausted due to the diminishing of his life-giving fluids. He fell to one knee but was able to rise and keep going. He wanted to get over the ridge, hoping that the fog would stay in the valley. He thought of his rifle. He hated to lose such a precious item but his life was more important. He drew a second gun from his belt, dropping the cork to the bottle of air, and fired it. A second hole punched through the mihstu but, like the first, it filled.

The pistol felt a burden in Ilyx's weakened state. He dropped it. He tried to climb the ridge but it seemed far steeper than he remembered. He fell to his knees, then to his stomach. The bottle of air tumbled from his hand. He breathed the mihstu into his lungs. The pain was alarming. Ilyx knew he was going to die.

He felt a ball of white-hot energy form in the middle of his solar plexus. He didn't know what it was or what caused it. It scared him. He thought it was a sensation that accompanied dying. It grew, knotting his gut. It expanded, filling his torso and limbs with sparkling energy. It burst out of him, blinding him with its light, deafening him with its sound. He saw no more of it, heard no more, because he was unconscious.

. . .

The summoning magic that long ago welcomed the mihstu to Golarion, that kept it there, even after Nex had gone, was undone. The link that kept the merciless hunter prowling the Spellscar Desert was broken. At once the mihstu was banished from Golarion and reappeared in its home plane, the plane of air. It was disoriented. Gone were the solids it had grown used to. There was no earth beneath it. One of Golarion's most powerful casters had summoned it. Thousands of years later, Nex's magic had been shattered.

. . .

Rava, a mutant gnoll, stood guard while the tribe ate, mated, and dozed. He saw a bright light breach the horizon. He glanced up at the moon, thinking, for a moment, it had birthed another. The light vanished but he could still see its afterglow. A moment later a boom rolled over him, frightening him, causing his ears to bend back from the sound. A second gnoll, Suyo, stepped up and studied the area where the light had been. The two gnolls looked at one another. Behind them the tribe started to yip, howl, and leap about, clanging their weapons together, their panicked excitement growing.

The Key, the Call

Geb's Rest, Yled, Graydirge, Mechitar, and various locations, Geb, and the Sea Bird, Quantium, Nex, Arodus, 4711

Geb floated six feet from the ground, his robes playing out beneath him, his ghostly light illuminating the grass and rocks nearby. A few feet away a sapling grew, a tree unlike any other. Geb paid the new growth no mind. As ever, he stared out over the Mana Waste, over the blasted countryside of Nex, into Quantium, at Nex's Refuge. As ever, his mind worked, plotting the path of revenge.

He turned his head a bit to the side, seeing something new. His robes stilled. His glow dimmed. He looked deep into the Spellscar Desert. His mind worked to comprehend what he had witnessed. Geb, who knew magic better than any in Golarion, had seen something he could not believe, something he did not think was possible. He had seen magic die.

He began to calculate the ramifications of what he had witnessed. He fitted them into the framework of his understanding. He plugged this new experience into his need to see Nex destroyed—and he knew. He spun and looked over his own kingdom, seeing it in its entirety. He sent out a call. At that moment every undead in Geb heard his voice. Every undead in Geb, except those who could match his will, was forced to obey.

What they heard was this: "Come to me—"

Geb was bound by his curse. He could never leave his own creation. The borders of Geb were the borders of his prison. But if those borders expanded, if Geb gained new territory by right of sword, then his prison too would grow. At that moment Geb, the man and the nation, made hot the long-chilled war with Nex.

. . .

No one—not even Kemnebi—had tallied Geb's wheat, oats, corn, and other crops. They were certainly in the hundreds of thousands. In each acre stood dozens of zombies. They stood like silent sentinels. They watched as the cereals grew. They waited, drenched by the rain, burned by the sun, pecked at by frustrated crows, crawled over by adventurous mice. Bugs made a home in their ragged clothes, in their hair, in their noses and mouths.

When the crops were ready, the zombies harvested them. The products of the soil of Geb, gathered by undead hands, headed to Nex to feed a people at war with their most important trading partner.

Crows slumbering on the undead farmhands' steady shoulders were shaken free. Mice scattered. Those bugs that were quick to leap or take flight did so as the zombies turned in unison and began to shamble from the fields. They did not, as was their habit, avoid the plants they tended. They trampled them underfoot, not intentionally, but because Geb did not care.

Half of the activated zombies headed directly toward Geb's Rest. The other half headed toward Mechitar. This first half stared at the horizon, looking for Geb's ghost. The second half scanned the ground under foot. When they saw a large stone, a stone that would be worth the effort to carry, they bent, picked it up, and took it with them.

. . .

Iztahuatzin sat on a crumbling throne, fawning undead kneeling before him. He was a deathsnatcher, a type of monstrous humanoid that claimed descent from demons. He looked demonic. He had a jackal's head, a vulture's wings, a rat's tail that ended in a scorpion's stinger and his four arms ended in dangerously clawed hands.

A deathsnatcher is a solitary creature. They rule over ruins inhabited by undead, which they create and cultivate for one purpose, to worship. Iztahuatzin thought himself a god and to his undead he was. He was shocked when his undead ceased chanting his name. They rose and turned to the northeast. He rose from his throne and watched, puzzled and angered, as his undead began to shuffle from the room, out into the collapsing remnants of an ancient settlement in the scrublands of the Shattered Range. He followed, studying them, his rage growing.

He stepped in front of a zombie but it turned and started around him. He grabbed it with his four hands and tore it into chunks which he tossed aside. A ghoul tried to dart past but he reached out and grabbed its shoulder, spinning it.

“What are you doing?” The ghoul twisted in his grasp, seemingly desperate to get free. “Answer your god!” The ghoul bit his hand. Iztahuatzin lifted it and flung it over a stone wall. “You!” he screamed at a specter that floated near. “Where are you going?” The specter did not respond. This enraged Iztahuatzin and he rushed to the incorporeal undead. “Where are you going? What are you doing?”

The specter did not look at him but moaned, “Geb calls.”

At the name Geb, Iztahuatzin stopped. The specter floated through the ruins, vanishing from sight.

“Stop! All of you! Stop!” His undead ignored him. “You obey me. I created you!” He reached out, grabbed another ghoul, lifting it from the ground. “Explain! Geb calls?”

“Geb calls," said the ghoul.

Iztahuatzin ripped the ghoul in half. "Geb calls *my* undead?" He looked toward the horizon in the direction that his undead now marched. "Damn you, Geb! You shall not get them!" He charged forward and began to tear his own creations to pieces.

. . .

The Bonewall surrounding Yled shuddered, knocking free the accumulated dust of a millennia, cracking the dried mud at its base, and alarming the great multitude of vermin that lived within. Spiders began to crawl free in such numbers that those close by fainted at the sight. A sound like a million cracking knuckles echoed over Yled.

The Bonewall straightened, no longer curling around Yled, and began to travel, in a serpentine manner, toward Geb's Rest. It was fifteen feet tall, fifteen feet wide, and thousands of feet long. It left a rut in the ground that would soon be followed by Geb's undead legions.

. . .

The fext, a type of undead born of battle, that resembled a heavily armored human soldier, but that, in truth, is an un-killable scion of war, shuddered when it heard Geb's voice. It shook off its stupor and looked around. It was surrounded by tens of thousands of skeletons, zombies, and other mindless undead.

A fext could smell war in the air, sense it in the heartbeats of the people. The fext—one of many newly awakened in the legions housed in Yled—felt a sensation akin to intoxication. There would be war, yes, it knew, a great war, perhaps the greatest yet. It began to laugh. Its fellows laughed, the sounds combining into an ominous chorus.

. . .

A cleric of Nethys, the dual-natured god of magic, stood on a low platform, giving a lecture about transmutation magic to a collection of priests and wizards seated before him in uncomfortable wooden pews. They occupied a small, low-ceilinged hall in the Mortuarium. A row of narrow, arched windows at the speaker's right-hand looked over the plains north of the Axan Wood.

The room was no longer perfectly level. Nex's twisting of the tower had put it out of true. As a result, neither the door nor the windows shut perfectly. A faint whistle slipped through the misaligned windows. Everyone had long ago gotten used to leaning slightly to one side or another, depending on which room or hallway they were in. Even the cleric of Nethys, leaning himself, and looking out over a leaning group of too-serious men and women, no longer even saw the comical postures of those before him.

A visitor, were there one, would no doubt find the sight humorous. All these pompous spellcasters leaning in unconscious compensation for the insulting magical effect that another—perhaps the most pompous of them all—spellcaster had forced upon them. It made for a grand joke. Perhaps that was why the Mortuarium allowed few outsiders to walk its un-level halls.

The cacophonous sounds of surprise and alarm rose up from the city below, drowning out the voice of the speaker. The cleric of Nethys tried to ignore the growing din (he was just getting to the good part) but those in attendance could not. Many turned toward the windows. A bit of hushed conversation began. Finally, acknowledging defeat, the speaker stepped from the platform and went to a window. His cry of surprise drew his listeners from the pews. Soon they were jostling to look down on the scene below.

The Bonewall was, by this time, a massive, bleached-white serpent slithering toward Geb's Rest. The legions were in the process of leaving the parade ground, moving in tight columns from positions they had held so long that the bare earth beneath them seemed unnatural. All this was seen by the light of moon, stars, magic, and torches.

The citizens of Yled filtered into the streets. Those who were asleep had been awoken by the cracking of the Bonewall, the cries of their neighbors, or by friends or family who didn't want them to miss a once-in-a-lifetime event.

Clerics, always quick to attribute worldly events to divine causes, began to search their memories and holy books for relevant scripture. They took to the streets proclaiming that—behold!—their god was at work. Those necromancers who remembered in whose nation they dwelt thought first of Geb.

The cleric of Nethys, as well as all of those in attendance, at once knew something terribly important was afoot. They looked at one another in surprise then each began from the room, intent on whatever actions he or she thought best, to rush after the legions or rush out of Geb.

. . .

None of the cities or towns of Geb could be called normal. Yet of all, Graydirge is perhaps the oddest. It is an ossuary, a place where the bones of the dead are deposited. Despite Geb's law, not everyone in Geb can be, or is, raised as undead. There are a multitude of reasons why, but in a nation like Geb a sorry fate is reserved for those whose remains are denied the blessing of necromantic magic. They are sunk in walls of cob as decoration, they frame windows and doors, they support table-tops, they *are* table tops; in other words, in Graydirge, bones do all the tasks that wood or stone would do better.

There are not all that many undead in Graydirge. There is a garrison of intelligent skeletons, a mix of other freewilled undead, and a coterie of vampires, but mostly there are living people in Graydirge. A good number of these are ranchers, their wives and children, and all those craftspeople that support life—simple country folk.

Sunk into this simple, back-country town is the Empty Threshold, a temple dedicated to Zon-Kuthon, a god—it would seem—that few would choose to worship, for he is an insane god, a god of darkness, envy, loss, and pain.

The Empty Threshold was constructed to be, and always has been, a form of punishment. Those who seek it out are after one thing, a life that mimics the profound loss of death. The temple is made largely of bones, held together by cob and bit of necromancy (for good measure). Those who walk its halls tread upon skulls. The keystone at the peak of every arch is a hip bone. The architectural uses to which the human spine has been put would astonish the most inventive architect, if she could divorce herself from the knowledge of its previous use.

Almost none of the ranchers and craftspeople of Graydirge worship Zon-Kuthon. They avoid the desolate structure that sits at the center of their town like a corpse at a wake, known but not recognized. Nor do the faithful of the Midnight Lord pay much attention to the country folk from whom they purchase their meagre fare. They do not try to convert them. No, they do not collect souls for their god.

They are the walking dead, or rather, the dying, or wish to be. They grind bones, mix the dust with psychedelic herbs and fetid water, and drink the foul brew to scour their minds. They are nihilist indulging in the act of self-annihilation.

The worshippers of Zon-Kuthon hardly noticed when the undead left Graydirge. Why would they? But the townsfolk did. They watched from their windows and porches as the garrison marched northeast, out into the vast fields of wheat. They gave silent thanks when the blood-suckers left, their eyes half-rolled back, walking stiff-jointed as if yanked by strings from overhead.

When the undead disappeared into the darkness outside of town the townsfolk emerged into the night. They spoke, they conjectured, they celebrated. The self-destroying followers of Zon-Kuthon got little sleep that night, for the temple of the Midnight Lord was surrounded by a spontaneous, joy-fueled midnight revelry.

. . .

She-mah-hon was tattooing Baya-Iza with glowing, magic-infused ink.

"Must you make it so painful, my dear?" asked the drow.

"That is the joy of it." She-mah-hon whispered.

"Joy you say?" asked Baya-Iza. "For whom?"

"Can you tattoo undead flesh?" asked Arazni.

Her entire clique were gathered in her quarters, as they often are, socializing, gossiping, entertaining one another, and most importantly being obsequious to their queen.

"It would be an honor," said She-mah-hon.

"Yes, but can you do it?" asked Jasmine.

"Sadly," said She-mah-hon, looking at Arazni, "you will feel no pain." She shrugged her shoulders. "It would be without joy."

"What a demented race," said Saskia. She was seated on the floor, her back against Arazni's bed. Arazni was lying on her back, her head over the edge, her hair falling down, observing the activities upside down. Saskia was running her fingers through Arazni's hair.

"It looks like a tea cup that's been fractured into a hundred pieces," said Arazni. "Even the handle's broken." She pointed.

Baya-Iza, worry clear on her face, looked down at her shoulder. She-mah-hon sat back and examined her work.

"You're looking at it upside down," said Saskia.

Arazni giggled. "Well, what is it?"

"A spider, I think," said Noreen Paisely, the Llorona, who stepped up and bent over the kyton's shoulder to examine the ongoing tattoo.

"It only has one leg!" cried Arazni, giggling.

Saskia playfully tugged Arazni's hair. "It's not done, you goof."

"Ow," cried Arazni. "You pulled your Queen's hair." She spun onto her belly. "Mother? What's her punishment?"

"Banishment to the ninth layer of Hell."

"For pulling hair?" asked Saskia.

"Not just any hair," said Lilith. "Royal hair."

"Yeah," said Arazni, touching her scalp. "Royal hair." She stuck her tongue out at Saskia, who returned the gesture.

"Now what does it look like, Queen?" asked Baya-Iza.

Arazni looked at the tattoo. "Oh, a spider!" She laughed.

"Good," said the drow. She looked at She-mah-hon. "I was about to banish *you* to the ninth layer of Hell."

"I've been there," said the kyton.

"Of course," said Baya-Iza, "I should have known." She chuckled and turned to Arazni. "You know—" But she did not continue because Arazni had an alarmed look on her face. She climbed up onto her hands and knees. At the same time Lilith stiffened, Jasimine, the Dead Bride, who was in the process of moving toward the bed, stopped and stood stock still. Noreen Paisely, like Lilith and Jasimine, was motionless.

Kimberly Silent Eyes, the Vishkanyas assassin, who was standing next to Araminta, studied her. Araminta too was motionless. "What's wrong with them?"

Saskia stood. "Arazni?" She looked at Baya-Iza, then to She-mah-hon, then to Kimberly. "What's going on?"

"Geb calls—" whispered Arazni. She climbed from her bed and stood, slightly wavering. "Geb calls." She looked at Saskia but was really looking in the direction of Geb's Rest.

Saskia reached out and shook Arazni by the shoulders. Arazni blinked and then actually saw Saskia. "Geb?" asked Saskia. "You said something about Geb."

Arazni smiled then hugged Saskia. She leaned back and looked into Saskia's face. "Didn't you hear him?" Saskia shook her head. Arazni turned and looked toward Lilith. "Mother? You heard him, right?"

Lilith, Noreen, Jasmine, and Araminta all began toward the door. They did not speak, nor did they move in their usual fluidly-animated manner. Instead they walked as if someone or something compelled them, because Geb had compelled them.

Baya-Iza stood. "Queen Arazni, what's going on?"

Arazni skipped from Saskia's arms into Baya-Iza's, a smile on her face. "Geb wants us, all of us." She giggled then sighed whimsically. "He needs us." She glanced at her grave knights. "Come, little brothers." She stiffened, adopting a serious attitude. "Daddy needs us. Let's go!" She laughed and fell in line with Lilith and the others. The grave knights followed. Baya-Iza, She-mah-hon, Saskia, and Kimberly Silent Eyes, all of whom were living, none of whom had heard Geb's call—he didn't need the living—stood staring out the open door.

"What should we do?" asked Kimberly. The women looked at one another.

"Well," said Baya-Iza, "I for one and damned curious." She started toward the door.

"I've always wanted to meet Geb," said She-mah-hon.

Kimberly shrugged her shoulders and followed.

"I haven't," mumbled Saskia.

. . .

The liches of the Whispering Way were gathered in the circular chamber beneath the Ebon Mausoleum. "What is he doing?" asked Masgava. "We haven't heard from him in—"

"The question of his motivation is irrelevant," said Eratosthenes. "We must consider only this, will we obey?"

"We must assume that our armies are under his control," said Neacal Aodhan.

Each lich in attendance had, in addition to his personal quarters under the Ebon Mausoleum, an estate somewhere within Geb, most being on the outskirts of Mechitar, where they kept their personal armies of undead and much of their wealth. The allure of the rather cramped space beneath the school was camaraderie, not of the social kind, per se, but more of an academic coming together.

The liches had advanced so far into the study of necromancy that they now encountered thorny problems. They often conferred, shared thoughts and experiences, and generally pushed each other to new heights (depths?) in their study of the dark art. Also, as many an academic, inventor, and artist knows, a pared-down living space spurs creativity and focus.

"They are," said Eratosthenes. "I can feel that I've lost control, that I am—diminished." He looked at his fellow liches. "Only the most powerful undead could resist Geb's summons."

"Could they be counted and known?" asked Ashoka.

"Hent-er-Neheh?" asked Ólchobar Yevan.

"Certainly," said Masgava. "Where is Cassius?"

"He could not resist," said Eratosthenes, who turned to Dagillus. "You did not hear Geb's call?" Dagillus shook his head.

"Only the undead?" asked Neacal.

"Geb has no need for the living," said Ólchobar.

"A shame that Cassius was not strong enough," said Masgava.

"It matters not," said Eratosthenes. "We shall join him."

"Do you decide for all of us?" asked Ólchobar.

"As co-chancellor I must go. As adherents of the Whispering Way you must see that the nation of Geb is not ruined by this." Eratosthenes paused, choosing his words. "I will not order you to join me. I will not ask you to join me. I will merely point out this fact, if you do not obey Geb's call, he will know."

. . .

Hent-er-Neheh sat in her usual chair at the end of the long, painted hall. The brazers burned, throwing both light and shadow over her. She had been conferring with the diplomats from Nemret Noktoria, Khamati at her side. Now she was alone. They had all heard Geb's call. His voice interrupted their strategizing and made them mute.

Khamati and the diplomats rose at once, without a word, and began the long march to Geb's Rest, where the master awaited them. Hent-er-Neheh felt an impulse to do likewise, but fought it off. It had taken all of her considerable willpower to do so. Not in her thousands of years as a mummy lord, not even in her days as a mortal, had she ever felt so strong a pull.

She replayed scenes from her long history with Geb. She remembered him as a boy, long-limbed, skinny, with a dangerous determination in his eyes. She knew he was destined for greatness even then, when he hadn't a single spell at his command. If she was honest, she was afraid of him, afraid of him even when he was a boy, afraid of the destiny so clearly and defiantly stamped on his features.

She wanted to be angry, so badly wanted it, but the emotion would not come. She had risen to be co-chancellor and would soon figure out a way to take the rod of rulership completely into her own hands, and now Geb had taken the rod away. He had shown that it was always his. She could rule nothing when he ruled all.

Hent-er-Neheh realized that the nation of Geb was an illusion. Everything that she and others had claimed as theirs was only free to be claimed because Geb had refrained from exercising his will. Now that he had, the false facade crumbled. The undead of Geb were merely on loan to them, they belonged to Geb.

"We thought we had power," she said to the silent hall and its flickering shadows. "We thought we were to be feared." She laughed. "But we are kings on a stage and you, nephew, are a king in real life."

. . .

Narcisse was savoring a mouthful of rice-wine, which had been imported from Tian at considerable expense, when an acolyte rushed in. He narrowed his eyes and watched as the acolyte, aware he was angering the one who had power over him, slowed his stride to a respectful walk, head bowed.

"I know what you've done," said Narcisse when the acolyte stopped before him. "You've ruined all the cocoa nibs I so laboriously had brought from the Mwangi

Expanse. You have! I can feel the guilt pouring from you like steam from a boiling pot."

"Master—"

"No, no!" interrupted Narcisse, wagging his finger. "Did I not tell you that the flavor of the chocolate depends on the care taken in the complex process of grinding, heating, and blending the nibs? If you cannot find your way around the kitchen then stay out!"

"But, Master, this has nothing to do with chocolate."

Narcisse sat back in his overstuffed chair, still skeptical. "The nibs?"

"Master, the nibs are fine, the undead are leaving!"

"The undead are—" Narcisse tried to figure out what undead, any undead, had to do with his precious cocoa nibs. He was unable to draw a connection. "How does this concern me?" He waved his hand and took up his cup of rice wine. "Nah-le-tah is—"

"He's leaving too!"

Narcisse set down his cup and eyed the acolyte. "I'm going to rise from this comfortable chair, in which I have only just now deposited my behind, go downstairs, and see to this madness you speak of. You know how I hate those stairs. If this," he began to rise, the acolyte quick to help, "is some kind of blown-out-of-proportion fantasy of yours," he grabbed and shook the acolyte, "I'll put you on a strict water and gruel diet. You'll forget the word 'flavor' by the time I'm done with you."

"But, Master," whispered the acolyte, "it's true—the undead, they're all leaving."

. . .

First, Narcisse went to see Nah-le-tah, but the hall contained only the sick. He waddled to the High Priest's chamber, where the many stone faces of Geb—and nothing else—greeted him.

"I told you—" Began the acolyte but Narcisse raised a pudgy hand to silence him. He went and stood beneath the rose window, looking up. Once he had mentally said a prayer to his goddess he went outside. He made it no further than the top step before he was stunned into inaction. He gripped both the railing and his acolyte's arm for support.

The streets surrounding the Church of Epiphenomena were packed with undead *and* living. The living were almost all necromancers or clerics of Urgathoa. He spotted Nah-le-tah and the other tomb giants in the crowd but he could not find his voice to call to them.

"By the will of the Pallid Princess," he said to his acolyte, "what is going on?"

"I don't know, Master."

Disorder ruled. The disorder was relegated to the living. The dead, there were so many of so many types, noticed Narcisse, were all making their way north, out of the city. The living, including powerful necromancers and priests, behaved as if they were children separated from their parents in a crowd of strangers. It seemed to Narcisse that they could not control the undead and, having lost a power which is most precious to them, didn't know what to do with themselves.

Nah-le-tah, seeing Narcisse, turned and began to force his way toward the church.

"A glorious sight," said the tomb giant.

"A confusing sight," said Narcisse. "Please do tell, what is all this?"

"Geb has called his undead to him."

"Geb has—" Narcisse looked from his fellow cleric to the multitude of undead. "Geb has done this?"

"Who else?" asked Nah-le-tah, his booming laugh reverberated from the church's marble.

"But—why?" asked Narcisse.

"Ask him."

Narcisse looked at Nah-le-tah. "Where are you—are you going to Geb?"

"Of course."

Something large, dark, and which radiated malevolent energy, flew overhead. Narcisse glanced up but looked back down, lest the thing wither his limbs or do Urgathoa-only-knew what else to him.

"Sthaga?" asked Narcisee.

Nah-le-tah looked north, down the crowded avenue. "Out there, somewhere." He looked at Narcisse. "He leads the advanced guard. He and his kind." The giant laughed.

"You find humor in the oddest things," mumbled Narcisse.

"Will you come?" asked Nah-le-tah.

Narcisse looked up at him. "I, ah," he glanced at his protruding middle, "I'm not built for travel."

A second tomb giant approached and spoke to Nah-le-tah in a language they shared, but which Narcisse was ignorant of. Nah-le-tah turned back.

"I'll do what I can to send news." He turned and began north, joining the ribbon of undead that led from the capital to the southeastern tip of the Axan Wood.

Narcisse released the railing and gripped the arm of his acolyte with both hands. "Quick, you fool, to the cellar for something stronger than rice wine. Oh, we must drink on this! Oh! Oh!"

. . .

Kemnebi and Elana were in bed, she lying atop him, kissing her way up his bare chest to his lips. He guided her with his hands on her back, awaiting her lips on his. When she arrived he kissed her with passion, their tongues mingling. Elana toyed with the tips of his canines, sliding her tongue under them, the danger of them an aphrodisiac. She pulled back and moved her head to the side, to kiss and bite his neck, to suck on the lobe of his ear, and finally returned to his lips, but he did not return her kiss. His lips remained as rigid as stone. Elana opened her eyes.

Kemnebi had a look of terrible concentration. Beads of blood were forming on his forehead. His body grew alarmingly hot under Elana, so hot she slid from him and looked. The muscles of his abdomen were hard. His entire body was rigid, his muscles tensed. She looked again into his face and saw that he was biting his lip, his fangs having punctured his flesh.

She was about to speak when he let out a low moan, his body relaxed, and he reached up to touch his lip. He wiped the blood from his lip and brow and turned to Elana. He did not speak. Neither did Elana, she waited.

"Geb." Kemnebi did not elaborate.

"Geb?" asked Elana.

Kemnebi sat up and turned toward the door. He looked at Elana then got out of bed, his nude body reflecting the dimly glowing magical lights in the room, and went to the door. He lifted the iron bar and set it aside. He yanked open the door and stepped out, looking right and left. He turned back. "Gone."

Elana stared back, confused.

"The vrykolakas. They're both gone."

Elana pulled the sheet up over her breasts. "They're —gone?"

Kemnebi came into the room and sat on the edge of the bed. He reached out and took Elana's hand. "A moment ago I heard Geb's voice. He called me to him." He shook his head. "I had to fight against it." He looked toward the open door. "They must have heard him, too. But, did he call to me *and* them? Why would he want them?" He looked at Elana.

"I didn't hear anything." She looked past Kemnebi through the door. "Is Geb—"

"He's out there, where he's been for—" He stood. "The vrykolakas—if they—" He shook his head. "Was he calling specifically to me?" He looked at Elana. "He didn't call me by name. If they went to him it means—"

"What?" asked Elana. "What does it mean?"

Kemnebi sat on the bed. "I don't know."

. . .

"I know," said the barmaid, smiling at Ahrhune. "Another?"

"One more, to send me to bed," said Ahrhune. He was seated at a small table in the Sea Bird, the sailor's bar and bunk house he found after abandoning the *Battered Skull*. He looked down at a map of Geb, the Mana Waste, and Nex spread out on the table. It cost him most of his remaining funds. The expense was worth it. The map was the most accurate he could find. Still, the majority of the Mana waste was blank. Only Lake Ustradi, the Ustradi River, and the major towns were noted. The four corners of the map were held down by empty mugs.

The waitress walked over, making her way effortlessly through the late evening crowd. She stopped and looked down at the map. She was uneducated so the names and shapes meant little to her, still, due to the detail of the map she was intrigued. "What's that?"

"Geb," said Ahrhune, pointing. "The Mana Waste," he moved his finger. "Nex."

"Oh," the girl laughed. "Where are we?"

"Quantium, here." Ahrhune planted his finger on the map, covering the capital of Nex.

"Wench!" cried one of the sailors.

The waitress rolled her eyes and gave Ahrhune a knowing look. She plucked one of the empty mugs from a corner and set down the full one. The sailor who hailed her reached out and grabbed her wrist, turning her. This jostled the mug and foam spilled over the mug's lip onto the map.

Ahrhune watched as the foam raced toward his finger. The sounds of the nearly full taproom fell away. The motions of the other sailors stilled. The details of the background faded into darkness. Ahrhune could both hear and feel his heart beating. He watched the foam advance, the bubbles climbing over one another as if battling for supremacy. He lifted his finger and the foam washed over Quantium.

Without knowing his own actions Ahrhune reached up and gripped the holy symbol of Sarenrae that hung around his neck on a gold chain. The colors and shapes returned to the room. The loud talking and laughter resumed. The barmaid returned to his table, pulling a towel from her belt. She began to blot the map.

"Oh, I hope I haven't ruined it." She cast a worried glance at Ahrhune. But he wasn't paying attention. He was watching her hand, watching the towel. "There," she said. "Doesn't look too bad." She smiled at Ahrhune. "That one's on me, eh. No hard feelings?" She hurried away. But Ahrhune was still staring at the map. Where Quantium had been was now a black smudge. It appeared as if someone had reached down like a god and wiped it from the face of Golarion.

Ahrhune realized he was gripping his holy symbol so tightly he was hurting his hand. He let go of it and looked from the map to his palm. Some features of the holy symbol had become implanted in his hand in the shape of angry red marks. He closed his hand into a fist and studied those in the room about him. For a moment he saw them as he had seen them in the prophetic dream Sarenrae had given him; he saw their bloody faces and hands, the wounds that caused their life to seep from them, and their blank eyes and he shuddered.

Home

The Spellscar Desert, the Mana Waste, Arodus, 4711

Mutant gnolls carried him wrapped in a filthy, flea-infested blanket. They knew where his kind could be found. They walked all night, heading toward the cliffs overlooking the Obari. The one carrying him threw the unconscious svirfneblin over his shoulder as he climbed down the cliff face. The gnolls passed him hand-to-hand, a hundred foot drop onto wave-blasted stones would be the result of a faulty grip.

They found the cave opening half way down the cliff face and entered, ducking beneath the salt-encrusted stone. They saw clearly in near-total darkness with the night-predator eyes of hyenas, their close kin. They watched as stones were moved by levers and from behind them tiny, dark-skinned figures, that, like themselves, had been touched by the wild, angry magic of the Mana Waste, looked out.

The gnolls held the blanketed figure, yipping excitedly. They pulled back the yellowed cloth to reveal his face. The gnomes recognized him as one of their own. They also recognized that the gnolls hadn't eaten him *and* that they handled him with something approaching veneration.

The gnolls set him at their feet. They laid his rifle and pistol next to him. Before they left the tunnel they touched him, imprinting the memory of his features onto their fingertips. The svirfneblin watched from behind the protective cover of their boulders but said nothing. They feared gnolls. The last of the gnolls knelt over Ilyx and looked into his face, he had never seen what he took to be a god before. He wanted to remember it forever. Finally he rose, still crouching in the low-ceiling tunnel, and followed his pack-mates out.

The svirfneblin did not further move the boulders until the gnolls had scrambled up the cliff face and were gone. They worked their levers and slid out into the tunnel, gathering around Ilyx.

. . .

Ilyx heard sobbing and opened his eyes. He did not see the stars above. He felt no breeze. He heard no sounds of insects, birds, or small mammals scurrying. He tried to sit up, but a sharp pain in his abdomen stopped him. He reached down to his hip and felt the empty holster. The sobbing increased and he turned. A figure advanced from the darkness and, much to his astonishment, he recognized her. It was his mother.

She fell over him, her good arm sliding under and partially lifting him. She kissed his face, his hands. Her twisted, useless arm hung in a sling. It banged against him as she moved over him. He reached up and pushed her back.

"Son, son!" she cried, her words slurred by her lisp. She reached up with her good hand and wiped the tears from her eyes. Ilyx's brother came into the room, dragging his swollen, misshapen foot, and hobbled up next to their mother. He smiled, revealing a jumble of yellow teeth.

"Bro-ther," he stammered. He tilted his head back and began to laugh; the sound like a wounded seal calling for help. Ilyx clapped his hands over his ears.

Is the boy—" called a voice Ilyx recognized as his father's. An elderly svirfneblin made his way into the room, feeling along the wall. His eyelids were concave, for he had been born without eyes.

"Son, son!" repeated his mother.

"Bro-ther!" cried his brother, again with the seal-sounds.

"The boy lives!" cried his father, feeling his way to Ilyx. He reached down and began to feel his son, touching his face.

Ilyx knocked his father's hands away. He reached out and covered his brother's mouth to halt the horrible sound. He tried to sit up but the pain in his stomach wouldn't allow it.

"Be still, boy," said his father. "You're hurt."

Ilyx reached down and began to tentatively feel his stomach but he could identify no wound, for it was within. He lay back and resigned himself. His mother bent over him, kissing him. His father's hands moved over his face. His brother bleated like a wounded seal.

Home," Ilyx said, a word he'd never wanted to utter again.

. . .

Ilyx sat on the edge of his fur-topped stone bed and drank fish soup from a ceramic bowl.

"We thought you had died above," said his father, who held one of his hands. "Under that burning ball of fire ain't no place for us."

"Son, son," said his mother.

"Yes, it' the boy," said his father, for the hundredth time.

"You're mother's in shock," said Ilyx's father. "She probably takes you as a ghost. The other elders wanted to throw you into the ocean." He laughed. "But only your brother's strong enough to lift you and they would never be able to convince him to do it." His father patted Ilyx's armor, then fingered the rifle's stock. "The chain I recognize," he said. "What's this?"

"Gun," said Ilyx.

"Hmmm. Something from the surface, I suppose. Surface dwellers have the damnedest ingenuity." He squeezed Ilyx's hand. "So, boy, you finally came home. I remember when you swore the lot of us to the Nine Hells. Glad you changed your mind."

"Didn't."

"Any idea why the gnolls acted as they did? Us elders are sure at a loss. They acted as if you were some kind of mythical god-spawn. You should have seen how they handled you. Of course, I didn't see it, but I was told." He laughed. "I suppose that bit of rubbish was their finest blanket. How did you convince them not to eat you?" He paused, but his son did not speak. "Silent as ever, eh? Fine then, keep your secrets. Oh, it's good to have you back, boy. Not that much has changed with us. The other elders will want to see you. They were always suspicious of you, you know. Seeing as how you aren't, well, like the rest of us."

"No."

"Oh, don't worry about them. They mostly want to gawk is all."

"Son, son."

"Yes, woman, it's your boy. Here." He held out his free hand. His wife came forward and put her wrist into his palm. He pulled her forward and she hugged Ilyx, who sat aside his now empty bowl. "I swear, she's half afraid you'll vanish again if she loves on you too much. He's back, woman, give him as many kisses as you've got. Well, boy, you seem to have recovered fairly quick. Must not have been hurt so bad after all. I suppose," he gripped his son's hand, "that means you'll be leaving us again."

"Yes," said Ilyx.

"Son, son!" cried his mother.

"Now, now, he ain't going this minute. He's got more heart than that. Ain't ya, boy?"

Ilyx did not respond.

. . .

"A mutation, gotta be," said his father, feeling his way back onto the room. "That's what we've decided." He made his way to Ilyx, who lay resting in his bed. "So, you're like us after all, just in some way we've never heard of or even imagined." His father sat. "Do you remember Langgevin's son, oh, now what is that boy's name, well, never mind that. He can shape clay into those little creatures that run around trying to bite everyone? A nuisance, but they keep the rats away. How can he do that? Or what about Dolca? You remember her, don't you? She looks like you, normal, I suppose, but she can create all those colored lights and all those strange sounds. Well, I remember magic, sure, and I suppose that's what they got. But you, boy, what you told us, well, is that magic?"

Ilyx grunted and shrugged his shoulders. His throat was hoarse from talking to the elders and he wanted something smooth and refreshing to drink, something more than dirty water.

"What a strange land," said Ilyx's father. "It's worked its way into us. Oh, why did our ancestors come up to the surface anyway? Curiosity? Well, look what that's done." He laughed but quickly grew somber. "Well, boy, we don't know much. We ain't got much. By the gods, I don't even understand these contraptions you've got with you. I don't think there's anything we can do for you and I know you ain't gonna stay." He grew emotional. "But until you're a father you'll never understand what it means to know your son is alive when you figured him for dead." He sniffled. "And your mother." He chuckled. "She's fifty years younger. I never knew how heavy a burden weighed on her heart." He turned toward Ilyx and squeezed his hand. "Stay a spell, boy, and let me soak you in. You can tell us about the surface, about your adventures, tell us anything you got to tell us, boy. We'll listen. Even the other elders are curious, and you know how they are about things."

"No."

"Boy, it ain't gonna kill you to say more than one word."

"No."

"You'll tell us," said Ilyx's father. "You'll tell us and you'll say your goodbyes and you'll leave, and none of us will ever know what happens to you up there." He squeezed his son's hand. "But you'll tell us about your life, you gotta give us that much."

The Burning Edge

Geb's Rest and the Axan Wood, Geb, Arodus, 4711

The coterie of vampires from Graydirge reached him first. They'd morphed into bats, flown a hundred miles, abandoning garrison skeletons and field zombies. They landed and took their natural shapes.

They were influenced by the fashions of the Empty Threshold, by the style of Zon-Kuthon. They wore black, tight-fitting leather outfits that She-mah-hon would appreciate, had she seen them. Steel spikes, rings, and bars pierced their flesh. Their hair was oddly cut and styled. No matter what color their hair had been before, it was now black, white, or silver, sometimes all three. They colored their eyes and lips black. None of them had ever seen Geb but now they stood close to him, not speaking, not even really looking at him. They waited, as he had instructed.

Geb faced northeast, as he had before, but he no longer stared at the Refuge of Nex, he watched the murderer of magic, the deep gnome. He saw him lying beneath the earth, among his kin. He had watched as the gnolls carried his unconscious form across the Spellscar Desert. He extended his will, his power, and, unbeknownst to Ilyx, kept him safe. Ilyx couldn't have been safer if a god had shielded him, but he would have been much better off.

If the Graydirge vampires felt—at some level—the approaching dawn, they didn't hide from it. They could have hidden amongst the discarded blocks of stone, wiggling like worms into the gaps between them. They could have buried themselves in the soil. They didn't. If they panicked inside they showed no sign of it outwardly. They did not look to the east as the sky began to glow. They did not change their expressions as the soft light of dawn fell upon their cheeks. When they began to smoke they showed no discomfort. Geb spared no effort to save them.

The horizon became a burning edge of light. Flames licked their flesh, dancing over black leather. Sunlight reflected from their piercings. The vampires' pale faces became as black as their painted lips. They did not scream. They did not lift their hands to block the sun. They waited, as Geb had commanded. They stood, silent and motionless, as the sun incinerated them. They had been the burning edge of Geb's army, the first to arrive, and they were the first to die for him. Not because he wished them to die. He simply hadn't cared enough to make an allowance for their weakness.

. . .

Sthaga and the wraiths of Mechitar were racing through the Axan Wood when rays of light began to filter through the leaves above. Sthaga knew the sting of sunlight. He had felt an approximation of it not long before, but the real sun was many times more oppressively violent. What he had felt before was an instant of pure light created by magic. Now he felt the real thing, the burning edge. It pressed down on him like a blanket of fire, smothering and inescapable. But, despite the threat of the sun, he could not stop. He could not retreat to safety. He could not seek the shadows. He continued to race through the trees, as did all of the wraiths.

The Axan's shadows were plentiful but not true darkness. They are pools of pink-gray and any undead who is slain by sunlight knows that they are a worthless refuge. As the sun rose higher and higher the shadows diminished. The wraiths, passing through clearings, or finding little pools of light, or moving from the shade of one tree to the next were vaporized.

The wraiths and other sunlight-fearing undead of Mechitar had entered the Axan Wood while the moon was high above. None exited, for the moon relinquished its celestial throne to the sun. All things in the cycle of time. Of course Geb did not care. His army would have no vampires, no wraiths, no sun-weak undead but so what. He had plenty of other soldiers at his command.

The same fate awaited all those undead in Geb that were harmed by the sun and who had succumbed to Geb's will. They died while answering his call. They died while racing to his side. He felt their loss yet cared not. They were the burning edge.

Geb Speaks, Nex Listens

Rhianna's Hunting Lodge, the Axan Wood, Geb, Arodus, 4711

Elana slipped from beneath the sheets, stood, and looked down at Kemnebi. He lay on his back, still, arms at his sides, eyes closed, chest silent. There were no windows in the room. She did not really know if the sun had risen. Judging from Kemnebi's state, she assumed it had. She walked softly to the iron bar, reached out, then recalled Kemnebi's wards on the doors and room. She could leave but she could not re-enter and she worried about that.

She lifted the bar and set it aside. She opened the door and stepped out, shutting the door behind her. The hunting lodge was empty and silent. She moved through its rooms, rooms filled with stuffed and mounted heads, weapons on display, and empty bottles of mead. She went to the back door and opened it. The sounds of the Axan Wood greeted her; the chatter of birds, the rustling of the leaves on the breeze, chipmunks chirped, darting into tall grass when the door opened.

A jack rabbit was sitting on the stones that made up the patio, a bit of clover in its mouth. It chewed and looked at Elana. She stepped out and shut the door behind her. The rabbit turned and hopped away.

Elana scanned the trees and bushes. She listened. She cast a spell that would enable her to detect the presence of undead but when she looked she saw nothing. She walked across the patio but did not enter the woods. She wanted to stay close enough that she could dart back inside if need be.

She pulled enchanted earrings from her bag and slipped them into her ears. She retrieved the enchanted necklace and clasped it around her neck. "Master

Castelli?" she asked, waiting. She looked skyward and estimated the time from the low position of the sun. She worried he was asleep. "Master Castelli?"

She went to a stone bench and sat, staring out into the Axan. The rabbit returned and sat chewing yet more clover, watching her. She called repeatedly into the necklace. A half an hour passed this way before he answered, his voice sleepy.

"Yes?"

"Master Castelli?"

"Yes."

"Geb speaks."

"Nex listens."

"Geb tried to call Kemnebi to him."

There was a moment of silence. Elana imagined Master Castelli sitting up in bed, rubbing the crust from his eyelids, waking up and trying to discern if what he had heard was a dream or reality.

"Say that again?"

"I was with Kemnebi—I am with Kemnebi—and last night Geb summoned him. He resisted."

"What did Geb say?" asked Master Castelli. "Tell me his exact words."

"I didn't hear, only Kemnebi."

"He—resisted?"

"Yes."

"Where is he now? Where are you?"

"At Rhianna's hunting lodge, in the southern Axan Wood."

"Tell me all that has happened since we last spoke."

Elana summarized events.

"One more thing, Master," added Elana. "Kemnebi created a pair of undead minions. They were guarding us. When Geb called him, those monsters, they left. Kemnebi said that Geb hadn't called him specifically, hadn't called him by name. I asked him what it meant that his creations had left. I asked him why Geb had summoned him. He didn't know."

A long period of silence followed before Master Castelli spoke again. "Is he—"

"Yes."

"Are you near him?"

"I'm outside."

"Who else is there?" asked Master Castelli.

"No one, we're alone."

"Leave—" Master Castelli urged. "Return to Nex."

"But, why? He's a valuable—"

"He is no longer chancellor. He has no power, no influence. He is exiled to the Axan Wood. He has no value."

"But, Master—"

"He is not worth the danger you're in," said Master Castelli. "Return to Nex."

"I can't, Master—I, we—" Master Castelli waited for his agent to continue. "We've been—intimate."

"Such a thing is to be expected. It is immaterial," said Master Castelli, his voice thick with authority. "Return to Nex."

"I—" Elana stammered. "I'm in love with him. I can't leave him. I won't."

"You're not safe, Elana," said Master Castelli. The authority in his voice had been replaced with fatherly concern.

"I'm safe. He's powerful. He resisted Geb."

"But Geb wanted him," said Master Castelli. "Geb will not be denied. I tell you, you're not safe."

"But I love—"

"Yes, and that love will get you killed. Listen to me, Elana. I'm not speaking to you now as your superior. You're like a daughter to me. Come home. Return to Nex. You are not safe."

"I won't. I'm sorry."

"We've no agents there, no support. You're down there alone."

"I know."

"Damn it," growled Master Castelli. He tried to focus on the importance of what had happened, on Geb's summoning of his former chancellor. He tried to guess why Geb had called Kemnebi. The added detail of the two undead minions' disappearance troubled him. Was it a coincidence? Was there someone or something other than Geb and Kemnebi involved? He couldn't afford assumptions—too risky in his trade—but interpreting facts was his job. He didn't have enough information and he hated that. "Stay close to him. I need you to figure out what Geb is doing, why he called Kemnebi. If he didn't call Kemnebi specifically I need you to figure out who all heard his call."

"I will."

Ask Kemnebi why his undead vanished—push him to unravel it."

"Yes, I will."

After a pause Master Castelli spoke again. "Elana—does he love you?"

"I—don't know."

"Does he know you love him? Have you told him?"

"I haven't said the words, but he must know."

"Has he said—"

"No."

"Elana, I want you to think rationally. Think about how much danger you're in."

"I've always been in danger." She chuckled. "Geb is dangerous."

"You know what I mean. You can come home. Your assignment is over." Elana heard his sigh through the enchanted earrings. "But if you stay, be careful."

"I will," said Elana. "And I will find out what Geb is up to."

"Geb speaks for real," said Master Castelli.

A Closed Door, an Open Door

The Bandeshar, Quantium, Nex, Rova, 4711

Master Castelli hurried down Warlock's Walk, the most prominent avenue in Quantium. He ignored the avenue's impressive sculptures. Some of them were even animated by magic, changing their poses to give the audience different views. They attracted tourists from all over Golarion, but he had other things on his mind. Not even the massive multi-sculptured fountain before the Bandeshar drew his attention and it was hard to ignore.

The fountain was Azlantian in origin. It had been found buried in the yard of a brewer, purchased at an astronomical price (the brewer started a well-funded, and therefore successful, distillery) and brought to the capital. Its arrival caused a regional renaissance in sculpture, the best examples of which Master Castelli had just passed.

He paused before entering the governmental palace and looked to his left. He could just see the sharp edge of the Refuge of Nex above the intervening roofs. The architecture—if it could be said to have architecture—of the Refuge was at odds with the overall theme of the city, a theme decided predominantly by one man, the city's Castellan, Elder Architect Oblosk, the ancient pech.

There was, at one time, a city park where the Refuge of Nex now stood. Nex walked to the edge of this outdoor space and raised his hand from his hip—slowly and deliberately—until it was pointed at the heavens. As he raised his hand a massive, dark red crystal, narrow and straight, rose from the ground until it stood two hundred feet high. It was semi-translucent. It cast a smoky red-gray shadow. It acted, ironically, as a sun dial that, looking down from the clouds, only the birds could read.

It wasn't a building at all; it was an unnatural crystalline growth. At the base of this crystal tower Nex had stonemasons build a set of plain stairs. At the top of these stairs he had blacksmiths mount against the red crystal a featureless iron frame and door. The door was without knob, lock, or key hole. The blacksmiths who mounted and secured it with iron bands that wrapped around the tower thought it was purely decorative—and woefully decorative at that.

Then Nex caused the door to open, revealing not the crystal beneath but an entirely different dimension of time and space. When the door closed behind him none knew if he would ever return or how to go in after him. As the years passed the crystal grew darker and darker, as if spilled ink slowly spread within.

Master Castelli had once stood before the plain iron door. Anyone could approach it. He was a young man then. He had come alone, just before dawn. He had even, in a sheepish mood, knocked on the door. His past impertinence no longer amused him.

He entered the Bandeshar and was escorted to a chair within a crowded room. He faced a large, ornate door. He knew that on the other side of that door the Council of Three and Nine were soon to meet. He was asked to be available, should they have any questions concerning the intelligence he had provided. He glanced around at the others who stood or sat. They were the assistants and aides to those within as well as those high ranking nobles who made it their business to be political gossips. Many were Arclords. They wore an expression of haughty impatience, feeling that they were on the wrong side of the door. Master Castelli identified with their sentiment, he felt the same way.

. . .

One of the twin doors on either side of the large white marble fireplace swung open and archmage Agrellus Kisk entered, tossing aside his open fronted robe, which an aid caught just before it landed on the floor. The aid retreated and shut the door, taking robe with him. Agrellus ignored everyone, even peers Iranez of the Orb and Elder Architect Oblosk. It was this trio who made up the "three" of the Council of Three and Nine.

The "nine" in the Council were in attendance too. This included Borume, the master alchemist of Oenopion, who had yet again successfully projected his consciousness into his gold and silver, alchemically-powered automation. The automation stood along one wall, facing Dunn Palovar's flesh golem opposite.

This was the flesh golem occupied by Dunn Palovar's projected consciousness. Few could say for certain, but many surmised, that Dunn had personally crafted the flesh golem to be as unsettling as possible. It was a mishmash of bloated, discolored human remains, stitched haphazardly together, offering glimpses of its bones and internal organs with every movement. Why had Dunn Pavolar gone to such lengths? Because he was an unpleasant man.

Equally unpleasant in appearance, but for entirely different reasons, was Master Phade. Actually, Master Phade could not be seen at all. He was an invisible stalker, a being native to the plane of air. In place of a material form he occupied an elaborate black leather suit that included boots, gloves, and an eyeless leather hood. Despite Master Phade's oddness he was unfailingly polite. What role did he play in the leadership of Nex? Master assassin, of course.

Seated in a chair, a piebald python playing over his hands, was Gen Hendrikian, the chief Riddler of the Scrivenbough, a temple and scriptorium devoted to the demon lord of serpents, magic, and forbidden lore. Gen Hendrikian was a nagaji, a race of ophidian humanoids said to be descended from nagas, those human-headed serpents who haunt ruins and nightmares. Like all nagaji, Gen Hendrikian had the forked tongue and lidless eyes of the serpent. Few enjoyed meeting his unblinking gaze.

While Gen was weird in an entirely obvious way the next of the nine was weird in a way few really understood. Elemion was a mutant, although he showed no obvious mutation. He appeared to be a middle-aged but still athletic and handsome Garundi. He was, however, only one-third of a tripartite being. His two other components were in the Mana Waste. Elemion represented the largest nomadic tribe residing in the Mana Waste. When he spoke it was unclear if the thoughts expressed came from the Elemion in attendance or one of the other two. Each could see, hear, and speak through the other, the three being one.

Astor Bizet, an androgynous elven man with flowing blonde hair, flawless skin, and large green eyes (although he sometimes preferred to be called a woman, and often dressed and acted unmistakably feminine), was the High Priest of the Church of Pharasma in the capital. His nature was fluid and could not be pinned down, not even by him (or her, depending). Astor Bizet had a personal following that came close to being a cult. He could be all to any, drawing everyone. He did not abuse this power, indeed, he seemed unaware of it. This made him all the more alluring.

Rixende Orth, a human woman in her late-middle years, was the High Priestess of the popular church of Nethys in the capital. She could pass for the wife of a baker with her plain looks, unflattering haircut, and somewhat dumpy physique, she was however a person to be feared as she was well acquainted with both halves of her god, the half which strove to preserve the world through the thoughtful application of powerful magics and the half bent on destroying the world through the malevolent application of same.

Fero Zetterling, a short, stout, balding man represented the wishes of the powerful and wealthy Merchant's League. Although he had no martial or magical might he, more than any other in the room, held the strings to a mighty purse. This power could command the other two, and often did.

The final member of the nine was the holy hermit Pyree, a worshipper of Irori, the god of history, knowledge, and self-perfection. Pyree occupied a cave near the Well of Lies, a particularly dangerous environ, especially for a hermit. None knew how to contact Pyree, yet he unfailingly attended the meetings of the Council, even emergency meetings like this, as evidenced by his unkempt presence.

"As you all know," said Agrellus, "I have just returned from the Mana Waste." He looked over the room's occupants. "Scrying into Geb has always been difficult, but, at times possible." He motioned to Iranez. "When we learned that Geb was becoming," he paused, "communicative, we tried to take a look at him. It was then that we learned that Geb, the man, is completely shielding Geb, the nation, from divination."

"Can you be certain that it is Geb?" asked Elemion. Agrellus shot him a dismissive look.

"Who else could accomplish that?" He strode further into the room and stood, feet wide, arms crossed over his chest. "I teleported to Alkenstar, changed my shape into that of a dragon," here he smirked, as few could manage such a feat and he enjoyed illustrating his power, "and flew along the border."

"Yes, we know—" Iranez said, her tone sharp with impatience. He continued, un-phased.

"I saw the undead amassing at Geb's Rest." He looked over the assembled council members for effect. "I watched as they crossed over the border and entered the Spellscar desert. Geb leads an army and he is heading directly," he pointed at the floor between his feet, "here. To Quantium."

All the members knew this. They had all been apprised. But to hear it from Agrellus carried more weight. A bit of murmuring ensued.

"An army of undead?" asked Astor Bizet. He meant this as a rhetorical question, which became obvious when he then suggested that, "we must call upon our respective faiths." He looked at Rixende, who sat close to him. "An army of undead falls to a smaller force of faithful clerics."

"A wise idea, Astor," said Iranez. "Any cleric of a good god who is willing to travel to Nex should be encouraged to do so. Can this call-to-arms be communicated through the churches?"

Astor nodded.

"Perhaps," added Rixende, "we should consider reimbursing those who we call upon, to encourage ease of transport."

"Yes, of course," said Agrellus, who wanted to take back over direction of the conversation. He was interrupted by Gen Hendrikian.

"There is a significant cult to the Dawnflower in Qadira," said the nagaji. "Sarenrae despises evil which cannot or will not be redeemed. Let us call upon them. Let Qadira send us her dervishes. We can put them to good use."

"Qadira," said Master Phade, he bowed to Gen, "if you will pardon my interruption." Gen nodded. "Wishes nothing more than to war against Taldor yet they cannot.

Have they a pent-up martial spirit? We have two baits, so to speak, with which to lure them."

Iranez spoke before Agrellus could re-capture the conversation. "Depending on how quickly Geb moves," she said, "only geographically close allies can have any hope of helping. We can reasonably count on Jalmeray, Katapesh, Osirion, Thuvia, Absolom, Taldor, Andoran, and perhaps Cheliax. It is an impressive but problematic list."

"Each poses its own—difficulties," said Agrellus. "Jalmeray is small and does not have much of an army. Kharswam is too weak and too concerned with tending his gardens and feeding his fowl to be upset at a neighbor's fate."

"There are many monasteries on the island," said Elemion. "The monks could be of aid. Who knows what strange feats they have mastered."

"We cannot expect much from Katapesh," said Fero Zetterling, of the Merchant's League. "They would relish seeing a commercial competitor laid low. Besides," he waved his hand dismissively, "they don't even have an army, only those odd constructs—"

"Aluum," interrupted Dunn Pavolar, who knew well the abilities of the Pactmasters when it came to his craft. He had tried, unsuccessfully, to reverse engineer the Aluums.

"Yes, thank you," said Fero.

"You must remember," said Iranez, "that if Nex falls to Geb, the southern border of Katapesh will no longer abut Nex, but Geb, a state of affairs they would not desire."

"Yes, you are right," said Fero. "If we point this out to them they would be more apt to send aid, if not soldiers and spellcasters, at least monetary aid."

"Ruby Prince Khemet," said Agrellus, "has been expanding Osirion's military. Perhaps he could be persuaded to lend some of these soldiers to aid an ally. It should be pointed out to him that this could be an opportunity to battle harden them."

"He could be counted on for monetary support, if nothing else," added Fero. "His ego would be pleased by spending his people's wealth on our behalf."

"Grand Prince Stavian," said Agrellus, "could be persuaded to send soldiers, especially for a price. The only question is getting them to Nex in time to be of use."

"Thuvia," said Pyree, speaking for the first time, "is a collection of city states and as such they will be unlikely to send much military aid. No city would want to empty itself of soldiers while others did not. However, each city may send some support."

"Will it arrive in time?" asked Astor. No one answered, as it was apparent to all that Geb was moving quickly, far quicker than any potential ally would or could.

"Our best hope," said Agrellus, "is to fortify our standing army with conscripts. Every male of fighting age will be conscripted. The women, children, and infirm will be evacuated to Oenopion."

"There is not room enough," said Borume. His voice was accompanied by the hissing of fluids through tubes and the light tapping of metal upon metal.

"Erect a tent village, if you must," said Agrellus.

"What makes you think," snapped Borume, "that Oenopion will not face attack?"

Agrellus turned to Borume's construct. "Why would Geb bother with Oenopion?"

"You've always under appreciated our—"

"Please," said Iranez. "We've made it this long without bickering, let's not start."

"How will we arm this conscript army?" asked Pyree.

"They must bring what they have," said Iranez. "We shall beat plowshares into swords if we must."

"How will we feed them?" asked Pyree. "Geb provides Nex with the majority of its grains. Certainly we have stores but we must consider the upcoming winter."

"We shall have to import from elsewhere," said Fero. "We'll begin working on that."

"Elder Architect," said Agrellus, "will you see to the physical defenses of the capital?" The pech nodded. "Thank you, Elder. Not only must we conscript every able-bodied man we must recruit every practitioner of the arcane and every cleric in Nex. We—"

"If I may again be so rude as to interrupt?" asked Master Phade. "Why not strike directly at Geb? Assassination? I would be happy to—"

"A fine idea under normal circumstances," said Iranez. "But Geb is a ghost. I believe only divine magic could harm him, and even then, it would take a powerful and brave cleric to assassinate him."

"An assassin would get no where near him," said Agrellus.

"What about Alkenstar?" asked Elemion.

"What about it?" snapped Agrellus.

"They could send out those cannons of theirs to harass and delay Geb's army. That would buy us, and our allies, time."

"Yes," said Agrellus. "I will command it." When he said this Iranez snickered but Agrellus wisely let it go.

"Borume," said Agrellus. "Send all of your alchemist to the capital."

The metal skull laughed. "We will turn the countryside into a marsh of alchemical agents which will dissolve Geb's army before it even reaches Quantium."

Agrellus turned to the flesh golem. "Dunn—"

"Yes, empty the Fleshforge." The flesh golem spoke with a deep, fractured voice. "I would point out that if you had given the kind of financial support I've been requesting for years that Nex would have enough golems to have prevented this in the first place."

"You think you're underfunded?" challenged Borume. "You would not believe how skimpy—"

"Gentlemen," called Iranez. She again successfully prevented a long simmering feud from boiling over. She turned to Agrellus. "If we draw away all protection from Oenopion and Ecanus we will leave their populations defenseless. This may encourage Geb to attack them, slay the living, and bring them back as undead."

"This would bolster his army," added Rixende.

"And be terrible for morale," said Astor. "Our conscript army would face the shambling corpses of their own wives, children, and elderly parents."

"No," said Agrellus. "Geb will not bother with them. His main advantage is speed. He will not detour, not even for soft targets. He will overrun Quantium. All else can be done after."

"In this I must agree with Agrellus," said Elder Architect Oblosk. "Geb is only concerned with victory. His surest path to victory is through Quantium."

"The Spellscar will hurt him more than he knows," said Elemion. "His own foul magic will have its revenge. It will decimate his army."

"Sadly," said Elder Architect Oblosk, "I must disagree. He will lose some, no doubt, but not enough to stop him."

"We have forgotten Nex," said Pyree. The other members of the council looked at him. "What if this threat draws him from seclusion, much as it has summoned me from my respite in the scrublands of the Shattered Range?"

“Perhaps it is fate,” added Astor. Pharasma was the goddess of fate, so he, as high priest, was more conscious of it as a force in the affairs of man than most. “The war between them has never been satisfactorily decided.”

“Will Nex defend his nation against his archnemesis?" asked Pyree. Everyone instinctively looked to Elder Architect Oblosk, who, of all in the room, was the only one who knew Nex personally. The pech thought for some time.

“We cannot put our faith in him.” He looked at the other council members. “As much as I would like to believe he would return to save his nation and his people,” the pech shook his head. “I would not count on it.” A moment of disappointment quieted the room. But the council members, long used to ruling without Nex’s aid, did not dwell on his absence.

“Agrellus?" asked Iranez. “How large is his army?”

“I don’t know.”

“Do dragons have poor eyesight?" asked Iranez.

Agrellus frowned. “We must focus on defending Quantium.” He looked at Borume’s construct. “Do not delay.” He turned to the flesh golem. “Either of you. Send everything you’ve got.”

“I will put out word and begin organizing the conscripts,” volunteered Iranez. “Who will take charge of evacuating the city?”

The holy hermit Pyree spoke. “I know well the way from Quantium to Oenopion. I shall lead the people.”

“Thank you," said Iranez.

Oblosk sighed. “I’ve got trenches to dig and walls to erect.”

“Let us speak to the faithful," said Astor to Rixende, who nodded.

“Mercenaries,” said Fero. “I know some people. The public purse will buy us many a sell sword.”

"Please see to it," said Iranez.

The group was about to disband when Gen Hendrikian spoke.

"Geb does more," everyone turned to the Chief Riddler, "than we think." He lifted the python's head and watched as its forked tongue tasted the air. "Or perhaps less." He looked from the python to Agrellus. "Is defending Quantium best?" He shifted his unblinking eyes to Iranez. "Let us present to Geb an open door." He looked back down at the python. "This is what he's coming for."

"This is no time for riddles," snapped Agrellus. "We've work to do."

A City Possessed by Joy, a House by Sorrow

The Church of Epiphenomena and Alexandr's Manse, Mechitar, Geb, Rova, 4711

As he'd carried Trevedic Faull, Kemnebi now bore Elana. She clung to him—terrified and exhilarated—as he skimmed the waves of the Obari Ocean. They turned a wide arc from the coast east of the Axan Wood, moving south then turning west until Mechitar shone like a land-fallen star. That it shone so brightly confused them both.

For a moment Kemnebi paused his flight, hovering a mile or two from the capital. He thought the city was aflame, so bright did it look. He hesitated to advance—not only do living things fear fire but many un-living things do as well. As they studied the capital they discerned that it was not aflame, merely well lit, more so than it had ever been.

They flew over, gazing at a sight neither could grasp. The entire city was alive with activity, and this after darkness had fallen. The people below were holding torches and lanterns, dancing, singing, and embracing one another freely and with great joy. The center of this activity was the square before the Church of Epiphenomena. Kemnebi flew low over the square, studying the scene below. He spotted Narcisse and landed behind him, setting Elana on her feet.

Drunken revelers swarmed, savoring a night once forbidden. The square was threaded through with priest of Urgathoa in their food-stained robes, busy chefs, and harried chef's assistants. One of these rushed to Narcisse, bowl-in-hand. Narcisse, who hadn't seen Kemnebi or Elana, so distracted was he, dipped a finger into the bowl and lifted it to his mouth, sucking the liquid from it. He coughed and turned red.

"Did you drop the entire container of cumin into the mix?" He grabbed the chef's assistant by the shoulder and shook him. "Your tongue is the most useless thing about you and that's saying something. By the grace of the Pallid Princess, I doubt the dogs would eat that but give it to them anyway and try again. Need I say—less cumin?" He shoved the man away.

"Narcisse" Kemnebi asked.

Narcisse spun, gasped, and lifted one hand to his heart, the other shooting out to grab Kemnebi's forearm. He was fully made up, face painted in garish colors, his hair elegantly coifed, his outfit the height of fashion, albeit a bit sweat-stained. He stood three inches taller in black leather boots. He did not wear his robes, desiring something more grand, but a bejeweled holy symbol, the iconic fly, bounced against his chest. "Is it? Can it be?" He laughed. "Chancellor?"

"I am not—"

"You might just be the only undead in Mechitar," said Narcisse. He pulled his hand from his heart and waved it out over the crowd. "Let no one say I cannot throw an impromptu feast." He smiled and looked at Kemnebi. "We've twenty-five boars roasting now. We'll feed every man, woman, and child in this city by dawn. I shall see a hundred boars on the spit if I see one." He squeezed Kemnebi's arm but paused and looked at Elana. "My eyes deceive," he said. "Surely no such beauty exists in this dead realm." He extended his hand, took up Elana's, and kissed it, leaving behind a smooshed ring of red lipstick. "Allow me to introduce myself. I am Narcisse, the former Duke between the Rivers and most-likely the new high priest of Urgathoa in Geb." He waved once more over the crowd. "And these are my people."

"Narcisse," said Kemnebi. "What is going on?"

Narcisse winked at Elana but kept a hold of her hand. He was still holding Kemnebi's forearm and seemed unlikely to release either. He was in a good mood and being so was even more touchy-feely than usual.

"Ah, Chancellor, what is going on is exactly this—Urgathoa has shifted her focus in Geb from un-death to gluttony. I am in the ascendant, praise her."

"Shifted?" Kemnebi asked. "What do you mean?"

Another chef's assistant rushed up, carrying a mug, foam spilling over the rim. Narcisse released both of his captives, excused himself for one moment, and tasted the ale. "How many kegs?"

"Twenty, Sir."

"How much does he want for the lot?"

"The gentleman mention two hundred scarabs, Sir."

"Damn him!" cried Narcisse. "He's a brigand. I should have him publicly whipped! Ah, but that's good ale. What's two hundred gold? Eh? Get them here on the double. The people must get sloshed!" Narcisse laughed but when the assistant tried to take the mug back he growled. The assistant retreated empty-handed. Narcisse turned back to his unexpected guests. "You, Chancellor, of all people, must know that Geb has called his undead to him. And so," he pirouetted, looking over the crowd, "the living have lit up the night." He smiled. "You must excuse me, I've been taste-testing wine since this afternoon. I abhor spitting it out. I've gotten a little—" He burped and giggled.

Kemnebi was staring over Narcisse's head. Elana looked from the bizarre priest to Kemnebi.

"Geb called them—all?" whispered Kemnebi.

"Narcisse," asked Elana, "are there really no undead in Mechitar?"

"Well, my darling girl, there *is* one." Narcisse looked sidelong at Kemnebi and laughed.

"Geb called every undead in Mechitar to him?" asked Kemnebi.

Narcisse's eyes narrowed and his grin became sinister. "No, Chancellor. He called every undead in his *nation* to him."

Elana grabbed Kemnebi's arm. "He's going to attack Nex!"

"Ah," said Narcisse. "Beautiful *and* smart." He laughed. "I wouldn't want to be a Nexian at this juncture in time."

Kemnebi looked from Narcisse to Elana. She began to cry. Although he didn't understand why she had begun to cry he recognized that he was equally as unsettled. He turned back to Narcisse.

"What about Queen Arazni, Hent-er-Neheh, Eratosthenes, the Blood Lords?"

"Gone, gone, and gone," said Narcisse. "All gone."

"The High Priest?"

"He serves two masters now," said Narcisse. He leaned into Kemnebi. "Although I personally suspect he always has."

Kemnebi looked to Elana. "Aleksandr?"

She wiped her eyes and looked up at him.

. . .

Only three servants remained in Aleksandr's mansion. They were his thralls, his most loyal retainers. They were huddled together on the floor before a couch, crying. They turned as Kemnebi entered, Elana trailing.

"Where is he?" asked Kemnebi.

"The Master has fled his house," said one of the three blood thralls, a Kelishite man of middle years with little hair upon his head but otherwise possessed of the unnatural beauty and vigor of vampiric blood. He rose, lifting the two others, both women, one Cheliaxian the other Garundi, both gifted with beauty.

"He was standing there," said the Chelaxian, pointing to a spot by a shelf of books, "when he jerked as if struck."

"He dropped the book he was holding," continued the man, "turned—" He seemed to struggle with emotion but was able to overcome it. "The Master's eyes were—blank."

Kemnebi looked at Elana. "Geb's call."

"The master went to the door, yanked it open, took the form of a bat and flew into the night," said the man.

"He gave us no instructions," said the Garundi. "The Master never leaves without giving us detailed instructions."

The Chelaxian woman began to cry and she gave herself to the arms of the Garundi. The man watched them then turned to Kemnebi. "We have learned of the call you mentioned. We know the undead have left Mechitar. The Master has left. What are we to do?" All three looked to Kemnebi.

"I'll let you drink my blood," Kemnebi said.

"When will Aleksandr return?" asked the Chelaxian.

Kemnebi shook his head.

. . .

"Kemnebi," asked Elana, after the three blood thralls had drank of his blood, been calmed by his words, and retreated to their quarters to further grieve the absence of their master. "If all the vampires in Geb have been called to Geb's Rest—" She thought for a moment. "Would they all have gotten there before dawn? If so, could they all sleep somewhere safe during the day? If not, if the sun rose while they—" She shook her head. "Would Geb—"

"Let them perish?" finished Kemnebi. "If he is building an army, one would think that he would ensure he had every soldier available. But," he looked at Elana, "I know Geb. It's entirely possible he doesn't care." Kemnebi thought for a moment. "Not only vampires are destroyed by the sun's light. Many kinds of undead are. To call them and make no allowance for this weakness would be—" He frowned. "But we are speaking about Geb."

"Do you think Aleksandr is with him?"

"He must be," said Kemnebi.

"I hope he survived the day."

Kemnebi looked at Elana. "Do you really think he's going to attack Nex?"

"Why else would he have called them?" Kemnebi did not answer but tried to divine Geb's thinking. "Kemnebi," said Elana, "can you stop him?"

Kemnebi looked up at her. "I don't know that anyone can stop him."

Elana hugged Kemnebi and looked up into his face. "You must try."

Kemnebi smiled but he was on the verge of tears. "It's ironic." He looked into Elana's eyes. "This all started because I told the Blood Lords there needed to be fewer violent undead in Geb. We needed the living and they were—prey." He turned his head to the side, listening to the sounds of celebration coming from the streets outside. "The predators have left and the prey celebrate." He looked at Elana. "I've gotten exactly what I wanted." He smirked, but it too was ironic. "Thanks to Geb."

"Kemnebi—"

"Geb has destroyed his own creation," said Kemnebi. "I wanted Geb to remain strong. I helped to build it, after all. I wanted us," he tapped his chest, "the undead, to continue to be the elite, the aristocracy. I wanted to secure our power and position. I didn't want to destroy Geb or even fundamentally change it. I wanted to ensure its survival among nations." He looked at Elana. "Now there is no Geb."

"What about Nex?" asked Elana. "Why is he attacking Nex?"

"He has always hated his rival."

"But Nex is gone."

"Maybe Geb has decided to finish what he started so long ago."

"But—why?" asked Elana. She let go of Kemnebi and walked a bit away, emotion clear in her movements. She spun and looked at Kemnebi. "Why now?"

"Maybe Nex has returned."

Elana shook her head. "I would know if he—"

"How would *you* know?"

Elana looked at him, a flash of panic on her face, but she recovered. "Wouldn't we all know?" She turned her back and seemed to be wrestling with her emotions.

"I suppose we would." Kemnebi looked at Elana's back. "They'll have to build a government from scratch. I could help them," Kemnebi smiled. "But they've had enough of undead rule. Besides, the war—if it is war—may be short and Geb may return. Their freedom may be short-lived. Geb may not be entirely ruined, but it is changed. Geb's awakening into action has ensured that."

Elana spun. "You have to do something. You have to stop Geb." She motioned violently. "He could be marching toward Nex right now." She burst into tears, turned, and walked hurriedly from the room. Kemnebi watched her go. He heard her open a door and close it behind her.

"What are you doing, Geb?" He asked aloud. "What do you want?"

Leaving Home, Not Going Home

The Spellscar Desert, the Mana Waste, Rova, 4711

"I'll never see you again—will I, boy?" Ilyx's father asked. They stood apart from the outcrop hiding the svirfneblins' village entrance. Ilyx was securing the straps of his pack, preparing himself for the long and dangerous trek back to Alkenstar. He did not look at his father. He did not look at his mother or brother, who stood with the other mutated svirfneblin in the protective shadows of the boulders. The sun was just dropping below the horizon behind him. "Ah, boy," said Ilyx's father, shaking his head. "You have no idea how much my heart aches." He squeezed his son's shoulder, clinging for guidance, support, and a final touch.

Ilyx yanked the last strap. He tugged on his rifle, making sure it was secure. He glanced at his father but didn't speak.

"Do the gods weep for our sorrows?" asked Ilyx's father. He turned toward his wife and other son. He couldn't see them but he could feel their presence and their emotion. "Thank you again for the coin." He turned back toward Ilyx. "Ain't got no one to trade with but I suppose someone will come around one day. Ain't no predicting that."

Ilyx was ready to depart. He stood before his father, staring at him with his ice blue eyes. His father could feel his son's nervous energy.

"Don't go, son." Ilyx didn't respond. "If I hadn't said it, your mother would never forgive me. Well, boy, don't just stand there. Give me a hug."

Ilyx let his father hug him. He even wrapped one arm around him.

"You have the food your mother made?"

Ilyx nodded. He knew his father couldn't see it but he imagined he felt the reverberations.

"I wish we could do more for you, boy. But we have so little. Besides," he felt his son's clothing, armor, and gear. "I suppose you got everything you need." Ilyx didn't speak. "Well, boy," his father stepped back and held out his hand. Ilyx's brother came up, bent, then stood so that his father's hand was on his shoulder. "Goodbye."

Ilyx turned and began down the sloping hillside, away from the svirfneblin's village. He faced a two-week trek to Alkenstar, and that was if everything went well and he made good time. He turned when the last rays of the sun were slipping beneath the horizon. The boulders were burnished gold on their tops but were deep purple below. He could just see the shapes of the svirfneblin. He raised a hand. A distant yell reached him.

"Bro-ther! Bro-ther!"

He lowered his hand, wiped the tears from his eyes, and turned into the setting sun.

. . .

The skeletons and zombies streamed past Geb. Their mass—a corrupted force of nature in size and ruin—teemed with countless undead. A lesser necromancer than Geb would be overwhelmed, if not outright terrified. Geb floated above them, surrounded by other ghost, who were attracted to him as are moths to a flame. They cast an eerie glow over those undead that passed beneath.

Geb stared into the Spellscar Desert. He knew that his nation had grown by two score miles since the first undead crossed over the previous border of Geb. He hadn't yet moved into his newly acquired territory. He had waited thousands of years to reach for his rival's throat. He wanted to savor every moment—of his hand closing around Nex.

He watched as the mutant svirfneblin, the murderer of magic, left his village on foot and headed west. He surmised, given the direction the deep gnome was walking and the fact he possessed firearms, that he was going to Alkenstar. Geb knew the svirfneblin would never reach that city of outlaws and gunsmiths.

A green glow colored Geb's wispy form. He glanced up and watched as an enormous skeletal dragon flew overhead. The dragon's bones were held together by necromantic energy, the source of the green glow. It was a ravener, a type of dragon that—when confronted by Death—cheated him. The dragon's name was Tykylainen and hundreds of years ago the ancient red dragon had come to Geb to bargain away his soul for everlasting un-life. Now Geb called in a favor, for he did not control Tykylainen. The ravener needed little persuasion to join in the great taking of life that Geb proposed. It was harder to convince him not to kill the sole life Geb wanted to keep whole, but to deliver him unharmed.

. . .

Ilyx leapt over the stone ridge, turned in the air, landed on his back in the sand and slid a few feet before coming to a stop, rifle pointed skyward. The green-glowing skeletal dragon swooped over the ridge and Ilyx fired. The bullet zipped between ribs, pinged off spine, and veered left. Tykylainen was unhurt. He flapped his skeletal wings and lifted. Ilyx got to his feet and began to reload his rifle.

Tykylainen turned, arced back toward Ilyx, and landed forty feet away. The ground shuddered upon his arrival. Ilyx lifted his rifle, aimed, and shot the dragon in the face. The bullet ricocheted off his orbital bone.

"You humor me, little one," thundered Tykylainen. "Put your stone-caster away. Do you believe you harm me with a child's toy?"

Ilyx turned, scampered up the ridge and began to run, all the time scanning for something, anything, to hide beneath or in. He heard the dragon laugh—an ominous sound if ever he'd heard one—and ran faster, looking over his shoulder to be sure the dragon wasn't right behind him.

Tykylainen leapt upwards, wings beating, and clumsily lifted into the air. He rose a bit before rolling forward and swooping toward Ilyx.

Ilyx ducked as the dragon passed over him. He drew his pistol, fired—it grazed the dragon's bony tail. He began to reload his pistol while running, dropping black powder and bullets.

Tykylainen turned and landed. Ilyx skidded to a halt and raised his pistol, but it wasn't loaded. "You've courage, little one," said Tykylainen. "How sweet your life-force would taste, ah, but I am denied." He studied Ilyx. "Do you not fear me?" He laughed. "Would you fear my maker? You should, but let us not speak in riddles for you shall soon meet him."

Ilyx looked down and tried to reload his pistol but his hands were shaking. The dragon was walking toward him, the green, necromantic energy pouring from him like poison dripping from an assassin's dagger. Ilyx looked down, steadied his hands, loaded his pistol, looked up and lifted it but before he could squeeze the trigger Tykylainen reached out and grabbed him, scooping him from his feet. He lifted Ilyx to his mouth, intent on devouring him but he paused and turned his head. "Why, Geb? Why is this one —" The dragon looked at Ilyx. He lifted his head to the sky and roared in frustration. He turned and hopped several times, his wings beating, then took flight.

A Home No More, a Home to Protect

The Cinerarium and Kemnebi's Pyramid, Mechitar, Geb, and various locations, Nex, Rova, 4711

Kemnebi knelt in his Cinerarium office, tracing the stump of his chair's broken leg. Elana stood behind him, watching and worrying. Kemnebi stood, turned, and walked out of his office. Elana followed. He went to Arazni's door and pushed it open. He paused before stepping in. The room was empty and silent.

"It's true," he said, turning to Elana. "Even she's gone to him." He walked to Arazni's bed and looked down at the scattered pillows and disheveled covers. "She despises him for what he did to her." He sat on her bed, elbows on his knees, chin in his palms. "She loves him for what he is to her." He glanced at Elana. "What did she feel when she heard his voice? What did she think?" He glanced at the floor, trying to imagine Arazni's response.

"Kemnebi?" He looked up at Elana. "What are we doing here?"

"I had to see." He sat upright and looked about the room. "No grave knights, no Lilith, none of the others," he turned to Elana. "No Arazni."

"We know where they are." She went to the bed and sat next to him, taking one of his hands into hers. "We have to go there. To stop Geb."

"Elana—"

She stood up and stepped away, her back to Kemnebi. "Are you going to let him destroy Nex?" She turned. "How many innocent people is he going to kill? And why? Revenge against an enemy long disappeared?"

"He can't be stopped."

"Yes he can!" Elana stepped to Kemnebi and fell to her knees. She grabbed his hands and pulled them to her chest, placing his palm over her heart. "*You* can stop him—you. Kemnebi, no one else is powerful enough. But you—"

"You think I'm as powerful as Geb?"

"If not you—"

"Only a few spellcasters rival him—Nex, Aroden, Old-Mage Jatembe," he said, squeezing Elana's hand. "But not me."

Elana was crying now. "You *have* to try."

Kemnebi stood, pulling Elana to her feet. She could barely stand so he held her. "We can rest at my house."

She looked up into his face. "There isn't time. We have to—"

You need food, drink, rest—you've endured too much."

Elana let herself be led from Arazni's chambers, from the Cinerarium, to Kemnebi's pyramidal home. Kemnebi fed her, gave her water and wine, then put her to bed. He sat next to her, stroking her hair, until she fell asleep. He went to his living room and saw the two depressions in the rug. He examined them and knew that they were footprints belonging to something tremendously heavy, but he didn't know what. He guessed something had lain in wait but was now gone.

He saw that the door to one of his cabinets was open and he rummaged through its contents. Only one thing was missing, the ancient medallion. It was another mystery, one he was unlikely to solve and did not even care to. He sat in the chair and thought.

'Can I stop him?' He shook his head. 'Not with Arazni, Hent-er-Neheh, and Eratosthenes with him. Impossible. Even without them—" He looked at the empty spot where the medallion had been. 'What will you do, Geb, when you conquer Nex? Raise up the dead and return home? Why bother? What do you gain by this? More undead? You already have a nation-full. To cause death and destruction? You could have done that at any time. Why now? Is Nex back? Has he returned to Golarion after all this time?' He banged his fist on the arm of the chair. "There has to be a reason," he growled. "I know you too well. You always have a reason for your actions. You are calculating, far-seeing, far-reaching. You never act on a whim."

He heard Elana turn in her sleep. 'She cares so much.' He thought. 'Her heart bleeds for Nex, for those innocent people.' He considered this. 'What kind of student of the Ebon Mausoleum feels that way? Who pursues the art of necromancy and yet feels so deeply about the loss of innocent life?'

He rose and went to his bedroom, where Elana slept. He stood by the bed and looked down at her. 'Who are you? Who are you, really?' He looked from her to the large shoulder bag she had brought. He went to it, picked it up, took it to the living room and emptied it on the carpet.

. . .

Hawwa lifted the hem of her robe, pulled the hood to shield her eyes from the sun and began down the rock-bordered path to the beach. She picked her way carefully among the stones and sharp-leafed grasses until she came to the thin, rocky shore. She paused and looked at Sa'ood, the master of the monastery. He was Vudrani, elderly, with long white hair, a long white beard, and deeply tanned skin. He sat cross-legged on a boulder, facing the ocean. He wore only a cotton wrapping. The spray, when the waves were tall, washed over him. Now, owing to a calm sea, he was merely spritzed from time-to-time.

"Come, Hawwa." He did not turn to face her, nor was she close enough he could have heard her over the ocean's low roar, still, he knew.

She approached. "Master—"

"No," he said, his voice quiet but stern, "I am no master, merely a traveler a bit further ahead on the path."

"There is war in Nex."

"Yes."

Hawwa was a bit startled by the master's response. He had been sitting on the boulder for a year, give-or-take, and he kept a strict solitude. She knew of no way that he could have heard of the approaching war. "They've asked for help."

"How can we help them?"

"They need soldiers, clerics, anyone and everyone that can—"

Sa'ood motioned to the ocean. "Do you know how many times the waves have knocked me from this slippery seat?" He turned and smiled. "More times than I can count. Should I shake my fist at them?" He lowered his arm and looked out over the water. "No, I must accept that it is their nature to crash upon the rocks, just as it is the rock's nature to resist. I have unwisely interposed myself into this dynamic."

"Master?"

"It is in the nature of men to war with one another." He glanced at Hawwa. "It is especially in the nature of Geb and Nex to war."

"Master, forgive my ignorance. What are you saying?"

"War has come yet again. Will there be needless suffering? Yes. Will there be loss of life? Yes. Is this regrettable? Yes." He looked at Hawwa. "Is this preventable?" He frowned. "Not until we, all living, thinking beings, experience a consciousness change." He looked out over the ocean once more. "That is the work we are called to do. Our work is not war. Our work is to erase the instinct to war from the universal consciousness. We must end all war, not one war."

"But, the Nexian people—" A gust of wind blew ocean spray onto them.

"I will not forbid, nor will I encourage," said Sa'ood. "Those who feel they must act to preserve Nex may do so. Those who continue to elevate their consciousnesses so that war is forgotten are free to do so."

Hawwa bowed, turned, and began back up the path. She doubted that many monks or nuns would travel to Nex, not just from her monastery but from any on Jalmeray.

. . .

Ruby Prince Khemet sat in his throne, looking over the heads of those who pleaded. He was a youthful and handsome man with dark hair, smooth features, and light brown eyes that glowed with the fire of his will. He was said to be a proficient spellcaster, favoring spells that brought forth the power of flame. He was comfortable in his throne, but seemed somewhat uncomfortable around large groups of people, an odd trait for a leader.

The man who addressed him was an Arclord from Nex, one of a rather large delegation, considering that their abilities would have been better used in preparing for war than in diplomacy. When the Arclords were finished making their request the Ruby Prince glanced to his left.

The Arclords knew—or thought they knew—at whom the prince looked. It was well known that Khemet was advised by a powerful elemental being, a being of fire, named Janhelia. Indeed, all of the Nexian retinue had to protect themselves against her heat with the use of protective magic. Even with this, the throne room was uncomfortably warm.

Khemet looked from the empty space—Janhelia was invisible—to the Arclords. "My father was weak and old when I forced him from power," said the Ruby Prince. "Yet he was loved by the people and they were angered by my actions, as were many of Osirion's allies. Yet he was no longer an effective ruler. Now that the people have an effective ruler they see how poorly things had gotten under my father. Now I am considered wise for my actions." He paused, for he was not one to talk over much and he was labored by his speech.

"As you mentioned," Khemet continued, "I have been building up Osirion's military. I receive criticism for this as well, but," he held up a ringed finger, "when Osirion has need of its military the people will say once more, 'he is wise to have done this.'" Khemet glanced at Janhelia, although no others could see her. He looked at the Arclords.

"If I send my military into Nex to be destroyed by Geb and his army of undead, which not even you can number, will the people say, 'he was wise to do this?'" He shook his head. "No. They will cry for their dead sons. They will fear their return as undead. They will blame me for getting involved in a war that is not ours." He could tell the Nexians wanted to speak but held up a hand to prevent them. "And yet, we are allies. And yet, if Geb is not stopped we must ask ourselves will he conquer Katepsh? Will he conquer Osirion?" He looked down, thinking, then returned his gaze to the Arclords.

"Geb was once ours, you know? A distant outpost. Geb himself once stood in this very room." He looked around. "These stones are that old." He looked at the Arclords. "But my military is young, as fresh as spring lambs. I will not send them to the slaughter." He held up his hand to stifle any interruptions. "Neither will I turn my back on Nex, for Osirion is a friend to Nex." He glanced at Janhelia. "We know many genie-kind." He looked back to the Arclords. "We have partnered with earth and fire. When you return to Quantium you will have with you those among us who can conjure the efretti and the shaitan and the elementals of earth and fire." He looked over the Arclords. "May the gods be with you." He nodded and the risen guards, his personal bodyguards, stepped forward and ushered the Arclords from the throne room.

. . .

"They cannot be sent outside of Katapesh," said Pactbroker Hashim ibn Sayyid, who spoke for the Pactmasters. "The aluums must stay within this nation. Their souls are bound not only to stone and steel but to the land itself, this is why they defend it so passionately." He smiled, which pushed up the ends of his busy, black mustache. "But Katapesh is home to how many mercenaries?" He laughed. "They have a guild—I direct you there with luck. Now, as to increasing our exports, I point you to the grain merchant's guild and again wish you luck. Coin is the law of the land, gentlemen. Coin can get you whatever you desire. If you need an army one can be bought here. If you need grain, again, the markets of Katapesh will provide. As for an army, no, we see no use in that. Why pay men to stand around when they could be earning?

"As to Geb," he continued. "We have no enmity with him, nor him with us. You say that if he is not stopped now he cannot be stopped later. I long ago gave up trying to time the market, it will be what it will be. When emotions run high it is wise to remove one's gold from the gaming tables. To the guilds, gentlemen, with our blessing. Please do not think me flippant, this is our way."

. . .

"Well," said Master Castelli, who had been teleported to Katheer, the capital of Qadira, by Agrellus. He stood at the docks along the Pashman River watching camels being loaded into ships. He turned to an assistant. "At least it's something."

"The madmen of the desert come," said a voice from behind. He turned. A bearded, sun-burnt man approached, his white and tan robes flowing, his sword banging against his hip. "They ride high in the saddle and carry swords of flame."

"Yussuf?"

The man stepped to Master Castelli and grabbed his arms. He smiled and pulled his friend in for a hug. "I heard you were in the capital."

"How? I've only been here three hours."

Yussuf stepped back from Master Castelli. "So you did not see my spies watching you? Ha! I take that as a compliment." He winked at his friend. "As for your spies, I've known about them for years."

"That explains why they've been so quiet," said Master Castelli.

Yussef patted Master Castelli on the arm. "Not every nation can have an intelligence service as skilled as mine." He looked at the camels. "What will you do with these?"

"I have no idea," said Master Castelli. "But Xerbystes was of the opinion they would solve all our problems. I couldn't refuse."

"They'll bring horses," said Yussef, "my madmen." He waved at the camels and laughed. "Eat these if you must."

"How many come?" asked Castelli.

"All the young men from all the tribes." Yussef looked at his counterpart. "They share one heart among them, a warrior's heart."

"Will they get here in time?"

"They ride the wind."

Master Castelli chuckled. "Will they solve all of our problems?"

"You only have one problem, my friend." Yusseff reached out and placed his hand on Master Castelli's shoulder. "But it's a big one."

. . .

Agrellus floated four feet from the paved courtyard. He was being held aloft by an up-flowing swirl of magical energy. The shifting, multicolored light of the magic filled the courtyard—splashing vibrant hues on the Bandeshar. It rose over Quantium like an enormous fountain. The noise was something like one hears in a diving bell, a roar known not only by its sound but by the pressure being exerted.

It was perhaps his greatest feat to date—and most obnoxiously public. He was at the center of a gushing font of magical energy that reached from Quantium to all four corners of the Inner Sea. This web connected dozens of churches and would allow clerics of many gods from many different nations to quickly travel to Nex.

He had not accomplished this feat alone, even if his ego ignored those who helped. He was surrounded by a circle of Arclords who, like him, chanted a complicated puzzle of arcane words and phrases powering the magic. Sweat beaded on their brows and moistened their mustaches and beards and clean cheeks—not all Arlords were male. A similar collection of Arclords were seated in the Arcanamirium in Absalom. A fountain of magic flowed from them, the two spouts connecting in the sky like a rainbow.

"Who would step willingly into that?" yelled Astor Bizet, over the roar.

"What?" yelled Rixende.

"The faithful," yelled Astor. "Will they have faith enough?" He pointed to Agrellus.

"What?" yelled Rixende.

. . .

Queen Galfrey, ruler of Mendev, stood in the courtyard outside of the Cruciform Cathedral, staring up into the sky. She was surrounded by advisors, bodyguards, and clerics of Iomedae.

We're stretched to the limit," she said to Franz Joseph, her trusted advisor. He was well past his fighting years but he wore field plate and carried a sword and shield. He too looked skyward.

"Aye," growled Franz Joseph.

"We're desperate to stop Deskari's demon hordes," said Queen Galfrey. "They're desperate to stop Geb's undead hordes." She frowned. "We can't both be desperate at the same time."

"No," growled Franz Joseph.

"If only we could send them all those damned low templars and get more men like you," she looked sidelong at her advisor, "minus your thirty-year accumulation of gray hairs."

"Aye."

Queen Galfrey pointed skyward. "By Iomadae, they did it. Here it comes."

An arc of brilliant, shifting, multicolored light raced down and ended ten feet before the Queen. It was a column perhaps twenty foot in diameter. Queen Galfrey looked from it to Franz Joseph. He studied the column, a look of worry on his face. He realized the Queen was staring at him, knocked his courage back into place, then waved a hand to the assembled clerics.

"Move yer asses!"

. . .

It was the largest tavern in Andoran. From the front steps one could see both the palace of the People's Council and the Golden Cathedral. It was also the largest temple to Cayden Cailean in Andoran. The architecture of the tavern amplified the volume of the drinking songs sung within, but at the moment it was silent and empty. The patrons were outside, in the Field of Concord. They weren't drunk, per se, but neither were they sober. They sang, of course—they loved to sing.

When the arc of magical energy sped into view in the sky above, the crowd cheered. Cayden Cailean's clerics gulped their ale, checked gear, and braced for travel. The arc touched down near the tavern. The patrons began to pat the clerics on the back, wish them luck and glory, and toast to their bravery. The clerics, their bravery properly lubricated, didn't hesitate to rush into the shifting, multicolored light.

The patrons fell silent as the men and women of Cayden Cailean were sucked up into the stream, lifted into the air, and whisked away. Moments later the magical stream retreated, leaving behind a reddish-orange glow which faded into the sun's dusty light.

. . .

Panos, a centaur, a hero building a legend, with a retinue of loyal and courageous warriors, a fervent follower of Ragathiel, the Empyreal Lord of chivalry, duty, and vengeance, looked down from the tree line of the Whisperwood, across the river Iseld, at Sensara, a town of roughly five thousand. This was in eastern Cheliax.

He hated the House of Thrune, the rulers of Cheliax. He hated Asmodeus, the god of the Chelaxians. He had worked all his life to frustrate and, he hoped, ultimately end their corrupt rule. He was contemplating a raid in the hopes of killing as many clerics of Asmodeus as he could find.

A flash of light caught his eye and he looked skyward. An arc like a rainbow, only closer and more vivid, raced overhead. He looked from it to his warriors, who stood in the forest shadows. He looked back to the faux rainbow. He could not believe what he saw next.

At first it was a dark blot within the beam. It grew in size and Panos realized it was coming closer. Finally it came close enough he saw what it was, a winged humanoid. It flew on wings of shimmering steel and wore elaborately carved full plate armor. A massive sword hung at its waist. What flesh could be seen under the armor and helm was unblemished white. Eyes like fire could be seen through the slits in the helm. The legion archon hovered twenty feet over Panos, who reverently bowed his head.

"A terrible call has gone over the land, uniting the forces of evil against an innocent people," said the archon, his voice rich in timbre. "An equal call unites the good. Go, now, Panos, whose deeds are known Ragathiel. Join this fight." The archon unstrapped his sword, floated lower, and tossed the blade in its scabbard to Panos, who, sensing motion, looked up and caught it. "Take my blade and our god's blessing."

The archon waved his hand and a bridge of golden light sprouted from the ground at Panos' hooves, climbed steeply, and connected to the rainbow bridge above. Panos charged up the archon's bridge. His warriors emerged from the trees and followed.

. . .

The magic of Agrellus and the Arclords branched to many places, populated and obscure. No one place sent a multitude but a multitude came. Thus did many brave and faithful men and women make it to Quantium in time to defend Nex against its immortal enemy. These included the faithful of Abadar, Cayden Cailean, Gorum, Iomedae, Nethys, Pharasma, Ragathiel, and Sarenrae.

Still more saw the rainbow above, heard its purpose, and went of their own accord to Nex. Would they reach the capital in time? They did not know, but they would try.

Geb

The Ebon Mausoleum, Mechitar, and Geb's Rest, Geb, Rova, 4711

Kemnebi, warded by protective spells, guided Elana through the Ebon Mausoleum. It was empty, even the librarian was gone, the doors to the library locked and chained. Kemnebi had no difficulty opening them. The pair went below the school and stood at the edge of the circular room, staring at the closed doors.

Kemnebi went to the opposite staircase and peered into the darkness below. "Stay here." He went down the stairs to the door at their foot. He didn't need divination to sense the door's magic; he felt it. Eratosthenes had locked and trapped the door. Behind it, Kemnebi knew, was the elven lich's most prized possession. He wanted to know what it was. He told Elana that it might possibly help them stop Geb.

Kemnebi began the careful and dangerous process of breaking down Eratosthenes's enchantments. It wasn't easy or fast, but free from threats, he focused—and that helped. It took him half an hour and many attempts but he finally broke through. The door popped open. A musty smell filled the air.

Is it," Elana asked, "safe?"

"Yes, but don't come down. There may be other traps." Kemnebi pushed open the door. The small, sparse room was lit by magical lights that floated in the four corners. There was a stone slab four feet in height, six feet long in the center of the rectangular room. A body lay on the slab, covered by a dark cloth. There was nothing else in the room.

Kemnebi cast a spell and scanned for the presence of magic. The body beneath the sheet and the magical lights glowed but nothing else did. He looked around the small space. There were no obvious mechanical traps. He stepped in and walked to the side of the stone slab. He cast another spell. The body beneath the sheet did not register as undead.

"Kemnebi?" called Elana, worry in her voice.

"I'm okay."

"What do you see?" He heard her coming down the stairs.

"Stay back." He heard her stop. He reached for the corner of the sheet and yanked it free, dropping it at his feet. He stared, stunned yet certain—it was Geb. His corpse had been preserved with necromantic magic. The self-inflicted wounds to his wrists, inner thighs, and throat were all still present, dark, gaping wounds. It was Geb's body, preserved at the moment of suicide. Kemnebi was so stunned he did not hear Elana come down the stairs. He heard her gasp and turned.

"Is that—"

Kemnebi looked down at the corpse. "Geb."

Elana walked into the room, stepped to the opposite side of the stone slab, and looked down at Geb's nude corpse. She looked up at Kemnebi.

"How—" She looked down at Geb's corpse. "Why —"

"I don't know how he got it. "I thought his suicide rites consumed it." He looked from Geb's corpse to Elana. "As to why," he looked back down at the body. "I wish I knew."

"Is *he* controlling Geb? Is that what—"

"Impossible."

"Kemnebi." He looked at Elana. "We have his body. You know necromancy as well as Eratosthenes—better." She looked at the corpse. "What can we do with this?"

"Nothing. Geb is a ghost. He's not tied to his body." He looked at Elana. "This is a—souvenir."

"No, it can't be just a—" She shook her head. "Eratosthenes has this for a reason. Kemnebi, think, damn it, is he controlling Geb? Is it Eratosthenes that is attacking Nex? Can *we* control Geb? Can *we* turn him back?"

Kemnebi sifted through all he knew of necromancy, of the undead, specifically of ghosts. He looked at Elana and shook his head. She banged her fist on the stone slab, looked at Geb's corpse, and yelled in frustration.

. . .

Geb watched as the dybbuk, a type of incorporeal undead with bloody hands and mad eyes, hovered over Ilyx's body. A stone from Geb's half-built pyramid served as Ilyx's unwilling bed. He was bound with his own rope. There was a clear circle, thirty feet in diameter, around the stone. Only Ilyx and the dybbuk occupied it. This clear patch was bordered by two hundred thousand skeletons, zombies, and other undead. Geb floated above, watching.

"Again," he commanded the dybbuk.

She looked up at him, her eyes bulging, and laughed. She floated close to Ilyx. "His heart weakens. He cannot—"

"Again."

The dybbuk looked at Geb then at her victim. She reached her bloody hands into Ilyx, causing him excruciating pain. He screamed but the sound gurgled to a stop. His back arched, lifting from the stone. He began to glow. The dybbuk fled as wavering light erupted in a blinding flash. When the light dissipated the dybbuk was gone, the necromantic magic that held her together disintegrated. Geb floated to the deep gnome and looked down.

"How?" he asked, but the unconscious gnome couldn't reply.

"The Spellscar has changed him." Called Tykylainen, who was seated amongst the undead. The ravener laughed. "You, Geb, and that other one, Nex—you are proud parents. This one, he is your twisted offspring." Geb spun to face the dragon but saw something else, his undead had parted.

Arazni rushed to him and skidded to a stop, tears in her eyes. She looked up at him, her hands on her heart. Her grave knights followed and behind them his aunt, Hent-er-Neheh, and Eratosthenes and the liches of the Whispering Way.

Geb glanced left—a giant loomed over the skeletons and zombies. It was skinless, its flesh flensed, its bulging muscles exposed. Geb motioned with a nod of his head and the ecorche stepped into the clearing, went to Ilyx, picked him up and held him. Geb reached down toward Arazni but he was not low enough for her to touch him, even though she stood on the tips of her toes and reached. The mixture of longing and pain in her eyes amused him but he had not brought her here to torture her.

Geb looked at Tykylainen. The ravener nodded and leapt into the air, his wings beating. The skeletons, zombies, and other undead turned and began into the Mana Waste. It was the bulk of his army and it spread as far as the eye could see in all directions. Now it headed toward Quantium. Geb floated along. The ecorche, carrying and guarding Ilyx, fell in-step. For the first time in centuries the grave knights left their queen. They formed a circle around the skinless giant. They too would protect Ilyx. Arazni, Hent-er-Neheh, Eratosthenes and all the others followed.

Trust Betrayed, Pride Made Manifest

Rhianna's Hunting Lodge, the Axan Wood, Rova, 4711

"Take all that matters," Kemnebi ordered Aleksandr's thralls. "Leave behind cutlery, rugs, artwork, and so on. I have no need of that. Go to my pyramid and gather everything of importance from there. Do not dally, but load a wagon and come to Rhianna's hunting lodge. Don't hire a driver—take his cart and horses. Overpay to buy his silence."

The trio nodded in unison. Kemnebi reached up and pulled off the necklace and amulet that denoted the office of chancellor. He handed it to the Garundi man. "Sell this. I have no need of it. Use the gold." He locked eyes with the man. "Let no one follow you."

"Yes, Master."

Kemnebi turned to Elana. "Come." He held out his hand.

The return flight to Rhianna's hunting lodge was somber. Even skimming the Axan's treetops couldn't lift their sullen mood.

. . .

"What are we going to do," Elana asked, "just stay here? Kemnebi, we—"

"Dawn approaches." Kemnebi closed the doors to Rhianna's bedroom and set the iron bar in place.

Elana fell silent. She hung her head, defeated. Kemnebi took her into his arms. "Elana?" He lifted her chin so he could kiss her. She did not return his affection. "I can do nothing now. Tonight—"

"Nex doesn't have much time," Elana whispered.

"Nex?"

"All those innocent people."

Kemnebi released her and stepped away, turning his back to her. "What drew you to necromancy, Elana?"

"Huh?"

Kemnebi looked over his shoulder. "The Ebon Mausoleum. A school of necromancy in the heart of a nation of undead." He turned to face her. "Why did you choose to come here?"

"I—" Elana began to weep. "Kemnebi." She stepped toward him but the look in his eyes warned her against intimacy.

"Why do you study necromancy?"

"I'm not a student anymore," whispered Elana.

"No!" said Kemnebi, his voice louder than he intended. Elana stepped back. "Why do you study necromancy? Answer me."

"I—" Elana sat on Rhianna's bed, her face in her hands, crying.

"You chose necromancy." He looked at her. "You chose the Ebon Mausoleum. You chose Geb. Why?"

Elana looked up, her cheeks wet with tears. She swallowed. "Power."

"Power?"

Elana looked at Kemnebi and nodded. She looked down at the floor.

"Power doesn't care, Elana," Kemnebi said, kneeling before her. He took her hands into his and looked into her eyes. "The powerful do not care about the powerless, even if they are innocent. Geb has power, Elana, the kind of power you say that you came here for." Elana couldn't keep his gaze and looked away. "Elana. Why do you study necromancy? Why did you come to Geb?"

She glanced at him but had to turn away.

"You didn't come here for power, did you?"

She shook her head.

"Why did you come to Geb?"

She looked at him, tears breaking over her cheeks. "Kemnebi—please."

"Why, Elana?"

"Please, don't."

"You're hiding something."

"No, please, Kemnebi. I love you. Isn't that enough? Doesn't that answer every question?"

Kemnebi released Elana's hands and stood. He went to her shoulder bag, looking down at it. "What's in this?"

"My stuff—from school."

He turned to face her. "You're lying."

"Kemnebi, please." She looked toward the door. "Dawn." She looked at him. "Dawn's coming. Please, lay with me. Can't we just—"

"Why?"

"Kemnebi—please. Please stop asking me. I—I can't tell you why. I can't."

"Who are you?"

Elana couldn't meet his gaze. It was too full of anger.

"Why do you care so much about Nex? Why do you want me to stop Geb?"

Elana looked at Kemnebi. "I love you."

"No!" Kemnebi lunged forward, grabbed Elana's arm, and threw her to the floor. "Stop saying that! Who are you? Why did you come to Geb? Answer me!"

"I'm Nexian—" Elana said, gazing up at him. "I'm from Nex. That's what I'm hiding. She climbed to her knees and reached for Kemnebi. "I have family, friends," she thrust her hands out to him. "I don't want them to die."

"The bag?"

Elana looked to the bag then back to Kemnebi. "Who cares about the—" She shook her head and wrapped her arms around herself. "I—don't have answers." She looked at Kemnebi. "I've fallen in love—"

Kemnebi slapped Elana across the face. She fell onto her side. "Why did you come to Geb? Why?"

Elana touched her cheek. She sobbed. It took her a moment to gather herself. She looked at Kemnebi. She sat and pulled her knees to her chest. "I'm a spy." She did not look at him. "I'm a Nexian agent." She glanced at him but had to look away. "I came to spy on Geb, not study necromancy." When Kemnebi did not respond she looked at him. He was motionless, his eyes unfocused. "Kemnebi, I'm not lying about—"

Kemnebi bent, wrapped his hands around Elana's throat, and lifted her from the floor. His rage possessed him. The beast held sway. "*You* told me to talk to them, to convince them. You!" He was squeezing Elana's throat so tightly she could not speak. "When I should have forced my will upon them *you* told me to coddle them, to be patient. Because of *you* they had time to move against me." He squeezed tighter. Elana's face turned purple. She reached up and tried to pry his fingers loose. "Because of you, it all crumbled—Aedha dead, Rhianna—"

An unwanted memory cut its way into his thoughts. He saw Leah's face. He saw her lips moving, denouncing him. He saw the angry slash of her brows over her narrowed eyes. She humiliated him before the assembled Blood Lords. He felt those ancient emotions as if they were fresh. He felt her betrayal. He looked up at Elana. "A Nexian— You betrayed me!" He squeezed as hard as he could, his strength fueled by irrational anger and the beast within. He felt her neck snap. Her fingers fell from his. Her body went limp in his hands.

Now he saw both Leah and Elana superimposed—both dead by his hand. He panicked. He lay Elana on the bed. "No, no!" He looked at her. "What have I done?" He stumbled back until he banged against the door. The iron bar rattled. He turned and lifted it, tossing it aside. He yanked open the doors, trying to flee from his sin, but the glow of the dawn filtered down the hall. He looked at the gray-gold light. He shut the doors and placed his palms against them.

Even deep in the lodge, he heard the Axan Wood's life stir. Dawn had come. He turned and looked at Elana. Her head hung to the side. She returned his gaze with lifeless eyes.

The Light of a Fire Reveals

Rhianna's Hunting Lodge, the Axan Wood, outside of Quantium, Nex, Rova, 4711

Kemnebi never learned a spell to restore life stolen away. He knew only spells to corrupt and animate the dead—necromantic puppets. Elana, he felt, did not deserve that. He built a funeral pyre, laid Elana on it, and used a spell to light it. Now he watched as the flames consumed her. He said no prayers. He watched and waited. He wanted the flames to reach their full intensity. He waited so he could step into the blaze and join her in death.

The flames illuminated the trees and bushes nearby. Something the flames revealed caught his attention. He glanced at the forest but, not seeing past his grief and confusion, looked back to the pyre. Again the flames showed him. He looked but did not see. He stepped closer to the pyre, ready to enter. He paused. He turned his head and looked at the forest around him. Whatever it was, whatever the fire's light was showing him, troubled him so much he was pulled from his self-destructive guilt.

He glanced at the fire then looked at the forest. He turned and walked to the nearby trees and bushes. Now he realized what it was the fire had revealed—the bushes, grasses, and flowers had been trampled. He realized who had done it. Geb's summoned undead had crushed the Axan Wood's undergrowth passing through. Only the trees had resisted them, everything else was crushed and dying.

Kemnebi looked at the fire. He could not see Elana within. The light was too intense. Some of the logs and branches collapsed and a shower of embers took flight. He watched them cool and blink out of existence. He stepped toward the pyre, ready to leap in, but paused. He backed away and looked at the sky. He looked once more at the flames, again at the sky, then at the trampled life all around him.

He took the form of a bat and flew up, riding the warm air current from the funeral pyre. He turned northeast and headed toward Quantium.

. . .

Ahrhune joined six clerics and a few archers on a platform behind the palisade. A wooden ladder had been pulled up and laid along the edge of the platform. The idea was that from this defensive position he and his fellow clerics could call upon the aid of the gods in defeating the undead while remaining somewhat protected. To Ahrhune it felt like cowardice.

The setting sun fused Geb's horde into one dread silhouette. Fires were lit in the Nexian ranks. Magical lights were called into existence. Elementals burned like roving bonfires. A boy lit a fire near the palisade. Ahrhune looked down at him. The night was not yet cool but the boy's hands were shaking. He stood next to the fire, not for warmth, but for security. The light from the fire revealed the tears on the boy's cheeks.

Ahrhune knew how the youth felt. He asked his goddess if this is what she really wanted of him, to die defending Nex. She hadn't answered. He had faced a hundred foes, but not a hundred thousand. He had lived a long enough life, he told himself, and he was ready to meet Sarenrae face-to-face, but his heart was still in his throat.

"You there—boy," Ahrhune called.

It took the boy a moment to realize that the speaker was above him. He looked up.

"How old are you?"

The boy was momentarily confused by the unexpected question. "Thirteen, sir."

"Are you afraid, boy?" called Ahrhune. Their dialogue, made in shouts, attracted the attention of those nearby. The youth looked self-consciously around but there was no use in hiding the truth. He looked up at Ahrhune and nodded.

Ahrhune lifted the ladder and set it against the rear of the wooden platform. When he had climbed down he motioned that those still on the platform should pull it back up. They did. Ahrhune walked over to the frightened youth. He peered down into the fire. He looked out over the sloping plain at Geb's undead horde. He turned to the youth and smiled. He tugged on his holy symbol, which hung by a chain around his neck, and showed it to the boy.

"See this, boy?"

"Yes, sir."

"This is Sarenrae's holy symbol. Me and her—" He let the holy symbol drop to his chest and held out his hand, his pointer and middle fingers crossed. "We're like this." He looked out over the undead. "Stay close to me and no harm will come to you." He looked at the youth and winked. The youth was not mollified. "Say, boy, while we're waiting, let me teach you a prayer." Ahrhune reached out and patted the boy on the shoulder. "It can't hurt, can it?"

The boy smiled.

The Calm Before the Storm

Quantium, Nex, Rova, 4711

Quantium lies just a hundred fifty miles from Geb's Rest. An army that does not tire, that can march day and night, can cross such a distance with bewildering speed. Even the Spellscar's wild magic can't slow them.

Calikangs tore zombies apart and smashed skeletons, but it didn't dent Geb's army. The bulk of undead washed over the calikangs like a tide. The tribes of mutant gnolls hid. Those who couldn't hide were killed, raised as zombies, and joined the march. The nomadic human tribes that roam the Mana Waste moved west. Those that couldn't move quick enough or far enough were slain, raised, and joined Geb's host. Not even the rare wild animal was spared, but fell to blade, claw, or worse, was raised as undead and added to the ranks.

. . .

Quantium, like Mechitar, was on the coast. The Obari lapped against its feet. Also, like Mechitar, a river ran north of Quantium, emptying into the bay. This was the Elemion River. Nex had never bothered to build a wall around his capital. The idea of a stone wall struck him as quaint. Why bother with stone, which could be smashed or sapped? Magic could do much better. A slew of mages was poised to raise a magic wall around Quantium to stop Geb's army but there were many other obstacles to overcome before this.

The open fields around Quantium had been transformed into a patchwork quilt of trenches filled with alchemical fluids that would dissolve Geb's legions, walls of sharpened spikes hid destructive spells that would trigger once the walls were breached, shallow valleys where Qadira's madmen could charge Geb's undead, defensive redoubts in which clerics were ready to blast their foes with positive energy—anathema to necromancy.

The standing army of Nex—fortified with mercenaries and volunteers—stood before the conscript army, forming a horseshoe shape with the Elemion on their right and the capital behind them. War barges, catapults on their decks, were anchored in the river. Hundreds of spellcasters waited, tense, clutching scrolls, wands, or staves. Once Geb commenced his attack a legion of summoned monsters would appear to stand in his way, from genies, to elementals, to celestials. Only Nex himself could better defend his capital in such short order. Yet, like Elder Architect Oblosk had predicted, Nex hadn't bothered.

. . .

Geb positioned his army a mile out from the city. It too formed a horseshoe around Quantium—a much thicker horseshoe. He arrived at dusk, awaiting full dark. He looked out over Quantium's defenses and smiled. They'd done well—better than he'd thought they would, given his swift strike. But it didn't matter and he knew it.

Geb had made a simple calculation. It didn't matter what they did. They could never neutralize his one advantage. He had numbers, unbelievable numbers. He could overwhelm any defense. It didn't matter if they destroyed two-thirds of his army or more. He'd raise every fallen Nexian soldier. His numbers were only limited by how many soldiers the Nexians had.

Only a simple plan works in war. His plan was as simple as he could make it, but it still contained one surprise. There was a reason he had waited at Geb's Rest. There was a reason he had held the bulk of his army back. He knew he was giving the Nexians time but it was a trade-off he was willing to make.

He wanted to give his stone-carrying zombies time. They had made the difficult journey and waited now, unseen. They would, upon his command, build a ramp out of those stones and climb it—a sneak attack. He looked out over the Nexian defenses. They all had one thing in common—they faced him. They faced landward. He flew high over his army, high over Quantium, and looked out over the Obari Ocean. The bay was empty of ships. The docks empty of men. He laughed.

Quantium would fall, though he didn't need it to. He only needed one thing and he was sure to get it. He looked down at the ecorche that cradled the mutant svirfneblin like an infant. All he needed was to get to the door, to control it completely, to make the ground under and around the Refuge of Nex his by right of sword. He needed the door—he already had the key.

The Storm Begins

Quantium, Nex, Rova, 4711

"What are they doing—why don't they attack?" the boy asked.

Ahrhune looked down at the fire, at the half-consumed logs. He looked up just in time to see a magical orb of light wink out. A wizard hastily cast a spell and a new light sprang into existence. Ahrhune studied the faces of the men and women around him in the light of this newborn globe. He watched them shift from one foot to another. He heard the groans given by those whose muscles were already exhausted by tension.

"Waiting."

"Why?"

Ahrhune looked down at the boy. "Because they can and we can't."

"I hope they don't attack."

"They didn't come all this way to stare."

"It sure seems like it," grumbled the boy.

. . .

Moonlight glinted off over a quarter-million decayed faces. Their eyes, those that retained them, shined in the moonlight, but lacked the inner glow of intelligence. A second light passed over. None of the zombies looked up to watch Geb as he floated over them, bathing them in a blue-white glow. He had never seen so many undead gathered in one place. The fields of Geb were empty, their bounty crowded beneath him. He wondered if Tar-Baphon, the Whispering Tyrant, had been able to field such an army. He doubted it.

Geb glanced up at the moon. He judged it to be midnight and, he told himself, he had waited long enough. He turned his gaze from the crescent above to a green light that circled near like a wayward star. Tykylainen, feeling Geb's attention on him, began a shallow dive that carried him close to the Nexian lines. His green, glowing necromantic energy rained down on the Nexians. It was harmless, but it foreshadowed what was to come.

Geb looked to Quantium. His gaze settled on the narrow, red-black crystalline growth that Nex had raised all those years ago. With a thought he sent his zombies forward.

. . .

"Damn," said Elder Architect Oblosk. He stood in the courtyard of the Bandeshar, before a low-walled, circular pool. The statue and fountain had been removed. The pool, twenty feet in circumference, was now used for scrying. Oblosk, standing on a newly erected wooden platform so he could take in the entire pool, turned and looked at an assistant. "I thought he'd strike key points, thrusting like spear tips," he said, turning to the pool. "But no, they come like a wave." He turned again to an assistant. "Dig the pits and raise the walls." The assistant nodded and ran off to pass along the Elder Architect's wishes to Agrellus and the Arclords. Oblosk turned back to the pool. "I've got a few surprises for you, Geb."

. . .

Three handsome, middle-aged Garundi men sat atop horses at the front of the Nexian lines. He was a Council of Three and Nine member, embodying one and three. Elemion, all three men, raised spyglasses to his eyes and scanned the plains surrounding Quantium. He lowered the glasses, each self eyeing the others.

Elemion was taking a risk bringing all three parts of himself to such a dangerous locale. He was of the thought that if any one of his many selves remained alive that, even if the other two parts were slain, he would live. He wasn't certain. He had never attempted—or desired to attempt—a test. He had brought his triplicate selves together as a symbolic act. He represented one of the largest nomadic tribes in the Mana Waste. They had come to Quantium's defense. He brought himself together, put himself at risk, to display his confidence that Geb's army could be defeated. He raised the spyglasses once more and, seeing the zombies crossing the mile-wide gap, wasn't so sure they could be defeated.

He lowered the glasses and was about to turn and speak to his people when a rumble passed through the ground beneath him, startling his horses. He raised the spyglasses and looked out over the plains. He saw, felt, and heard the earth crack open before the zombie horde. A deep ravine now separated them from their enemy. Elemion watched as, on his side of the ravine, jagged, towering rocks erupted from the ground, making an unscalable wall. He could no longer see the zombies. He lowered the spyglasses, turned, and looked toward Quantium. He raised his fists and cheered, a three-part yell, wondering if the ancient pech could hear.

. . .

Geb floated high above his army and looked out over the battlefield. He saw the front edge of his army disappear into the ravine. With a thought he directed his zombies to intentionally enter the pit, but only at a single point. He would fill the pit at this point with their corpses, making a gruesome bridge. The same efforts would be used to scale the wall. The zombies would make a ramp out of themselves.

. . .

Agrellus was at the far end of Warlock's Way, a the edge of the city, surrounded by Arclords. They had erected a field camp that consisted of a multitude of tables and shelves. So many magical tomes had been stuffed together that the shelves groaned under their weight. Scrolls piled on tables, overflowing onto cobblestones.

"Walls of fire," Agrellus pointed to a pile of scrolls.

"Sir," argued one of the Arclords, one confident—or rash—enough to argue with the archmage. "Walls of ice. The fires will burn our own—"

Agrellus raised a hand as Oblosk's assistant skidded to a halt in the makeshift, open-air wizard's study. Agrellus and the Arclords waited for the messenger to catch his breath.

"He says blow the wall," the messenger panted.

"So soon?" asked the Arclord who was advocating for ice over fire. Agrellus glanced at him and smiled.

"I told him it was practically useless, a mere gesture." He looked at the messenger and nodded. The messenger rushed back to Oblosk. Agrellus turned to the Arclord. "But when he said I could blow it up." He smiled, turned to face the battlefield, and began to cast a spell.

The Arclord began to cast a spell as well, one he had forgotten to cast in the haste and confusion that proceeded the battle. A small magical box, the size and shape of a lantern but made of arcane energy, materialized. A second box appeared a few feet from the base of Oblosk's platform.

"Hello?" asked the Arclord.

"Uh, yes?" called an unknown voice from the other end.

"No need to run back and forth," said the Arclord.

"Oh, um, yes, of course," said one of Oblosk's assistants.

. . .

Borume sat alone in a small, dark chamber in his home in Oenopion. Only a port window admitted light and fresh air. The iron door was locked and barred. Outside stood two heavily armed guards. His home was surrounded by armed soldiers. Borume wasn't taking any chances.

Oenopion was strained to the breaking point by refugees from the capital and countryside. He didn't care for people. He found their irrational moods maddening. He found their sensitivities annoying. He was not so concerned with driving Geb from Nex as a civic duty, he was motivated to get these strangers out of his town.

He thrust his consciousness into a silver and gold construct that now stood outside of Quantium. His senses of sight, smell, and hearing were all tied to the construct, leaving only taste and feel to him. The construct examined a newly made feature of the plains outside of the capital. It was a shallow, snake-shaped pond made of highly caustic chemicals. They'd already eaten away the grasses, flowers, bushes, and insects, leaving only rocks and soil.

He directed the construct to turn and look to left. There he saw the last of the specially coated barrels being emptied and rolled away. He looked at one of the low walkways that led over the slurry. He looked up and saw Oblosk's jagged wall. He scanned the top and watched as zombies toppled over, landed—breaking bones—get up and shamble toward his pond. If Borume could have made his construct smile, he would have.

. . .

Word travelled fast through the Nexian lines; pull back behind Borume's pond. Those casters and their guards who had ventured out to pester the Gebbian army with spells now turned and retreated over the wooden walkways. They were careful. Even though the walkways had railings the idea of falling off and landing in the caustic—the smell nauseated them—slurry encouraged thoughtful movement.

The earth elementals, those who still existed—the zombies had torn many apart—went into the soil and glided toward the walkways. When the last Nexian crossed, the elementals reached up and smashed the walkways. They glided back toward the stone wall and waited until they were needed.

. . .

Borume's construct was the only Nexian anywhere near the caustic pond. Everyone else was at least a hundred yards back. Borume had no fear of chemicals. First, he wasn't physically present. Second, his construct was not only made of resilient metals but was enchanted to resist the kinds of chemicals that were likely to corrode or otherwise harm it. Finally, Borume knew what he was doing. He had been mixing chemicals since he was a boy. He watched the zombies fall and gather, wondering just how long Agrellus was going to wait.

. . .

Agrellus was once more floating on an updraft of arcane energy. He needn't be. The spell would work without such a showy display of power but he found that he not enjoyed the sensation but that the visuals ensured that others knew damn well he was the most powerful caster in Nex, or, if not, he certainly passed for it. As before, he was surrounded by Arclords who aided him. He had the thought that they were getting good at the shared casting of spells. He was curious what all could be accomplished by that methodology. He told himself that once Geb had been sent home like a scolded pup, tail between his legs, he would explore it further.

The spout of arcane energy shot into the air and formed something like a cloud above Quantium. It was the strangest cloud anyone had seen, roiling with arcane energy, lighting curling within, and humming like a tuning fork. The cloud moved toward Oblosk's stone wall. It spread out and took a similar horseshoe shape. It dropped down and became a fog that clung to the rocks. It seemed to dissipate without effect.

A few of the Arclords began to whisper. They looked at Agrellus. He could almost feel their concern. He could hear their murmuring: had the spell failed. He knew it hadn't. He was holding it in, reveling in the sensation. It felt like he was holding a mountain chain aloft in his hands. If he shifted a muscle the mountains would tumble to the earth. He had never felt anything like it. He wanted to savor the moment.

. . .

Rixende Orth was seated on a low, cushioned bench, a spell book in her lap. She could cast both arcane and divine magic. She was reviewing the correct wording for a spell that would transmute mud (a component of almost all battlefields throughout war's long history) into stone. It was a spell she had copied into her spell book years prior but hadn't cast more than twice since.

She looked up when the light and sound of Agrellus' cloud passed overhead. She had with her several of the higher ranking clerics within the church. The rest of her clerics were dispersed throughout the ranks. Rixende and her clerics watched as the cloud seemed to soak into the jagged stone wall. Nothing happened.

"He's failed," said Sebastian, one of her closest advisors and the second highest ranking cleric within the church. "We should have never believed his boasting. Agrellus is—" The remainder of Sebastian's critique was drowned out by a sound like an earthquake. The stone wall exploded into massive shards.

. . .

The ground shook and many were thrown down, but not Geb. The dust cloud that floated from the shattered wall obscured his vision. He waved a hand and a supernatural breeze blew over the battlefield, carrying the dust away.

He scanned his line. By his reconning a tenth of his zombies either fell into the ravine or had been intentionally cast in. Another tenth had just been torn to bits by the explosion. This did not dismay him. It gave him an idea. He began to cast a series of spells.

. . .

"Finally," said Borume. His voice issuing from the gold and silver construct. He directed it to turn and walk to the Nexian line. There it joined a contingent of alchemists from Oenopion. He stood for a while in silence, watching the zombies advance. A thought struck him and he turned to the alchemist nearest. "The smell will be atrocious."

The alchemist, never having seen such a construct let alone spoken to by one, stared back, mute. Finally, she turned and looked out over the alchemical pond. Borume and the alchemists from Oenopion watched with a mixture of horror and awe as the zombies began to wade into their pond. The chemicals at once began to dissolve their legs. It splashed onto their thighs, their torsos, and their arms. Everything the alchemical mixture touched began to dissolve. Borume was correct, the smell was overwhelming. Even a hundred yards back they smelled it. Many began to vomit.

The first zombies to enter the pond never left it. In fact, almost nothing existed of them. Borume figured there was a million gallons, if not more, of caustic chemicals in the pond. He had emptied every store, public and private, in Oenopion to create it. At its deepest point it was two feet, at its shallowest mere inches. As he watched the zombies, he knew he needed four times as much as he'd had to really make an impact. He knew they were going to fill the pond, turning it into little more than viscous sludge.

. . .

The zombies clogged the unnatural, stinking pond with their dissolved remains. It was, as Borume knew it would become, a disgusting—but no longer dangerous—slurry. Ahrhune held a scarf to his face and scanned the line before him. He could not say how many zombies had succumbed to the alchemists' unnatural waters. It didn't matter, because they still came. He pulled the scarf away from his mouth and looked to the sky.

"Sarenrae, help me with this one." Ahrhune stepped forward, leaving the Nexian line. He looked to his left and right and saw hundreds of casters, both arcane and divine. He began to intone the proper words and move one hand in an intricate pattern. With his other hand he, along with hundreds of others, produced a tiny bag containing a small candle. These material components would be consumed in the spell.

Once the words were said, Ahrhune pointed. He watched, slightly amazed (he hadn't cast much in his short time as a cleric of Sarenrae), as an ant the size of a pony materialized. Its dusty red skin glowed with celestial light. It turned and glanced at Ahrhune. He waved his hand, "Go, go, taste zombie flesh!" The ant turned to face the zombies and, along with thousands of similarly summoned monsters, from dire rats to a cloud giant, rushed forward. Meanwhile, Ahrhune and the other casters retreated behind the lines.

Ahrhune went to the boy and slapped him on the shoulder. "It worked! How about that?"

A bright light flashed overhead and he ducked. Countless fireballs arced over Nexians, hammering zombies with arcane fury. The volley of fireballs, cast from scrolls, wands, and memory, would continue for a solid five minutes before the roar died down. After this, a maze of walls made of fire sprang up. Sadly, these walls injured not only the zombies but the summoned monsters. But Agrellus was not one to be easily persuaded.

. . .

Geb finished the series of spells. The collected remains of his destroyed zombies began to coalesce. The sight was appalling. Severed limbs, bits of flesh, caved-in skulls, and other disembodied parts flopped, crawled, slithered, and rolled to a central point. It took some time for them to gather. They passed underfoot. They were stepped on by those zombies who still shambled forward or by those summoned monsters that fought them. The bits of bodies formed a massive pile.

When the pile contained all it needed it shuddered. The dead flesh began to adhere to itself, held by Geb's spells as if glued together. A roughly spherical shape rose from the center, followed by something like shoulders. A colossus of undead flesh rose up to a height of sixty feet. It weight one hundred and fifty thousand pounds. It turned and "looked" at its creator. Geb nodded and the flesh colossus turned and began toward the Nexian lines.

Geb watched from his lofty vantage point. He was impressed with the volley of fireballs. It reminded him of Nex's long ago meteor shower attack. That memory fueled his need for vengeance. He studied the blasted battlefield. The massive, burning graveyard that the plains outside of Quantium had become pleased him. He had lost three-fourths of his zombies, but they had done their job. They'd overrun the more devastating Nexian defenses. They'd absorbed hundreds of spells. And, most importantly, they'd revealed weak spots in the Nexian lines.

With a thought he sent forward his skeletons. Although a much smaller force than his zombies had been, this was a more dangerous force for within the ranks of the swift moving skeletons were ghouls, ghast, mummies, and mohrgs. Supporting these undead were clerics and necromancers. Baykoks flew overhead, firing bone arrows from accursed bows.

Baykoks were a nasty type of undead—not that there are any pleasant types. They can release a blood-curdling howl that paralyzes with fear. They spawn endless bone arrows, never needing to worry about ammo. Finally, and this is their most frightening ability, they can consume the soul of a nearby dying creature, of which there would be plenty. They make use of the poor victim's soul to heal themselves. Baykoks were normally solitary hunters, but hundreds had answered Geb's call.

This second wave would cross the ravine on the zombie bridge but would focus on attacking the weak points with the goal of breaking through the lines. Before they could do this, however, they would be tested by the madmen of the desert, the efreet and shaitans of Osirion, the spellcasters of Nex, and the clerics of half a dozen gods.

. . .

A tent flap opened and a bearded Ulfen lying on a cot—his legs hung over the end, from the knee down, so tall was he—lifted his head. A young woman stood in the opening.

"You said to get you when the skeletons came."

"Well?" asked the Ulfen.

"They're here." She chuckled. "And something else, something you'll have to see to believe." The Ulfen emitted a dismissive sound. This prompted the woman to add, "Something bigger than you."

The man nodded, laid his head back down, and closed his eyes.

"Rouse the boys and girls," he said.

The woman grunted and left.

"What's that, Gorum?" asked the Ulfen. He opened his eyes and lifted his head. "Aye." He stood but had to remain bent, for the tent was not tall enough to accommodate his full height. His mithril chainmail rustled at the movement. He reached to the side and grabbed his enchanted war hammer (it struck with the added bite of the northern cold). He exited the tent and looked out over the battlefield. He couldn't see much except the rear of the Nexian line and the protected, elevated platforms for the spellcasters. There was one thing he could see, a tower of flesh that lumbered forth like a dead god. He figured that was a problem for the spellcasters to solve. Besides, he thought, if that colossus got close enough to be of worry it didn't matter how he felt about it, he would be dead.

The sounds of battle—he thought of it as a song, his favorite one at that—came to him. As he stretched, a hundred heavily armed and armored men and women approached. He turned, saw the mercenary company he led, and smiled. "You've already received half your pay. I hope you remembered your kinfolk and didn't waste good Nexian gold on booze and loose women, or," he chuckled, rubbing his hand over his chin, "beardless youths." Several of the women among his ranks laughed. "When this battle is won you'll get your other half plus whatever loot you can carry from," he turned and waved his arm over the battlefield. He turned back to his mercenaries then pointed to the north.

"The Bloody Blades are up yonder." He turned. "The Heaven Sent." He pointed south. "But we're the Nephilim and we're the best." He smiled. "I talked to Gorum. He said it was a glorious battle already, but that we needed to get off our asses and join." The mercenaries cheered. "Well," said the Ulfen, "they came to Katapesh and hired the best. Let's give them their money's worth."

. . .

Astor Bizet sat side saddle on a milk white steed. His white and pink robes fluttered about him, as did his long hair. Like Rixende Orth, he had near him the elite of his church. Like Rixende's, the rest of his clergy were spread through the lines. He closed his eyes and began a prayer. His goddess held dominion over fate. He asked her the results of Geb's attack. He received, in answer, both weal and woe. The following words came to his mind, *the battle will be lost and won*, and he didn't know if they were his own words or Pharasma's.

He opened his eyes and looked out over the field of battle. The zombies were a fraction of what they were before. He thought their number insurmountable but the magical defenses prepared by him and his fellow members of the Council of Three and Nine, as well as a multitude of helpers, had accomplished the seemingly impossible. In their wake rushed skeletons, with broken blades and rusted armor, a foul light in their empty sockets. The skeletons were not alone, their boney mass hid much worse. He turned and looked down at his clerics.

"Prepare yourselves for battle." He slipped from the saddle and waved up a squire. "Take this beautiful creature back to the stables." He ran his palm down the horse's muscular neck. "Such beauty doesn't deserve," he glanced toward Geb's army, "to be destroyed by such ugliness."

The Unexpected

Quantium, Nex, Rova, 4711

Fero Zetterling tugged on the hem of his ill-fitting breastplate. He was too rotund for it but the armor smith had, upon being pressed by Fero's agent, admitted it to be the best protection and so it had been purchased—including a surcharge for refitting—gold Fero now considered wasted. He turned to one of his employees.

"Damn it, what's going on? Did the fireballs wipe them out?"

Fero and his young hires—outfitted for war out of charity and self-interest—stood at the conscript army's rear. They could, with a quick jog, reach the homes and businesses at the edge of Quantium and find shelter from the storm. This had been a consideration in their placement.

"I'll look," said Fero's youthful employee. He ran to the nearest elevated platform and called for the ladder. A cleric of Abadar, the god of cities, law, merchants, and wealth (the clerics of whom seldom found themselves so engaged) leaned over the wall and scolded the pestering youth. When the youth motioned to his employer the cleric lowered the ladder, albeit with some displeasure. The youth scrambled up, produced one of Fero's spyglasses from his pack and looked over the battle. He came down, the ladder went up, and the youthful employee returned to his employer.

"The zombies are nigh, engaging the front—skeletons follow."

"What?" cried Fero. "They still come? After all that?"

"Sir, if I may?"

"Well, go on."

"There is something quite large just coming onto the field of battle." The youth pointed and Fero looked just in time to see the colossus rise to its full height. He'd later claim he fainted from restricted blood flow, blaming the breastplate. For now he lay in the mud, at peace with the world.

. . .

Gen Hendrikian, the nagaji and Chief Riddler of the Scrivenbough, the Temple to Abraxas, was waiting in the courtyard before the temple. He was full of confidence, despite the worrying updates that periodically reached him concerning Geb's successes. He scanned the faces of those clerics remaining with him, the majority being spread through the ranks, despite the fact that they could not channel positive energy or drop their chosen (requested via prayer) spells for healing spells. Abraxas was not a good god but an evil demon lord. Still, his clerics could do much to frustrate the enemy.

"All is done, Chief Riddler," said an acolyte, who ran from the open doors of the temple. "Our most rare and precious artifacts shall not fall into Gebbian hands."

"The treasures afforded us by Abraxas have never been under threat by Geb."

"Sir?"

Gen turned to face his acolyte. "Geb is not coming here, nor are any of his followers."

"Sir, then why—"

"In every war-torn city there are looters," said Gen. "I'm not concerned about the Gebbians, but our own. There are many Arclords who desire those books and scrolls. They might feel, having defended our great city, a certain entitlement to them."

Gen turned toward the battle. "We've delayed long enough. An uncertain fate awaits us. Let us greet it." The shortest route to the front lines took him past the Refuge of

Nex. He motioned the opposite direction, toward the harbor. "Let us follow the Obari to the Elemion and approach from Geb's flank. Serpents sneak and attack unseen, they do not charge forward."

Even though this wisdom was enough for his clerics, who fell in step behind him—after closing and locking the temple doors—Gen Henrikian glanced at the smoky red crystal shard in which Nex had taken refuge. He wanted to steer clear of it at all cost.

. . .

Master Phade left his full-body, black leather suit on its stand in his quarters. He was as nature had made him, invisible and almost immaterial. He flew over the field of battle, searching for Geb's elite. They eluded easy discovery. They were not, like most elites, hidden at the rear of the line, but were embedded with their foul creations.

The invisible stalker had located Geb, he was easy to see, floating, as he was, hundreds of feet above his army. Phade spotted a small contingent held back at Geb's rear. These were surrounded by the Bonewall. It was a small but potent force. Why Geb held it in check he did not know, but it worried him.

Master Phade, a being of air, was the first to feel the beating of powerful wings. He looked at the undead dragon but saw that he was diving, his wings pinned to his rib cage. Master Phade looked and saw, just coming into view, a pair of dragons. They flew in from the north. He went toward them, hoping to get a better look. He was curious if they had come in support of Geb or Nex.

His curiosity was satisfied when he saw that one of the pair sported shimmering gold-colored scales, the other, its scales glowing with the moon's reflected light, was silver. They flew in straight and fast and, upon surveying the state of battle, made for the colossus of corpses and strafed it with fire and ice.

The colossus, so perturbed, lifted a maul-like fist and swung at them, to no avail. The ravener, having himself breathed fire upon the Nexian line, and, having seen the two dragons in the air, beat his wings and sped to them, no doubt, thought Master Phade, desiring that they pay dearly for polluting *his* sky with *their* presence.

. . .

Long ago Nex had set two golems in orbit around Quantium. One had an emerald hue, the other ruby. They carried massive swords. Their armor was of an archaic style (although the height of fashion when Nex created them). The earth around Quantium had been worn into a rut with their ceaseless passing. No one could command them, except Nex. All through the preparations for battle and so far through the battle itself the golems had not ventured from their circuit. It seemed to all of Nex that the ancient prophecy, the one that said the golems would come to the capital's defense, was, like so many other prophecies in this Age of Ill Omens, false.

. . .

Iranez of the Orb forsook her stylish dress for practical attire. She had volunteered to oversee and protect a massive field hospital that was set up not far from the docks, in a series of spacious warehouses. The wounded had begun to filter in not long after Borume's pond had become a stinking slurry.

She was hurrying from one warehouse hospital to another when something caught her attention. She looked around but nothing obvious greeted her. She soon realized what it was and looked.

The ruby-hued Quantium Golem stood nearby, motionless. It turned and faced its opposite, the emerald-hued, who was likewise motionless and staring. As Iranez watched a silent communication passed between the two golems. The ruby-hued golem stepped out of the track and headed toward—much to Iranez's alarm—her. The emerald-hued golem too stepped from the track and headed toward the flesh colossus.

As if this hadn't stunned her well enough, yet another unexpected sight came to her. A zombie, dripping wet, rounded the corner of a building and began down the avenue. It was followed by several of its kind, all wet and —she now noticed—trailing seaweed behind them.

. . .

Elder Architect Oblosk, bent over the railing of his platform, commanded with a gesture the scrying to focus in on the two new arrivals. He turned and looked down at one of his waiting assistants. "They're with us!" He laughed and was about to turn back to the pool but he saw something that alarmed him. All of the streets that led to the harbor were clogged with undead. He pointed and yelled. His assistants turned and looked.

Oblosk hurried down the steps and went to the magical lantern-shaped box. "Undead inside the city!"

"Say again," came a voice from the glowing box.

Oblosk turned and squinted. He turned back to the box. "Zombies, they're coming out of the Obari. Don't ask me how."

Oblosk heard chatter through the box. One snippet mentioned walls of ice. He turned to his assistants. "It's not safe here." He glanced around, remembered where a secret tunnel was, and motioned. "There, through that arch and to your left. Go, go!" Before he abandoned the magical communicator he issued one last request. "Agrellus? Agrellus, can you hear me?"

"Yes, Oblosk, what is it? I'm busy."

"Dump Ecanus on them."

Laughter came through the magical box. "With pleasure."

. . .

Dun Palovar, despite his years, remained a striking physical presence. He had broad shoulders, a muscular chest, back, arms, and thighs, a well-kept beard of white and a thick mane of white hair. He stood erect and moved with a purpose. Despite his obvious physical stamina it was the power of his intellect, which shone in his gaze like crackling energy, that intimidated people. When those who knew Dun Palovar personally spoke of his intellect they used words like "intimidating," even "punishing." While Agrellus was flamboyantly arrogant, Dun Palovar was intensely arrogant.

Dun Palovar stood just before the main building on the sprawling campus that composed the Fleshforges of Ecanus. He was not one to suffer from impatience but he was annoyed. He did not know how well or poorly the battle for Quantium went. He only knew to be ready. His patience was rewarded when the air began to hum.

At first a single oval-shaped portal opened. This first was followed by half a dozen more and a dozen after that. The oval portals enlarged until they were the size of barn doors. Dun Palovar nodded. His fellow flesh forgers pulled open the massive doors of the buildings nearest. Forge-crafted golems and beasts surged forth.

. . .

Geb watched the gold and silver dragons behave like pestering flies, annoying his flesh colossus. The sight amused more than it worried. He was deciding whether or not to personally intervene and kill the dragons. He relished picturing them as raveners or wyrmwraiths—undead dragons—but their creation took time and was power-draining, even for him. He needed to conserve power for what was to come.

Before he was able to decide, a collection of glowing doorways appeared behind his skeletons. The magical portals began to enlarge. Geb knew immediately what they were and what their purpose was. He attempted to dispel them but it was too late. He abandoned his casting as scores of flesh golems and monstrous beasts poured through and began to attack his lines from the rear.

His mood took a decidedly sharp downturn.

. . .

A lifeless salt plane extended to the horizon in every direction. An eclipsing moon hung overhead, offering only a weak light. Szuriel, the Horseman of War, knelt over a being that, at first glance, seemed her twin.

Szuriel was a perfect physical specimen. She was tall, athletic, well-proportioned, and hauntingly beautiful. Her skin was milky white and flawless. Her blonde hair flowed like pure honey. She wore a short skirt of dark gray silk hemmed in gold and a sleeveless, scarlet-colored silk top.

Her sword, which every horseman of war had wielded, was buried to the hilt in an angel's chest. The angel lifted its head and tried to speak but blood spat out in place of words. The angel dropped its head onto the hard-packed salt and died. Szuriel began to laugh but stopped short. She lifted her head and looked up. Blood seeped continually from her eyes, staining her cheeks, falling onto her breasts, soaking her shirt.

"You again?" she asked. She heard a familiar voice from far, far away. "Is that so?" She rose, yanking her blade, the *Lamentation of the Faithless,* from the angel's dead breast. She looked down at the angel then glanced to either side. Two dozen corpses, all angels, all dead by her hand, were scattered in the salt. She looked back up. "I'll own you, Geb. I'll own you for eternity."

. . .

The portals that Agrellus and the Arclords created remained open, monsters filing through, but they were joined by others. These portals were like angry, bleeding wounds in the skin of reality. The creations of the Fleshforges were terrifying to behold but they struck one as practically soothing to the eye when compared to what came from these new portals.

A large humanoid-shaped daemon emerged, his head like a vulture's, his body pierced by dozens of weapons. It surveyed the battlefield, selected an appropriate weapon, and drew it from his body. He then stepped away from the portal and waited for others to join.

The purrodaemon didn't have to wait long but it did have to hurriedly step aside, for the next daemon through was gargantuan. It resembled nothing more than a massive sphere set upon four stout legs, adorned with twisted, razor-sharp horns. Four long arms extended from its sides. These ended in massive, clawed hands. It was an olethrodaemon, the most powerful of the daemon breeds. It was half the size of the colossus and a tenth of its weight, but twice as dangerous.

Many types of daemons poured from the wound-like portals. Some resembled insects with a multitude of legs and claws, some apes with hooves for feet, horns atop their heads, and clawed hands. Some appeared to be snapping maws with little by way of bodies. Most disturbing, perhaps, were those few daemons that appeared in the form of innocent children. They were indistinguishable from the little boys and girls they appeared to be until one drew close and saw that their throats had the appearance of being slit but that the wound had become a fang-filled maw seeping blood.

Szuriel, the Horseman of War, sent these daemons at Geb's request. They spread over the battlefield like a contagion and at once met with the constructs of the

Fleshforges. Although, more than a few could not help themselves and made directly for the Nexian lines, drawn by the life forces of living opponents more so than Dun Palovar's un-living creations.

The Deluge

Quantium, Nex, Rova, 4711

Ahrhune wove through pikemen and shield bearers to join clerics and casters at the square's heart. Several clerics prayed. The Nexian battle casters readied scrolls, if they had any left. They had already used the majority of them in the volley of fireballs.

Ahrhune understood the logic of the Nexian army. It consisted mostly of pikemen, shield bearers, and battle casters. These formed into squares of four hundred men, mostly pikemen. The formation was defensive. The idea was to protect the casters and let the arcane might of Nex do the heavy lifting. The pikemen kept the enemy at bay. The shield bearers protected the casters from incoming missiles, be they arrows or magic. The battle casters, carrying shoulder bags filled to the brim with scrolls, provided the offense.

The bane of such a formation was the archer. But Ahrhune surmised that the range of the Nexian spells was greater than that of any normal archer and so this threat was largely neutralized.

As he watched a mass of Qadirian horsemen circled before the pikemen, turned, and charged once more along the Gebbian line. They leaned low in the saddle and swiped at the zombies, skeletons, ghouls, ghasts, and mummies with their flaming swords. Before the undead had a chance to strike back, the Qadirians, many chanting the name of Sarenrae—which pleased him to no end—had raced away.

The shield bearers and pikemen to his left squeezed in and a mercenary company, led by a towering Ulfen, passed along side. Several such mercenary companies had taken the field. They went out ahead of the pikemen but gave room for the Qadirians to work their maneuvers.

Ahrhune had never participated in a land battle of such size and scope. He usually fought on narrow decks, the floor beneath him rolling on the waves. He dealt not with the obstruction of shield bearers and pikemen but with rope and barrel. He had seen plenty of the supernatural but the sights he had seen this day were well beyond his experience.

The pikemen moved back into place and called out. The remaining zombies and second wave—skeletons and worse—were fast approaching. The pikemen thrust their pikes into the zombies. The casters began to cast. Ahrhune, who was not yet confident in his casting, drew his sword. He realized it was of little use where he stood and sheathed it. He began to channel Sarenrae's divine will, and, after a moment of concentration, released it in a blast. This healed the wounded nearby and harmed the undead.

The zombies, now skewered, began to pull themselves down the hafts of the pikes with the intent of clawing and clubbing the pikemen. Ahrhune saw that even though his channelled energy destroyed many, the undead still came.

The skeletons were even less impacted by the thrusting tips of the pikes but the pikemen realized that by whipping the tips of their weapons back and forth they could snap bones with ease.

Ahrhune watched, in horror, as a group of ghouls leapt onto the pikes and began to clamor over them, reaching out with diseased hands. The weight of the ghouls on the pikes pulled them from the hands of their wielders. However, the pikemen adjacent were quick to stab the offending ghouls. Their suicidal attack had temporarily opened a hole in the defensive wall and into this stepped a corpse wrapped in filthy linens.

The mummy moaned and turned its malevolent gaze on the pikemen. Fear and despair gripped their hearts and many dropped their pikes, leaving further holes to be exploited. There were plenty of pikemen however and even the mummies, as terrifying as they were, could not absorb a dozen pike thrust without succumbing.

Ahrhune once more began to call upon his goddess and once more channeled her divine might. The wounded were healed, the undead harmed. He stepped up and reached past a shield bearer to grip the shoulder of a slender pikeman.

"Boy—you doing okay?"

The boy, his mind focused by battle, did not hear Ahrhune's words or feel his touch. He thrust the tip of his pike into a ghoul. The ghoul turned his gaze on the boy and began to pull himself along the haft, reaching for the boy's face. The boy almost panicked but three more pikes thrust into the ghoul and it ceased to move. The pikemen pulled their weapons free and sought new targets.

. . .

The Ulfen jogged twenty yards ahead of the pikemen and stopped. His Nephilim spread out around and behind him, forming three well spaced lines. The skeletons were already clamoring over them and the Ulfen and his crew gleefully swung their swords, axes, and hammers.

The Ulfen swung his two-handed war hammer in a wide arc, destroying three skeletons and knocking aside a ghoul. He chuckled to himself at how easy this was going to be but the thought vanished when he saw what was behind the skeletons he had just destroyed.

It was the husk of an enormous and very much dead spider, twice as tall as he and four times as broad. Although the spider's husk was split along the back and clearly hollow it was animated, not so much by necromantic magic (although it was) but by thousands of smaller spiders. These spiders crawled all over the animated husk, coating it with protective webbing and, although the Ulfen didn't know it, acting as its hive mind. It was a deathweb, a type of undead that populated terrifying children's stories. The Ulfen frowned. He hated spiders.

. . .

Fero Zetterling stirred awake. He realized that he had lost considerable esteem in the eyes of those who looked up to him and worried that his employees were soon to abandon him. He therefore directed his men forward, himself in the lead. The little group of merchant marines did not make it far before what they took to be a black fog swept over the Nexian lines and headed directly toward them.

Even though the sounds of war were deafening, Fero and his employees heard the mad screams and maddening wailings of the caller in darkness, for the fog was no fog at all, but a black cloud of a dozen insane souls. The swirling vortex of madness and despair moved down and settled on Fero and his men. It reached into their minds with ghostly fingers and tugged at their sanity.

. . .

Rixende Orth began to cast the spell which would transmute mud to stone as soon as she saw a giant, severed hand skittering toward the pikemen before her. The hand was truly giant, or had belonged to a giant at some point. She was well aware that such undead existed but the pikemen were more than a little shocked. The hand was not alone, it was being escorted by hundreds of skeletons and a smattering of other undead, mostly mummies and—although she could not yet see them—mummified monsters.

The spell worked—the giant crawling hand stuck fast, the tips of its five fingers now incased in stone to the first knuckles. The pikemen cheered, as they no longer had to contend with the absurd hand. Their cheer was short lived as the mummies revealed themselves. Rixende began a new spell, one that would create a barrier of whirling blades before the oncoming undead.

. . .

Khamati climbed atop the giant hand and looked down on the Nexians before him. He screamed to draw their attention and those who looked at him were paralyzed with despair. This made him laugh. The words of a potent divine spell rose above his laughter and the din of battle. He recognized the spell and looked hard at the caster. He ventured out onto the middle of the giant hand's fingers, knelt, and exhaled a blast of super heated sand. The cone shaped, burning, supernatural sandstorm scalded the first several rows of pikemen but didn't reach the caster.

A moment later her blades appeared and began to cut his mummies and pets to shreds. This angered Khamati and spurred him to his own casting. He spoke part of the spell in ancient Osirion. He pulled his gem encrusted holy symbol from around his neck and held it aloft. He pointed it at the woman who had summoned the blades, he could see that she was a cleric of Nethys, and when his spell was complete his holy symbol transformed into a black ray that shot into the woman's body.

. . .

Immediately after Rixende summoned the barrier of blades she began to channel positive energy. She never completed it as a black beam sliced into her chest. It was pure hatred given energy and form. She tried to scream but she was disintegrating from the inside out. She heard a name in her mind, the name of an ancient, forgotten god.

The spell destroyed her, utterly and completely, consuming her in unholy fire. It left no remains.

. . .

The ghouls pushed the armored skeletons before them, using them as shields. The pikemen whipped their pikes, knocking the skeletons aside. The ghouls leapt on the pikes, climbing over them. The pikemen bunched together and began to stab the ghouls. None of the pikemen saw that beneath their muddy, blood-soaked boots a black circle was forming. The circle was made of necromantic energy. It formed a shadowy disk edged with arcane runes.

The disk burst into a circle of black fire forty foot in diameter. Immediately the life forces of two dozen pikemen were snuffed out. They dropped dead where they stood. This opened a huge hole in the line which was filled by undead.

. . .

Baya-Iza, the drow necromancer, laughed when the circle of death spell completed. She'd caught more victims than she'd hoped. She was protected by four potent bodyguards as well as scores of skeletons, ghouls, and so forth, and thus was at ease and enjoying herself. She looked once more at the berbalangs that protected her, a gift from Arazni. They were humanoid undead, looking not unlike ghouls, with massive bat wings. She pondered which spell to cast next but couldn't decide between black tentacles or waves of fatigue.

. . .

Kimberly Silent Eyes crouched on the back of a vrykolakas. A second of the serpent-tongued undead, they had been created by and taken from Kemnebi, but she didn't know that, stood nearby. She'd adopted the pair, seeing them as useful steeds. She saw an explosion of divine light and thought to herself that a juicy target was presenting itself. She could not control the vrykolakas but, much to her satisfaction, they were drawn to the powerful divine caster just as she was.

The vrykolakas began to weave their way through the skeletons and ghouls. Kimberly saw the pikes drop and the leading edge of the Nexian line destroyed. She saw casters bring protective circles around them. She saw the undead before her burned with searing light. She saw all this and was certain she was going to score a valuable kill.

. . .

The pikemen square surrounding Astor Bizet and his clerics was beginning to crumble. Despite all their efforts there were simply too many undead. Astor finished a spell, pointed his holy symbol at a group of three mummies, and commanded a pillar of fire to strike down on them. When the pillar had come and gone the trio of mummies were little more than charred husks. Despite the satisfaction this gave him, he was worried, for the pikeman's square was compromised. He pushed aside the shield bearer guarding him, rushed forward, knelt, and began to cast a mass healing spell.

Before he could complete the spell his instincts alerted him to danger and he looked up. A pair of dark-skinned, deformed undead with long necks, forked tongues, and hatred-filled eyes rushed toward him. He stood just in time to be knocked down as one of the vrykolakas tackled him, pinning him beneath its clawed hands.

The vrykolakas leaned down and hissed in his face. Astor could taste the rancid breath. He tried not to look at the monstrous undead pinning him but strained to reach his mace. A beam of white light struck the side of the vrykolakas and in the light Astor saw something dark leap overhead and land nearby. He turned his head just in time to see a dagger swing toward his face. He tried to roll out of the way but the vrykolakas had him pinned.

In that moment—a poison-soaked dagger arcing toward him—Astor felt a serene calm. The words of a spell came to him. It was the most potent spell Pharasma had granted him. Thankfully, it required nothing more than to speak the sacred words.

Astor looked up into the slit-eyes of the woman bent over him. He spoke with calm assurance because he spoke with the voice of a goddess. The dictum took but a moment to speak but in that moment fate was altered.

A pure white light shone from Astor's face and hands. It flashed out in a forty-foot radius spread. The two vrykolakas, the skeletons fighting the pikemen, the ghouls clamoring over the dead, and Kimberly Silent Eyes all felt —in that moment—the authority of a god.

The divine might lent to Astor's voice shattered the skeletons. The purity of the divine light radiating from his skin burned the ghouls to ashes. The twin vrykolakas tried to leap to safety but they too were consumed by divine wrath. Kimberly staggered in reverse. She dropped her daggers and raised her hands to her ears in an attempt to silence the deafening roar of Astor's voice. She tripped over a corpse, fell onto her back, and lay paralyzed.

Astor stood, stepped forward a few feet, knelt and resumed the casting of his mass healing spell. One of the pikemen who had witnessed the entire episode—although it took but a few seconds—stepped up, drew his short sword, and decapitated the High Priest's would-be killer.

. . .

Hent-er-Neheh was being carried by a dozen skeletal champions in a liter. A circle of mummies surrounded her lofty, mobile seat. She cleared the way with spells. What she wanted was to beat Eratosthenes into

Quantium. She had no idea how he felt about the issue, or if he even cared, but for her it was a point of pride.

She had collected about her a significant number of powerful undead which she controlled. This was no easy feat, as Geb's grip was supreme. But she created these undead after he made his call and they were hers. It had taken her hours to create the skeletons, mummies, and various other undead. She was especially proud of her devourers.

They were always problematic to make as they required the lost souls of fiends or evil spellcasters, a difficult commodity to secure. They were ten feet in height but were a measly two hundred pounds, being a dry, emaciated corpse.

What was most interesting about devourers was that locked in their otherwise empty rib cages was a tormented ghostly form. This was the soul of the last victim to succumb to the devourer's touch. What made devourers so potent was their ability to cast a range of spells at will, their resilience against magic, and most appallingly, their ability to devour souls, which unwillingly occupy the ribcage prison. These trapped souls could then be used by the devourer to heal itself or harm others. On this day, many souls made the horrific passage from a living being into the devourer's unnatural prison, only to be consumed to heal the devourer or to reflect a spell back on its caster.

Hent-er-Neheh saw a flash of light a hundred feet before her and sat up to examine it closer. It appeared to be two jets of fire but she couldn't detect the source. She commanded her retinue forward, overcome by curiosity, despite her dislike of fire.

. . .

Borume's construct had outlived, if such a term can be applied, the alchemist and soldiers that once surrounded him. He was on his own and that was perfectly fine with him as he needn't worry about collateral damage. With no allies to get in his way he could use the most potent of his weapons. Attached to each forearm was a large tank of liquid. Attached to the back of each wrist was an igniter. With the correct movement of his hands he opened a valve and forced the liquid through a pump and nozzle that shot it over the igniter and created a twenty foot long jet of fire. He was running out of liquid but was having great fun using it up.

He cleared the field before him with his twin jets, then looked down to check the volume in his tanks. He figured he had one or two good sprays left then he would have to go back and refill. When he looked up he saw a group of undead approach. As he watched, four tall, thin undead floated before the rest and came toward him. He looked past them and saw a group of mummies. He could hardly tell one undead from another but he certainly knew that mummies hated fire.

He stepped to his left and kept walking in a semi-circle. His idea was to draw the tall, floating undead out of the way, then rush back and spray the mummies. So far the undead were acquiescing to his plan. When the four floating undead were sufficiently to one side he rushed back to his right, turned—his legs could carry him one way while his torso faced another—and sprayed the mummies with fire.

When the twin jets of fire lit up the field before him, Borume saw that yet another mummy sat in a liter at the center of the group. He lifted his arms and tried to spray her but she was too far back.

. . .

"What's this?" yelled Hent-er-Neheh when the silver and gold construct (she worried it was some kind of golem) tried to spray her with fire. She looked to the mummies and saw that they were burning. This angered her. She looked at the devourers, pointed to the silver and gold flame-thrower, and commanded, "break that thing!"

Not only are devourers potent casters and horrifying undead they are also, despite their seeming frailness, incredibly strong. They turned and floated toward the offending construct.

. . .

Borume was so taken with his burning of the mummies that he had neglected the tall, floating undead, a type he could not identify. If he knew what they were he would have paid them more heed. His attention was drawn to them when one reached out, grabbed his wrist, and bend his hand to the side. He couldn't feel the construct's metal bend but saw his hand twist, the metal screeching in complaint.

He swung his free arm and punched at the devourer's in face only to realize the undead's arm was much longer than his. He succeeded only in hitting empty space. A second devourer reached and grabbed his other arm. It pulled and he heard the heads sheering from the bolts that held his shoulder together. The two other devourers came up, grabbed what they could, and began to bend, twist, and break him.

. . .

Borume's consciousness snapped back into his body and he slumped against the wall. He felt his heart in his throat. He felt the sweat beaded on his brow. He even felt lightheaded. He took a series of deep breathes and reminded himself that he was unharmed. He rose, wobbled a bit, steadied himself, then lifted the bar behind the door and set it to the side. He opened the door and stepped out. His guards turned, surprised to see him.

He did not acknowledge them but walked across the room, pulled open the door, and yelled down the stairs. “Claudia?” He heard talk and movement from the floor below. A voice called back to him. He answered. “Wine!” He thought for a moment then added, “and something to eat, something comforting.”

. . .

“This is childish,” scolded Nah-le-tah. He stood with his hands on his hips, watching his fellow tomb giants gather the boulders which had been cast by the war barges in the Elemion River. “What are we, hill giants?”

“We’re conserving our spells," said one the giants.

“These are as effective as anything else we’ve got," said another.

“We look like fools when we throw—”

“Admit it, Nah-le-tah,” interjected another of the giants, “you’ve a bum shoulder, otherwise you would be doing likewise.”

“I do not—” But Nah-le-tah’s protest was drowned out by laughter.

. . .

“Stay back,” Master Castelli yelled to the axemen who were advancing toward the burning undead that came into the intersection. He lifted and activated his enchanted staff. A cone of ice-cold wind and sleet issued from the staff’s tip and shot toward the combusted. When the miniature blizzard passed the once burning undead lie in the street, their fires suppressed by a coat of ice.

Master Castelli turned to Iranez. They were in an intersection near one of the field hospitals. A group of axemen, saying they were Heaven Sent, had brought their wounded to the hospital and now stayed to defend it.

“Iranez!” Master Castelli pointed.

Iranez of the Orb turned and watched in horror as a little girl, her once white dress now soaked in blood, a wickedly curved dagger in hand, turned the corner. She stopped and held out a hand to Iranez. “Mommy?” But while the child's voice was heard her lips hadn't moved. The sound came from a gash in her throat. The vulnudaemon tilted her head and looked at Iranez. As she waited, a swarm of red, multi-eyed, orbs flew around her. They opened their fang-filled maws. "Mommy, can my friends come over and play?"

Iranez began a spell which she finished just as the first of the cacodaemons reached her. A branching chain of lighting issued from Iranez's pointed finger, travelled through the cacodaemons, bouncing from one to the next, before finally ending in the vulnudaemon. Daemons were somewhat resistant to electricity but Iranez's spell was so potent it overcame their resistance.

The red, horned orbs fell from the sky and flopped on the cobble stones like fish. The little girl shook, animated by the voltage coursing through her muscles. When the electricity left her she wobbled, began to smoke, then fell forward, landing face-first on the stones, her dagger skittering into the gutter.

"No," said Iranez. "You're grounded."

. . .

Master Phade was able to identify the lich by the potent spells she cast and by the aura of power she gave off. She was mixed in amongst various other undead but she was most certainly a Blood Lord, he could sense it.

He stalked her and studied her. She was casting recklessly. She made no effort to conserve her power. She took no care for her own defense. He waited for a moment when she was between spells and flew before her. He was shocked to see that her gaze held no intelligence, no self will. She gazed forward as if in a trance. He studied her for a moment then flew around behind her.

Master Phade hovered behind the lich and waited. He wanted to see if she would feel his presence or if she was insensitive to her personal surroundings. Once he was certain that she was more or less oblivious he slammed a fist into her lower back. She stumbled forward but continued to cast, not turning, not even actively responding to his attack. He floated along behind her, keeping pace, then slammed his fists into her several times. He felt her ribs splinter, her spine crack. She dropped to one knee and lost the spell she was casting.

Master Phade waited. The lich regained her feet and began to cast. He struck her on the side of her head, knocking her off balance, cracking her skull, and causing her to lose yet another spell. The lich stood, silent and motionless. The undead all around them continued forward, continued to attack, but Master Phade and the lich did nothing.

The lich jerked into motion and resumed her advance into the Nexian lines. Bodies were scattered all around her. She stepped on them and over them. She began to cast a spell and Master Phade lifted both arms and slammed them on the lich's shoulders. He felt her collar bones snap. Her arms went limp and the spell was lost. Again she stood without thought or action.

Master Phade floated around to her front and stood before her. Her eyes were blank. He lifted both arms and brought them down on the top of her head. Her skull caved in. Her body crumpled to the ground and turned to dust.

. . .

At the northern tip of the Icerime Peaks in north eastern Brevoy, roughly twenty miles as the crow flies from the city of Skywatch, along the northern edge of the Little Icerime River, stands an ancient castle. It is still occupied, and has been for many generations, by the Lermontov clan, cousins to House Lodovka of Acuben Isle.

The Lermontovs, like their cousins, are warriors comfortable fighting on iced decks in the Lake of Mists and

Veils. They are noblemen who have for a device the eagle pulling a carp from cold water.

But unlike their cousins, they keep a controversial secret, for beneath their castle a spiral staircase leads deep into the stone. At the base of this staircase is an enchanted iron door. Behind this door is a spacious chamber filled with tomes, scrolls, enchanted wands and staffs, and enough gold and precious stones to keep the Lermontovs in wealth for many generations to come. There's also, oddly, a well-appointed bed—albeit one covered in a layer of dust.

There is a secret door carved into the back wall of this chamber and behind it is a mithril box, sealed and trapped by magic. In that lockbox are several strips of vellum on which Lilith Lermontov transcribed the last lines of the spell that completed her transformation into a lich. This is Lilith's phylactery, hidden about as far away from Geb as one can get and still remain within the Inner Sea region.

Unseen by anyone the phylactery began to glow. Within the box the words on the vellum crackled with arcane energy. The air was filled with a high-pitched whine. A lump appeared under the coverlet on the bed. Its shape was like that of a cat curled up under the blanket but it was no feline, it was Lilith—the beginning of her new body.

It would take up to ten days for her body to recreate itself. When she opened her eyes, ten days hence, and saw where she was she would be struck by several thoughts. Chief among these would be her last clearly held memory, that of being in Arazni's chambers, joking with the Queen and her coterie. She would have no memory of Geb's call, the journey across the Mana Waste into Nex, or the ensuing assault on Quantium. She would have no memory of who or what had destroyed her. She wouldn't learn these things until she returned to Geb, *if* she returned to Geb.

The Breach

Quantium, Nex, Rova, 4711

Ahrhune hunted for the boy he'd vowed to protect. The pikemen were scattered. Many had dropped their pikes and ran into Quantium, seeking the safety of their homes. He had lost sight of the boy in the confusion. Only a few casters remained. They held short swords in their hands. Fear shone from their wide-open eyes. Ahrhune studied the corpses underfoot. Ashes blew into his eyes and he had to lift his sweat-soaked scarf to wipe them. When he lowered the scarf he saw a light moving toward him. He raised his sword, bracing for the worst.

The light moved on wings. It wasn't a globe of light but a pure white dove that shone with divine brilliance. For a moment Ahrhune was stunned. He had not expected to see a bird on a battlefield, crows maybe, after the fact, but not—and then he realized what the bird was and dropped to his knees, pressing his forehead to the blood-soaked earth.

The bird fluttered overhead, close enough that the tips of its wings touched him. He rose and spun. The dove landed on a body, turned, and looked at him as if beckoning. Ahrhune approached, watching the dove as he did so. Only when he was certain that what he saw was a symbol of Sarenrae's favor, a divine messenger, did he think to look at the corpse. He dropped his sword and dropped to his knees. He reached out and pushed the hair from the boy's face. Tears came to his eyes.

The dove made a mournful sound and Ahrhune looked. The bird tilted its head and Ahrhune had the thought to say a quick prayer for the boy. He again looked at the bird. It turned and looked to the left. A sound like rolling thunder came and the divine dove took wing.

Ahrhune turned just in time to see a pack of headless horsemen charging. He leapt out of the way. The dullahans trampled Nexian corpses under hoof as they passed. They were heading into Quantium.

Ahrhune regained his feet just as a second rolling wave of thunderous sound approached. He tried to dodge again but a muscular arm grabbed him and plucked him from his feet. Ahrhune was deposited on a centaur's back.

"Panos!" the centaur shouted over his shoulder.

Ahrhune grabbed the centaur's armor and held on. "Ahrhune." He yelled back.

"Ragathiel," the centaur yelled.

It took Ahrhune a moment to comprehend what was being said and why. He called back, "Sarenrae."

"Hold on," yelled Panos.

"I am!"

The centaurs charged after the dullahans, following them into Quantium.

. . .

Kemnebi flew for hours, flying over Geb's Rest—which Geb had forsook for activity—crossing the Mana Waste, crossing southern Nex, following the trail of lifeless earth that Geb's army had left behind them.

He was thankful that he did not feel fatigue for if he had he would be exhausted. He had just seen the last of the volley of fireballs on the horizon. The smell of burnt corpses wafted over him as he approached Quantium.

He took in the battlefield and was appalled. He did not know that the mountain of body parts he saw had been a colossus, not that it would have changed his opinion. He saw the Nexian army split—half pressed to the Elemion, half to the Obari. To his surprise the Gebbian army did not press their advantage but seemed content to contain the Nexians.

Kemnebi flew low and saw something he never would have expected. An undead dragon was lying on its side, as was a gold dragon. Both were dead, the ravener being only a skeleton lying in a pool of green, glowing—but fading—necromantic energy. They held each other by the throats and seemed to have fallen from the sky. A silver dragon lay not far away, its side smashed in as if a giant maul had struck it.

Kemnebi landed near the smashed silver dragon and took his human form. He scanned the plains, searching for Geb's ghostly form. Ghosts drifted across the plains, harassing those pikemen or casters who yet lived. He saw the Bonewall, it could be nothing else, slithering toward a large group of undead and followed.

. . .

Geb floated into the gap and paused. He studied the buildings of Quantium. He glanced at the tallest amongst them, if it could even be called a building. He turned and looked to his left and saw Eratosthenes. The liches of the Whispering Way had divided the Nexian lines and now held the gap so he could pass. Not that any enemies closely pressed. Eratosthenes stared back. Several of the liches who had accompanied him gathered and studied Geb.

Geb had the thought that he was looking at his nation's new master. He had the notion to tell Eratosthenes about the gift he was soon to bequeath him but ultimately he didn't care. While he studied the elven lich a pair of grave knights passed between them. A shadow blocked the moon and Geb looked. The ecorche stepped up and stopped, staring forward and waiting.

A bejeweled skull surrounded by a shimmering cloud of magical energy raced past and—spotting a living victim—shot twin beams of ruby-hued light from its ruby eyes. The Nexian, struck in the back, for he was running away from the mass of undead, stumbled and fell. His soul lifted from his body and was pulled back by the retreating beams. It was deposited in one of the demilich's gems. The demilich laughed and flew into the city. Geb smiled, taking it as an auspicious sign.

He held out his arm and Queen Arazni stepped up and slid her arm under it. It was a symbolic gesture, for Arazni could not really lock arms with Geb, giving he was a ghost, but it filled her with pride to accompany him at this moment in time, the moment of his ultimate victory over Nex.

. . .

The undead ignored Kemnebi. They didn't even look at him, for their eyes sought out only the force of life; which, they longed to quench. He walked among them, stunned by what he saw. He saw a white shimmer approach and began a spell but the ghost was not Geb and, like all the other undead, it ignored him. He abandoned his casting as the ghost passed.

Kemnebi saw movement and turned. Once again the Bonewall was moving. Once more he followed. He lost the Bonewall as it made its way into Quantium. He ran but came to a halt when he saw Eratosthenes. For a moment he was alarmed and began to cycle through meaningful actions, from turning into a bat to casting a spell, but when Eratosthenes turned and looked at him, Kemnebi saw no reason to flee or attack.

"Why?" asked Kemnebi. "Why has Geb done this?"

Eratosthenes looked to his left, in the direction Geb had gone. He looked back at Kemnebi. "Ask him."

Kemnebi looked at Eratosthenes, attempting to discern if the lich was honestly going to let him pass. He looked toward Quantium then back to Eratosthenes. He turned and ran into the city.

. . .

Geb paused. The ecorche, who was right behind him, turned and hunched, protecting the captive deep gnome from threat. Three grave knights rushed forward, as did the Bonewall, which circled in front of Geb. The last thing Arazni saw before the Bonewall cut off her view was a group of Nexian casters step out into the avenue and begin casting.

. . .

Agrellus and the five Arclords that remained with him continued to cast, even though a fifteen foot tall wall of bones cut them off from their targets. A trio of grave knights rushed them. They finished casting and six sword-shaped shimmering planes of energy blinked into being. They flew toward the three grave knights and slashed through them. The grave knights did not cry out but they were obviously injured by the mages' swords.

"Geb!" screamed Agrellus. "Show yourself, you coward!"

. . .

Ahrhune tried his best to fight from horseback but, even though he could keep his footing on a rolling deck he had no skill in the saddle, not that there was a saddle. It didn't take long for him to be thrown from Panos's back.

He was momentarily stunned but had enough sense to roll away before he was trampled. The dullahans turned on their centaur hunters. Their swords poured forth cold. They swung their laughing, decapitated heads from leather thongs. But the dullahans had their fill of battle. What they wished now was to terrify and the centaurs were proving impossible to scare. So the dullahans scattered, charging down the streets of Quantium, howling bloody murder.

Panos and his centaurs charged after them, leaving Ahrhune alone. Ahrhune wasn't sure what to do. He scanned the area around him but saw only empty streets.

He heard screams of the dying, echoing off buildings. He wasn't sure which way to go. He heard movement and spun. A door opened and a man motioned that he should enter. He went to the door.

"Have you any injured?"

"They've died," said the man. He scanned the street. "Hurry."

"Got wine or beer?" Ahrhune asked, realizing his throat was parched.

The man grabbed Ahrhune's scarf and yanked him into the small house. It took a moment for Ahrhune's eyes to adjust to the darkness, for those within kept no light. The only illumination came from his own holy symbol, which was glowing, although he didn't know why. He had cast no spell upon it.

"Are you a holy man?" asked one of the room's occupants.

"Yes."

"Why have the gods allowed this?" asked the same man.

"I—"

"That serves no use," growled the man who had yanked Ahrhune within. "Wine, bread, those things serve a use. Give." He held out a hand and a bottle was placed in it. This he passed to Ahrhune. A moment later he handed Ahrhune a chunk of brown bread. Ahrhune drank, ate, and drank again.

"Thank you."

"We were—" The man paused. "We—" He looked at the others within the room.

"It's okay," said Ahrhune. "We're all afraid."

"What will happen to us?" asked the same man who doubted the gods.

"I don't know."

"What *do* you know?" snapped the man. At that moment Ahrhune's holy symbol fell dark. Everyone in the room fell silent. A dim light shone through the gaps under and above the door.

"What is it?" whispered Ahrhune's questioner.

"Ghost?" asked the man who had offered wine and bread.

Ahrhune went to the door and listened. He heard a mournful wail. The light moved away from the door. The wail lessened and was lost. Ahrhune's holy symbol began to glow. He turned and looked at the men. "Stay here."

"Where are you going?" asked one of the men.

"To help whomever I can."

Fear and Faith

Quantium, Nex, Arcanamirium, Absalom, Rova, 4711

Kemnebi knew only the wealthy and powerful adorned themselves with such gems, jewelry, and rich attire that the three men wore. He could feel the enchantments coming from their rings, belts, and robes, but for all this, the three Arclords lay dead in the street. They had no visible wounds but with his keen vision he could see that the blood in their veins was black, a sure sign of necromancy.

He ran deeper into Quantium, came to an intersection, looked to his left and saw that the next intersection was blocked by a wall of bone. He started toward the wall but a familiar voice called his name. He stopped, spun, and readied a spell. Arazni stood in an alley, clutching a dying Arclord. She dropped the wizard and looked at Kemnebi.

"Why did you come here?"

"To stop Geb."

Arazni looked at the Arclord at her feet then back up to Kemnebi. "Too late." She stepped out of the alley. Kemnebi backed away. "You have no place here."

"I'm going to destroy Geb," said Kemnebi. Arazni laughed. Kemnebi began a spell. Arazni stopped laughing and looked at him but the emotions displayed on her face weren't what he expected, she looked as if she were lost in thought. This caused Kemnebi to pause in his casting. "Arazni, help me." She looked at him. "Help me destroy Geb." Arazni tilted her head, either confused or intrigued, he didn't know which. "You can finally be free of him. You can—"

"No!" she screamed. "I won't let you!" She began to cast a spell.

Kemnebi resumed his own casting. His spell was a gamble but one that, if it paid off, would end things. When he was done casting he pointed a finger at Arazni and commanded her to halt. She ignored him.

Arazni reached up to her left ear and ripped the diamond earring from her lobe. As a result of the spell the diamond shattered into a fine, sparkling dust. As she completed her spell the dust swirled around her, falling onto her, and clinging to her flesh, hair, and dress. She balled her fists and walked toward Kemnebi. "I won't let you take him from me."

Kemnebi backed away while beginning a new spell. Arazni rushed him and clawed his face but he kept the spell. He pushed her back and finished the incantation. He pointed and drew an imaginary square at her feet. Vertical bars, made of force, rose from the ground. She realized what spell he was casting and leapt over the rising bars. She clipped her feet on them and tumbled forward, falling into Kemnebi. They both fell onto the cobblestones but rolled apart.

Kemnebi sat up and looked at Arazni. She got onto her hands and knees and looked at him. "The problem," she said, rising, "with two powerful undead necromancers fighting is that far too many necromantic spells won't work." She began to cast.

Kemnebi remained seated, feigning helplessness. He studied Arazni's motions, listened to the words she spoke, and was able to identify the spell. He changed shape into a bat just before she completed her spell. He flapped his wings and was just able to rise above the rays of scorching fire that emanated from her fingertips. She growled and searched for him. "No!" she yelled. "Don't flee!" Kemnebi flew over her and changed his shape. She spun just in time for him to strike her, knocking her to the ground.

"Why do you protect him?" He motioned toward the Bonewall. "Why help your tormentor? I don't understand. After everything he's done to you, why—"

Arazni kicked at him forcing him to leap back. She began to rise but paused, half hunched over, head twisted, face angled up, eyes wide. "I won't let you take him from me!" She stood. "I need him, don't you understand that?"

"Arazni, why?" Kemnebi shook his head. "I don't understand. No one needs Geb. He's a blight on Golarion. He—"

"No!" screamed Arazni. She rushed Kemnebi, reaching for his face.

Kemnebi shoved her back and began to cast. Arazni too began to cast, but Kemnebi had the jump on her. He cast his own fire spell, sending three rays of scorching heat at her. He'd forgotten, though, that she had protected herself against spells. The diamond dust that coated her deflected the rays away.

Arazni abandoned her spell and instead leapt onto Kemnebi, knocking him onto his back. She scrambled on top of him and slammed her fists into him. Her strength had been increased by lichdom, but his durability had been increased by vampirism. The punches, those that connected, hurt but they were not dangerous. He could not be knocked unconscious. Arazni spoke and sobbed as she flailed on him.

"I can't die! Don't you understand that?"

"Arazni, you're already dead," said Kemnebi between blows.

"I can't face her again—I can't be judged!"

Kemnebi bucked his hips while at the same time reaching up, grabbing Arazni's shoulders, and tossing her aside. He stood. Arazni lay in the street, sobbing, her face in her hands. Kemnebi knelt.

Arazni shook her head. "I'm afraid, Kemnebi."

"What are you afraid of?"

Arazni lifted her head and looked up at him. "Death."

"We've conquered death."

Arazni smiled, but it was an expression of sorrow. "You could never understand." She looked down at her hands. "I stood by Aroden. I helped him." She looked at Kemnebi. "We did wonderful things together. We," she began to cry.

"Then Geb did this to you. I know. That's why we have to stop him."

"Help me up." She reached out.

Kemnebi took her hand and helped her to her feet. Her sudden embrace startled him. He wrapped his arms around her to steady her. "She's waiting for me. She's been watching me." She looked up into his face. "She watches all of us."

"Who?"

"Hold me, Kemnebi. I'm scared."

"Arazni? Who watches us?"

She studied his face. "Pharasma. She sits in judgment."

Kemnebi chuckled involuntarily. "Pharasma?"

Arazni lowered her gaze, as if embarrassed.

"Arazni," said Kemnebi. She looked up into his face as he spoke. "You aren't to blame for what Geb's done to you."

She turned her head and looked into the alley, at the Arclord she had killed with her own hands. She looked down. "I've—done things." She looked up into his face. "Terrible things."

"It's not your fault. It's because of what Geb did to you. He made you this way."

Arazni reached up and touched Kemnebi's cheeks with her fingertips. She studied the features of his face. She smiled, closed her eyes, pulled his face to hers and kissed him. She pulled back and looked at him, her eyes searching. Her features turned and she thrust her thumbs into his eyes. "I'll kill you," she growled, "then you'll see!"

Kemnebi reached up and grabbed her wrists. He struggled to pull her hands away from his face. Her considerable strength was made still greater by the powerful emotions she was feeling. "Arazni!" Her hands were now an inch from his face. He turned her arms to the side and flung her away. She fell to her knees, brought her hands to her face, and resumed sobbing. Kemnebi backed away from her. He reached up and felt the blood flowing from his eyes onto his cheeks. His vampiric healing was already closing the cuts her thumbnails had made, but he could barely see through the wash of blood.

"I have to destroy him." He looked at her, only able to make out her hunched form. "Don't make me destroy you."

Arazni sat up. She was profile to Kemnebi and did not turn her head to look at him. She too wiped her face; the sleeve of her dress soaking up her tears. "I've thought a long time about how to kill you, Kemnebi." She looked at him and smiled. "A master vampire," she looked forward. "A skilled necromancer." She smirked. "I played a little trick on Rhianna." She frowned. "It wouldn't work on you."

"I must stop Geb before more innocent people die."

Arazni turned. "Innocent?" She smirked. "No one's innocent, Kemnebi."

"Will you let me pass?"

She looked at him. "You can't destroy Geb. But if you want to try—" She shrugged her shoulders.

Kemnebi gave her a wide arc as he passed. He heard her rise behind him but didn't turn, his attention was drawn to the sounds of battle coming from the other side of the Bonewall.

"You see," said Arazni. Kemnebi stopped and turned. She stood in the street, arms at her sides. "I finally figured out how it works with you vampires. Everything you do relies on the blood you steal from your helpless victims."

An explosion sounded and shards of bone rained down on Kemnebi and Arazni. Kemnebi looked behind him and saw that a section of the Bonewall had been destroyed. He could see through the gap that Geb, the grave knights, and a clutch of ghosts were in a pitch battle with a ruby-hued golem and two wizards he knew by sight, Agrellus and Iranez of the Orb. Agrellus and Iranez were surrounded by a small group of wizards and soldiers, all of whom fought valiantly against Geb and his undead.

"Kemnebi, are you listening?"

He turned back to Arazni.

"I was saying, without blood, you're powerless."

"Arazni, don't—"

Arazni began to cast. Kemnebi too began to cast. This time Arazni was quicker. Kemnebi's spell was disrupted by an intense pain. He fell to his knees and clutched his chest. He had only experienced pain akin to what he felt now once before, when Tcha-n-hebu drained the life from him.

He looked at Arazni and tried to speak but blood poured from his mouth. It did not smell like blood, but smelled sharp, offensive, and dangerous. He tried to stand but he couldn't. Arazni watched. He raised his hands to his mouth in an attempt to staunch the flow. The blood gushed past his fingers.

"What, have you done to me?" he spat out.

"I turned your blood into acid." She walked toward him and knelt. "Don't try to change into any other form, you'll burst open. I've seen it. It's horrifying."

"Arazni—"

"This is your fault, Kemnebi. You didn't have to come here. You could have stayed in Rhianna's hunting lodge with that little tart."

"Arazni—"

She pressed a finger against his lips. "There's nothing to say." She stood and looked down at him. "I can never go before Pharasma. Not ever. Geb is the only one powerful enough to ensure that." She looked up at the battle. "He needs me." She looked down at Kemnebi. "I need him."

. . .

Agrellus fell to his knees, clutching his chest. He was disoriented by the effects of two spells. One had been cast by Geb. He didn't know what it was, but it had leached the life from him to a dangerous degree. The second spell was his own, a failsafe.

He looked around him. He was in a small, wood paneled room. A magical orb of light floated overhead, otherwise the room was empty. Upon seeing where he was, he knew what had happened: he had been teleported. Before the battle for Quantium had begun he placed a contingency spell on himself. If his life was in peril, if death hovered near, his contingency spell would automatically teleport him to safety. This was not all, for a third spell now completed. This spell had been prepared by Astor Bizet and added to the contingency spell. A powerful divine spell now bathed Agrellus in healing energy.

Agrellus stood and yanked open the door. He stormed out of the windowless room, yelling at anyone who might hear. "I need teleported back to Quantium!" He rushed down the halls of the Arcanamirium and grabbed the collar of the first wizard he saw. "You! Can you teleport me to Quantium?"

"Sir?" The wizard looked at the fist that crumpled his collar. "Why, I never—"

"Damn it," growled Agrellus.

. . .

Ahrhune heard an explosion followed by the pelting of debris on nearby rooftops. He ducked under an eave as bits of bone rained down. He looked at the white shards in the street, stunned by the quantity. He stepped out into the street and went toward the sound. He rounded a corner, then ducked back behind it.

He stood with his back to the wall and peered around the edge. A woman stood in the street, looking down at a man coated in blood. She said something then walked off, heading toward the partially shattered wall of bone. As Ahrhune watched she stepped through the breech in the wall. It re-knitted itself behind her.

Ahrhune ran to Kemnebi and knelt. He tried to assess Kemnebi's wounds but didn't see any. He took off his holy symbol, held it over Kemnebi's chest, and began to pray. He'd exhausted his limited divine energy but he willing to believe in miracles and, judging from the blood loss, he thought a miracle was the only magic sufficient to help Kemnebi.

When he felt a hand on his forearm he opened his eyes. Kemnebi shook his head.

Don't give up!" Ahrhune urged. He closed his eyes and resumed praying.

"It won't," Kemnebi coughed up acid-laced blood, "work."

Ahrhune opened his eyes and looked into Kemnebi's face.

"I don't have," again he coughed, "much time left." His hand slipped from Ahrhune's arm and fell onto his thigh.

Ahrhune felt the thump of Kemnebi's hand. He also felt the hardness of the vial in his pocket when Kemnebi's hand struck it. He put the holy symbol back around his neck and dug in his pocket. He saw colored lights and looked up. Whatever was transpiring on the other side of the wall of bone, he knew, involved potent magic. He turned his attention back to Kemnebi. He pulled the vial of sun orchid elixir from his pocket and looked at it. He looked at Kemnebi, who was lying on his back, eyes half open.

Ahrhune drew his dagger and cut the wax seal on the vial. He re-sheathed his dagger and popped the cap of the vial. He lifted Kemnebi's head and placed it on his thigh. "Drink this."

"No—healing—" Choked Kemnebi.

"It's not a healing potion," said Ahrhune. He placed the vial on Kemnebi's lower lip and tilted it up. The elixir was as thick as syrup. It poured slowly over Kemnebi's lip. "Come on, come on, damn it," growled Ahrhune. "Don't let it spill out. Swallow it."

When he was certain Kemnebi had swallowed the elixir he laid his head back down. A sound like thousands of nails dragged across cobblestones hit him. He looked up. The wall of bone was slithering to the side. The battle was done. There was a group of people standing, facing him, waiting for the wall. At the center of this group was a ghost.

Ahrhune dropped the vial onto Kemnebi's chest. He picked up his scimitar and stood. He pulled his holy symbol from around his neck and held it out before him. "Sarenrae, I could use some help here."

The group, led by Geb, advanced down the street toward him.

Refuge

Quantium, Nex, Rova, 4711

Four square blocks around the Refuge of Nex teemed with undead, mostly zombies that had climbed up the ramp of stones they had carried into the Obari Ocean. The Bonewall surrounded the area around the dark red crystalline tower. Two grave knights stood at the base of the stairs, watching Geb. The others had fallen to Agrellus, Iranez of the Orb, and the brave Arclords and warriors with them. to Agrellus, Iranez of the Orb, and those Arclords and warriors brave enough to stand with them. Geb had routed them, forced them to flee. Now he floated before the tower, looking up at it.

Arazni stood next to Geb, looking at him, not at the crystal tower. She didn't understand why they were there. She glanced at the tower, wondering if Geb planned to destroy it. Geb looked at the ecorche. The skinless giant walked past, stepped directly onto the platform and knelt. He turned and faced Geb.

Arazni saw, for the first time, the dark figure cradled in the giant's arms. "Geb?" she asked, turning to look at him. He did not answer but nodded to the ecorche. The giant knelt, holding Ilyx in the palm of one hand. He looked at Geb, who again nodded.

The ecorche dragged its fingernails across Ilyx's chest. Ilyx opened his eyes and screamed. Geb looked at the two grave knights. He glanced at the two grave knights. They eyed the ecorche, then retreated to safety.

"Geb," Arazni asked, "what are you—" She stopped when she realized he wasn't listening.

The ecorche kept tearing at Ilyx's flesh. As he did so the bits of flesh clung to him. They began to stretch over his bloody muscles and tendons in an effort to form new flesh on him. It was one of the giant's more terrifying abilities.

Ilyx screamed and tried to fight off the giant's raking nails, but there was nothing he could do. Finally, bloody and near death, he passed out. The white glow began to pulse from what remained of his skin. The ecorche stopped and waited. The light became a shroud, pulsed out, drew in, then exploded in a blinding flash.

When the light faded, leaving only an afterglow, the ecorche was gone. Ilyx lay on the platform, unconscious. Geb floated to the base of the steps and looked up. He floated up the steps and went to the door. It was cracked open. He traced the door's edge with ghostly fingers, laughing. He drew his hand back. The door opened.

Arazni ran to the base of the steps and looked up. She could see that behind the door stood a swirling vortex of energy. Geb?" she called, stepping up and reaching for him.

Geb floated through, reaching back to close the door behind him.

To Realize, to Rally

Quantium, Nex, Rova, 4711

Arazni rushed up the steps and dug her nails into the seam of the door. She yanked it open. All she saw was dark red crystal. She stood, stunned. The vortex was gone. Geb was gone. She reached out and placed her palms on the crystal, unable to believe what she saw. She glanced down at the grave knights, but they'd pivoted and marched off. She turned and looked at the crystal. "Geb!" She pounded the crystal. "Geb!"

. . .

Eratosthenes and the liches of the Whispering Way turned and looked when the brilliant white explosion momentarily lit up the sky over Quantium. A moment later they looked at one another. They looked at Eratosthenes. He looked at his fellow liches. They all turned and began the long trek south.

. . .

"I can pick them out," said one of his warriors, the same woman who had woken him at the start of the battle. "You don't have to—"

"Cut it," said the Ulfen.

The woman looked at his long blond hair. It was full of spiders. "But it's so beautiful."

"Cut it."

She drew her dagger and grabbed a handful of spider-infested hair.

A man ran up. "Sir."

Both the Ulfen and his field-barber looked.

"You have to see this."

The Ulfen looked sidelong at the woman holding the knife. He frowned and picked up his war hammer, the handle of which was leaned against his thigh.

. . .

"There," said Astor Bizet. He was wrapping a bandage around the arm of a wounded soldier. "Come to the temple tomorrow and we'll finish this—"

"Temple?" asked the soldier.

Astor glanced the direction of Quantium. He frowned and looked back at the wounded soldier. He patted him on the shoulder. "I'll find you."

Astor dipped his sleeve into a basin of water and wiped his brow. He ducked under the canopy of the makeshift field hospital and looked out over the battlefield. The Nexian army had been divided into two parts. He stood pinned between the Elemion River and Quantium's edge. He turned and walked to the edge of the Elemion. He knelt and washed the blood from his hands. He stood and wiped his palms against his once fine robe. He looked along the length of the Elemion and saw movement downriver.

A woman in a blood-stained dress was standing at the shore, perhaps thirty yards upriver. She was clearly undead, he could see that her flesh was unwholesome, even at that distance. She was carrying a soldier in her arms. The man was either dead or near death, for he was limp. She knelt and placed him in the water. She pressed on his chest, submerging him. After a minute, she rose and looked up at the moon. She looked down at the drowned man, turned and walked away, heading south.

"High Priest?" an acolyte called. Astor tore his gaze from the strange woman and looked at his acolyte. "They're leaving."

"Who?"

"The undead. Well, some of them, the others—you just have to see."

Astor looked upriver but the woman was gone. He followed his acolyte to the edge of the Nexian lines and looked. He couldn't believe what he saw.

. . .

Saskia studied the skeletons around her. They stood stock still. She heard movement and looked. A winged undead that resembled a ghoul was crouched atop a pile of bodies. Saskia threaded her way through the motionless skeletons toward it. The berbalang heard her and looked. It hissed at her, its long, pointed tongue uncoiling. It grabbed a fresh corpse, launched into the air, and flew south.

Saskia looked and saw that droves of undead were fleeing. The unintelligent undead merely stood, inactive. The intelligent undead, no longer under Geb's control, fled the coming of the dawn.

"Saskia?" She turned. "Saskia?"

"Here."

Baya-Iza came into view, a magical staff in one hand, the glow of a spell illuminating another. "Come on, let's go."

"What's going on?"

"It's over."

"But," Saskia looked at the skeletons. "What's happening?"

"I don't know, but it's over." Baya-Iza looked to the south. "Eratosthenes," she pointed with her staff. She looked back at Saskia. "Everyone's leaving."

"What about Arazni? What about Geb?"

"Dead? Gone? Who knows?" She started to the south, speaking over her shoulder. "Come on."

Saskia looked to the east, to the sky. The dawn was beginning to break.

Reconstruction

The Bandeshar, Quantium, Nex, and Rhianna's Hunting Lodge, Axan Wood, Geb, Lamashan, 4712

Master Castelli sat in an overstuffed chair in his office in the Bandeshar. His wound was bothering him. He lifted his shirt and looked. His midsection was wrapped in cotton strips where the ghost's hand had passed through him, corrupting his flesh. He could've had it healed by a cleric but refused. So many others needed their attention. He would live, he told himself. He pulled his shirt down over the cotton wrappings.

Iranez of the Orb worked next door, issuing orders to underlings. The commotion in the room, people coming and going, people talking over one another, was a pleasing accompaniment to his work. He looked up when Iranez appeared in the doorway. Her battle with Geb and his undead minions had done nothing to diminish her beauty. She smiled at him.

"Sorry for the noise." Before he could respond she closed the door.

In the resulting silence he heard hammering, sawing, and men yelling over the sounds of construction. He rose, with a groan of pain, and went to the window. He pushed it open and looked out. A pair of men passed below, carrying a length of wood on their shoulders. A mason was mixing a batch of mortar in a large tin bucket, scraping the side with his paddle.

Master Castelli heard the sounds of spellcasting and—for a brief moment—was alarmed. He called a spell to mind, calmed himself, and looked. A woman cast a spell, conjuring a magical disk. A group of workmen began to stack bricks onto it. The debris of a destroyed wall were being cleared away.

Rain, Master?" the woman called, spotting him.

Master Castelli looked at the clouds, then to the woman. "Not today."

The woman looked up at the clouds, then to the workmen, then to Master Castelli. "Good, we've plenty enough to do. Agrellus is planning a big celebration for Winter Week." She looked at the debris around her. "Think we'll be ready?"

Master Castelli smiled and nodded.

. . .

Kemnebi stood in the clearing, looking at the pile of ash. He turned and looked at the mound of freshly dug earth. He looked at his hands, at the dirt on them, and at the color in his flesh. Sunlight glinted off them as he gazed up. He was sweaty and he smelled. That pleased him. He went to the grave and knelt. He reached down and set the empty vial on Ahrhune's chest. He sat on his heels, looking down into Ahrhune's face.

"I wish I knew your name," he said, gazing at the trees. Their leaves had changed and were now red, gold, yellow, and brown. He marveled at the color, at the sunlight shining on their surfaces. He had forgotten how beautiful light and color was. The birds sang. He'd forgotten them, too, the pure joy in their melodies. He saw movement and looked. A hare leapt into view, eyed him, clipped a stem of clover, and sat chewing it. Kemnebi looked down at Ahrhune.

"I'm sure you would rather be buried in a churchyard. I'm sorry for that. But, after what you've done for me, I figured I should tend to your grave myself, honor it—honor you." He looked at the vial. "Sun orchid elixir, that," he looked at Ahrhune, "or you performed a miracle." He looked at the hare. It clipped another stem of clover and sat chewing contentedly. He looked down at Ahrhune.

"I didn't understand what undeath was," he closed his eyes and tilted his face toward the sun, "until I felt the sun warming my face as I lay in the street of a ruined city." He looked at Ahrhune. "Undeath is a trade off. What you get, what I got, with undeath was certainty—the certainty of having defeated death. What I traded away—what I lost —was everything that makes life worth living: the ability to experience, grow, contribute," he looked at the ashes and thought of Elana, "to love."

He looked down at the holy symbol that once belonged to Ahrhune but that he now wore around his own neck. "I don't know if I've been redeemed but I know you've given me a second chance." He looked at Ahrhune. "I'm going to use everything I know about necromancy, about the undead, about the Blood Lords, to fight them. Geb the man is gone. Geb the nation must follow him into oblivion. I'm going to make that happen." He reached down and placed his palm on Ahrhune's chest, "thank you, friend."

. . .

Ahrhune heard the lapping of the waves on the shore. He felt warm sand beneath him. He opened his eyes and saw a clear blue sky above. He half sat up, tucking his elbow beneath him, and looked out. The debris of *The Destiny* was floating near, some of it had washed ashore. He laughed at his good fortune.

He became aware of another presence on the beach with him and looked. Coming out of the sun was a woman with long, dark hair. She wore only a loose fitting white dress held with a golden belt around her thin waist. She walked barefoot in the sand. An ocean breeze blew her dress and hair.

She came close and looked at him. Her eyes shone with golden light. He stood, brushing sand off his backside. He looked at the woman. She was perfection—

unblemished, radiant. She held out one hand, an offer to him, and brushed the hair from her eyes with the other.

"Welcome home."

Author's Afterword

Some people may be curious about how all this came to be. The original kernel was buried in *Pathfinder Campaign Setting: The Inner Sea World Guide*, a book I consulted so frequently during the construction and writing of this story that the cover fell off. There were many tantalizing statements in the section defining Geb and Gebbian society. I got to thinking. How would a society of undead *really* work?

I am a student of many disciplines—all writers must be. I study history, sociology, psychology, philosophy, economics, and more. When I asked how these factors—especially law, order, and economics—would function in Geb's society I realized that a tremendous story was available to me.

I began to construct the story, using every storytelling technique I knew. I spent six months alone working on the premise, plot, theme, characters, conflicts, etc. I spent a year writing the rough draft. I spent another six months revising and editing it. All told, I've spent two years crafting this story, living as a starving artist then and now.

Not only did I do this. I had to teach myself how to make a website in order to distribute this story. I overcame my deep dislike of social media to share this story. I had to design a cover and make this document available in multiple formats.

I did this knowing I couldn't sell it or earn remuneration. So be it. As I said in the foreword, the writing is—and has been—its own reward. I also realize that in the time I've been working on this a second edition of the Pathfinder Roleplaying Game has come out. This includes a new campaign setting guide. Plus, new material about Geb has emerged, including an adventure path. I have not consulted this new material. I didn't even know it existed until I was almost done with the rough draft.

Part of me worries that Paizo, the publisher of the Pathfinder game, will not appreciate this story and will want to prevent it from seeing the light of day. If they did, I'd have lost two years of work. Imagine the doubt a writer feels when he thinks all his efforts are for naught. Sadly, many writers know this feeling. Paizo is well within their rights to do this. If they did I would be saddened but not angry. If they do not, well, then the fear becomes that no one will read it or that it will be lost in the noise. A writer has many fears, yet we must overcome them and create anyway.

All I ask of you is to share the story. If you appreciate my fiction search for more of it. If you like it, share it. There are only two types of marketing that work. One is spending millions to build a brand and saturate the market. The other is word-of-mouth. I wish I had millions but since I don't I have to rely on word-of-mouth. That means relying on you, dear reader, to share your enthusiasm for a story well told. Do that for me, and I'll owe you.

H. Rad Bethlen

Glossary of People and Places

Abadar: the god of cities, law, merchants, and wealth.

Abaddon: An Outer Plane, home to the Horsemen of the Apocalypse.

Abbey of Nerves: When the kytons, the original natives of Hell, were forced to flee, they went to the Plane of Shadows, led there by Aroggus. Aroggus created a massive cathedral to house his homeless race. Not only is the Abbey of Nerves an ever-shifting maze of rooms, halls, and corridors—to confound would-be attackers—it is a place of torture, pain, and suffering where the kytons are free to explore their twisted art.

Abraxas: The demon lord of forbidden lore, magic, and snakes.

Absalom: Perhaps the most famous city in all of the Inner Sea, Absalom is also the wealthiest. It is rumored that Aroden created the island and city of Absalom. It is home to the artifact known as the *Starstone* as well as the *Spire of Nex.*

Abyss, The: One of the Outer Planes, home to the demonic races and the demon lords, as well as many evil deities.

Aedha "Weeping Tree" Nijis: An elf, born in Kyonin. She ventured into the Axan Woods seeking the Twilight Unicorns. She did not find them, instead, she was nearly killed by evil fey of that forest. She saw Rhianna's hunting lodge and asked for aid. What she got was undeath. She became Rhianna's lover and in time a Blood Lord.

Agrellus Kisk, Archmage: Leader of the Arclords and one of the three of the Council of Three and Nine, the rulers of Nex.

Ahrhune ag-Hashid: A Garundi born in Thuvia. He was a pirate under the protection of Prince Zinlo. Upon retirement he became a cleric of Sarenrae.

Aleksandr Kovalenko: Born in Cheliax, he made his way to Ustalav where he met and fell in love with Rhianna Ceinwen. He would later travel to Geb where he was embraced by Kemnebi. He is a Blood Lord.

Alkenstar: A city in the Mana Waste, founded by and named after a refugee from Nex. It is home to many forges and other heavy industry.

Aluum: A type of golem created by the Pactmasters of Katapesh, powered by the souls of slaves.

Andoran: A fledgling democratic state on the northeast corner of the Inner Sea. It is considered a revolutionary country due to its free-market ideology and military abolitionist philosophy.

Apollyon: The horseman of pestilence.

Araminta, a Carnival of Death: Once a Varisian (and a changeling, not wholly human) who traveled as part of a caravan, she was a harrower, a type fortune teller that uses specially designed cards with symbolic meanings. She was killed by Lilith and raised as a zombie lord. She is a Blood Lord.

Arazni, Queen: Once a herald of Aroden, she was ripped from the afterlife and forced into undeath by Geb. She became his queen and is the nominal leader of Geb.

Arcanamirium: One of the most powerful institutions of magic in the Inner Sea region. It was founded by the Arclords and is in the Wise Quarter in Absalom.

Arclords: This group of spellcasters trace their lineage to the household servants of Nex and claim they represent his true beliefs and intentions. However, they stood apart from Nexian politics until one of their own gained a powerful seat on the Council of Three and Nine.

Arlantia: A dryad and resident of the Southern Fangwood in Nirmathas. She was corrupted by Cyth-V'sug.

Aroden: A powerful wizard who raised the *Starstone* and became a living god. Despite his divinity he died in the year 4606, one hundred and five years previous to current events.

Arodus: The eighth month of the calendar year, a summer month, named after Aroden.

Aroggus: A kyton demagogue, he led the kytons out of Hell and made the Abbey of Nerves to hide them from their foes.

Ashoka: A member of the Whispering Way, a lich, and a Blood Lord.

Asmodeus: The ruler of Hell and the god of contracts, pride, slavery, and tyranny.

Aspenthar: The second largest city in Thuvia, ruled by Prince Zinlo.

Astor Bizet: High Priest of the temple to Pharasma in Quantium.

Avistan: A continent on Golarion. Avistan is divided from Garund, which is to the south, by the Inner Sea.

Axan Woods: A forest in central Geb.

Axanir (River): A river that flows from the Shattered Range Mountains to discharge in the Obari Ocean just north of Mechitar.

Azlant: A continental empire whose collapse led to the Age of Darkness.

Azlanti: The people of the Azlant Empire, now extinct.

Bandeshar: A sprawling mansion in Quantium, home to the Council of Three and Nine.

Barrier Wall (Mountains): A long, east-west mountain range in northern Garund. South of the range is the Mwangi Expanse. North of the range is Rahadoum, Thuvia, and Osirion.

Basimah Pareja: Daughter of Castelli Pareja.

Baya-Iza: A drow and native of Zirnakaynin. She is now a resident of Mechitar and a Blood Lord.

Bhavya: A catfolk who is also a merchant in Mechitar. He runs a pawn shop with his business partner, Xylia.

Birth of Light and Truth, The: The holy book of Sarenrae.

Blackmarrow Altar: A powerful artifact made of black skulls which can create a set amount of undead every day.

Blood Lords: Part of the ruling elite of Geb, along with Queen Arazni and Chancellor Kemnebi. There are sixty Blood Lords, only nine of which are mortal, the rest being undead.

Bonewall: A massive—and animate—wall of bones created by Geb to protect the city of Yled.

Borume: The Master Alchemist of Oenopion and one of the nine of the Council of Three and Nine, the rulers of Nex.

Brevoy: A nation in the northeastern corner of the Inner Sea region, bordered in the north by the Lake of Mists and Veils. Lilith is a native of Brevoy.

Calikang: A blue-skinned, six-armed giant used by Nex in his war against Geb. They now roam the Mana Waste in a futile attempt to right the long-ago wrongs of Nex and Geb by restoring the aberrant magic of the land to its natural state.

Casmaron: A continent of Golarion which lies to the east of Garund.

Cassius Allius: A member of the Whispering Way, a lich, and a Blood Lord. He is also a ratfolk who achieved lichdom not through necromancy but through alchemy, with a touch of necromancy.

Castelli Pareja, Master: A member of the Nexian intelligence service whose chief area of concern is Geb. He is also a spellcaster and crafter of magic items.

Catfolk: A feline humanoid race.

Cathedral of Epiphenomena: A church devoted to Urgathoa, located in Mechitar, Geb.

Cayden Cailean: The god of bravery, ale, freedom, and wine. He was once mortal and became a god through the *Test of the Starstone*.

Changeling: A race of humanoids with hag blood in their ancestry. Their eyes are different colors and, depending on the type of hag, they have other defining characteristics.

Charon: The horseman of death.

Cheliax: A powerful nation devoted to the worship of Asmodeus.

Chevonde Garron, Marquis: Born in Galt, his family, like that of Narcisse's, was wiped out in the revolution. However, by this time Chevonde was already a vampire residing in Katapesh. He is Kemnebi's grandchild. His sire was Leah Ben-Reuven. He is a Blood Lord, the only Blood Lord allowed to reside outside of Geb.

Cinerarium: A pyramid constructed by Geb in Mechitar. It is home to Queen Arazni and houses both Chancellor Kemnebi's offices and the meeting hall for the Blood Lords.

Council of Three and Nine: Nex's rulers—the Three (Iranez of the Orb, Elder Architect Oblosk, Agrellus Kisk) and the Nine (Borume, Dunn Palovar, Master Phade, Gen Hendrikan, Elemion, Astor Bizet, Rixende Orth, Fero Zetterling, and Pyree).

Cruciform Cathedral: A cathedral devoted to Iomedae in Nerosyan, Mendev.

Cyth-V'Sug: The demon lord of disease, fungus, and parasites.

Dagillus: An instructor at the Ebon Mausoleum and member of the Whispering Way. Not yet a lich but on the path to becoming one, led to that destination by Eratosthenes. Despite his association with the Whispering Way and his powerful allies, Dagillus is not a Blood Lord.

Darklands: A vast series of tunnels and caverns beneath the surface of Golarion.

Daughter of Urgathoa: A rare type of undead created by Urgathoa to reward her faithful.

Deathsnatcher: A type of monstrous humanoid that can create and command undead.

Deskari: The demon lord of chasms, infestations, and locust.

Desna: The goddess of dreams, luck, stars, and travelers.

Destiny, The: A pirate ship once captained by Ahrhune ag-Hashid. It was destroyed by a div.

Div: A relative of the genie. An evil spirit.

Dread Wraith: A large and more powerful wraith.

Drow: An offshoot of the surface-dwelling elven race that now resides in the Darklands. Unlike their cousins, drow are almost universally evil.

Dryad: A type of fey that protects nature.

Dunn Palovar: The Chief Fleshforger of Ecanus (he crafts golems) and one of the nine of the Council of Three and Nine, the rulers of Nex.

Dwarf: One of the races in Golarion, stout, often surly, and tradition-bound. Dwarves primarily live in mountain strongholds. They are known for their love of stone and metal work.

Earthfall: An event in which the *Starstone* fell to the surface of Golarion, creating the Inner Sea.

Ebon Mausoleum: A school of necromancy located in Mechitar, Geb.

Ecanus: The second largest city in Nex, known for the Fleshforges.

Ecorche: A type of undead giant without flesh. It flays its victims and temporarily wears their flesh.

Elana de Oliveira: A native of Nex. She is a student at the Ebon Mausoleum and assistant and companion to Saskia Kalff.

Elemion (Individual): A mutant from the Mana Waste. He is a tripartite being. He is a member of the nine of the Council of Three and Nine, the rulers of Nex.

Elemion (River): A river that flows from the Brazen Peaks to discharge into the Obari Ocean just north of Quantium.

Elf: A long-lived and noble species of humanoid, adept at magic.

Empty Threshold, The: A temple to Zon-Kuthon in Graydirge, Geb.

Encarthan, Lake: A lake in central Avistan.

Erastil: The god of family, farming, hunting, and trade.

Erastus: The seventh month of the calendar year, a summer month, named after Erastil.

Eratosthenes: An elven lich from Kyonin. He is a Blood Lord and the leader of the Whispering Way in Geb.

Fangwood: The Southern Fangwood is the largest forest in Nirmathas. The Northern Fangwood is in Lastwall. The Fangwood is vital to Nirmaths's economic, military, and cultural survival.

Fero Zetterling: An agent of Nex's powerful Merchant's League and one of the nine of the Council of Three and Nine, the rulers of Nex.

Fetchling: A semi-derogatory nickname for the kayal race.

Fext: A type of humanoid undead born of battle and death. It is exceptionally hard to kill and can only be wounded by obsidian. It "lives" for war.

Final Blade: An artifact used in executing the revolution's enemies in Galt.

Fleshforges: A complex of magical workshops in Ecanus which are used to create golems and other unnatural beings.

Galfrey, Queen: The ruler of Mendev.

Galt: A nation enduring a bloody terror, a revolution gone wrong. Both Chevonde and Narcisse are refugees from this failed state.

Garund: A continent on Golarion. Garund is divided from Avistan, which is to the north, by the Inner Sea.

Garundi: A dark-skinned, proud yet friendly human race found in Absalom, Geb, Katapesh, Nex, Osirion, Rahadoum, Thuvia and elsewhere.

Geb (Individual): One of Golarion's most powerful necromancers. Born in Osirion and a founding member of the death cult that arose amongst the Pharaoh's royal embalmers. Geb was exiled from his homeland and went on to found his own nation. He is the mortal enemy of Nex. When Nex disappeared into his Refuge, Geb committed ritual suicide. However, he was cursed to return to Golarion as a ghost.

Geb (Nation): The nation founded by Geb, ruled by undead.

Geb's Rest: A remote location near Geb's northern border. Geb waits here, for what and why, only he knows.

Gen Hendrikian: A nagaji, cleric of Abraxas, and Chief Riddler (equivalent to High priest) of the Scrivenbough.

Ghoran: A plant-based humanoid that reproduces via a seed grown in the abdomen.

Ghoul: An intelligent type of humanoid undead that consumes the flesh of corpses.

Giant, Tomb: A race of giants concerned with death and the undead.

Gnoll: A hyena-like humanoid, intelligent yet feral.

Gnome: A humanoid race of short stature, descended from fey.

Golarion: The third planet from the sun, home to many forms of life. The Inner Sea region resides on Golarion.

Gorum: The god of battle, strength, and weapons.

Gozran: The fourth month of the calendar year, a spring month, named after Gozreh.

Gozreh: The god of nature, the sea, and weather.

Grave Knight: A type of undead bound to its armor.

Graydirge: A town in central Geb, just northwest of the Axan Wood.

Groetus: The god of empty places, oblivion, and ruins.

Hag: A humanoid female, usually hideous in appearance but not always, which can command powerful magics. Hags are loners and evil but they occasionally gather to cast potent spells.

Half-Elf: A mixed race of human and elven origins.

Hell: A deep, multi-layered pit in the outer planes, ruled by Asmodeus and his archdevils.

Hent-er-Neheh: The daughter of Nakht-Neb-Tep-Nefer and Geb's aunt and initial instructor in magic and necromancy. She was mummified by her father and is a mummy lord. She was one of the founding members of the death cult in ancient Osirion. She is a Blood Lord.

High Isgerian: An architectural style modeled after the architecture of Hell.

Horsemen of the Apocalypse: Four god-like beings who are the instruments of death and destruction. They reside in Abaddon. They are: Apollyon, Charon, Szuriel, and Trelmarixian.

Ilyx: A svirfneblin solo adventurer who uses firearms.

Inner Sea (Region): A collection of nations that surround the Inner Sea and occupy the northern half of Garund and western half of Avistan.

Invisible Stalker: A creature native to the Plane of Air. It is comprised of air and is impossible to see and difficult to injure.

Iomadae: The goddess of honor, justice, rulership, and valor.

Iranez of the Orb: A witch and member of the three of the Council of Three and Nine, the rulers of Nex.

Irori: The god of history, knowledge, and self-perfection. He was once mortal and became a god through self-perfection.

Isger: A nation beholden to Cheliax, its neighbor to the west.

Isle of Kortos: An island in the Inner Sea, home to Absalom the nation and Absalom the city.

Iztahuatzin: A deathsnatcher that lives in the foothills of the Shattered Range Mountains in western Geb.

Jalmeray: An island nation off the coast of Nex in the Obari Ocean.

Jasmine, the Dead Bride: A zombie lord and Blood Lord of Geb. She died on her wedding day and still wears her blood-stained and tattered bridal dress, thus her name.

Kaltessa, Lady: A noble woman who lives in Isger. She is the high priestess of the archdevil Mammon in the Inner Sea region.

Katapesh: A nation, the northern neighbor of Nex. Also, the capital of this nation.

Kayal: A humanoid race from the Shadow Plane.

Keleshite: A people of the desert, arrogant yet able. They are a human race found in Katapesh, Nex, Osirion, Qadira, Taldor and elsewhere.

Kemnebi: The Chancellor of Geb. He was once a student of Geb's. He descends from an advisor to the Pharaoh and studied under Geb. He is a vampire and the leader of the Blood Lords.

Khamati: Cousin to Geb, nephew to Hent-er-Neheh. He is a mummy lord, cleric of a god long forgotten, and a Blood Lord.

Kharswam: The ruler of Jalmeray.

Khemet, Ruby Prince: The ruler of Osirion.

Khufnu: A distant relative of Geb's. He is a mummy lord, a worshipper of Shax, and a Blood Lord.

Kimberly Silent Eyes: A Vishkanyas assassin who killed her employer (a former Blood Lord) and took his place.

Kyonin: A nation of elves that was once abandoned by them, although they have now returned.

Kyton: A humanoid race given to extreme body modifications. They were the original inhabitants of Hell but were betrayed and have removed to the Shadow Plane.

Lamashan: The tenth month of the calendar year, a fall month, named after Lamashtu.

Lamashtu: The goddess of madness, monsters, and nightmares.

Land of the Linnorm Kings: A nation in the northwest of the Inner Sea region. It derives its name from a dragon-like creature called a linnorm that inhabits the frozen plains and mountains of that region.

Latitia, the Diseased: One of the highest ranking priests to Urgathoa in Geb. She was changed from a human into a Daughter of Urgathoa. She is a Blood Lord.

Leah Ben-Reuven: One of Kemnebi's children (a mortal he embraced a.k.a turned into a vampire). She is Chevonde Garron's sire. She was killed by Kemnebi.

Lich: A powerful type of undead. Becoming a lich is a long, arduous process. Most fail.

Lilith: A lich and advisor to Queen Arazni. She is called "Mother" by Arazni and many of those who surround the Queen. Although a lich and a Blood Lord, she is not associated with the Whispering Way.

Llorona: A type of undead that drowns its victims in rivers. Llorona are created from mothers who drown their own children.

Mammon: The archdevil of avarice, watchfulness, and wealth. He rules the third layer of Hell.

Mana Waste: A region between Geb and Nex. This was the battleground for the war between those two god-like wizards. The land is filled with aberrant magic and magic dead zones. The eastern half is largely unstable and dangerous, home to roving tribes of mutants. The western half is more stable. Alkenstar, Dongun Hold, and Martel are all in the west. The Grand Duchy of Alkenstar is nominally under the control of Nex, although it has a great deal of independence.

Masgava: A lich, member of the Whispering Way, and a Blood Lord.

Material Plane: The known universe and all that resides within.

Mauxi: A people native to the Mwangi Expanse, although descended from the Osirioni people.

Mechitar: The capital of Geb.

Mendev: A nation on the western shore of the Lake of Mists and Veils, occupied with a crusade into the World Wound.

Mohrg: A type of undead that resembles a skeleton but retains its digestive tract, which it uses to consume the living, for which it has a great hunger.

Moira the Disowned: A refugee from Galt. A human wizard and Blood Lord. She was disowned by her family, prior to the revolution, due to her study of necromancy.

Molthune: A nation run by a military oligarchy. It is the northwestern neighbor of Isger.

Mummy: Mummification was originally a religious ritual meant to prepare the body for the afterlife. This ritual has been corrupted to turn the corpse into a type of undead.

Mutant: The aberrant magic of the Mana Waste has mutated the region's inhabitants. Many are born with debilitating defects, although some have strange and even useful "powers."

Mwangi Expanse: A dense jungle nation surrounded on three sides by mountain chains.

Naga: An intelligent monster with a serpentine body and a humanoid head.

Nagaji: A race said to be descended from or created by nagas. These serpentine humanoids have lidless eyes and are not widely trusted by other races.

Nah-le-tah: A tomb giant, cleric of Urgathoa, and Blood Lord.

Nakht-Neb-Tep-Nefer: The great uncle of Geb and one of the original founders of an ancient death cult in Osirion. He is a mummy lord and a Blood Lord.

Narcisse, the former Duke Between the Rivers: A refugee from Galt who conspired to murder his own family and steal their wealth. He is a cleric of Urgathoa and Blood Lord.

Neacal Aodhan: A lich, member of the Whispering Way, and a Blood Lord.

Nemret Noktoria: An ancient necropolis beneath the sands of Osirion.

Nethys: The god of magic. He is known to have both a good / protective side and an evil / destructive side.

Nex (Individual): One of the most powerful wizards ever to exist on Golarion. He founded the nation of Nex. He fought Geb to a standstill. He finally left Golarion, disappearing into the Refuge of Nex. He has not been seen since.

Nex (Nation): The nation created by Nex. It has a high density of spellcasters.

Nirmathas: A war-torn nation comprised of a distinctly independent people.

Noreen Paisely: A llorona and a Blood Lord.

Obari (Ocean): The ocean that separates Garund and Casmaron.

Oblosk, Elder Architect: A pech and one of the three of the Council of Three and Nine, the rulers of Nex. Of all the council members, only Oblosk knew Nex personally.

Oenopion: The third largest city in Nex and home to both a large ooze colony and a great many alchemist.

Ólchobar Yevan: A lich, member of the Whispering Way, and a Blood Lord.

Oppara: The capital of Taldor.

Osirion: One of the oldest continually inhabited regions in the Inner Sea. The birthplace of Geb.

Pactmasters: The secretive ruling elites of Katapesh.

Pashow: A town in south central Thuvia, near the Barrier Wall Mountains.

Pech: A type of humanoid fey that lives underground. The pech are known for their shyness and their stonework.

Phade, Master: An invisible stalker and member of the nine of the Council of Three and Nine, the rulers of Nex.

Pharasma: The goddess of birth, death, fate, and prophecy. It is Pharasma who judges the souls of the dead.

Pharast: The third month of the calendar year, a spring month, named after Pharasma.

Pyree: A holy hermit and worshipper of Iroiri. He is one of the nine of the Council of Three and Nine, the rulers of Nex.

Qadira: A nation on the western coast of Casmaron. It is on the eastern shore of the Obari Ocean, across from Osirion.

Quantium: The capital of Nex.

Ragathiel: The Empyreal Lord of chivalry, duty, and vengeance.

Ratfolk: A humanoid race of bipedal rats.

Ravener: A type of undead dragon.

Refuge of Nex: A crystalline tower erected by Nex that leads to a different dimension. After Geb attacked Quantium with a killing fog Nex entered the tower and has not been seen or heard from since.

Rhianna Ceinwen: A vampire, the child of Aleksandr Kovalenko, who was once her lover and a Blood Lord. She sired Trevedic Faull after being asked to do so by Aleksandr.

Rixende Orth: High Priest of Nethys in Nex.

Rova: The ninth month of the calendar year, a fall month, named after Rovagug.

Rovagug: The god of destruction, disaster, and wrath.

Sands, The: The first pirate vessel that Ahrhune ag-Hashid sailed on as a youth.

Sarenith: The sixth month of the calendar year, a summer month, named after Sarenrae.

Sarenrae: The goddess of healing, honesty, redemption, and the sun.

Sarkosis: A nation that was destroyed by the arrival of the World Wound.

Saskia Kalff: A native of Taldor who was later orphaned in Qadira and transported to Katapesh to be sold as a slave. She was purchased by Chevonde Garron who molded her into a courtesan and spy. It was Chevonde's intention to place her close to Queen Arazni but Lilith discovered his plot and took Saskia as a student. She is a Blood Lord and the mentor to Elana de Oliveira.

Scrivenbough: The temple to Abraxas in Quantium.

Sellen (River): An east-west river that runs along the northern border of both Galt and Kyonin.

Serving Your Hunger: The holy book of Urgathoa.

Shadow (Undead): A simple-minded type of incorporeal undead that is little more than its name implies.

Shadow Plane: A plane of existence that darkly mirrors the Material Plane.

Shattered Range (Mountains): A long, north-south mountain range in eastern Garund. West of the range in the Mwangi Expanse. East of the range is Katapesh, Nex, the Mana Waste, and Geb.

Shax: The demon lord of envy, lies, and violent or sadistic murder.

She-mah-hon: A kyton and emissary of Aroggus. She is a Blood Lord.

Shoanti: A war-like but proud people who inhabit Belkzen, the Lands of the Linnorm Kings, Varisa and elsewhere.

Skoan-Quah (Skull Clan): One of the clans of the Shoanti people. They have a fascination with death.

Southern Fangwood: See fangwood.

Sovyrian: Little is known about the land to which the elves escaped from Kyonin before Earthfall.

Sovyrian Stone: The gate through which the elves of Kyonin escaped before Earthfall.

Spellscar (Desert): A desert on the eastern side of the Mana Waste. It is known for violent and unpredictable weather and other magic-fueled geological features and hazards.

Starstone: An artifact that fell to the surface of Golarion (much like a meteor), creating the Inner Sea and initiating the Age of Darkness. It was later brought to the surface by Aroden. It has the power to grant divinity to those who past its test, few do.

Starstone, Test of: Anyone may attempt the *Test of the Starstone*. Anyone who passes the test is granted divinity. Those who fail die. Each test is unique to the individual who takes it. It is unknown who created the *Starstone*, why, or how it came to fall on Golarion.

Stavian, Grand Prince: The ruler of Taldor.

Sthaga: Sthaga was once a human cleric of Urgathoa but has since become a dread wraith. He is the High Priest of the Church of Epiphenomena in Mechitar, Geb.

Stilgar: A dwarven wizard and owner of Stilgar's Scrollworks.

Stilgar's Scrollworks: A business that creates scrolls to order and scrolls for sale to the general public. It is located in Oenopion, Nex.

Stormflood (River): A river in southeastern Galt.

Styx (River): A supernatural river that flows through Abaddon and the Abyss. The waters of the Styx can erase a person's memory.

Sulah, Bones of Wood: A ghoran who was corrupted and is now a unique type of undead. She is a Blood Lord.

Svirfneblin: A type of ebony skinned gnome that lives underground.

Szuriel: The horseman of war.

Taldor: An imperialistic nation in the southeast corner of Avistan.

Tanglebriar: During the period when the elves had abandoned Kyonin a demon named Treerazer was exiled to the southern forest of that nation. His presence has corrupted the forest, earning it its current name. The elves have so far been unable to dislodge him.

Tar-Baphon: A powerful lich and tyrant who was imprisoned.

Thuvia: A desert nation in northern Garund.

Tian: One of the natives of Tian Xia.

Tian Xia: A continent on Golarion which is difficult to reach from the Inner Sea.

Tiefling: A humanoid with demonic blood somewhere in his or her lineage, revealed by physical markers such as wings, horns, barbed tails and so forth.

Treerazer: A powerful demon that inhabits the Tanglebriar in southern Kyonin.

Trelmarixian: The horseman of famine.

Trevedic Faull: A kayal who came with his clan group from the Shadow Plane to Taldor. He later went to Geb to study at the Ebon Mausoleum, at which he now teaches. He met Aleksandr Kovolenko and the two became friends. He was embraced and made a vampire by Rhianna Ceinwen. He is a member of the Whispering Way, a worshipper of Nethys, a necromancer and a Blood Lord.

Twilight Unicorns: A group of unicorns residing in the Axan Wood. They are unlike unicorns found elsewhere in that they are not inherently good and they have the ability to prophecy; although, few have been able to locate them in order to make use of their gifts.

Tykylainen: A ravener, who bargained with Geb for the boon of undeath.

Ulfen: A tall, blonde haired, pale skinned race of humans found in Irrisen, the Lands of the Linnorm Kings, Varisa, and elsewhere.

Uoser: The apprentice and personal assistant of Hent-er-Neheh. He is a mummy lord and a Blood Lord.

Urgathoa: The goddess of disease, gluttony, and undeath.

Ustalav: A cursed land on the north shore of Lake Encarthan. It is home to many undead.

Vampire: A type of undead that both survives on and draws power from the blood of the living.

Vennonius: A ghoul and one of the diplomats to Geb from Nemret Noktoria.

Viratus: A ghoul and the chief diplomat to Geb from Nemret Noktoria.

Vishkanyas: A somewhat serpentine humanoid race. They are known for their ability to produce poison which they often coat their weapons with using their long, forked tongues.

Vocorix: A ghoul and one of the diplomats to Geb from Nemret Noktoria.

Voradni Voon: A warlord who sieged Absalom twenty two years after Aroden had created it. He failed.

Wamukota: A Zenj and a native of the Mwangi Expanse. He is one of Kemnebi's blood thralls and his most loyal and trusted retainer.

Well of Lies: A dangerous dungeon complex in southwest Nex. Nex himself explored the dungeon and ordered it sealed.

Werewolf: A lycanthrope, a cursed humanoid that changes shape into a wolf and a wolf-man hybrid.

Whispering Way: A secret cult dedicated to undeath, especially the achievement of lichdom.

Whisperwood: A large forest in eastern Cheliax.

World Wound, The: Once a nation known as Sarkosis, now a blasted region surrounding a rift that connects Golarion to the Abyss.

Wraith: A type of incorporeal undead that drains the life force from its victims.

Xylia: A gnome, native of Nex, who now runs a pawn business in Mechitar with her catfolk business partner, Bhavya.

Zenj: One of four distinct peoples of the Mwangi Expanse. They are the most numerous. They inhabit the central area of the expanse.

Zinlo, Prince: The ruler of Aspenthar in Thuvia.

Zirnakaynin: The largest drow city in the Inner Sea region. It is located in the Darklands.

Zon-Kuthon: The god of darkness, envy, loss, and pain.

H. Rad Bethlen has been compared to Isak Dinesen (*Seven Gothic Tales*) and Fritz Leiber (*Swords and Deviltry*). He is known for his work in the fantasy and horror genres as well as his non-fiction. He has been published in Europe and America.

Enjoy the story?

If you liked what you read, please take a moment to **leave a review on Amazon**! Your feedback helps other readers find this story. It only takes a minute but it makes a huge difference. The Amazon algorithm requires 30-50 reviews before it will pick this book up and promote it to like-minded readers. Your review is instrumental in helping that happen!

www.ingramcontent.com/pod-product-compliance
Lightning Source LLC
LaVergne TN
LVHW020646110826
845149LV00012B/1931

9781965650271